# ORBITAL DECAY

# ALLEN M. STEELE

# ORBITAL DECAY

ACE BOOKS, NEW YORK

ORBITAL DECAY

An Ace Book/published by arrangement with
the author

Quality Printing and Binding by:
Berryville Graphics
P.O. Box 272
Berryville, VA 22611 U.S.A.

*This one's for* Linda
*because of all the right reasons*
*And for her favorite band,*
The Grateful Dead

# Acknowledgments

The author extends his deepest gratitude to the people who helped make this novel possible: *Rick Dunning,* who designed Olympus Station and aided in the design of Vulcan Station, and otherwise acted as an unofficial science adviser in the creation of the backgrounds and technology; *Jim Ball* of NASA's Public Affairs Office at the Kennedy Space Center, who gave me a first-class tour of the facilities and answered many questions about flight operations at the Cape; *David Moja,* also of the Kennedy Space Center, who lent me an enlightening half-hour of his time; *Joye Patterson* and *Roy Fisher* of the University of Missouri School of Journalism, for enabling me to take off on a couple of off-campus trips to the Cape and Washington, D.C., which allowed me to gather material while conducting postgraduate research at the same time; *Ken Moore, John Hollis,* and *Dan Caldwell* of the Nashville Science Fiction Club, who supplied me with invaluable insights, criticism, and magazine articles during the genesis of the book (and to Ken's cats—Avco, Big Black, Pinhead, and Toker—for educating me in feline psychology); *Ginjer Buchanan,* who rescued this novel from the slush pile and gave me encouragement when it was needed the most; *Ian Ralph,* who volunteered to be the novel's first reader and survived the experience to give me a critique; and, definitely not the least, *Linda,* for back rubs, patience, beer runs, and all the other big and little things.

September, 1983–October, 1986;
*Columbia, Missouri;*
*Nashville, Tennessee;*
*Washington, D.C.;*
*Worcester, Massachusetts*

"Just as the oceans opened up a new world for clipper ships and Yankee traders, space holds enormous potential for commerce today. The market for space transportation could surpass our capacity to develop it. Companies interested in putting payloads into space must have ready access to private sector launch services. . . . We will soon implement a number of executive initiatives, develop proposals to ease regulatory constraints, and, with NASA's help, promote private sector investment in space."

—President Ronald Reagan
State of the Union address
January 25, 1984

". . . In recent years there has been an increasing amount of interest and speculation in the area of space colonization and space habitation. . . . It is only fair to point out, however, that far too much space colonization work has been pure utopian dreaming; historically, there is nothing wrong with this if you keep fact and fiction delineated. Similar utopian dreaming heralded the opening of the new frontiers of the past. Cathay was once a magical kingdom with great wizards and magic that were really advanced technology beyond the comprehension of visitors. Far Araby was a place of jinns, flying carpets and odalisques ready to do your every bidding. America was a land of milk and honey where the streets were paved with gold and even if they tossed you in jail it was in golden chains. California was a land of perpetual sunshine where it never rained. And the space colony offers us a pastoral existence with trees, grass, grazing livestock, happy farmers and dancing children eating goat cheese. . . . But opening a frontier is a deadly, difficult, gut-tearing job that requires the best people that the human race can produce and demands its toll in lives and property."

—G. Harry Stine
The Space Enterprise

"Sure, we had trouble building Space Station One—but the trouble was people."

—Robert A. Heinlein
"Delilah and the Space Rigger"

# ORBITAL DECAY

# PART ONE

## *A Hard Day in the Clarke Orbit*

Some day soon—perhaps tomorrow, perhaps a week or a month, maybe as long as a year from now if they're really lazy about it—they're going to find this crevasse. It won't be very difficult, because the tire tracks from my tractor will remain indelibly printed in the gray lunar soil. There are no winds on the Moon to shift dust over the tracks, no erosion save for the impact of stray micrometeorites. My trail will remain fresh even if they delay the search for a decade, and it will lead across the Descartes Highlands east of the Abulfeda Crater until it ends, quite abruptly, at the lip of this crevasse within sight of Argelander Peak.

When they shine a spotlight down here, they'll discover the wreckage of my tractor, looking like one of the junked cars one sees from the highways in Pennsylvania. When they lower a couple of men down by cable, they'll find my footprints in the dust at the bottom of the crevasse. They'll follow those lonely footprints as they lead for a mile and a half northwest, the steep walls of the crevasse rising to either side like enormous hedgerows of ancient volcanic rock. It's dark down here, even during the high noon of the two-week lunar day. Their helmet lanterns will cast ghostly circles of light along the walls and in the deep impressions of my footprints. They will feel the cold lonesomeness which is destined, in these last hours of my life, to be my dying impression.

Actually, I understand that oxygen asphyxiation is not a bad way to go, relatively speaking. There's worse ways to die in space. In the end I'll probably babble my head off, gleefully talking about moon worms as my lungs fill with carbon dioxide. I'll go out crazy as a shithouse rat, but at least I'll be happy. I think.

When they come to the end of my tracks, they'll find me sitting on my rump with my back propped against a boulder, quite dead. They will also find the greatest discovery ever made. I'm serious. It's down here in this crevasse with me, and the search party would have to be blind to miss it.

I only wish I could be around for the moment. I wouldn't be able to see the expressions on their faces through the reflective coating on their helmet visors, but I can imagine what words will pass through their comlink.

Although, now to think of it, even hearing what they had to say would be impossible. If my suit radio, or the radio in my poor wrecked tractor was still working, I wouldn't be sitting here now, waiting to die.

Life is just full of little ironies, ain't it?

I wonder which will go out first: the oxygen supply, the batteries in my life-support system, which keep me from freezing to death, or the microcassette into which I'm dictating these last thoughts. Theoretically I shouldn't be wasting precious air in speaking; I should be conserving it in hopes that a search party from Descartes Station will find me in time. Rescued in the nick of time, la la la. Sorry, that stuff only happens in science fiction stories. I know damn well that the guys back at the base, inert bastards that they are, won't even think about looking for me until I'm several hours overdue. These two-week days tend to distort time like that. I'll be long dead by the time someone peers over his Marvel comic book and says, "Hey, what happened to Sam?" It'll be another hour before someone else says, "Hey, y'know, I think Sam's overdue from his trip out." And it'll be another hour after that before someone finally says, "Well, gee whiz, maybe we ought to take another track out and go find ol' Sam; he might be in trouble or something."

You sons of bitches. I'm gonna get you for this.

At least there's the consolation, the posthumous booby prize, that someone may eventually transcribe these taped recollections and publish them as an article about the man who made the greatest discovery. After all these years, after all those reject slips, I'll finally get something of mine in print. The last words of a failed science fiction writer; maybe it'll even get in *Analog* or *Omni,* one of the mags that turned down all the other stuff I wrote. It may even spur some publisher to print *Ragnarok Night,* the SF novel that no one would touch while I was alive.

I can always daydream, can't I?

Yeah, life is just full of them crazy little ironies. Death is too, I suppose.

So, to pass the time until my oxygen or suit batteries peter out, I'll tell you a story, you who will someday separate this tape from my suit recorder. A spaceman's memoirs, if you will. How Samuel K. Sloane, who got a job with Skycorp so he could go to space to get authentic background for his science fiction novel, ended up making the Great Discovery.

Of course, that isn't all there is to it. There was also the stuff that happened on Skycan and Vulcan, like Doc Felapolous and his cats or the run-in between Virgin Bruce and Cap'n Wallace, and Jack Hamilton and orbital decadence, and the day we messed with the plans of the National Security Agency and stuck a banana in the Big Ear, so to speak. That all came first . . . which of course means that I had best start at the beginning, like you do with all good stories.

First, you have to understand that outer space isn't all that it's cut out to be. . . .

# Homesick

The days began the same way after a while: adventure made mediocre through repetition, the vastness of space a stale background against which their tedious lives were played.

A dozen men floated in the narrow cylindrical compartment, all facing in the same direction like automatons waiting to be activated. Even in weightlessness their aluminum space armor and enormous MMU backpacks seemed to hang on them like heavy burdens; they slouched under their packs, their shoulders bent, their helmeted heads hanging low, their hands moving slowly as they replenished their oxygen tanks from hoses dangling from the wall. The compartment was filled with the sound of hissing air and the thin crackle of suit radios being tested, of muttered comments and complaints and the clink of tools nestling together in the cargo pockets of their overgarments. Behind them a technician, wearing a T-shirt with a rock band's name stenciled on the front, floated from man to man, checking suit joint seals, turning intake valves they couldn't reach, rescuing runaway gloves and power tools from midair. There were no windows. CRT screens overhead displayed job assignments for the day, and TV monitors showed scenes inside the construction shack's main bay and outside, where the work was going on. No one paid attention to the monitors; everyone knew what it looked like out there and didn't want to be reminded.

They were all in there on that shift. Virgin Bruce, singing an old Grateful Dead song, his raucous laughter ringing through the whiteroom. Mike Webb, smiling at Bruce's jokes, trying for the umpteenth time to get the suiting procedure right, always having to get Julian, the technician, to help him. Al Hernandez, moving efficiently, telling another interminable story about his family in Miami, his brother in the FBI, his son who wanted to join the Marines, his wife who kept asking when he was coming home (everyone, hearing these things, nodding, silently asking, *what's new, Al?).* Hank Luton, who would be in the command center and not have to wear a suit for the next four hours, bugging everyone about little details—a joint in one section that needed to be rewelded, a bend in a truss which meant the beam had to be replaced, all the stuff the computers had picked up since the last shift—and being rewarded with surly grunts and mumbled apologies. And the rest of the handful of space grunts who called themselves beamjacks—because it sounded like "lumberjack" —who for some reason were thought of as pioneers instead of everyday Joes trying to make it through another dogass day.

One by one, they managed to make it out of the whiteroom, through the hatch at the end of the compartment into the next inflated plastic cylinder, moving in a ragged single file toward the airlock. Now and then someone had to go back because a suit sensor detected a slow leak or a weak battery. The airlock was a big metal chamber which they were herded into by another technician. When he sealed the hatch they stood for another few minutes, their feet gripped to the floor by magnetic overshoes, everything colored candy-apple red by the fluorescents in the ceiling. No sound now, except the whisper of air inside one's helmet and conversations overlapping in the comlink, received through their snoopy helmets' earphones.

The opposite hatch of the airlock slid open, and Vulcan Station's main construction bay lay before them like an airless basketball court, paper-thin aluminum walls offering scant protection from the void. They shuffled out onto the deck, some heading for the beambuilders, some for the construction pods docked nearby, some for the hatch leading outside the shack.

Those who went outside, one by one, gripped their MMUs' hand controls, pushing them forward and letting the little jets push them away from Vulcan. Once this had been exciting; now it was just the first part of the job, getting out to the powersat. It lay before them like a vast metal grid, a flat rectangle bigger than the towns some of them had been born in, larger than anything that had ever been built on Earth. They floated away from Vulcan, little white stick-men against the overwhelming darkness, the shack's blue and red lights outlining them as silhouettes. Earth was a blue, white, and green crescent beyond the powersat. They tried not to look at it, because it never did any good; if you thought about it too much, you got depressed, like Popeye. Just do your job; punch the clock and hope you make it through the shift alive.

Once or twice a week, when he had a few minutes to spare at the end of his lunch break, the beamjack the others called Popeye would float down to Meteorology for a look at Earth.

Not that it was impossible to see Earth any time he wished; he saw the planet every time he went on shift. From 22,300 miles away, it was an inescapable part of life, always there, always to be there. It was something no one could ever forget.

Yet sometimes Popeye Hooker *did* find himself forgetting. There came times—while on the job, while lying awake in his bunk, while climbing into his suit for another work shift—when he tried to recall what standing on real ground was like, how fresh air tasted, and found himself unable to remember.

Sometimes he could not remember Laura's face. Part of him didn't want to remember what she looked like, and it might have been for the better if he could not; yet Popeye had to remember Laura, for reasons he could not comprehend. It was those instances when her face disappeared from his mind's eye which scared him the worst.

So, when he could, he would head for the weather station to borrow a few minutes on the big optical telescope. Once or twice a week, although if he could have, he would have visited Meteorology every day. But his being allowed to use the telescope at all was a personal favor extended by the bogus meteorologists and he didn't want to risk overstaying his welcome.

The weather station was at the south polar end of Olympus Station's hub. To reach it from the rim, Hooker had to leave the four adjacent modules comprising the mess deck and walk down the catwalk until he reached the gangway leading down into the western terminus. On this particular day he had fifteen minutes before the beginning of his second shift, so he had to hurry. Hooker grabbed one of the two ladders in the terminus and began to climb up through the overhead hatch into the western spoke.

As he ascended, he passed fluorescent light fixtures, fire control stations and color-coded service panels set in the cool, curving metal walls. Along the inside of the spoke were taped-up notices of one kind or another: the announcement of the Saturday movie in the rec room, reminders of deadlines for filing W-2 forms and absentee voter registration, announcements for union meetings, and ever present "Think—Safety *First!*" signs. The second ladder ran directly behind him; another crewman passed him, heading down to the torus, his soles clanging on the ladder rungs, echoing in the utilitarian cool.

Soft music from an occasional speaker set in the walls accompanied his journey to the hub, the Muzak that was piped through

Skycan. Hooker gritted his teeth as, for perhaps the tenth time that day—he had lost count, if he had ever kept it—he heard "If I Had A Hammer" segueing into a syrupy version of "Yesterday." Elevator music for a place that didn't have elevators; it was another sign of his lapsed mental condition that he couldn't laugh at this irony.

By the time he had climbed halfway up the spoke, most of the one-third normal gravity experienced on the rim of the station was gone, and he was not climbing the ladder so much as pulling himself forward. "Down" as a direction became meaningless; the spoke's shaft took a horizontal rather than a vertical perspective. By the time Hooker reached the hatch leading into the hub he was clinging lightly to the ladder, experiencing zero gee. It was a sign of how long he had been on Skycan—how long, too, he had trouble recalling—that he became almost instantly acclimated, with only the slightest feeling of queasiness.

The spoke ended at the entrance to the hub, in a central passageway running perpendicular to the rim. Another hatch opposite to the one he emerged from led to the east spoke leading back down to the other half of the torus. In one direction, the passageway led to Command/Communications and the airlocks. In the other, toward the south pole, were Power Control and Meteorology. The soft hiss of air from the vents was drowned out by "Yesterday," reverberating off the metal walls.

By the time he reached the weather station at the end of the hub, passing the yellow radioactivity warning signs on the hatches leading into Power Control, the Muzak had segued into "Close To You" and Hooker was feeling closer to the edge than before. The hatch at the end of the corridor was marked "METEOROLOGY—Authorized Personnel Only." Popeye grasped a handrail and pressed the button on the intercom by the hatch and waited, trying to shut out the saccharine violins and chorus. Impending insanity was soundtracked by the Carpenters; there had to be better ways to lose one's mind.

The intercom crackled and he heard the voice of one of the bogus meteorologists. This one called himself Dave, but no one knew their real names. "Yeah? Whoizzit?"

"Claude Hooker," Popeye said. "Hey, is the telescope free now? For a few minutes?"

The intercom was silent for a moment. Popeye imagined Dave consulting with the other two men in the crowded compartment beyond the hatch. *Popeye's out there. Wants to use the telescope. Any incoming transmissions?* He hoped things were quiet in Cuba and Nicaragua today.

The intercom crackled again. "Yeah, okay, Popeye, for a few minutes. Give us a chance to straighten up in here first, okay?"

Hooker nodded, forgetting that Dave could not see him. The "straighten up" line was a tired old shuck. In microgravity there was no place for carelessly misplaced items; a compartment in Skycan's hub always had to be kept shipshape. Dave and his companions were doubtless putting away long-range telephotos of Soviet silos and submarine bays and troop movements, transcripts of messages from Washington and Langley and Cheyenne Mountain.

In a sense, the three men in the weather station did serve as meteorologists. If asked, they could confidently explain current weather patterns in the Western Hemisphere, tell a listener a high pressure system hanging over the American Midwest was causing St. Louis to feel like an anteroom of Hell or why a front coming in from the Pacific was dumping rain over northern California and Oregon.

But everyone in Olympus Station's hundred-person complement, except for the occasional greenhorn who happened to ask why the three meteorologists generally kept to themselves, knew that Dave and his companions Bob and John were National Security Agency analysts. They were weathermen of the world's geopolitical climate, rather than the natural. Their meteorologist roles were rather weak covers for their spending long hours in a compartment crammed with telescopes and radio equipment.

Their cover story had never been very solid. The phony weathermen knew that the rest of the crew knew their real purpose aboard Skycan, and the crew knew that they knew that as well. No one made an issue of it, though, or at least as long as little favors were extended by the NSA spooks. Sometimes it was getting them to transmit, via their private communications downlink, birthday and Christmas greetings to friends and relatives on Earth, or allowing a homesick space hardhat a few minutes at one of the few optical telescopes aboard, and the only one kept fixed on the planet.

For the NSA weathermen the little favors could be written off as good public relations and a guarantee that no wise-aleck beamjack would stop by their table at mess and loudly inquire about how every little thing was in Havana today.

The hatch opened from the inside, held open by Dave, his feet held to the carpet by his Velcro-soled sneakers. He stepped aside as Hooker gently pushed himself into the weather station. The other two guys—John and Bob, or whatever their names were that week— were seated before consoles, ostensibly studying photos of a storm front gathering over the West Indies; there were no photos or computer printouts anywhere in sight. The three of them looked almost like brothers who had all gone to Yale, down to their cleanshaven faces, closely cropped hair, and neatly pressed uniform coveralls, which almost no one else bothered to wear or had modified by cutting off the sleeves or sewing on various unofficial patches. The weathermen were so cleancut, in fact, that whenever Skycorp's front office in Huntsville sent a request for publicity photos to illustrate press releases, the snapshots sent back were usually of Dave and John and Bob at work in their neat little compartment, dressed in their neat little uniforms, with a caption like "Olympus Station scientists at work uncovering the secrets of the universe." Everyone else aboard Skycan looked like the Three Stooges.

The weather station was a hemispherical bulge at the end of Olympus' hub, which was kept permanently pointed toward Earth. Half of the dome was windowed with thick Plexiglas, permitting the best view of Earth available on the space station. Arrayed around the window were various consoles and screens, the largest of which was the TV screen belonging to the telescope.

The telescope itself was a smaller version of the big space telescope in orbit near Skycan, which was used by the astrophysics lab. It was positioned outside the dome on a yoke and was operated by a joystick on the console below the TV screen, which turned the box-shaped instrument in the direction desired. Whatever was captured in the telescope's three-inch lens was transmitted to the TV screen inside the dome.

Hooker attached his own Velcro slippers to the carpet and walked to the bucket seat in front of the telescope console. As he sat down and strapped himself in, Dave bent over next to him and put his fingers on the console's touchpad controls.

"What'll it be today, Popeye?" he asked pleasantly. "There's clear skies over the Rockies. . . . I got a really stunning view of the Great Divide this morning. Can you believe there's still some snow up there? Bob managed to see a whale pod swimming off the coast of Nova Scotia a little while ago, too."

"Gulf of Mexico," Hooker replied. "Off the coast of Florida. Panama City area, northern part of the state."

"Kinda overcast over Florida today, Popeye," Bob said.

"He's right," Dave said. "There might be a hurricane developing in the Caribbean. We've been keeping an eye on it for the past couple of days."

"You'll have to make it short," said John, the gruffest of the trio. "We have to track the thing, y'know."

Hooker wondered if they were watching the hurricane or the movements of Soviet subs near the Dominican Republic. Besides, it was early summer down there, not exactly hurricane season yet. But there was no sense in irritating the bogus meteorologists with those notions. He noticed that the Muzak had not penetrated the sanctum of the weather station. Apparently John, Dave, and Bob, with their exalted government status, had escaped Cap'n Wallace's means of improving crew efficiency and morale.

"Try it anyway, please," Hooker prodded. "I won't stay long."

Dave shrugged and tapped instructions into the telescope's range finder.

Watching the TV screen, Hooker saw the Earth leap toward him, the thousands of miles peeling away as if he were sitting on an accelerating rocket hurtling down the gravity well. He stopped four hundred miles above the ground. Patchy clouds filled the screen, indistinct at first but becoming more defined as Dave adjusted the focus. Through breaks in the shroud he could see brown and green edged by sapphire blue. Dave checked a computer simulation on a smaller screen beside them.

"We're over Louisiana right now," he told Popeye. He sniffed the cool, conditioned air. "Mmm-*mmmmh!* Can't you just smell that Cajun cooking!" he said theatrically, trying to imitate a deep southern drawl with his New England accent.

"Never could stand coon-ass country myself," Bob said from his console across the compartment. "The girls are nice, but some of those redneck types there . . ."

"Hang on, Popeye," Dave said, noticing the beamjack's restless fidgeting. "Lemme just recalibrate the . . ." His fingers danced across the glowing keys as he watched the computer simulation. "Ah, there we go."

The screen blurred as the scene shifted to the right and closed in, tracking across the southern tier of states as it simultaneously zoomed in. Earth spiraled around, 22,300 miles away; from this part of Olympus it looked as if the planet were constantly in a slow tailspin. The telescope's computer corrected this illusion caused by Skycan's own revolution, giving observers a steady picture of the surface that didn't induce vertigo.

"We're in luck," Dave said. "Found a break in the cloud cover. We're somewhere over the Gulf near northern Florida. We want to . . . ?"

"Yeah, let me handle it."

He gripped the joystick and gingerly maneuvered the telescope. It wasn't much different than handling the hand controls of an MMU backpack, requiring the same delicate touch, and he had already done it a couple of previous times when he'd been down to the weather station. Watching the screen, he glided above azure waters thousands of miles away, yet so seemingly close he could imagine himself in an ultralight plane sailing above the ocean. His body tensed, and he stared at the afternoon sunlight glinting faintly on the gentle wave caps.

Suddenly a tiny sliver coasted into view: a boat, trailing whiskery lines of wake behind it. "Zoom in more, please," he murmured, his eyes fixed on the screen.

Dave obliged, leaning over Hooker's hunched shoulders to tap instructions into the telescope. The screen zoomed in closer and the white sliver enlarged to become a twin-mast sailboat, its sails filled with wind, its bow plunging in and out of the surf.

The deck was a white oval. For a second he could see—he *thought* he could see—a tiny, thin brown spot on the foredeck. A woman sunbathing near the bow. At least, so it seemed.

Hooker strained his eyes, almost pushing his face against the screen. There was no longer a carpeted floor under his feet; he felt the varnished, slippery deck. For an instant the air changed, becoming warmer, the most remote hint of fish smell mixed in with salt. . . .

He thought of Laura.

*She leaned against the rail on the starboard stern; blue halter top, faded jeans, chestnut brown hair blown back by the warm autumn breeze, highlighted by the orange setting sun, a tumbler of Scotch on the rocks in her right hand. Laughing . . .*

He remembered what her face looked like, that afternoon.

*A glint of gold against the blue, sinking, swallowed by the deep blue. Gone, forever gone . . .*

He shut his eyes.

*Cold, as only Atlantic waters can be cold. Salt water in his mouth. The night so dark, dark as death. Flames on the water, crackling in the distance, consuming a dark lump in the center, smoke rising against the starlight.*

He reopened his eyes. White clouds had scudded into view, blocking the view on the screen. The boat, the girl—all vanished into the puffy white. Gone, forever gone, like gold vanishing into the deep, deep blue.

"Go swim for it," he whispered.

"What'd you say?" Dave asked.

Hooker settled back into the chair, letting out a breath he hadn't realized he had been holding. "Never mind. Nothing."

"Nice view there for a little while, huh? How'd you like that boat?"

"Uh-huh. Nice boat." Hooker unfastened the seat belt, let himself float out of his chair. The third shift would be starting soon; he had to get to the airlock to catch the ferry over to Vulcan Station. Besides, John was giving him a dirty look, as if to say that he had worn out his welcome in the dome.

Dave laid a hand on his shoulder. "Hey, pal, you okay?"

Hooker felt depressed as hell. "Yeah, sure. I'm fine. Thanks for letting me take a look through the scope again."

"Sure, Popeye." The NSA meteorologist smiled. "Anything to help out a homesick swabbie."

# 2

# Ear Test

After Dave had closed and locked the hatch behind the departing Popeye Hooker, he was chided by Bob and John for allowing the beamjack inside. After all, they were expecting a classified transmission from the NSA's headquarters in Fort Meade, Virginia, material rated "Top Secret-Eyes Only" of which only a few people in the federal government were even aware. If Popeye had overheard the transmission, he could have spread word around Olympus Station that something called Big Ear was being tested.

"So big deal," Dave said, pulling himself hand over hand back to his chair. "Everyone knows about the Ear. You can pick up a newspaper down there and read all about it."

"You know what I mean," Bob replied, glaring at him from his seat beside the communications console. "It isn't just the Ear."

"Yeah, uh-huh. I know what you mean. But, y'know, if we were to let the cat out of the bag . . ."

"Five years in Leavenworth, like that." Bob snapped his fingers. "Unauthorized disclosure of security-sensitive information. Don't even think about it, Jarrett."

"No, I mean if *someone* were to release that, uh, info . . . y'know, if that happened, and someone were to take a poll and ask everyone how they felt about it, I'd bet that most people would say this was the right thing to do."

John blew out his cheeks derisively. "Yeah, I bet. You know what kind of shit would hit the fan if this got out? What Congress would say? The ACLU? The UN? Come back to reality, pal. . . ."

"Besides, if it got out, it'd just render the system useless," Bob added, nodding his head. "Something like this has to be kept secret for it to work."

He paused, staring up at a CRT screen over his head displaying a graphic representation of low-orbital space above Earth. "Okay, birds One and Two are coming into position. We should be hearing from Meade any minute now." He pulled his headset up from around his neck and fitted it over his cranium, pulling the microphone into place in front of his mouth.

"Anyway, so I feel sorry for the guy," Dave continued, gently lowering himself into his own chair and strapping his torso into place. "I think he's really getting nutty for going back home."

"So who isn't?" John said. He adjusted his own headset and touched glowing buttons on his console, which changed its liquid crystal display. "Man, I've been up here nine months now and my wife and kids still think I'm in Ecuador."

Dave said nothing. He gazed through the big port in front of him at Earth spiraling below them. He spotted a wink of reflected light moving across the planet, just above the Caribbean. That would be the Freedom space station, orbiting three hundred miles above the equator.

"Hey, when are they going to switch command and control over to Freedom?" he asked.

"When all the tests are done," John replied, working at his console. His fingers wandered across the pressure-sensitive LCD keyboard. "I think they're talking three or four months from now, whenever Skycorp get done building the module."

Bob looked at them both sourly. "That's classified, Knox," he said to "John." "I don't want to hear either one of you chitchatting about it, understand?"

Dave turned away to keep Bob from seeing the expression on his face. Christ, working with Piers Pauley—whom everyone aboard Skycan knew as Bob—was a major pain in the butt. The man was career NSA through and through; the Agency was his first priority at all times. Dave suspected that Pauley had taken this post as a steppingstone to advancement in the Agency, that he had ambitions of becoming a senior administrator in NSA's space-based intelligence operations. Dave himself only wanted to stay on as long as it took to amass enough savings in the bank; then he would retire from the Agency and move back to his native New Hampshire, perhaps open up a restaurant in North Conway. The hell with cloak-and-dagger, and the hell especially with the Big Ear.

"Incoming transmission from Meade," Bob said. He touched buttons on his console. "You're patched in Knox. Scrambler working."

"Big Dog, this is Olympus Weatherman," John intoned. "We're green for Ear Test. Do you copy?"

*Roger, we copy, Weatherman,* an equally monotone voice said in their earphones. *The Ear is in place. Send activation code and stand by for program transmission.*

John picked up an envelope that had been magnetically tacked to his console and tore it open, drawing out a red slip of paper. "Bob, the activation code is one, seven, seven, nine, foxtrot gamma tango," he read from the paper. Bob entered the code on his communications console keyboard.

An instant later: *Roger, Weatherman, code received and authenticated. Now transmitting program.*

All three men moved their fingers over their terminals' keyboards, touching controls which cleared their systems. The LCD's, which had displayed meteorological commands, went dark, leaving empty black glass surfaces. A few moments later a completely different set of command keys, controlling the new program just transmitted from Virginia, appeared on the consoles.

"Big Dog, we've received program," Bob said. "Awaiting commencement of test."

*We copy, Weatherman. Test begins in thirty seconds.*

Dave touched silver keys on his console, watched them turn gold. "Recorder activated," he said. "Source locator on standby."

"Locator slaved to Big Dog feed," John said.

"Signal locked with Meade and Big Ear," Bob said. "Comlink status green."

"Big Dog, Weatherman is green," John said.

*Roger, Weatherman. Test begins now.*

Instantly, small green lamps appeared on each display, lighting the words SYSTEM TEST. Dave glanced at the cassette loaded in the recorder by his elbow, affirmed that the machine was working, the reels moving. Okay, now to see how long it would take for the Ear to hear something.

At that second, a digital numeral 2 appeared on their displays. "Holy Mother," he murmured to himself, "that was quick."

"Big Dog, this is Weatherman," Bob said. "We have two possibles, over."

*We copy, Weatherman. Please monitor.*

John touched buttons on his console and immediately all three men heard new voices in their earphones—a conversation between two men, as clear as if they had picked up an extension phone in one of their houses:

*. . . I'm telling you, he's no damn good. We should have never elected him, never believed a word he said. It was all campaign bull-*

*shit, all the time. Now the bastard's sending troops to Central America
and you can bet Stevie's one of them.*

*Yeah, A-right. I told Stevie she shoulda split to Canada. . . .*

*Canada's just catching 'em and shippin' 'em back to the States.
Doesn't do any damn good to run from the draft now. I'm telling ya,
Jeff, the only way to stop that crazy fucker is to kill him before he gets
us further into this mess. . . .*

A thread of print appeared on their screens: SAN DIEGO, CA. MAX
A. HILLMAN 2206 OCEANSIDE 6198750646; SAN DIEGO, CA. ROBERT
P. ROSE 1117 PALMETTO 6190324201.

"Big Dog, Weatherman," Bob said into his mike. "Intercepted
telephone conversation in San Diego. Possible discussion of Presidential assassination. Location and identities verified." He glanced
over his shoulder at Dave; Dave nodded back. "Conversation recorded."

*Roger, Weatherman. Data received. Monitor second possible, please.*

John cut off the first conversation, touched buttons that brought
the second phone call Big Ear had netted into their earphones.

A child's squeaky voice; it could have belonged to either a boy or a
girl, no more than six or seven years old: *So my daddy says there
could be a nukey bom' put in, put in a big city, y'know, an' if someone
wanted to call the Pres'dent and say you gimme a hunnert zillion
dollars or I'll blow it up and kill everybody and the Pres'dent would
have to say okay 'cause if he din't all those people would get kilt and
he wouldn't get re'lected. . . .*

Another child's voice: *Yeah, yeah! But y'know, y'know, y'know
whatta work better, huh?*

*If, if, if . . . if you gotta nuk'la bomb and we put it in the base-
ment of the school, huh? An' we called Miz McDaniels an' said, you
better stop Jeff and Mike and the other third grade guys from beating
us up an' we getta watch TV during arithmetic, or we . . .*

The three men began to howl. When Bob switched the comlink
back to the Fort Meade channel they could hear the reciprocal
laughter from the men in Virginia. "Big Dog, that call originated in
Jackson, Tennessee. Do you want a fix?"

*Ah, that's a negatory, Weatherman. I don't think we have a threat
to national security there.*

"We copy, Big Dog." Bob paused, studying his display. Dave
checked his own screen and saw that three more possibles were being
registered by the system. "The Ear's picked up three more bogies,"
John said. "Do you want us to monitor?"

*Negative, Weatherman, we can analyze them here. Big Dog calls his chowtime good eating and our compliments to the chef. Ah, Surfer Joe is ready to hang three in a few weeks.* "Surfer Joe" was the code name for the Vandenberg AFB launch site, the point from the which the next cluster of SIGINT satellites would be boosed into polar obit. *Erase data and terminate link. See you, Big Dog out.*

"Weatherman out, Big Dog," Bob said.

"Woof woof," John murmured, and typed a sequence of commands which both erased the key display and wiped the one-time program from the computer.

As Dave shut down his keyboard and wiped the program Fort Meade had sent up, he glanced at the recorder he had just shut off. On that tape were two conversations: one between a pair of irate but not necessarily harmful Californians, the other between two kids somewhere in Tennessee. Private phone calls, which the NSA had monitored, recorded, and determined their points of origin. The guys in San Diego—especially Robert P. Rose, who had offhandedly mentioned shooting the President—were about to come under investigation by the Agency. . . .

For saying things they thought had been said in the privacy of their homes. Dave frowned as he worked. *And I thought sedition laws had been found to be unconstitutional. . . .*

Big Ear. When the system was complete and fully operational, being able to locate and intercept phone calls that seemed to threaten national security would be just a drop in the bucket.

Suddenly, Dave found himself getting worried: *What in the hell am I helping to create?*

# 3

# The Wheel

I don't know why we didn't call Olympus Station "the Wheel." In one of those grand, corny old science fiction movies of the 1950's, *The Conquest of Space,* there was a torus-shaped space station, and its crew called it the Wheel, but that's not what we called ours.

Maybe it was because the crew in that movie and the crew of Skycorp One had fundamental differences in attitude. Cap'n Wallace got a videotape of *The Conquest of Space* shipped up to us once, to show in the rec room on Saturday night. We all got a big laugh out of it, which annoyed Henry George Wallace because he took it seriously. There was no way we could. Spit-and-polish Air Force officer types going around saluting and eating food capsules—that wasn't us by a long shot, with the possible exception of the NSA spooks in Meteorology. It embarrassed Wallace because that was his fantasy of how we were supposed to be, and that episode made him all the more reclusive—but I'll get to that later.

We called our wheel in space "Skycan," which aptly summed up the living conditions. The Federation starship *Enterprise* it wasn't. In fact, I can't imagine a more boring place to live, except maybe for the Moon.

Does it come as a surprise that living in space is boring? That the image of happy, enthusiastic spacemen giving their all for the future of stellar conquest is an idealistic myth? I think a few of the crewmen who slipped out and had to be sent back home did so because of the shock that space life is not the picnic it's cut out to be. The guys who stayed, and kept their act straight, did so because they found ways of coping with Skycan. Wallace had his fantasy world, of the intrepid commander leading his men boldly forth where no man has gone before. I had my SF to read and write, a similar escape, if not quite as obnoxious. Other people came up with other ways, and I'll get around to telling you about that. But let's start with good ol' Skycan.

As the name implies, it was cramped. A new extreme in coziness, you might say. Each bunkhouse module was about twenty-four feet long by six feet wide, with eight bunks per module, four on each side. The bunks had accordian screens across the open sides; each bunk had its own locker, intercom, viewscreen, and computer terminal. And, except for the modules occupied by Doc Felapolous, Wallace, and Hank Luton, the construction foreman, that was the maximum amount of privacy one could get in the station. Not even the showers and johns were that private.

Speaking of the showers: Because we had to be water-conservative, we often went days—and sometimes weeks—without bathing. You got used to it. After a while.

From the outside, Skycan looked like a huge stylized top hanging in geosynchronous orbit. As one got closer, as during an approach from Earth or from one of the other stations, smaller spacecraft could be seen continuously moving around it: orbital-transfer vehicles up from low Earth orbit, ferries transporting men to and from Vulcan Station, on occasion a Big Dummy or a Jarvis bringing up supplies from the Cape.

The station consisted of forty-two modules linked together by interlocking connectors and rail-like rims running above and below the modules. On the inside of the wheel was an inner torus, an inflated passageway which connected the modules, called the "catwalk." At the center of the wheel was the hub, a converted external tank from a *Columbia*-class shuttle that had been brought into high orbit by OTV tugs and transformed into the station's operation center. It was connected to the rim modules by two spokes, which ended at terminus modules at opposite ends of the rim.

All the modules were the same size, and had been brought up, three at a time, by Big Dummy HLV cargo ships. The modules, built at Skycorp's Cocoa Beach facility, each had certain specialized functions. Besides the sixteen bunkhouses, there were four modules for the wardroom, or mess decks; two for Data Processing, where the computers were maintained; two for Sickbay/Bio Research; two for the rec room; five for Hydroponics, where the algae and vegetables were grown; three for Life Support, where water and air quality and circulation was controlled; two each at opposite ends of the station for Reclamation, which purified and recycled the water and solid wastes from the bunkhouses; one for the Lunar Resources lab; one for the Astrophysics lab; and two for Skycorp's offices, which doubled as comparatively spacious living quarters for Wallace and Luton.

The hub was about one hundred and fifty-five feet long and twenty-eight feet wide. Through the center ran a central shaft that connected the levels; the spokes ran into it at the center of the hub. At the bottom was Meteorology; above that was Power Control, which housed the RTG nuclear cells that powered the station. Above the spoke intercepts was the Command deck, the largest compartment on Skycan except for Power Control, containing the work stations for the crewmen operating Traffic Control, Communications, and other functions. Above Command was Astronaut Prep—better known as the "whiteroom" from the old NASA days—where crewmen went to prepare for EVA or for boarding spacecraft. The last level was the Multiple Target Docking Adapter, better known as the airlock or the Docks, where up to five spacecraft could dock with Skycan.

Olympus spun, clockwise in reference to Earth, at 2.8 rpm, which produced at the rim an artificial gravity of one-third Earth normal. There was only microgravity, or zero gee, at the hub. When a ship prepared to link with the Docks, operators at Traffic Control activated motors that turned the module counterclockwise at 2.8 rpm. This produced the illusion that the MTDA was standing still while the rest of Skycan continued to turn, making it possible for the craft to connect without wrecking itself or the Docks.

Living up there produced a funny kind of orientation. At the rim, in one of the modules, "up" was in the direction of the spokes and the hub. At the hub, "down" was the modules. We had also divided the station's rim into two hemispheres, for purposes of designation in an environment where, when one walked down the catwalk, one eventually came back to the place from which he or she had started. So Modules 1 through 21 were in the "eastern" hemisphere, with the spoke leading from that half of the station being the east spoke. Modules 22 through 42 were in the "western" hemisphere, with the spoke in that half of the station being the west spoke.

The modules were designated by numbers, but for easy identification along the catwalk small colored panels had been affixed to the walls beside the access hatches in the floor. The modules were thus color-coded: The bunkhouses were dark blue, Hydroponics was brown, the Wardroom was yellow, Life Support and Data Processing were both gray, Sickbay was white, the rec modules were green, Reclamation was amber, the terminus modules were light blue, and the science modules were scarlet. Fortunately we didn't have problems with colorblind personnel, since Skycorp weeded those people out in its selection process.

The color-coding of the modules was the only bit of color one could find on Skycan. Everything was painted a flat, utilitarian gray. It added a great deal to the monotony. There were no windows except in the hub; TV screens near the ceilings next to CRT displays gave the only views of what was going on outside. Most of the furniture was bolted to the floor, and little of it seemed to have been designed with the human body in mind. Pipes and conduits ran across the ceilings and most of the walls. The lighting was white and harsh, from fluorescent tubes in the ceilings. Since the hatches were heavy and hard to shut, they were left open most of the time, except in Hydroponics and Data Processing, where certain temperatures had to be maintained, and in Reclamation, which reeked like an outhouse.

Muzak played constantly from the speakers in the modules and in the catwalk and in the spokes—Henry's idea of improving morale, which did exactly the opposite. Sometimes you found a couple of guys on the catwalk throwing Frisbees, making them bounce off the floor and the curving Mylar walls. In the rec room you could work out on the gym equipment or stare at the wide-screen TV or play video games, but that was about it.

We had books and magazines, but we had read them all because there were not very many. There were members of the opposite sex aboard, but in such cramped quarters there was hardly any chance to get laid with any privacy. While getting it on in a bunk with the curtains closed, one might expect to hear people outside, murmuring, laughing, making obscene noises.

We had video cassettes sent up to us, to show on the rec deck, but it was most G for General Audiences stuff—Walt Disney nature flicks, unfunny sitcoms, space adventures and so forth—that H.G. Wallace thought was best for our morale. I've lost count of how many times we saw the *Star Wars* movies, Goldie Hawn flicks, *The Pat Robertson Story* and *The L-5 Family: Part III.*

No vacations for the guys on one-year tours of duty. One vacation to Earth for the guys on two-year contracts. It cost a thousand bucks per pound to get something up to the Clarke Orbit, so if it cost nearly $200,000 to send an average-sized person to Olympus Station, including the cost in job training and life support, you can bet Skycorp wouldn't bring 'em back to Earth for a week just because he or she was getting a little bored. As stated in the fine print on the job contract, only a death in the family or a severe medical problem could get you sent temporarily back to Earth. Some of the guys with two-year contracts didn't even bother to take their vacations; it just wasn't worth having to go through readjusting to low-gravity life, with the usual recurrence of spacesickness that went along with it.

So there were one hundred and thirty of us aboard that wheel in the sky: building the powersats, putting up with the boredom and cramped quarters, making money the hard way to support families or start small businesses like restaurants or game parlors when we got back home. Working, eating, sleeping, working. Getting bored.

People started doing strange things after a while.

# 4

# *Virgin Bruce*

A few minutes after Popeye Hooker, in an even more funky mood than before his visit to Meteorology, floated up the hub's central shaft to the Docks, a crewman on the Command deck stared at his console's main CRT and murmured, "What the hell?"

His screen displayed the whereabouts of all spacecraft in a three-dimensional region of space around Olympus Station and Vulcan Station. Although the screen was two-dimensional, computer graphics depicted the spacecraft as existing in a sphere sixty miles in diameter. Each blip on the screen was designated with a different color according to its type. Small print above each blip showed the craft's location and trajectory on the X, Y, and Z axes.

What the space traffic controller noticed was a craft enroute from the construction shack to the main station. This was not unusual in itself; at least a dozen ships made the fifty-mile trip between Vulcan and Olympus each day. What was odd was that this craft was a construction pod, and they never—absolutely *never*—made trips between the two stations.

If one of the beamjacks at the powersat needed to return to Olympus, he never rode over in one of the OTVs that served as interorbital ferries. The construction pods were difficult to pilot; most of the guys who were trained to operate them preferred not to make the delicate docking maneuver more than they had to during a work shift.

More importantly, though, the pods' fuel supplies were limited. Someone attempting to make a run back to Skycan in a pod ran a high risk of running out of fuel on the way over. Being set adrift was more of a nuisance than it was a danger. It just meant that someone else had to drop what he was doing to go out in another spacecraft to tow the unlucky pod back to Vulcan Station. But because this meant lost time and productivity, using construction pods for commutes between Vulcan and Olympus was strictly against regulations. With the exception of a single pod that was kept at Skycan for maintenance jobs around the station, most of the pods remained in the vicinity of Vulcan Station and SPS-1.

Yet, there one was. The white blip on the controller's screen was a Vulcan construction pod, and its coordinates and bearing showed it to be heading for Skycan.

The controller raised his headset mike to lip level and touched a button on his intercom. "Communications? Joni? This is Rick at TC."

Communications was located a half-level below Traffic Control. If the controller glanced over his shoulder and down, he could have looked through the open-grid metal flooring and seen the radio deck, about fifteen feet away. More than once, he wished his station could have been closer to Joni's station. In fact, having her sitting in his lap would have been just close enough.

*Communications. What's up, Anderson?* Joni's throaty voice responded in his earphones. A lovely voice, Anderson reflected. The kind you could fantasize about hearing at night, in your bed. He just loved to talk to Communications when she was on duty.

"Ah, I have a construction pod on my screen, bearing nine, three, three, on course for Olympus. Have you had any radio contact, love?"

There was a pause. *A construction pod, Traffic Control?*

Anderson wished she would be a bit less formal with him. Oh, *mon cheri amour,* perhaps even informal enough to take your clothes off for me? He glanced at his console again, to be sure. "That's confirmed, ah, Communications." But why rush things? "That's construction pod Zulu Tango on direct course for Olympus. Have you received radio confirmation?"

*Opening comlink and signaling, Traffic Control. Stand by.*

Anderson heard the familiar whisper of the primary channel being opened and lovely Ms. Lowenstein's voice saying, *Construction pod Zulu Tango, this is Olympus Command. Do you request emergency docking instructions? Over.*

A pause. Nothing. No response from the approaching pod.

Her voice again. *Construction pod Zulu Tango, this is Olympus Command. Do you copy? Over.*

Anderson checked his screen again. The pod was still on a beeline for Skycan. From the data the computer was giving him, it was a little less than fifteen miles from Olympus and closing. He glanced up at an overhead TV monitor, but couldn't make out the pod's navigational lights from the stars in the background. Anderson figured the little spacecraft had to be running on its fuel reserves by now.

*Zulu Tango, this is Olympus,* Joni Lowenstein said again. *Do you copy? Please acknowledge contact.*

What's going on with this asshole? Anderson wondered. Is his radio out?

As if in reply, a new voice came over the radio link. *Olympus Command, this is Zulu Tango, over.*

*Zulu Tango, you're in Olympus traffic zone. Do you wish to dock? Over.*

*You're damn straight I want to dock, Olympus.* The voice had a distinguishable sneer in it. *Clear Bay Three, over.*

Anderson felt his temper rise. Who did this jerk think he was, demanding docking space for a pod at Olympus? "Open the channel, Joni," he snapped. When he heard the click of the frequency being opened to him, he said, "Pod Zulu Tango, this is Olympus Traffic. What the hell are you trying to pull?"

*Listen, pencil-neck Olympus Traffic,* the voice snarled, *don't gimme any shit and get that bay open* now!

Anderson, gasping for breath, could have sworn he heard the communications officer stifle a laugh. Her voice then came back on the line. *Zulu Tango, is this an emergency? Over.*

*Lady, there's going to be an emergency if you don't get pencil-neck to gimme a clear place to park this bug. I'm decelerating now, and I don't want anything between me and Bay Three 'cept ten miles of nothing, or I'm going to stomp on his head. Over.*

Anderson reeled back from his console, staring at the screen and the white blip on it, which now seemed as big as a golf ball. What manner of maniac were they dealing with here? A ferry to Vulcan about to go out, another on approach from the shack, an OTV bringing up a cargo canister from low orbit—and here was a pod with no business being there at all, demanding an airlock all to its own. H.G. Wallace was going to have a duck. . . .

The voice from Zulu Tango came over the link again: *And while you're at it, Olympus, get Wallace and tell him that Neiman wants words with him when I get in. Thank you, sweetheart . . . over and out.*

The string of insults Anderson had prepared disappeared from his mouth. Neiman. Of course, it would be Neiman. His lip curled in disgust, but he felt his hands quiver slightly, and he hurried to clear the other traffic away from Bay Three.

He now knew what manner of maniac with whom they were dealing.

The construction pod was a squat cylinder that looked vaguely like a bumblebee; indeed, the yellow and black stripes running horizontally along its midsection added to its metaphorical appearance. Its primary electrical supply, at the rear, came from a long bank of solar cells resembling wings. The large spherical fuel tanks near the bottom could have been pollen sacks; the polarized canopy windows on its front, multifaceted eyes; the docking adapter on its top perhaps the bee's jaws. Most insectile were the two long, articulated arms thrusting out from either side of the cockpit, which looked like a bee's front legs. The pod moved by means of thrusters arranged around the fuselage, and depending upon the skill of the pilot, it tended to behave like a flying insect, with sharp, apparently erratic movements.

Classed technically as a FFWS—Free-Flier Work Station—its manufacturer had tried to peg the little space vehicle "work bees." Yet too many of the beamjacks had seen the movie *2001* for the name to stick. As long as there were wags to mumble, upon approaching for a docking, the immortal phrase—"Open the pod bay door, Hal" —the FFWS's would be known as pods, manufacturers' metaphors notwithstanding.

Pod Zulu Tango made its final approach to Olympus' third airlock in the MTDA at the top of the station, its thrusters flashing as its pilot gently brought it in. While the station's rim and hub continued to rotate, the pilot's eyes and the simulation on his navigational computer both told him that the MTDA was stationary, an illusion caused by the backward rotation of the module itself.

As it closed in on the airlock, Dave Chang, the Chinese-American who served as the whiteroom chief, glanced out a porthole, saw the pod's hatch in the center of the docking adapter, and knew at once that they were all in big trouble.

Chang had been given only a brief warning from Anderson down in Traffic Control that a construction pod from Vulcan was making an unexpected rendezvous at Skycan. The instructions had been few; an order from Command that, under no circumstances, would the pilot be allowed to leave the Docks before Security Officer Bigthorn and Doc Felapolous arrived. Anderson had not told Chang who exactly it was inside the pod, negligence which Chang now believed to be the result of his having fleeced Anderson at a blackjack game in their bunkhouse a couple of weeks ago.

Anderson, obviously, was trying to set him up for a big surprise. But Chang had worked in the whiteroom at Vulcan before being sent over to Olympus, and thus knew all of the beamjacks. He was also aware that many of the workers who were assigned to fly the pods had their own preferences as to which of the machines they operated. Technically, regulations did not allow such preferences, but Luton quietly let them get away with rule-bending the way Wallace wouldn't allow, so some of the pod pilots were given dibs on the machines with which they were most comfortable.

These pod pilots sometimes painted things on the hatches, which was also supposedly against regulations. Some of the pods thus had names ("Pod Person"; "Magic Fingers"; "Bertha"; "Smilin' Ed") and designs (Scooby Do sitting on a rocket; a buxom blonde winking seductively; a kid running along with a pizza under the slogan "We Deliver!").

What Dave Chang saw on Zulu Tango's hatch, illuminated by the pod's running lights, was a grinning skull emblazoned with eagle wings. Painted below the skull, in red paint, were the words "Ride To Live, Live To Ride."

"Oh, boy," Chang said, "we are in deep shit now."

"What?" asked Harris. The kid was strapped into a chair near Chang's head; Chang was floating upside down next to the console Harris was attending. The kid was wearing a headset and had not clearly heard what Chang had said.

Chang looked at Harris. "I said, 'Why don't you go up and see if he needs help with his suit?' "

Harris studied Chang curiously. "I thought you said something else."

Chang shook his head. "You misunderstood me. I'll take over there. Why don't you go and help the beamjack out of his pod?"

Bob Harris was new on Skycan, having arrived for his twelve-month tour only two weeks before. He had grown up in San Francisco and had thus known Chinese-Americans all his life; he considered them to be the most straightforward and sincere people around. He was therefore willing to do anything his Chinese-American supervisor told him to do, and in fact regarded Dave Chang as his best friend on Olympus Station.

Chang, on the other hand, had long since grown tired of Harris' puppyish devotion, considered him a putz and thought he should be abused at any opportunity. He just smiled and nodded toward the hatch leading to the Docks.

"Sure thing, Dave," Harris said, returning the smile. He unbuckled his chair's belt, floated upward and grabbed a pair of handholds, then began pulling himself toward the hatch. Chang settled into the chair and watched as Harris waited for the lights above the hatch to indicate that the MTDA had been pressurized. When the lights flashed green and a bell chimed, Harris undogged the hatch and pulled it open.

Once Harris had floated into the chamber, Chang pushed himself toward the hatch, pushed it shut, and turned the locking wheel. After all, he mused, the orders had been not to let the beamjack out until Mr. Big and Dr. Feelgood arrived. He then went back to the console to watch the show on the TV monitor.

The Docks was a narrow compartment about the size of one of the rim modules. There were five docking bays there, equilaterally separated by handrails and storage compartments. It was forever cold in the compartment, exposed as often as it was to vacuum. Only a few minutes earlier a ferry taking beamjacks out to the construction shack had departed from Olympus, so the heater had yet to take the edge off the chill.

Puffing little clouds, Harris made his way to the third airlock; he could see the locking wheel turning as the pod pilot began to let himself out.

He coasted in front of the hatch and grabbed hold of a rail overhead, hovering in front of the airlock as it swung open. As it did, he said cheerily, "Hi. Can I help you . . . ?"

A fabric snoopy helmet was flung through the open hatch with such force that it smacked into Harris' chest. The young crewman, who had played a lot of basketball, instinctively made to grab it with both hands. His letting go of the rail and the impact of the helmet was enough to send him sailing into the bulkhead wall behind him. Fortunately he had developed enough zero g reflexes to grab another handrail before he bounced into another hard surface.

With the rail gripped in one hand and the snoopy helmet—which, he now noticed, was trailing loose wires—clutched under his arm, he stared at the open airlock and watched the pod pilot clamber out.

The man who emerged was small, even by the standards of beamjacks, who never reached a height of over six feet. Five-five, probably the shortest admissible height for a Skycorp employee, but an awfully mean-looking five-five. With thin black hair combed straight back and a spade beard covering most of his lean face, the space worker would have looked filthy stepping out of a shower and ravenous coming away from a four-course meal.

He pushed himself through the airlock with the practiced ease of a long-timer. Eyes as black as his hair fixed on Harris, and his gaze made the kid think of rattlesnakes he had seen in zoos.

"Yeah, you can help me," the pod pilot said, in a voice that was surprisingly soft. Floating in the middle of the compartment, he began to climb out of his spacesuit, releasing the top and bottom halves and pushing himself out of them. "You can help me by getting Cap'n Wallace's ass down here so I can chew it off, you dig?"

"Cap'n W-Wallace?" Harris stammered.

"Y-yeah, Ca-Cap'n Wa-Wallace," he mimicked with a sneer. He discarded his spacesuit carelessly, leaving it hanging in the air like a discarded carapace, unbelted his urine collection cup, and began to unzip his long underwear. Underneath he wore a black T-shirt and a pair of nylon gym shorts. "And if I don't get him, I guess I'm just going to have to chew your ass instead."

"Uh-huh. Right away, ah, sir." Harris hastily moved toward the compartment hatch, still carrying the damaged helmet under his arm. He grabbed the handle, but found it immovable. Chang had locked the hatch from the outside.

Watching on the TV monitor in the whiteroom, Chang relished the expression of trapped fear that suddenly etched itself upon Harris' face. "Meet Virgin Bruce, you little wimp," he snickered.

Bruce Neiman grabbed an overhead rail and swung himself closer to Harris, backing the kid against a bulkhead until their eyes were only a foot apart. "Looks like you're locked in here with me, kid," he said, his voice no longer so soft. "Maybe Wallace is already on his way up here to see me. Why don't we take the time to get to know each other better."

"Uh, ah, yessir. My name's . . ."

"Shut up. My name's Bruce. Like it says here."

He pointed to a tattoo on his left bicep, just under the T-shirt's sleeve. Harris stared at it; it was a heart with a dagger thrust through it. A scroll underneath read "Virgin Bruce."

Virgin Bruce grinned, displaying a gold-capped front tooth. The rest of his teeth looked as if they had been kicked at, many times. "Ain't it pretty? What's your name, kid?"

"B-Bob Harris. I . . ."

"I don't give a shit. Where're you from, B-Bob Harris?"

"San—California—I mean, San Francisco . . ."

"San Francisco!" A wide grin suddenly spread beneath the spade beard. "That's the Grateful Dead's town. You know the Dead, Harris?"

Harris swallowed. He was familiar with the Grateful Dead, even if it was only from listening to his father play their old records every night of his childhood. Once the old man had taken him to a Grateful Dead concert, to see the band—which now included younger musicians teamed with the graying survivors of the original group— but the music had never stuck on him as it had on his father.

"Yeah," he quickly agreed. "I, uh, really like the Dead . . . man," he added. This guy couldn't be as old as his father, though, could he . . . ?

The grin stayed on the beamjack's face. "Yeah. You're awright. Shit, you couldn't live in Frisco without liking the Dead . . ."

He gave Harris a slap on the arm, which almost sent him sailing into the wall again, and unexpectedly began to sing. "Red and white . . . do, *dooh* . . . blue suede shoes . . . do, *dooh* . . . I'm Uncle Sam . . . do, *dooh* . . . how do you do do? . . . doom-da-do-de-doom . . ."

It was a Grateful Dead song. For the life of him Harris could not recall the title or the way it went, yet Virgin Bruce was clearly trying to get him to sing along. Harris flashed onto the absurdity of his situation: confined with a madman in an airlock thousands of miles from Earth, his life dependent upon remembering the lyrics to an old rock and roll song.

Virgin Bruce, in the midst of singing, thrust out his hand, palm spread upward. "So gimme *five!*" he sang.

Five? The beamjack was staring at him expectantly, waiting for something. Harris thrust his hands into his coverall pockets, searching for a nickel, and found he didn't have any change with him.

"Umm . . ." He swallowed what felt like a rock. "I . . . don't got any change, uh, man. . . ."

The light in Virgin Bruce's eyes disappeared as if it had been cut off by a switch. He glared at Harris and the younger man suddenly pictured himself being thrown out, screaming, through one of the nearby airlocks. Virgin Bruce himself looked tough enough to endure a few minutes of exposure to hard vacuum.

"Never mind," he grumbled instead, looking disappointed more than anything else. "No one can remember all the songs all the time."

He grabbed the wires dangling from the snoopy helmet he had hurled at Harris and wrenched the helmet out of the crewman's grasp. As it floated in front of Harris' face like an Indian's captured scalp, Bruce said, "You know what really pisses me off, though?"

"N-no, what . . . the helmet?"

"No, goddammit! The Muzak!"

"The music? The Dead?"

"Fuck, no, not the Grateful Dead! The *Muzak!*" His mouth stretched into a grimace. "Man, if they piped the Grateful Dead into my earphones I wouldn't be over here! I'd love hearing 'Truckin' or 'Hell in a Bucket' while I was out there pushin' girders around. I'd be the happiest dumb son of a bitch they got hired on this orbiting funny farm!"

He hurled the helmet across the compartment. It bounced off a locker with a dull *thump* and drifted in midair near the empty spacesuit he had cast aside, looking like a decapitated head. "But, oh *no,* Cap'n Wallace decides that if he's going to give any music to us hardworkin' Joes spending eight hours every day shoving around beams and welding cross sections with our feet, it's gonna be music that he likes . . . *dentist chair music!*" His voice rose to a scream. "Bullshit guaranteed to drive us out of our fuckin' *minds!*"

"Yeah," Harris mumbled hurriedly, "I can understand . . ."

"*Understand?*" Virgin Bruce shouted. "You can *understand?* Do you know what it's fucking *like?* Christ! You're out there sweating out trying to hold two beams a hundred feet long together with those claws and weld 'em together before they both drift off to Mars, getting that sweat frozen on your forehead 'cause the heater's on the blink again and it's twenty degrees inside that thing, and one of your buddies is on the radio having apoplexy 'cause he can't do what he's gotta do till you're done and out of the way, and Wallace and Luton are giving everyone hell 'cause the whole project's four months behind schedule . . . and what do you hear in the background on your headset, some faggot string section playing 'Born Free'! Don't tell me you can *understand, kid . . .*"

"Uhhh . . ."

"And you know why Wallace wants that crap piped all over the station, on the main comlink channel for the beamjacks? It's supposed to be calming, and to make us more efficient!"

"Ahhh . . ."

Whatever reply Harris might have managed was interrupted by the compartment hatch being unlocked and swung open. He and Virgin Bruce looked around to see two men pulling themselves through the hatch. One wore a uniform coverall bearing the shoulder insignia of Skycorp; on his breast was a patch that read "Security." A taser was strapped to his belt. He was also the biggest crewman on Olympus, and probably the biggest Navajo anyone on the station had ever met. Phil Bigthorn, a.k.a. "Mr. Big," had biceps the size of some guys' thighs.

The other newcomer wore a golf shirt and raggedy Bermuda shorts and, while not quite in Mr. Big's class, had a large, muscular build. Doc Felapolous' hair was prematurely gray, as was his mustache, which he kept waxed so that it tipped upward at the ends. In his early fifties, his age pushed the limit for Skycorp's space employees. His darkly tanned skin and deep wrinkles gave him the appearance of a desert rat, which fitted in with his Arizona upbringing.

Grasping a rail with one hand Mr. Big immediately started pulling himself toward Virgin Bruce. His other hand was reaching for his taser unit. Bruce grabbed for a handhold and swung himself around, bracing himself. Between them, Bob Harris looked as if he were trying to melt into the compartment wall.

Felapolous lightly grabbed Bigthorn's arm. "Hold on, Phil," he said calmly. "Let's just let ol' Bruce get a chance to explain himself."

His gaze went to the beamjack. "Now, Mr. Neiman, would you kindly explain to us just what in the blazes you're trying to prove?"

Virgin Bruce, meeting the security officer's cold stare, replied, "Would you explain to me what ape-shape is doing here?" A corner of his mouth twisted up as his eyes locked with Mr. Big's. "What's the matter, Phil? Looking for another dance like our one in the wardroom last month?"

Mr. Big smiled a smile completely devoid of any humor. "You want a fight, Brucie, you got a fight. This time you don't get a tray to bash me with. . . ."

"Gentlemen, you're beginning to behave like my nephews," Felapolous said, still as calm as an afternoon in the Sonora. "Besides that, you're about to give our friend here an anxiety attack." He looked at Bob Harris. "Son, unless you'd like to learn what it's like to be caught between two mad dogs, my advice to you as a physician is to get the hell out of there."

Harris glanced at the men on either side of him, then grabbed for a rail over his head and squirmed from between them. Doc Felapolous looked at Virgin Bruce, raising an eyebrow inquisitively. "To answer your question, Mr. Neiman, I suggest that you examine your own actions. You come blasting in here in a pod, against regulations, demanding docking space and turning the channel blue with your language. You threaten the traffic control officer and tell the com officer to send Mr. Wallace up here so you can 'have words with him.' When you get here, you pin the first person you see against the wall. . . ."

"Hey! I never touched him!" Virgin Bruce looked at Harris. "You tell him! I never laid a head on you!"

Harris shook his head vigorously. Felapolous barely gave him a glance. "All right, I'll take that back, although you did seem to be a bit intimidating when we came in here a second ago. At any rate, you've managed to create quite a stir. Considering your reputation . . ."

"Reputation!" Bruce shouted. "Listen, Doc, lemme tell you about my reputation. Check my record. Who pulls more double shifts than any other beamjack? Who manages to get four hundred square feet of that powersat built every three days? Who went out and rescued Jobe's ass when his tether broke?"

"Who did we catch trying to smuggle a case of beer up by bribing a shuttle pilot?" Mr. Big said. "Who once tried to hook into a comsat and attempted to transmit an obscene birthday message to the chairman of the board of Skycorp?"

Virgin Bruce started coughing, putting his hand over his mouth. Felapolous noticed the snoopy helmet with the torn out wires floating nearby. "Despite your propensity for sophomoric antics, I've never recalled an instance of you damaging equipment before," he said. "You want to tell me about it?"

"Well, yeah," Virgin Bruce said. "That's why I'm here, Dr. Feelgood. See . . ."

Felapolous raised a finger admonishingly. "Bruce, I would appreciate it if you didn't use that nickname someone has managed to pin on me. I may be known for dispensing various and sundry painkillers, but as a licensed physician and member in good standing of the AMA, I prefer that you call me 'Doctor' or 'Doc' or 'Felapolous' or 'Edwin' or any combination of the aforesaid. 'Dr. Feelgood' makes me sound like the guy who used to be the President's personal physician." He paused, gasped hugely, and sneezed into his palm. "You may continue. And please hurry; this place is cold."

Mr. Big's eyes rolled upward for a moment. Dr. Feelgood had never been known for brevity of speech. Harris hung from a rail and stared at them all. Trapped in an airlock with three guys called Mr. Big, Dr. Feelgood, and Virgin Bruce. What had ever compelled him to leave San Francisco?

Virgin Bruce continued. "What I was coming to, uh, Doctor, is a case of the crazies from having to hear that damn dentist-chair music —no offense—being piped into my helmet while I'm trying to work."

Felapolous wiped his hand on his shorts and touched a finger to his lips. "Ah. You refer to the Muzak."

"Yeah, I mean the Muzak. I hate hearing it in the station, I hate hearing it when I eat, when I'm trying to sleep, and I especially don't like hearing it when I'm trying to do my job."

"So you decided to take it up directly with your project supervisor, correct?"

"Damn straight. It's his idea, after all. I got mad and took off my helmet and ripped out the wires, but then I had to hear communications over the pod speakers, which aren't worth a damn. So I decided to come over here straightaway and, uh, take this up with Wallace himself."

Doc Felapolous shrugged. "Somehow I can't argue with the principle of the idea, to tell you the truth. I don't particularly like that stuff myself. That's why I have a tape deck in my office, so I can play my Mendelssohn and Mozart tapes. I have my wife send up cassettes every month or so."

"Yeah, good idea. Except my weight allowance when I came up here wouldn't let me bring up a deck. So I gotta listen to this wimpy stuff all the time."

"Hmm. Yes. I suppose I can see your problem." Felapolous stroked one waxed end of his mustache. "All right, Mr. Neiman, I'll give you your choice of prescriptions."

He had been holding his left hand close to his body throughout the conversation. Now he raised his hand, displaying the syringe he had kept hidden in his palm. "This is filled with enough happy juice to keep you sedated long enough for Phil to get you to a restraining bed in sickbay. I ought to give you that prescription, considering that our friend here doesn't seem too happy with your attitude or your previous assessment of his physique."

Mr. Big smiled humorlessly again; his expression tacitly said that he would have liked nothing better but to have a doped-up Virgin Bruce strapped down on a couch for a couple of hours, at his disposal.

"The alternative," Felapolous went on, "is for you to get another helmet from a locker, have this poor fellow whom you've frightened half to death refuel your pod, and go back to work at Vulcan, where by your own account you're too valuable to have missing for very long."

"Yeah, uh-huh." Virgin Bruce crossed his arms. "And what about my complaint?"

Felapolous gave a little smile. "My profession decrees that I must remedy pain, so I'll take your complaint into consideration. I have an extra cassette player in sickbay, a small pocket version which was supplied to me so that I could take verbal notes. Since I generally write everything down, I wouldn't miss it. I could give it to you on an indefinite loan. You may install it in your pod. You'd have to find your own tapes, though. I won't lend you mine, and besides I rather doubt you'd enjoy listening to Italian opera or 'Tales From the Vienna Woods.'"

"Uh-huh, I see." Virgin Bruce nodded his head slowly. "And about my idea to take this up with Wallace?"

"Not part of the prescription, sorry. I never recommend that my patients attempt to treat themselves for their complaints." He cocked his head toward Mr. Big. "Anyway, the difficulties you might have in that treatment could be detrimental to your health."

Virgin Bruce glared at Mr. Big. "I doubt it."

Mr. Big spoke up. "Hey, listen, Doc, I was told to . . ."

Doc Felapolous silenced him with a wave of his hand. "Mr. Bigthorn, concerning matters medical, I have the last word on Olympus, not the Project Supervisor. You've just heard me give Mr. Neiman treatment for his complaint."

"Yeah? I haven't seen you give him any medicine."

Felapolous reached into a pocket of his shorts, fished out a tin of aspirin and opened it. He handed two tablets to Virgin Bruce. "Take these with water and get out of here," he said. "Come back for a checkup when you get off your shift and I'll fill out the rest of your prescription for you."

He turned to Bob Harris. "Son, if you can quit grinning like a jackass, you can get Bruce's pod refueled and ready to go. Also, please have Mr. Chang come to see me about his back problems." He turned to leave. "I think he's missing a spine. Come along, Phil."

# Tall Tales

Every January 28th at about 11:30 A.M. EST, regardless of how much work had to be done, there was always someone in Olympus Station's hub, watching through the telescope for the reappearance of the Challenger Ghost.

It always appeared at exactly the same time, at 11:44 A.M. off the Florida coast near Cape Canaveral. Whoever was watching through the telescope would see against the dark Atlantic waters a brief bright white-hot flash of light, like an explosion was occurring in the high atmosphere downrange from the Kennedy Space Center. Almost as quickly as it appeared, the flash would fade, leaving the watcher feeling confused, and slightly chilled.

Undoubtedly, what one had seen was the explosion of an airborne object in the vicinity of Cape Canaveral. The logical explanation, given the apparent altitude and bearings of the flash, was that a spacecraft just launched from the Cape had exploded over the Atlantic. However, in a sacred tradition dating from 1986, no manned or unmanned rockets were ever launched from the Kennedy Space Center on January 28—the anniversary of the *Challenger* disaster.

When the phenomenon had first been noticed, no one on Olympus Station recognized the significance of the date or time. An urgent radio message to the Kennedy Space Center was made by Olympus Command, inquiring if one of the cargo rockets which regularly lifted off from the Cape had exploded. After a longer than usual delay, the following message had been received:

CANAVERAL 1156 TO OLYMPUS RE LAST INQUIRY:
WE NEVER REPEAT NEVER LAUNCH ANY
SPACECRAFT ON THIS DAY. NO EXPLOSIONS HAVE
BEEN SPOTTED DOWNRANGE BY GROUND
OBSERVERS OR BY RADAR. CAPE WISHES TO

INFORM OLYMPUS SOURCE THAT HE/SHE HAS A
SICK SENSE OF HUMOR IF THIS IS BULLSHIT AS WE
SUSPECT. CANAVERAL OUT.

Later, once Olympus Station assured the NASA administrators at
the Cape that a nasty joke was not at the heart of the matter, both
Skycorp and NASA began quiet investigations of their own. Yet
nothing could be definitively proved or disproved until a year later,
when January 28 rolled around again. On that day, a team of pho-
tographers, space historians, and scientists—including a couple of
parapsycholgists—were gathered at the Cape, monitoring by both
optical telescope and by cameras sent aloft on Air Force planes the
area of airspace nine miles downrange from the Cape where the
*Challenger* had been destroyed by a malfunctioning solid-rocket
booster. At the same time, a small group of Olympus crewmen gathered in the Meteorology compartment of the as-yet uncompleted
space station to watch the event. A third group of observers were
aboard the airplanes circling the area of the Atlantic Ocean where
the sighting had been made. All three groups were recording the
event with video cameras—and one of the parapsychologists was an
esper who concentrated her thoughts on the approximate area of the
explosion.

Nothing was seen from the ground or from the sky, or was registered by any of the cameras, but the flash *was* seen from space, at
exactly the same historical moment when the *Challenger* was con-
sumed in a ball of fire. A weather satellite's pictures confirmed the
eyewitness reports of the Olympus crewmen, and subsequent computer enhancements of those pictures showed a definite explosion,
down to faint streaks showing what appeared to be two solid-rocket
boosters beginning to arch away from the center of the explosion.
But no one on the ground or in the air saw anything unusual; that
information was confirmed by the camera footage. The parapsychol-
ogist who was attempting to gather an ESP impression at the crucial
moment had to be told when the event had occurred; she registered
nothing in her mind.

But from space, it had been seen. Still later, a NASA investigator
making a check through satellite footage, which happened to have
been taken of that area since 1987, noticed that similar white spots
were evident in all pictures taken over Florida's Atlantic coast on
those days when the sky was not overcast and the satellites' cameras
were pointed in the right direction. The ghost light, therefore, could

be registered by either human or artificial eyes . . . but only from outer space.

There had to be some significance to that detail, but whatever it was, it was too subtle for anyone to deduce.

New crew members aboard Skycan, when they asked why there were cats on the station, were frequently told that they had been brought aboard to control the cockroaches that stowed away in the food containers. The food—which was supplied to Skycorp by a distributor of airline in-flight meals—was bad enough to give that story some credibility, but that was not the reason why a half-dozen felines now wandered through the station's modules.

The fact was that Doc Felapolous' assistant, a University of Tennessee med student named Lou Maynard, who was completing his degree in space medicine aboard Skycan, had brought the first two cats up as test animals. Originally called OST One-A and OST One-B, the cats were respectively a young male and a young female, and it had been young Dr. Maynard's intention to study their reactions and degrees of adaptation to reduced and near-nonexistent degrees of gravity. His initial hypothesis had been that even though the cats' instinctive ability to right themselves while falling would be disturbed under such conditions, their nervous systems would eventually adapt and the cats would learn to regain their sense of balance.

The hypothesis, alas, was a bust. Neither cat ever became completely adapted to Olympus Station's various degrees of gravitational pull. In the hub they yowled and flopped about crazily, clawing madly for anything, or anyone, that represented to their eyes a fixed point, and in the rim modules the Coriolis effect made them perpetually clumsy, missing jumps and crashing into things when they ran. At least Maynard was able to collect enough new observations to publish his results in *The New England Journal of Medicine* and in *Science,* but the real advances that the experiment made were unintentional. Sometimes, as Doc Felapolous later observed, this is the way scientific inquiry works.

Although OST One-A and OST One-B were at first kept in cages in sickbay, it is impossible to keep cats locked up for very long—as any cat owner knows. Sooner or later, they *will* get loose. When the cats did manage to escape, they found themselves welcomed by most of the station's crew, who fed them and pampered them and played with them and hid them in bunks and in lockers when the distraught Dr. Maynard came searching for them. They would get locked away in their cages again and again, only to be set loose by a beamjack who was a born-again cat fancier. Once the cat was out of the bag, so to speak, that there were *pets* aboard Skycan—no one except Maynard and Felapolous referred to them as lab animals—OST One-A and OST One-B were adopted as crew mascots. They were given names: OST One-A became Spoker, for his tendency to escape under a ladder into the bottom level of one of the hub spokes, and OST One-B was named ZeeGee, for the amusing (albeit dangerous) antics she performed while in the microgravitational conditions of the hub.

This caught Doc Felapolous' interest as an unlettered psychologist of the armchair variety. When H.G. Wallace became upset about the cats' presence on his space station—"There's no place for house pets aboard a space station," he said to Felapolous sternly—Felapolous was able to reply, "Oh, but there is!" He pointed out the subtle role which pets play in people's lives, as familiar living objects who will accept people no matter what they are like, who can be talked to, stroked, played with, confessed to, loved and admired. Felapolous pointed out that clinical psychologists had known for decades that pet therapy was an important tool in dealing with depressed patients, and that some prisons had successfully experimented with allowing long-term inmates to keep pets.

"The men are bored," Felapolous said to Wallace. "Let them keep the cats as pets. It'll be good for them."

"How can they be bored?" Wallace retorted. "They're participating in the ultimate human adventure. They're making the conquest of space."

"Henry," Felapolous replied, "man can't live on starlight alone."

The deciding factor in the argument, however, rested in the instinctive behavior of the cats themselves. Put a male cat and a female cat together for a little while, and guess what happens?

Unfortunately, Lou Maynard was unable to follow his first paper, "Observations On The Adaptive Behavior of Domestic Cats To Microgravity" with a hot sequel, "The Results of Feline Inbreeding In Microgravitational Conditions." Like humans, Spoker and ZeeGee desired privacy for their mating practices; unlike the male and female crew members on Olympus Station, they got what they wanted. Six months later, a crewman named Ralph Conte came off his shift, went to his bunk in Module 14, opened the curtain, and was surprised (and, to his credit, even somewhat excited) to find ZeeGee nursing a litter of six tiny kittens, born while he was out on the powersat welding girders together.

This event was almost enough to cause a mutiny when H.G. Wallace let it be known that he considered two to be company and eight a crowd, and that he intended to ship the whole bunch back to earth in the next OTV destined for rendezvous with a shuttle in low Earth orbit. By the time it filtered down through the crew, scuttlebutt had it that Wallace secretly intended to throw all the kitties out through an airlock in the Docks. Had Doc Felapolous not interceded and acted again as the station's mediator, it is possible that the first full-scale mutiny in space would have occurred, with perhaps H.G. Wallace being the one who would have gone spacewalking without the benefit of a tetherline—perhaps without a spacesuit as well.

In the compromise which was reached, ZeeGee and Spoker were sent back to Earth once the kittens were old enough to be weaned. It was also agreed that the two males of the litter would be neutered before they reached reproductive maturity, to prevent any further increase in the feline population. Wallace grumbled a little because his vision of stellar conquest did not include cats among his stalwart crew, and the male members of the crew blanched somewhat at the mention of other males becoming eunuchs, but a compromise was better than no agreement at all. When Skycorp questioned the logic of keeping the offspring aboard, Dr. Maynard told them that his next research project was to be the adaptive behavior in microgravitational conditions of felines born outside an Earthlike environment, *et cetera*.

New crewmen who were being broken in as beamjacks were issued a chest control unit for their spacesuits, which included a recessed button covered by a sliding safety plate. Asked what this button was for, the Vulcan Station crewman fitting them into their suits would say, "Oh, that. Well, I'm not supposed to tell you this, but if anything goes drastically wrong—I mean, *really* wrong, where nothing you can think of helps you and no one else can do anything for you —push that button."

Once in a while the rejoinder was, "Oh, yeah, I've heard that one before." But most of the time, the next questions were "What is it? What does it do?"

The whiteroom assistant would wink knowingly and say, "That's the panic button. It'll bring help." No one ever believed it immediately.

Now and then, greenhorns would find themselves in a situation in which they felt helpless and beyond assistance: becoming untethered while on EVA, having a girder slip out of hand and go floating away out of reach, finding themselves in an uncontrolled roll or pitch because of a misfire by their MMUs. After trying everything they had been taught, and after yelling fruitlessly for help over the com-link, sometimes they would in desperation slide back the little cover and shove their gloved finger down on the red panic button.

Nothing would happen. Nothing could happen. The button was a dead switch, wired to absolutely nothing in the chest control unit, not so much as a light. But it made people who were panicky feel like something was being accomplished; occasionally, it had the effect of buying time for confused people to think out a solution. No one knew where the idea of a panic button originated, but most agreed that it was a nifty idea.

# 6

# Hooker Remembers
## (A Night on the Town)

A few minutes before Virgin Bruce docked at Olympus Station, an interorbital ferry set out from Skycan and headed for Project Franklin.

The ferry was a modified OTV, its stern engine removed and replaced with a docking adapter matching the one at the front, its propulsion coming from thrusters arrayed around its cylindrical fuselage, piloted by remote control from Olympus Station. The interior resembled the cramped interior of a Greyhound bus; twenty acceleration couches left over from its service as a shuttle's passenger module were arranged in two rows down the length of the compartment. There were no viewports, only a single TV monitor at the forward end; really, there was nothing to do during the fifteen-minute trip to Vulcan except stare at the back of the couch in front and breathe the oxygen pumped in to offset decompression sickness. If anyone were allowed to smoke in space, the cabin's NO SMOKING signs would have been lit, and everyone knew better than to unbuckle their seat belts while the ferry was under thrust. It all made for a boring fifteen minutes.

Hooker sat in the back of the compartment, plastic time-card in hand, and stared at the back of another beamjack's head, his eyes following the aimless drift of a lock of hair that bristled out from under the band of the guy's cap. Another beamjack, Mike Webb, was sitting next to him, but Hooker didn't feel like carrying on small talk. He simply sat and waited for the trip to end, pondering his own dark thoughts.

For some reason the trip to the meteorology deck had left him more depressed than he'd been before he'd gone there. That had never been the case in the past; a few minutes with the telescope used to refresh him, used to remind him that there was still a Gulf of Mexico waiting for his return from two years in space.

He remembered when he could daydream about it, that day of coming home: feeling the thump of the landing gear cranking down, the slight wobble as the elevons airbraked the final approach, then the smooth jar of the shuttle's touchdown on the Cape's landing strip, the spaceship whisking past palmettos and Spanish bayonette, white sand kicking up in the noonday sun; then, finally, climbing out of the cool white metal womb into tropical heat, feeling the coastal breeze on his skin. He would bum a cigarette from one of the ground crew and wander off down the runway, sauntering away from the slow ticking of cooling metal and the whine of machinery being moved into place. *Where're you going, Popeye?* someone would ask. *Out to the beach. I'm goin' fishing,* he'd reply. *Don't you want your check?* someone else would ask, as an awed silence fell over the processing area. *Send it to my bank,* he'd throw over his shoulder.

Somehow, he had stopped having that daydream. It had happened at about the same time he had started losing track of the days.

Hooker stared at a loose rivet on the couch in front of him. He remembered looking at the sailboat through the telescope. Had he seen a girl on the boat, a sliver of suntanned skin against the white-washed deck? She had blond hair and wore a blue bikini; she was lying face down with her arms crossed under her head; there had been sweat on her back, small thick beads beginning to roll down the cleft in her buttocks, where it disappeared into her bikini bottom. He could see that sweat from twenty-two thousand three hundred god-damn miles away, so he knew for bloody sure that it was Laura lying on the deck of that sailboat, Laura smiling softly as she improved her tan, Laura who was . . .

It had not been Laura. There had been no girl lying on the deck of the sailboat.

Hooker clenched his hands on the armrests of his couch. His eyes squeezed shut tight, his head lolled back against the couch. Unbidden, uninvited, the memories came.

By some miracle—probably its location in the northern part of the state, where it still got cold in the winter—Cedar Key had managed to escape the devastating effects of the boom which had hit Florida during the twentieth century. It had never become a major tourist attraction, even as a coastal town.

A couple of hotels had been built near the beach, it was true, and the long boardwalk near the municipal marina included the usual seashell shops and overpriced restaurants found at any surfside location. But the weather in northern Florida could be as cold and damp during the winter months as it was in New Jersey or Missouri, so the snowbirds from Trenton and Jefferson City tended to stay away from lonely little Cedar Key, heading instead for the plastic sprawl of Panama City Beach or the urban familiarity of Ft. Lauderdale. This left Cedar Key as one of the few places on the Florida coast, even in the early twenty-first century, which still retained a vestige of its charming old-time squalor.

So it was to a still undeveloped, underpopulated Cedar Key that Claude Hooker made port that cool January evening. He brought the *Jumbo Shrimp II* into the marina shortly after eight o'clock, avoiding the anchored sailboats and other shrimp boats lined up at the jetties. A steady breeze from the southwest blew through an open window on the bridge, ruffling his thinning hair. Over the low rumble of the boat's diesel engines he could hear the faraway rumble, from miles away over the Gulf, of the approaching thunderstorm that had chased him and the other fishermen home early from the night's work.

Within an hour Hooker had tied up the *Shrimp* and battened down the trawler for the coming storm. There was no catch in the live hold below the aft deck, so he left the nets in the hold and spread a canvas tarp over the hatch to prevent the hold from flooding. Checking the lines to make sure they would keep the boat at the dock, but weren't so tight that they would snap in a heavy wake, he noticed soft orange lights glowing in the cabins of some of the other shrimp boats tied up nearby. Other captains staying with their boats overnight, he decided, hoping the storm would break and pass by later in the night so they could head out and try to get at least a few hours fishing in by morning.

Lightning flashed on the horizon, briefly outlining the thunderhead's forbidding mass in the night sky. Satisfied the *Shrimp* was secure, he jumped onto the dock and walked toward the gravel parking lot nearby. He felt a little guilty for not hanging by, as the other shrimpers on the boats were doing. The hell with it, he thought. If he missed a night's work, it wasn't fatal. There was money in the bank. For once, the bills were all paid at least long enough to keep his creditors off his back, and it had been weeks since he had given himself a night off. Perhaps the storm was a blessing in disguise. Hooker smiled. Maybe it was God's way of telling him to go get drunk in town tonight.

He was still smiling as he fitted the key into the door lock of his old Camaro. Yeah, maybe it was a good night to head over to Mikey's Place. Hanging out in the bar sipping cold ones and playing pool was preferable to going home and watching TV all night. Maybe he could even find a young lady, so when he did go home it wouldn't have to be alone. For all the good that it had done, things had been a little lonely since Laura had moved out.

Hooker's mouth twitched as he settled into the driver's seat and fitted the key into the ignition switch. If he was lucky, perhaps the storm would keep his ex at home tonight.

The storm's squall line hit the town just as Hooker opened the bar's wooden front door. He pressed the door shut against the wind and rain as patrons nearby howled irritably, then turned and looked around the inside of the place.

Mikey's was having a big night. The place was nearly jammed to capacity with Cedar Key locals, half of whom had already departed from sobriety. It was a small and dimly lighted bar, with rough pine furniture, old fishing nets suspended from the ceiling, and boathooks fastened to the walls between plastic beer signs and framed sailing prints. A musky scent hung permanently in the air, beer and tobacco mixed with crusted salt and sand from the boots and sneakers of the fishermen who made this their hangout.

Over the long bar and liquor case behind, next to a holograph of a tall ship, a video screen showed an old *Pink Panther* movie played on an ancient videodisc system beside the cash register. Peter Sellers' voice was drowned out by rock and roll music from a decrepit Wurlitzer in the corner, John Fogarty belting out an old blues number he and Creedence Clearwater Revival had revamped many years ago. Mikey, an oldies fan, allowed nothing in his jukebox less than thirty years old, which suited most of his regulars just fine; besides, the oldies were back in style, since the New Wave of the last few years of the twentieth century had finally bankrupted itself into Hollywood schmaltz. Sidestepping his way through the crowd, Hooker glimpsed Sellers being attacked by a Chinese assassin while the Wurlitzer banged out "The Midnight Special." Somehow, the combination made aesthetic sense.

Then the screen was obscured by a figure: A short man with his shirt pulled open, exposing a flopping beer gut and extreme sunburn, had climbed up on the bar and commenced dancing to the Creedence song. He lip-synched the words as his dirty tennis shoes stomped along the polished wooden surface, sending an ashtray skittering off to crash on the floor. His performance brought yells and laughter.

People sitting at the bar hastily grabbed their glasses and bottles from his path, and a plump young woman reached up to tuck a folded dollar bill into his waistband. He leered at her and pumped his fat thighs suggestively, and was rewarded with a high-pitched giggle from her and a dark glare from the man sitting next to her.

An elbow bumped Hooker's. "Kinda looks like Mikey's is in good form tonight, huh, Hook?"

Hooker looked around, saw Whitey Cuzak standing next to him. Hooker shrugged and grinned. "Place hasn't changed much since the last time I stopped by," he murmured under the music. "Hey, Cooz. Who is that fat fool anyway?"

"I dunno his name, but I hear he's in from New Orleans. It figures it would have to be some ragin' Cajun."

"New Orleans? Don't they keep those tourists over at the Belle la Vista Lounge?"

Whitey shrugged and took a sip from his schooner. "I don't think he's a tourist. Somebody told me he's a fishing guide. Takes the Okies out on the water to show 'em swordfishing ain't the same as fishing for cat on the Big Muddy."

"The Mississippi doesn't run through Oklahoma, Cooz."

"It doesn't? Well, what the hell do I know. I grew up in this state."

The Creedence single ended just as the bartender grabbed the arm of the New Orleans fishing guide and tried to drag him off the bar. Then a J. Geils Band song—Hooker recognized the synthesizer and percussion intro to "Freeze-Frame"—segued in, and the guide howled in delight and recommenced his erratic hopping on the bar top.

Whitey sniggered from behind the lip of his beer mug. "I also hear he wrestles sharks."

"What?" Hooker wasn't sure he had heard his fellow fisherman correctly.

"Yup. Someone was telling me that he takes people out at night to go fishing for shark." He leaned closer to make himself understood over the blare from the juke box. "Story is that, when they catch a little one, like a nurse or sand shark, he likes to put on a little show for the tourists. You know how you never bring a live shark into the boat, how you drag it into a net in the water and then shoot it or take a hammer to its brains? Well, that crazy asshole takes a skinning knife and jumps down into the net with it."

"While it's still *alive?*"

"While it's still alive." Whitey shrugged, grinning like a fox. "He wrestles around with it for a while, hanging onto its dorsal fin where it can't bend around and take a bite out of him, playing Tarzan. Scares the shit out of everyone in the boat for a few minutes doing that, before he takes the knife and puts it in its guts. After that he scrambles out of the net and gets a gun and blows the poor bastard's brains out. I hear it makes him popular with the people who've come down from Minnesota. They love having their picture taken with him."

There was a crash from the bar, which made them look up. The bartender and the bouncer, a big black guy nicknamed George the Goon, had grabbed the shark wrestler's legs and yanked him off the bar. One of his flailing arms had toppled a bottle from the liquor case; he was bleeding and screaming obscenities as George the Goon got him in a headlock and started dragging him out the back door.

"Nice guy," Hooker observed. "I'll make a point of avoiding him this evening."

"Hey, why? If George doesn't break his legs, you oughta go meet him. He's been buying everyone drinks all night."

Hooker smiled and put a hand on Whitey's shoulder. "Y'know, Cooz, what I really had in mind was a nice, pleasant girl, who can make intelligent conversation, has a good sense of humor, who's charming and has an intelligent perspective on life . . ."

"Has small firm breasts, a tight ass, and could give a vacuum cleaner a run for its money," Cuzak interrupted, grinning broadly.

"Now, I didn't say that. . . ."

"But I know what you meant. Thank God my daughter's off in college where she doesn't have to be around your type." Whitey hesitated, his smile fading. "I guess I should warn you, though . . ."

"Whitey, damn it, I haven't even *seen* Becky since . . ."

"No, uh-uh, I didn't mean that, Claude. Laura's here tonight."

"Oh, goddammit. She's *here?*"

"Last time I saw her, she was over at the other end of the room, near the pool table. That was only about five minutes ago."

"Great. I'll make a point of avoiding her, too. Maybe she and Bluto the Shark Killer will get together and leave me alone. They'd make a nice pair." Hooker looked over Cuzak's shoulder, scanning the crowded barroom. "Well, the place is packed. Maybe she won't spot me in all these people."

"Come to think of it." Whitey said, "she and that guy were hanging around with each other when I saw 'em."

"See? What did I tell ya?" Whitey grinned and gave his arm a slap, then moved off into the crowd. Hooker inched his way across the room to the bar, where he found Kurt the bartender sweeping up the debris left by the fishing guide's bar-top boogie. The sour expression on the bartender's face stopped Hooker from making a wisecrack. Seeing him approach, Kurt put aside his broom and fetched a shot of tequila and a Dos Equis.

"Laura's been looking for you," he said as he measured a dose of José Cuervo into a shot glass.

"That's nice. I'm not looking for her."

"I told her a giant squid had attacked your boat and you were reported missing, but I don't think she believed me."

"Well, good try anyway. Where did you see her last?"

"Over by the pool table. She was with Rocky. Her taste must be getting weird."

"Rocky? Who's Rocky?"

"Rocky the dancing geek. The guy George the Goon just dragged out of here. Did you see that?"

"Yeah." Hooker shrugged. "Very entertaining. You guys should give him a job, and put up a sign outside 'Live Dancing'. . . ."

Kurt flashed him a sour look. "That was going to be on the house, but for that crack you can pay up."

Hooker closed his eyes and raised his eyebrows, and slipped his bank card into the pay slot on the bar. Kurt entered the charge on the cash register, and a receipt started to ticker out on the printer. "Go ahead and keep my number in the machine, Kurt," Hooker said. "I plan on being here a while tonight."

"Awright. Good luck avoiding your ex."

"If you see her, tell her that a squid really *did* get me."

Hooker hung around near the bar, staying away from the side of Mikey's where the pool tables were situated. He chatted with a few friends, drank a couple of more beers, watched the end of the *Pink Panther* movie. He had wanted to shoot some pool, but since his ex-wife was over there, the idea was out of the question. Instead, he drifted over to the video games near the front door.

It was on his third game of *PsychoKiller* when he met Jeanine and indulged his monthly habit of falling madly in love.

Although she never explicitly mentioned either her age or background, Hooker managed to figure her out at least to an approximate degree. Her soft, unlined face and firm figure put her in her early- to mid-twenties. Her poise and taste in clothes gave her away as being from an upper middle-class family: a country club refugee, given to slumming during weekends away from Everett and Richard and the rest of the horsy bunch. Her manner of speech—grammatically perfect, hardly a contraction or a split infinitive to be found—indicated that she was college educated, possibly from an Ivy League school. Although she tried to pass herself off as being an old salt from the local area who happened to drop into town now and then, Hooker recognized her as being a fairly common type found in Cedar Key now and then: affluent, bored with champagne society, conservative Republican family, tending to take off to the boonies in search of freewheeling good times and perhaps a brief romantic interlude with someone who would show her a better time than dinner at the Oak Tree and being pawed in the back of the old man's BMW.

But despite all this, Jeanine was fun. She was beautiful to look at, took the ruckus brewing around them in stride, could hold her Scotch and make easy conversation about homicidal video games and weird fishermen who danced on bar tops, and had a nice laugh for his stupid jokes. And, as best as he could sense, she was clearly interested in having him take her home that night.

It seemed as if that was what he was going to do, until he excused himself to go visit the john. The last he saw of Jeanine's smiling young face was when he said, "Stay put, I'll be back in a sec."

When he came back a few minutes later, Jeanine was gone, and he found Laura waiting for him.

"Looking for your friend?" she asked him sweetly.

Hooker stopped when he saw her and simply glared. *God damn it, she has done it again.*

"What did you tell her this time?" he asked, after giving himself a moment to simmer down. "That I had a contagious social disease? Or did you think of something more clever, like I was the reincarnation of the Boston Strangler?" He didn't even bother to look around Mikey's for her. Jeanine, he knew from the moment he saw Laura standing in her place beside the *PsychoKiller* machine, was gone.

Laura shrugged, her brown hair falling over her narrow shoulders in a way which had once been provocative and had since grown to be merely irritating; tomboy grown up to be mischievous siren or smartass harpy, depending on circumstance, personal outlook, and the day of the week. "Nothing much, really," she said soothingly. "I just slid up to her and suggested that rumor had it you were into bondage, sodomy, and cigarette burns."

She paused. "To tell you the truth, I think she was rather turned on about the bondage and sodomy, but I don't think she anticipated the bit about cigarette burns."

No, Hooker thought, there wasn't even any point in trying to catch up with Jeanine. Trying to pursue her would only convince her that she had nearly gone home with a sadist. "Thanks a lot, Laura," he said, picking up his beer from where he had left it on top of the video machine and draining it. "Considering that we've been separated for . . . is it ten months now? . . . you're really going out of your way to continue with your wifely obligations. Especially making sure that hubby stays celibate."

Laura crossed her arms and leaned against the *PsychoKiller* machine. "Just looking out for you, Claude. Did you really want to take home that nice bit of jailbait? Jesus, she was almost young enough to be your daughter."

"She was older than that," he responded angrily. "And even if she wasn't, since when did you get the job of making moral decisions for me? That's the third time you've . . ."

"And not without good reason," Laura snapped. She had suddenly turned serious. No longer the smartass honey, she had become her professional, schoolteacher self. She began ticking off the reasons on her fingertips. "The first time, that woman did have a contagious social disease. Things like that get around the ladies' room, y'know. I don't think you would have enjoyed finding little lesions on your privates a month after having a one-nighter with her. The second time, the lady in question was married. Maybe you didn't notice, or maybe you just ignored it, but she had a little gold band around her finger. I saw it."

She stared him straight in the eye, fixing him with her aquamarine gaze, the first thing which had fascinated him when they had met. "Maybe we're not married anymore," she said, "but I'm still your friend, and friends don't let each other get hurt."

Hooker was quiet for a moment. He glanced down at the slender hand resting on the controls of the video game. "I see you haven't taken off *your* ring yet," he mumbled, looking for a way out of the impasse.

Laura tilted her hand up to gaze at the slender gold band around her ring finger. "I keep it on to remind me that marrying a sailor can get you shipwrecked," she said softly, studying it with a slight smile on her face.

Neither of them said anything for a moment. Laura gazed wistfully at the wedding ring she had not taken off, and Hooker gazed at her looking at the ring. The harpy was gone, and for some reason he couldn't explain he was no longer mad. *I wonder why I ever left this beautiful woman,* he thought, admiring the way the video game's gaudy flashing lights reflected on her face, her hair, her eyes. *I must have been a crazy son of a bitch, giving up this beautiful woman for horny-ass teenagers.*

Laura sniffed hard, rubbed her finger against her nose, and laughed abruptly. "Yeah, listen to *that.* Uh, and it also works pretty well as a pest repellent."

"Too bad you had to turn into such a pest yourself," he caught himself saying. *Oh, shut up, Hooker.*

Her eyes dropped. "You're really pissed off at me this time, aren't you, Claude?"

"Forget it," he muttered. "Look, just . . . forget it." He struggled to find something else to talk about. "Hey, if that works so well as a pest repellent, what were you doing hanging around with that bozo?"

"What bozo?"

"The bozo who was dancing on top of the bar. Uh—Rocky. Kurt told me you and he were hanging around together a little while ago."

"We're friends." She shrugged offhandedly. "He's funny even if he gets blitzed easy, but he's a nice guy. I run into him when he drops into town. Why, you don't think I have a thing going for him, do you?"

"No, I was just wondering," Hooker replied. He felt a little confused, because Cuzak had told him that Rocky was from New Orleans. Well, by water, Cedar Key and Louisiana were not that far apart. "I just hadn't seen him around here before."

"That's because you don't come here that often yourself, anymore. You spend all your time on the *Shrimp.*"

She changed the subject. "Are you really that pissed off at me, Claude?"

"Well . . . no," he lied. "But don't you think I have a right to be pissed off? I mean, sometimes it's hard enough seeing you, let alone having you act like a den mother or something."

"Hey, it's my town too, y'know. I mean, I got a teaching job here. You know how hard it is to get a job teaching anywhere these days? Besides that, I like Cedar Key. It's one of the nicest places I've ever lived in. A divorce isn't going to make me move. C'mon, Claude, lighten up, will you?"

"Yeah," he said. "Uh-huh. I'll lighten up. Excuse me, but I think I'm going to go get drunk and see if I can lighten up."

Hooker started to turn away, but Laura grabbed his wrist with both hands. He tried to pull free, but her grip was surprisingly strong. Not so surprising, when he thought about it. Laura was a lifelong outdoorswoman. She had chopped firewood for the better part of her twenty-seven years, when she had grown up in the boonies of Vermont.

Yet those were tender hands as well. His skin remembered her palms stroking his back in the middle of the night, her fingers clutching his ass at the height of her orgasm. Flesh remembers.

As if she were reading his mind, Laura pulled him closer. "Look," she said softly, "if you really must get laid tonight, well, y'know, I'm not doing much. . . ."

"Jesus, Laura . . . c'mon. It's supposed to be over. We're not married anymore."

"I didn't say we were," she replied, shaking her head. "I didn't say we had to get married again. But, shit, we slept together for a year before we got married, and I don't see . . ."

*Okay, go on,* he thought. *Let's hear the rest of the speech.*

"I mean," she continued, "here we are, both in this little town, and it's not like we're both seeing other people. We're still friends. Can't we do what, y'know, some friends do?"

*She's going to keep it short this time,* he thought. *Nothing about how much she's missed me, or how she loved watching the sunrise from my porch, or the way I made scrambled eggs in the morning. Repetition makes for brevity, I guess.*

Laura laughed. "Hey, look, I'll admit it, I'm kinda horny myself. And there isn't another guy in the place who looks better."

Hooker looked down at the floor, but instead of seeing the floor, all he could see was her. Damn it, she was still wearing the calfskin boots he had given her for her birthday a year ago, just before they got married. His mind remembered. His flesh remembered. His mind was fogged after the beers and tequila, but the flesh never forgets.

She was following a script they had read through a couple of times before; the next line was his.

"I think there's a bottle of wine in the fridge back at my place," he said quietly. "Go on. Get your coat."

She smiled, and leaned forward to kiss him. As she did, Hooker wondered why—when they were divorced, when seeing her was something he tried to avoid—he could not stop from sleeping with her.

# 7

# Getting Some Sun

Does it seem funny to you that I'm so obsessed with the names we put on the things we built and used in space? Perhaps it should be strange, but it's only a reflection of how the people who worked up there felt about their jobs, their environment, their living conditions: a cross between a nostalgia for futures past, and cynicism for what shape the future had taken. How we name things is an indication of our true feelings.

Take, for instance, the formal name given to Skycorp's orbital construction shack in the Clarke Orbit. When it was still in the design and development stages, Skycorp simply called it "the Construction Shack," in the same way NASA went for the longest time calling its first permanent space station simply "the Space Station." But when it finally was built, shortly after Olympus Station was finished, the company decided to christen it with something less generic.

They picked the name Vulcan, the P.R. people said, because it fit in with the mythological origins for Olympus, the name of the main space station in geosynchronous orbit; that is, Olympus being the home of the gods, and Vulcan being the tool-making deity, the omnipotent blacksmith. It makes sense that way, of course, but note: NASA had used mythological nomenclature—Mercury, Apollo, Thor, Athena, et cetera—during its first years, now regarded as the halcyon, pioneering days of spaceflight. Seen in that context, this tends to make the use of names like Olympus and Vulcan a commentary on how Skycorp's leaders felt about their work, as taking further pioneering steps into that great, high frontier.

Second point. In the TV series of the twentieth century, *Star Trek,* what planet did Mr. Spock come from? Skycorp never came straight out and admitted that this bit of trivia from modern mythology had anything to do with its choice of name for the construction shack, but one can't but help notice that a lot of the company's aging execs were old-time SF fans and trekkies, that long before they had risked their financial assets with McGuinness' fledgling commercial space enterprise they had parked themselves in front of the tube to watch the continuing adventures of William Shatner, Leonard Nimoy, and DeForrest Kelly. And before you scoff at this premise, remember: The first space shuttle NASA built had its name changed from the *Constitution* to the *Enterprise* because of pressure from the trekkies.

Speaking from a strictly aesthetic viewpoint, it makes sense that an old SF television series had something to do with the christening of Skycorp's construction shack. Of all the big structures built in space, Vulcan Station alone had that funky, semi-streamlined, designed-by-committee look that typified the spaceships on *Star Trek,* a look which reminded one of common household objects. The TV *Enterprise* looked like an old Whammo Frisbee with a toilet-paper core and two crayons attached; the Romulan battle cruisers looked like dinner trays; the Klingon ships were reminiscent of the plastic mallards your uncle the duck hunter used to have hanging over his cabin fireplace.

Vulcan Station looked like a telephone receiver. Not the ones which came into common usage by the end of the 80's; the big ones with round ends that Bell Telephone put in every house and office after the end of World War II. It might have been strictly a coincidence of design, but I rather think an engineer, sitting up late in his office, trying to come up with a practical design for the construction shack, stared at an old phone on his desk and went—"Eureka!"

Essentially, Vulcan was an elongated bar between two hemispherical modules. The modules, called Module A and Module B, were flattened at the bottoms. Most of Vulcan was unpressurized except for the command deck in Module A and the inflated modules that were strapped on the outer skin of Module B—colloquially called "hotdogs" because of their sausagelike appearance—which served as temporary areas for the beamjacks to suit up and rest in.

The rest of the shack was uninhabitable, exposed to hard vacuum, including the main construction bay between the two modules, where much of the work was done. In contrast to the designs made for construction shacks by earlier designers, though, these areas were not skeletal, open areas; a thin aluminum skin, not much thicker than tinfoil, was stretched over the whole superstructure. The point was to protect the construction supplies—including the aluminum sheet rolls sent from the Moon at great expense—from micrometeorite damage. This gave Vulcan its unexpectedly streamlined appearance.

The underside of Vulcan, in the long cross section between Modules A and B, contained a wide-open hatch, the main construction bay. The shack hovered above the powersat, tethered in place by cables, with the hatch over the unfinished end of the powersat's structure.

The beam builders were contained in the main bay. They were like the ones designed by Grumman and NASA in the 70's: big rectangular machines each weighing nearly a hundred tons on Earth. Their mass alone was formidable in space, when it meant lowering and raising the fat bastards in and out of the bay. Three large rolls of aluminum sheet, made on the Moon, were loaded on rollers on the outside of a beam builder, one on each of the machine's three sides. The sheets were fed in and molded into spars and joined with cross-spars with laser welders. What came out was a perfect tetrahedral beam, a hundred feet long, which could be joined with other beams to form one of the main spars.

To join the beams together, beamjacks in MMU backpacks and in pods would glide between and under them, inserting trusses and reinforcing seams. It was long, slow work, because guidance lasers in Vulcan were focused down the length of the satellite. With them, Command could tell whether the giant structure was being built straight. If it wasn't—a common occurrence—then beamjacks would have to get it straight. Imagine trying to build something several miles long as straight and even as a laser beam, and you can see one of the reasons building the thing was such a heartache.

On the end of Module A was a ramp where more guys worked at assembling the two microwave transmitting dishes which would eventually be fixed to rotary joints at each end of the completed powersat.

The construction pods were housed within Module B, near one of the two freighter loading bays on the upper half of the shack, just across from the main airlock leading to the hotdogs. During changes in the work shifts, which occurred three times daily, this area was always the most crowded. One shift coming in, one shift going out, pods maneuvering in through their bay adjacent to the main construction deck for refueling and taking on relief pilots, sometimes with the added confusion of a freighter from the Moon or Earth unloading materials. Every eight hours it looked like a Chinese fire drill performed in zero-g.

The focus of all the activity—when there was a focus—was the massive structure floating underneath Vulcan. When the White House and Skycorp and NASA announced its inception, they called it Project Franklin, after old Ben who allegedly discovered electricity by flying a kite with a key on the end into a thunderstorm. This name was almost as pretentious as if they had called it Project Prometheus, and so most people forgot about it as one of those names a Republican administration in the White House would devise.

SPS-1, or the powersat as it was more conveniently called, was planned to be about 13.3 miles long and 3.3 miles wide. It resembled a vast flat gridwork, with the construction shack hovering over one end, men and work pods skirting around it like tiny white insects. Eventually it would be covered with sheets of protovoltaic cells manufactured on the Moon, transforming it into a massive, rectangular mirror.

You know the rest. The cells capture sunlight, transform it into electricity which in turn is transmitted through microwave beams to rectennas in the Southwest, supplying five gigawatts of electricity to the U.S., the cost of which shows up on your electric bill each month. Frankly, I don't think it's my place to say whether that cost is high or low, except to say that the forests in the northeastern states and Canada look much prettier since the acid rain problem has been obviated and school kids in Pennsylvania history classes have to struggle to remember what the fuss in the 70's over Three Mile Island was all about.

Since grabbing the sun's energy was what all of the expense and R & D and manpower had been for, perhaps the government and Skycorp should have called the whole shebang Project Prometheus. It fit with the rest of mythology, but . . . well, it wasn't used after all. All the science fiction writers had already overused the name.

# 8

# The Whiteroom

Hooker's reminiscing was interrupted by the inaudible yet tactile *thump* of the ferry docking with Vulcan Station.

"Al right, coffee break's over!" someone up in the front of the narrow compartment said loudly. "Everybody, back on your heads!"

There were just as many crewmen asking what was so funny as there were who were snickering at the punch line of the old joke. Seat belts were unbuckled and the men in the spacecraft began to float out of their couches, each reaching up to grab the rail running the length of the compartment's ceiling. It took a moment for Hooker to bring himself back from the remembered evening in the bar. For an instant, as he took in the weird sight of crewmen gently floating above his head, he found himself weighing this reality against that mind's eye vision. The former was sorely lacking in appeal.

Unfastening his own seat belt, he pushed himself up with the toes of his sneakers and grabbed the overhead rail. He bumped into Mike Webb, the beamjack who had been sitting next to him, and muttered an apology. From the front of the cabin he could hear the slow hiss of the hatch being undogged and opened. The line of crewmen began to ease toward the airlock hatch, pulling themselves hand over hand along the rail. It was then that Hooker realized he had made a slight mistake upon boarding the ferry.

The problem was that he had been one of the first to board the spacecraft at Olympus. It was something most of the men who worked shifts at the powersat project tried to avoid; he could only blame his lack of forethought on the crummy day he'd already had.

The first crewmen to board the ferry had to go to the back of the cabin to get seated. Because there was only one hatch in the ferry, at the bow, it meant that the last beamjack aboard at Olympus was the first to get out at Vulcan. It made no difference when the ferry was returning to Olympus from Vulcan; one simply crawled out into the Docks and headed for the rim modules. But the crews coming aboard Vulcan had to be processed through the whiteroom, and there lay the rub.

The whiteroom was in the second hotdog affixed to Vulcan's outer skin; four such modules were attached to Module B, joined together by metal sleeves, and anchored near an airlock in the construction shack. Vulcan had been designed so that the modules could be moved about the space platform as necessity dictated, since pressurized areas were a secondary consideration aboard the construction shack.

The whiteroom, like the rest of the hotdogs, was a narrow compartment in which only a few crewmen could fit at a single time. It was where the beamjacks climbed into their suits and replenished their oxygen tanks before going to work on the powersat. Suit-up was a long, clumsy procedure. Even the comparatively lightweight suits worn by the pod pilots took five or ten minutes of work to don; the bulky hard suits worn by the men, doing EVA jobs took as long as twenty minutes to struggle into, depending on the dexterity of the individual.

Which meant that the last guys aboard the ferry when it came over from Olympus sometimes had to hand around—literally—for up to an hour, waiting for the persons ahead to suit up, pressurize, check themselves, clock in and cycle through the airlock. Once, Command had tried to control the situation by giving beamjacks revolving numbers for their boarding rank and docking work—time for the minutes wasted in the whiteroom; but the first part of this arrangement fell apart when crewmen started ignoring the boarding rank (because of apathy, or feeling as if they were getting the same bad seats over again). The second part fell through when the union found out about it and raised hell with Skycorp.

Popeye had forgotten to arrive late to get aboard the ferry. It was a game the beamjacks sometimes played: Who could find an excuse to board the ferry last? Popeye winced at his dumbness. Hang around indeed, while your arm muscles got cramped from holding the rail and your eyes got tired of looking at the back of your buddy's head . . . or ass, if he was turned upside down.

He looked around and saw his own expression mirrored on Webb's face. Webb grinned painfully and rolled his eyes up in his head: *Boy, I guess we fucked up again.* Popeye nodded and looked away, never dreaming that his luck had just changed.

He had had a lousy day up to now. But while space does not often forgive mistakes, sometimes it may let one slide your way. Because of his error, Hooker was given the opportunity to make more during the rest of his life.

# 9

# *Zulu Tango Approach*

For once, Virgin Bruce felt good. Absolutely on top of the whole damn world. Not only that, but he was feeling good he was on the clock, a miracle in itself because he hated to work. He felt so good he could sing, and so he did:

> "What in the world ever became of sweet Jane?
> "She lost her sparkle, you know she isn't the same;
> "Livin' on reds, vitamin C and cocaine;
> "All a friend can say is ain't it a shame."

When he received the cassette recorder Doc Felapolous had promised him and had it installed in the instrument panel of his pod, he wouldn't have to sing Grateful Dead songs to himself. He would get some tapes shipped up to him—surely one of his few remaining friends in St. Louis or Kansas City wouldn't begrudge him that small favor—and then he could ride in style and never mind the syrupy versions of "Moon River" everyone else was subjected to day in and day out.

> "Truckin', like the doo-dah-man,
> "Once told me 'Gotta play your hand.
> " 'Sometimes the cards ain't worth a dime
> " 'If you don't lay 'em down.' "

As he sang he glanced through the canopy, checking his trajectory by eyeball-reckoning his distance from the powersat. The computer screen in front of him, which displayed a graphic simulation of his approach angle to the huge satellite, told him that he was just under a mile away—of course, the numbers were actually in metric figures, but he had long ago become used to making the mental conversion to yards and miles, because he was an *American,* goddammit—yet for an experienced pilot nothing could replace eyeball navigation. Bruce pushed the yoke forward a tad and gave the throttle a little push, and one of the RCR's on the fuselage fired, braking his approach. The powersat floated upward a bit. He glanced down at the screen, making sure that the navaids computer agreed with what his eyes told him, and confirmed to himself that he was on a steady course for the construction shack. Nice shooting, guy. Who needs the computer? Satisfied, he grinned and resumed singing.

"Arrows of neon and flashing marquees down on Main Street . . ."

Another construction pod passed before him, carrying a load of rebars in its claws, its spotlights dazzling him briefly with their glare.

"Chicago, New York, Detroit, and it's all on the same street."

Chicago, he thought. What a hell of a town. I used to love cruising my bike down Lakeshore Drive, checking out all the rich dames in their spiffy threads. What a trip that was.

"Your typical city involved in a typical daydream,
"Hang it up and see what tomorrow brings . . ."

*Vulcan Control to Pod Zulu Tango. What the hell do you think you're doing, Neiman?*

Virgin Bruce sucked in his cheeks and widened his eyes, the way he remembered Eddie Murphy doing when Bruce was a kid watching *Saturday Night Live* on TV: "Uh, oh, it's the landlord!"

Virgin Bruce reached up to his chin and made sure his headset mike was adjusted, then reached to the communications panel to switch it on. To his chagrin, he found that it had already been switched on. Oh, hell, he thought. I must have been singing to the whole shift!

Recklessly, his lips stretched away from his teeth in a huge grin. Nothing to do but brazen it out. He started in on the next verse.

"Dallas got a soft machine;
"Houston too close to New Orleans;
"New York got the ways and means . . ."

*Neiman, we got the ways and means to can your pay for the week if you don't shape up and fly right. Now you come back with something other than sing-a-long or you and me are going to have a major disagreement, if we don't already have one. Do you copy?*

"I copy, Hank, I copy," Bruce snarled into the mike. "And what's this crap about flying right? My trajectory is as clean and regulation as you're gonna get, man."

*Bullshit, Neiman. Take another look at your screen. You just cut off a Big Dummy coming in on final approach to Vulcan. The pilot had to waste fuel braking so he'd keep the safe minimum distance from you and your hotdogging.*

Neiman frowned. Hank Luton, the construction supervisor, wasn't fooling this time; he was mad. Virgin Bruce punched a couple of keys on the computer and got a wide-angle display of the space around his pod. Sure enough, it showed an HLV from Earth on an approach trajectory to the construction shack. A quick glance at the coordinates told him that his pod had zipped straight in front of the big freighter. He felt instantly sorry; he, too, had been forced to make unnecessary firings to correct for careless flying by other space pilots in the crowded sphere of space surrounding Vulcan Station.

"Hey, Hank, I sure as shit am sorry about that," Virgin Bruce said, genuinely apologetic. "I just didn't see that guy. Tell him I'm . . ."

*I don't give a goddamn how sorry you are, Neiman!*

Virgin Bruce winced. Luton *must* be mad; no one shouts into a mike like that unless he's full-fledged furious. It was enough to make his ears ring. The construction supervisor kept on, in just a slightly quieter tone of voice. *I don't like this crap you just pulled, you got that? I don't like you taking off to Olympus without getting authorization, and I don't like what you just tried to pull over there! You're nothing special to us, Neiman, and you put on your pants the same as the rest of us! You think you got a problem, you take it to me, I'm your boss and not Henry Wallace! You got that, pal? I mean do you got that?*

"Loud and clear, Hank," he murmured. Hell, this was on an open channel. Everyone on the shift, and on Olympus—even on Earth, if they were hooked up with the right equipment—must be hearing this chew-out. "How many times do you want me to say sorry, Hank?"

Silence for a minute. Then Luton's voice came back, authoritative and cold. *Neiman, you're relieved of your shift. I want you to dock at Vulcan and meet me in the hotdogs. You and me are going to have a talk about your job, pal.*

"Job? What do you mean, talk about my job?" Bruce almost yelled back. "Listen, Hank, who's done the most shift-hours up here? Who's . . ."

*Zulu Tango, this is Vulcan Traffic.* Luton's Alabama-accented voice was replaced by Sammy Orlando's Brooklyn nasality. *We have you on course for docking at Vulcan. Do you acknowledge? Over.*

Virgin Bruce checked his own bearings. No, he was not on course to dock at the construction shack; in fact he was heading a mile away from Vulcan, out to a section of the powersat most of the shift's crew had been working on all day. Sammy was too good a traffic control officer to miss that; he was subtly letting Bruce know that he didn't have a choice as to his destination. Not if his job mattered.

"Roger, Sammy, that's an affirmative," Bruce growled back. "Request docking at Vulcan Beta. Over."

*We copy, Zulu Tango. Proceed for docking in the garage. Vulcan Traffic out.*

" 'Ride to live, live to ride,' " Virgin Bruce said, his customary sign-off. "Tango out." He snapped off the comlink, squeezed his eyes shut for a moment, and murmured, "Oh, shit."

He would have to handle this carefully, as gently as laying down a bike at sixty in a cow pasture, otherwise that was what he was going to get up smelling like: shit. He opened his eyes and began to make the necessary course corrections that would bring him in toward Vulcan Station. The long, huge grid of the powersat began to glide past the top of his windows. He could see the tiny forms of space-suited beamjacks clinging to its underside, their helmet beacons making tiny moving spots of light along the silver girders. *Very carefully,* he reminded himself as he flipped to autopilot. Otherwise it was goodbye space and hello Missouri.

Actually, it wasn't the thought of getting fired and shipped back to Earth that bothered him so much. He was sick to death of space. He wasn't particularly stuck on beamjack work, and sometimes he thought he would gag if he had to swallow any more of the freeze-dried guano they served in the mess deck. He wanted to go back, but the time wasn't right yet. The heat hadn't blown over down there yet. If he went back now, it would only be a matter of time before the Exiles found out where he was and tracked him down.

It was a nightmarish fantasy, which had haunted him for over a year now. He would be in a room—maybe an apartment he had rented, maybe a seedy motel room in Texas or Maine or Colorado, where he thought he was safe. Maybe he would be expecting someone to come by—a friend he had made in a bar, or some nice chick with full tits and ass-length hair he had been laying—and he'd go answer the door, but the buddy or the babe wouldn't be standing there. There would be four or five of them standing at the door. The light of a twenty-watt bulb would be shining dimly on their leathers and the chains they'd be carrying. Maybe one or two of them would be grinning with savage humor, but the others would have the dark, vicious glower they all too often fixed on those stupid enough to say the wrong thing or make the wrong move. Maybe he'd try to slam the door; maybe he wouldn't even bother, knowing they could bash their way through in seconds. "Hello, Brucie," they'd say. "Long time no see."

Then they'd stomp him into the floor so far the cockroaches would have to get shovels to find him.

Take it easy with Hank Luton, man, he told himself, grasping the stick firmly with both hands as he headed the pod toward Vulcan Station. Tell him you're sorry. Tell him it won't happen again. Let him chew you out and don't give him any shit back. Do whatever you got to do, man, but don't let him think the best thing for him to do is to send you back to Earth and get a replacement, because you know the Exiles have put an APB out for you with the Angels and the Outlaws and all the rest, and they can find you if you come up from hiding too fast. Do what it takes to survive, Bruce man. . . .

A blinking red light on the communications panel caught his attention. He frowned; it was the priority alert for the comlink, informing everyone that there was something on the main channel that everyone on active duty needed to monitor.

He flicked the monitor switch, and instantly he heard the high beeping whine of the general alarm, which all but drowned out the sound of several voices chattering at once in an almost indistinguishable garble. Bruce's eyes went wide, and this time he wasn't playing Eddie Murphy.

Something had just gone seriously wrong on Vulcan Station.

# 10

# An Inch Away From Eternity

Outer space is an environment that seldom forgives mistakes. It is the most relentless environment into which man has ever ventured. It is an engineer's nightmare, a hell in heaven for the foolhardy and the stupid. Although to enter, live, and work there demands perfection in every detail, it is in man's nature to make mistakes, and therein lies the rub.

During the first decades of spaceflight most of the mistakes were made in the comparatively soft and safety-redundant environment of the launch pad. The mistakes led to long delays in launches and scrubbings of flights and, in the instance of the Apollo 1 fire in 1967, the death of three men who were being groomed to walk on the Moon. But although there were near-fatal accidents in orbit during the first years of the American and Soviet space programs, it was a long time before anyone died in space. The worst failures of man and machine were caught on the ground, where the consequences were less terrifying.

But mistakes always happen. They always have; they always will. No matter how sophisticated space technology became, flaws slipped in. Sometimes men died as the result, sometimes the consequences were less serious. A radio transceiver not switched on, a tether not securely fastened, a misfire of an MMU backpack in the wrong direction, a too-hard docking of a spacecraft, careless entry of a program into a computer, a lost tool during EVA, misunderstood communications between spacemen, miscalculation of body movement in zero g, any imaginable combination of dumb jerk boo-boos: These mistakes, which were either corrected or buffered by safety programs, were more often measured in nuisance value than in their contribution to early graves being dug.

Yet there were other types of errors which were not easily avoidable. Bad engineering on the ground; mistakes made in design or manufacture of items on Earth, which would later be carried into that place of no atmosphere, no gravity, and extremes of heat and cold. Those mistakes killed.

A construction pod undocked from Vulcan Station and began to head toward the powersat. Its pilot, a young beamjack named Alan McPhee, gently steered the tiny spacecraft around the bend in Vulcan's bell-shaped Beta module, heading toward its underside on a course that would take him beneath both construction shack and solar power satellite. McPhee was a good pod pilot, but his skill was not enough to cope with a flaw in his spacecraft.

A fuel cell, a sphere the size of a gymnasium medicine ball, which was strapped to the outside of the pod's fuselage, had a weak skin. It had been manufactured by a small aerospace company in Illinois, which subcontracted to Skycorp. The fuel cells were supposed to be carefully inspected by X-ray equipment for weak points, yet this one had slipped through because the technician in charge had been thinking too much about her impending breakup with her boyfriend. A couple of months later, the faulty cell had been repressurized in the construction shack's pod garage almost a dozen times. Each time additional pressure had been put upon a thin spot in the cell's lining, which was absolutely undetectable to the naked eye.

This time, when McPhee took his pod called "We Deliver!" out for another shift, carrying rebars to beamjacks around the powersat, the soft point on the cell's skin yielded to the internal pressure from the liquid-fuel mix.

Soundlessly, the fuel cell exploded in space, just as the construction pod was passing the hotdog modules.

Claude Hooker clamped the tubes leading from his life-support pack into the sockets on his suit's midsection and gave them a clockwise twist that locked them in place, then took the helmet off the overhead rack and tucked it under his arm. Grabbing a rail with his free hand, he slipped the toes of his boots free from the foot restraints on the floor. Now floating free in the narrow compartment of the whiteroom, he began to pull himself toward the hatch leading to the next compartment, where technicians would ease him into an MMU pack before he would cycle through the airlock and head to work.

He passed Mike Webb, the beamjack who had sat next to him on the ferry, and another spaceman, a new guy whose name Hooker couldn't remember. Webb was notorious for being slow in the whiteroom, and the rookie was as inept at getting ready for EVA as only a tenderfoot could be. Webb gave Hooker a quick thumbs-up and a silly grin as a technician struggled to wiggle the beamjack's legs into the lower half of his spacesuit. Hooker shrugged, managed a weak smile, and returned the thumbs-up. The new guy was trying to retrieve a glove that was floating away from him, and Hooker absently batted it back with his free hand. The rookie, whose name-patch read HONEYMAN, nodded and said, "Thanks, Popeye."

"No sweat, Honeyman," Hooker replied. As he passed the optical scanner near the hatch, Hooker paused to hold his right wrist in front of the lens, allowing the computer to read numbers printed on the card strapped to the cuff and clock him in. A green light flashed on and Hooker started to enter the hatch, gently rotating his body to a horizontal position so that he could fit through the narrow aluminum sleeve.

"Hey, Popeye, hold on!" someone called behind him. Hooker grabbed a handhold next to the hatch, stopping himself, and looked around. Julian Price, the young black kid who worked in the whiteroom as a suit tech, was pushing himself up alongside. Price reached over to Hooker's left leg, reached under the cuff of the overgarment, and relocked the loose ankle joint above the boot.

"Be careful there, man," he murmured. "You could get in trouble that way, big time."

"Thanks, Julian. Wasn't thinking."

"Always gotta keep thinkin', Popeye," Julian said, giving Hooker's suit a quick once-over inspection. "They don't look at you when they're putting on your pack over there, man, and I can't check everything you're doing when you're suiting up. I mean, I can do my job, but it starts and ends with you, man. . . ."

"Yeah, uh-huh," Hooker grumbled. "See you later, Julian."

"Check ya, Popeye," Price finished, letting him go. He seemed mildly stung. "I mean, don't be too appreciative or nuthin' now."

Hooker paused again, looking back at Julian. "Sorry, Julio. Didn't mean anything. I owe you one."

Julian's grin returned. He gave Hooker the thumbs-up. "No offense taken, Popeye. Be careful out there."

Hooker returned the ancient gesture and pushed himself through the hatch into the connecting sleeve, wanting to kick himself for being short-tempered with the kid. God damn it, Julian looked out for all the beamjacks going out of EVA like the manager of a high school football team making sure the shoulder pads fit and the jocks were washed. It was a thankless job, but someone had to do it, and Julian did it well. He had probably caught enough loose suit joints, badly connected air hoses, and minute cracks in spacesuit armor to keep an army of beamjacks from blowing out their guts in sudden decompression accidents. No one here had the right to snub him.

Ah, hell, Hooker thought. I'll find a way to make it up to him. Hooker had plenty of telephone time logged to his credit that he had never used; there was no one on Earth he needed to call. I'll let him make a call to his mom and dad in Washington, D.C., Hooker decided. That'll make up for . . .

There was suddenly a roar from far behind him, like a shotgun blast—a thin, reedy whistle that sounded like someone trying to play a broken flute, and, moments later, the electronic warbling sound of an alarm going off. He instinctively convulsed in midair like a man trying to duck a gunshot; his head banged against the side of the sleeve and he saw stars for an instant.

He then realized that the roar had come from behind, from the other whiteroom, adjacent to the one he had just left. The alarm that was warbling was one he had heard only once before during his duty tour, during an instruction drill when he had first come aboard. He twisted around, performing a cramped somersault within the sleeve, and caught a glimpse of a miniature cyclone ripping through the compartment he had just vacated. Logbook pages, loose pens, overgarment segments and other loose items were being caught by the wind and being thrown around in the unnatural gale. He saw the emergency hatch seal on the hatch on the other side of the whiteroom iris shut like a closing sphincter.

*"Blowout!"* he heard Mike Webb scream. *"It's a blowout!"*

But if it was only the far whiteroom which had been affected, then where was that high, reedy whine coming from? Something else was wrong. . . .

Julian Price floated past the sleeve hatch, his back turned to Hooker, his hands flailing as he tried to grab hold of something the way Webb and Honeyman had, grasping suit racks against the gale raging inside the compartment. Without really thinking about it, Hooker reached through the hatch and grabbed Price's ankle just above the top of one of his sneakers. The kid yelled as Hooker yanked him into the sleeve as hard as he could; he bounced off Hooker as both of them were crammed into the narrow space, slamming Hooker against the side of the sleeve.

At that moment the emergency hatches on either side of the sleeve irised shut, trapping the two men inside. It was suddenly quiet, except for the dull sound of the emergency Klaxon from the whiteroom. A single, recessed bulb by Hooker's left shoulder threw an amber glow across their faces.

Julian Price forced his right forearm up between him and Hooker; the two men were squeezed together as tight as if they were both lying in the same sleeping bag. There was an intercom unit strapped to Price's wrist, and he clumsily jabbed at the TALK button with his chin. "Mayday! Mayday!" he yelled into his headset mike, which miraculously had not been torn off during the decompression hurricane. "Price to Control, blowout in Modules One and Two!"

Sammy Orlando's voice came through the headset earphone; Hooker could hear it tinnily. *We're aware of that, damn it! Get off the line! There's nothing . . .*

It was replaced by Luton's voice. *How'd you get out of there? There's total decompression in both compartments! Everyone who was in them are dead already!*

"Bullshit!" Price yelled back. "I just got out of Number Two! There's two men trapped in there; you gotta get 'em out!"

*Our instruments tell us it's total decompression . . . something pierced both those hotdogs. There should be no one left alive in either one!*

"And I'm telling you, man, there's two men stuck in Number Two!" Price hollered. "I dunno about Hotdog One, but Webb and Honeyman are still in Two! They've just got a slow leak in there or something, but they're still alive, you gotta—!"

"I'm wearing a spacesuit, Julian!" Hooker shouted. "I can get 'em out! Tell 'em to open the hatch!"

*"Hank, Hooker's wearing a suit and he says . . ."*

*Are you wearing a suit, Price?*

"Negative, Control."

*Then forget it. You two just sit tight.* Luton paused. *I don't want to risk one man because the other might have a chance. Those guys only have a few minutes. I don't want the body count to go up any more than it has. Where're you two, in a sleeve?*

"Roger!"

*Then just stay there. We'll get someone to get you out soon. Forget those guys, son. I hate to say it, but they're dead men.*

"Screw you, asshole!" Price screamed. "Open the goddamn hatch!"

"Zulu Tango to Vulcan Command, do you copy!"

He waited a moment, then tried it again: "Zulu Tango to Vulcan, do you read, dammit!"

Virgin Bruce didn't know if anyone had even heard him. The main comlink channel was a confusion of voices; most of the other channels he had scanned were similarly garbled. Whatever had happened at the shack, it had occurred so quickly that no one seemed to know exactly what the nature of the emergency was, or what they were supposed to do.

*Command, something's blown in Hotdog Two, I'm seeing oxygen vapor coming from—!*

*Repair shifts to Hotdogs One and Two! This is Command, repair crews on shift to Hotdogs—!*

*Holy shit, there's a body out there! We need a medic at the shack!*

*Vulcan, this is pod Romeo Virginia. I've had an explosion on my aft side fuel cell. I have loss of control and I'm in tumble. Repeat, Vulcan, this is Romeo Virginia, I've got a problem . . .*

*Romeo Virginia, what the hell are you . . . ?*

*Goddammit, Hank, get that fucking hatch open or I'll . . .*

*Where's the damn repair crew!*

*This is Romeo Virginia! I've got one of the kits!*

*Romeo, get to the hotdogs! There's been a blowout on One and Two! One's lost, get Two!*

*For the love of Pete, Luton, open the fucking hatch and I can get . . .*

*Squelch Hooker, Sammy. Romeo, get to—!*

*Negative, Hank, I got no control! My fuel cell blew up and . . .*

*Oh, my God, that's Luke, that's Luke's who's—!*

*Everybody, goddammit SHUT UP! Who's got the repair kits! Who's on the shift—!*

Virgin Bruce sank back into his couch, staring straight ahead. Now, in the gleam of the shack's navigational lights a mile and a half away, he could see a phosphorescent, tiny white cloud of water and oxygen forming near Module Alpha. Something had blown out one of the hotdogs; two, if what he had heard was right. He didn't want to think what the larger objects he could pick out dimly in the tiny cloud might be.

*Command, this is the main bay, we've got stress on the beambuilder assembly! The whole shack's shaking—!*

*This is Caldwell, Command! I've got the other kit, but I'm way out on the powersat on tether, repeat, I don't have a pack . . .*

*What the hell are you doing without . . . never mind, who's got a sealkit!*

Jesus! How could have he forgotten! Virgin Bruce craned his neck back and checked the ceiling space above and behind his head. Strapped to the bulkhead, next to the first-aid kit, was the sealkit, a compression tank with a foam nozzle. He had been issued an emergency kit last time around, but had forgotten to turn that kit over to another pod pilot; he had been too pissed off about the elevator music.

*Sammy, turn off the damn alarm!*

*Command, I'm too far out here, I can't . . .*

Abruptly, the emergency horn ceased to split his ears. Eerily, things suddenly seemed as if they had gone back to normal, except for the yelling on the main channel.

*Medic, we need a medical crew . . .*

*Screw it, George, they're dead!* Hank Luton said harshly. *Who the hell has a—!*

Bruce stabbed at the switches on his communications board, bringing himself back on line. "Hank, this is Zulu Tango! I've got a kit and I'm going in!"

*Oh, for Christ's . . . Bruce, you don't know what the hell you're . . .*

"Hey, fuck you, Hank! I got a sealer, so get off my back and lemme get those guys . . .

*Bruce, you only got a couple of minutes maybe!* This was Sammy Orlando's voice now. *Haul ass, man!*

"Right, Vulcan," he snapped, Hell, if Luton wanted to play games while men were dying, he'd take Sammy's word as the go-ahead. "Get a fix on me and clear the traffic on a line between me and it. I'm comin' through!"

*Neiman?* Hank Luton's voice again. *You've got the go-ahead. But if you fuck this up, pal, I'll . . .*

"Get outta my ear and lemme work, Hank!" Bruce yelled into his mike as he switched off the autopilot. "You just tell me where to go, I'll do the rest!"

*You got maybe three minutes, Neiman, maybe not that. Make it count, you son of a bitch.*

"Sammy, kill the rest of the bells, will ya? I don't need to be reminded how bad the situation is."

Vulcan's command center was a dimly lit compartment with a low ceiling, crowded with control consoles in every available space except for a narrow deck lined with stirrup-like foot restraints. When the shit had hit the fan Hank Luton had lifted his toes out of his restraints and he was now floating horizontal to the floor, holding onto rungs on the bulkheads. It was easier to get to things in a small compartment that way, if you were used to zero g and could swim in it.

The last of the alarms—it seemed as if a dozen had all gone off at once, warning of explosive decompression, emergency hatches being shut, loss of orbital stability, and other simultaneous emergencies— went silent, leaving only the chatter of voices from the comlink channels. Sammy Orlando, his skinny frame still harnessed into his chair in front of the communications board, was listening intently to something through his headset. He looked over his shoulder at the construction supervisor.

"Hank, I just heard from the Korolev cosmodrome," he said. "The Russians have picked up our signals and are offering rescue assistance."

"Oh, swell. That's great news." Luton ran a free hand over his balding forehead; the sweat that hadn't caught in his kinky hair rubbed off into beady droplets which hung in the air. The Soviets were also maintaining a station in GEO orbit, but even by a straight-line trajectory it was still several thousand miles away. The best they could do now was to send over another pod to serve as a meat wagon for the dead. . . . "Tell 'em thanks, but no thanks," Luton replied. "Tell 'em we got everything under control, thank-you anyway."

"Sir, the Space Rescue Treaty . . ."

"Damn it, Sammy, I'm not going to play UN right now! Tell the Russians to take a hike and keep an eye on what Neiman's doing!"

He turned his head to look over Sammy's shoulder at the traffic control screen. One white spot on the screen indicated where Virgin Bruce's pod was located; it was moving closer to the center as he watched. Another white spot, Alan McPhee's pod, was hanging nearby; a blue line between Neiman's pod and the construction shack showed that Zulu Tango would come close, but not intersect, the point where Romeo Virginia was floating dead in space. "How bad is McPhee's drift?" he asked.

Orlando made a quick computation on his computer. "A few hundred meters per minute. Want to send a rescue pod?"

"Negative. He sounds okay, just a little shaken. Keep an eye on him, that's all." He found himself smiling. "If he gets too far away, get the Russians to rescue him, if it'll make 'em feel important."

The communications officer looked over her shoulder. "I'm getting a message from Hooker and Price. They wanna . . ."

"I heard, I heard!" Luton yelled. "Julie, keep listening to them, and if it sounds like they're running out of air, get Mike to open the other hatch and let 'em out, but I don't want to hear their crap again. Mike, how're they doing?"

"I think they'll make it for a few minutes," the chief engineer said. "I'm worried about the beam-builders."

"Shit. Didn't you get those things cut loose?" Without waiting for a reply, Luton somersaulted to face the wide port that overlooked the main construction bay.He could see that the massive machines had been disengaged from their telescoping supports and were now drifting below the construction shack at the ends of the beams they had been processing before their shutdown. "I see 'em. What's the problem?"

"They might break loose."

"Oh, great." The beam-builders cost several billion dollars and had required separate shuttle flights to get them into space, due to their size and mass. Losing one of them would be almost worse than having a man killed.

But not quite. "Just keep an eye on them," Luton snapped impatiently. "Put a man on each of 'em if you get a chance. I'm not worried about . . ."

"Hank! I'm getting something from Number Two!" Julia Smith yelled.

"They're still alive?" Luton attempted to roll over again in midair, but he did it too fast and his torso slammed into an overhead panel. He swore again and glanced down to make sure no important switches had been thrown. "What's going on, who's that, what's he . . . ?"

"It's . . . incoherent." Julia's pretty eyes were squeezed shut. She had listened to long strings of profanities from beamjacks on duty without scarcely batting an eyelash, but what she was hearing now was giving her pain. "He's . . . he's panicking, Hank."

Who wouldn't? Luton thought. Who couldn't? He remembered what he had (cruelly, he now realized in spontaneous hindsight) told Hooker a minute (had it been that short a time?) ago: *They're dead men.* "Try to talk to them," he rasped. "Tell 'em to hang on . . . or something. Help's on the way."

He craned his neck to glance out through the port. Out beyond the hemisphere of Module B, where earthlight shone on the skeleton of the powersat, he could see the growing spotlights of pod Zulu Tango approaching the shack. A strange, bitter irony: The end of this sudden, deadly nightmare rested with a man he had been half-intending to fire ten minutes ago. Everything depended on a sleazy biker from Missouri: It was as disgusting as it was horrifying.

"Sammy, just make sure he's on course and nothing's in his way," the shift supervisor said, his eyes locked on the approaching construction pod. To himself, he murmured, "Bruce, for Christ's sake, don't fuck up this time."

It was hard to breathe now. The air inside the whiteroom had become so rarefied that he had to gasp for each lungful. The cyclonic wind which had ripped through the compartment had settled some, which made Webb realize that most of the air was already gone. Soon, it would all go through that inch-long slit in the fabric wall. When it did, he and Honeyman would die.

Webb hung with one hand to an overhead rail and took deep gasps of cold oxygen. His fingers were turning numb and the upper portion of his body—the part that was not encased in spacesuit armor—was becoming chilled, since the heat had been sucked out along with most of the cabin pressure. He doubted he would freeze before he suffocated, however. Even though the bit of shrapnel which had punctured the hotdog was wedged in the wall fast enough to prevent explosive decompression of the type that had killed the two guys in Hotdog One, the leak was fast enough that he knew he and Honeyman would die in a couple of minutes, three at most.

He almost envied those guys. They had gone out quick. What was that old movie-poster line? "In space, no one can hear you scream?" He *had* heard them scream, just before the emergency hatches had irised shut. But Webb knew that they must not have screamed for very long. Now Honeyman was doing enough screaming for them all.

*"Get us out of here!"*

The rookie beamjack was hanging to a handhold near an intercom panel, howling at it in stark terror. Tears had streamed from his eyes and were floating around his face in fat globules. "Goddammit, you bastards, I don't want to die, get me out of here!" His voice was turning hoarse and, in the decreasing atmospheric pressure, tinny, as if he were farther away than fifteen feet. Webb noticed that Honeyman's chest was heaving with the effort to sustain his howling. He also noticed, in disgust, a dark splotch in the crotch of the beamjack's jumpsuit where he had urinated in fear.

"Shut up, damn it!" Webb forced himself to yell. He didn't want to die, either, but he was damn sure not going to go out like a coward, or in the company of one if he could help it.

The absurd part of it was, there he was in a spacesuit bottom, with other parts of a suit floating around the compartment, and there wasn't any way he could use them. Not in time, anyway. Getting into a suit was a long procedure. Even half-dressed as he was, Webb would still need ten to fifteen minutes to struggle into the top half, join the halves, connect the hoses and adjust the air supply, put on the gauntlets and don the helmet. This was even if he omitted steps like adjusting and switching on the interior water-cooling system or donning the overgarment. Parts of the spacesuit had been scattered all across the compartment by the escaping pressure; just gathering them would take a couple of precious minutes. . . . It wasn't even worth trying.

"You fucking shits! You rat-fucking bastards! Get me—!"

"Shaddup, Honeyman!" Webb snapped. He thought of the first American astronauts to die in a spacecraft. Gus Grissom, Ed White, and Roger Chaffee. The Apollo 1 fire at the Cape, way back before the first Moon landing. Even at the end, when the fire in the tiny command module was reaching for their bodies and their lungs were filling with smoke, they had been trying to undog that hatch the engineers had made so well it couldn't be opened quickly in an emergency. They had screamed, that was for certain, but they had fought for their lives until they lost consciousness.

Bad engineering and lack of foresight was going to kill him and Honeyman as well. Whoever had designed the hotdogs, in trying to conserve space inside the cramped little compartments for suit racks and TV monitors, had apparently decided that rescue balls were not needed here, and that sealkits should be given to the astronauts working outside the hotdogs, not put inside. No way to seal the hole from inside. . . .

Or was there?

A flash of inspiration hit him, an old Dutch legend he had learned in childhood. My mind must be going, Webb thought. My life is passing before my eyes, to recall something like that now.

Yet he glanced around and spotted what he was looking for: a spacesuit glove, floating in midair a couple of yards away. Without allowing himself time to think through what he was going to do, to consider the dangers—no time, no time—Webb let go of the rail and pushed himself toward the glove. Grabbing it as he passed, he shoved his right hand into the thick gauntlet as he automatically braked his plunge through the compartment with his feet. The glove fit snugly on his hand, and for the first time since he had been a beamjack, Webb didn't mind the tight fit. He would need that snugness, every fraction of an inch of it, for what he was about to pull off.

*If* he could pull it off. Webb took another deep lungful of rapidly thinning air, then pushed off again with his legs. Arms thrust in front of his head, he launched himself toward the hole.

Julian Price had taken care of their air supply before the situation in the sleeve had become critical. Disconnecting the air hose from Hooker's spacesuit and adjusting the regulator on his chest pack, the whiteroom technician had transformed Hooker's backpack oxygen tank into an oxygen source for both men. Now that they didn't have to worry about asphyxiation, they only had to wait for someone to rescue them from the sleeve.

The waiting was the hardest part. Vulcan Command was no longer listening to them since Hooker's outburst, so there was no point in trying to communicate with Sammy or Hank. Julian had tried to cheer the beamjack up with small talk, but Hooker had stopped listening. They floated together in the sleeve, pressed against each other like lovers, yet Hooker wasn't seeing Price's face any more. Eyes half shut, breathing shallowly—his momentary hysteria had drained him both emotionally and physically—the beamjack's mind was far away in time and space. . . .

*He lay on his back in a rubber boat under a jet-black night sky, feeling the ocean's tides gently rock him back and forth. Eventually the waves might carry him back toward shore—he wasn't that far from land—or he might eventually sit up and use the boat's plastic oars to get him home. For now, though, he didn't care; his only concern was his pain.*

*He turned his head slightly and looked across the bow. The boat was still burning, a charcoal on fire on the ocean's surface a couple of miles away. Eventually the rest of the hull would sink below the waves and the gasoline would consume itself, and the little tongue of flame that still glowed on the ocean would be extinguished. He stared at it for a while, remembering how a glint of gold vanished into the ocean —gone, forever gone— Then he turned his eyes away, to stare up at the clear night sky.*

*The stars had come out, brilliant and white. Mars stood out as a reddish point near the horizon, and the Milky Way was a gauzy, breathtakingly huge swath across the heavens. He realized that he had never seen anything as beautiful as the night sky over the Gulf.*

*Staring up at the stars, he felt the pain in his heart beginning to ease, to be replaced by a deep yearning. How could he have forgotten that which he had felt as a kid, the frightening beauty and wonder of infinite space? If only he could be there now, one with the stars, far away from this tragic and painful Earth.*

*He noticed, then, that one of the stars was moving, steadily rising from the horizon. He watched it move. No, it wasn't an aircraft; judg-*

*ing from its trajectory, it had to be a spacecraft, probably a launch
from Cape Canaveral, hundreds of miles away on the other side of the
Florida peninsula. Recognizing it for what it was, he looked above the
moving star, and spotted its probable destination, a couple of bright
lights almost directly above his head. Those would be the space stations, Olympus and Vulcan.*

*Unexpectedly, he found himself smiling. . . .*

He felt a hand grasping and shaking his shoulder. Julian Price's
dark face replaced the starscape. "Hooker! Popeye! Wake up, man,"
Price was saying. "I think something's happening out there!"

Virgin Bruce tried not to look at the bodies. One was floating close
to one of the construction pod's canopy. The corpse was wearing a
jumpsuit that was blotched with frozen red blood, and Bruce was
glad that at least he couldn't see the face. Explosive decompression
was a grotesque way to die. It may have been sudden, he realized,
but the beamjack must have had a long, final minute of horror and
agony. . . .

Forget it, he told himself. Forget that the stiff was probably a
friend of yours. Concentrate. He ran his gaze over the bank of instruments above the viewports, making sure the pod's cabin was depressurized and that all the engines were safed, then quickly glanced at
the tiny bank of lights within his helmet, just above the rim of the
visor. Everything was green. Virgin Bruce then grabbed a lever on
the left, next to his seat, and pushed it forward. The hatch directly
over his head undogged and opened to space.

The construction pod was held by its arms to the hull of the
construction shack, an emergency maneuver only seldom rehearsed
and never, in his memory, actually put to use in a real-life crisis. His
seat harness was already undone; Bruce planted his feet on either
side of his seat and pushed himself upward through the hatch. He
propelled himself out of the pod faster than he had anticipated, into
the red and white glare of the navigational beacons arranged around
the shack's hull. They dazzled his eyes for a moment, and he raised
the handjet blindly to shoulder-length and squeezed the trigger. The
spurt of the jet slowed his momentum and he blinked furiously,
trying to clear his vision. Christ, he had not expected it to be so
bright outside. . . .

*Neiman, what's going on?*

"I'm outside the pod, Hank," he said. It had been a long time
since he had gone EVA, not since he had tested with a pod and
satisfied the supervisors that he was competent with the buglike ma-

chines. For an instant he felt vertigo, and he forced it down. "I'm about"—he squinted his eyes and peered at the rounded surface of the shack's B module below his feet—"fifteen, twenty feet above the hotdogs."

*Your pod secure?*

"Roger." Actually, he hadn't checked since he had left it, but if the magnetic shoes on its claws had not held and it had started to drift, he was not about to go back and fool with it at this point—Let the damn thing drift. "Now shut up and lemme work."

*Bruce*— Then Hank Luton shut up. His vision cleared, Virgin Bruce started easing himself downward toward the hotdogs. If he had known this was going to happen, he reflected, he would not have taken the spare snoopy helmet with its built-in communications headset from that kid in the Olympus whiteroom. Of all things now, he didn't need Luton giving him the mother hen treatment.

Never mind, he thought. Forget that dipshit. Save those poor bastards' skins. Going headfirst, he steered his body around until he faced the hotdogs. Through the visor he could see the debris caused by the accident—torn scraps of Mylar and aluminum mesh, odds and ends blown out from Hotdog One, tumbling in microgravitational orbit around the shack. He hadn't spotted the body of the other crewman killed by One's explosion yet, and he prayed that he wouldn't. That was all he needed now to completely freak him out; his stomach told him again that it had been a long time since he had last gone spacewalking.

Nothing to grab onto on the shack's hull; he had to rely completely on the little handjet, something he had used only once before, during the initial week of training. Probably no one had used one seriously since Olympus had been built six years ago. He felt his mouth going dry, but he didn't dare distract himself to sip from the water straw inside his helmet; those guys could be fighting for their last gasps now. He forced thoughts of the immensity of space around him from his mind. The inside of the suit chafed at his skin. "Busted, down on Bourbon Street . . ." he sang absent-mindedly.

*Come again, Zulu Tango?*

He ignored Julia Smith's inquiry; an old Grateful Dead song was the only thing keeping his head on tight. "Set up . . . like a bowlin' pin . . . knocked down, it gets a wearin' thin . . ."

He made it to Hotdog Two and the first thing he could grab, the hemisphere of struts holding the rubbery cylinder in place. He grabbed a strut with his free hand and started to ease himself along, pulling himself carefully so as not to accidentally push himself away and off into space. Glancing down, his eyes widened as he saw that the tightly stretched multilayer fabric of the temporary module was already beginning to sag inward, like an inner tube being leaked. It could only be a matter of seconds now. . . .

*Neiman, where are you?*

"I'm on the hotdog, Hank. Shut the hell up already!" Okay, he had arrived, now where was the damn hole. . . .

His helmet lantern swept the area and caught a small, ragged edge protruding from the side of the module. There is was! "I got it!" he yelled. It was only a few feet away now. "Hang on . . . hang on . . ." he mumbled.

*Neiman . . .*

"Will you shut the hell up, Hank. I'm trying!" Virgin Bruce yelled. He yanked himself forward and almost threw himself off the strut in his haste. He had to stretch his hand just to grab the next bar.

He was almost on top of the rip and was reaching for the sealkit where he had strapped it to his right thigh, when he noticed something peculiar: a jagged piece of metal, glinting in the light, slowly tumbling away from the rip. It was obviously a piece of the fuel cell which had exploded—he could tell from its general shape and form —but if it was, why had it not lodged itself in the hotdog when it had come so close? Indeed, why was it drifting *away* from . . . ?

Oh, my God, he thought. It's the piece that was lodged in the skin. It had to be. But if it had become dislodged, when why wasn't the hotdog exploding?

He looked down at the rip, and saw a stubby white cylinder sticking out of the hole. It was effectively stopping the rip like a cork in a bottle. Amazed, he stared at the object for a long moment under the glare of his helmet lantern's beam. There was something familiar-looking about that thing, yet he couldn't quite put his finger on it. . . .

Suddenly, he began to laugh. He heard Luton's voice in his headset: *Neiman, listen, it's okay. Mike Webb's inside the hotdog and . . .*

"I know, Hank, I know!" he nearly shouted. "I can see it! It's his damn finger!"

# 11

# Huntsville

Skycorp's corporate headquarters was located in Huntsville, Alabama, in that part of the western side of the town where the aerospace contractors traditionally nestled up against the George C. Marshall Space Center. That part of the little Southern town had begun to grow in the 1960's; the boom had continued into the 1990's, when NASA and the U.S. government had been the western hemisphere's largest purchaser of aerospace goods and services. The facilities of Boeing, Rockwell, and General Electric constituted their own city-within-a-city, a high-tech enclave on the doorstep of Marshall Center, waiting for the next major contract.

But by the last years of the twentieth century, the contractors had begun to go into business for themselves instead of for NASA. McDonnell Douglas started it first, when it followed the early success of its Project EOS space experiments to develop a space-manufactured pharmaceuticals industry. North American Rockwell and several smaller companies began to launch their own rockets as the result of Government deregulation and White House encouragement, and soon private launch services in the United States were able to successfully compete not only with the original commercial space-carrier, Europe's Arianespace, but even with NASA and the Soviet Union, in providing reliable, economic launch facilities for commercial industry.

It was only a matter of time before someone in the space business took the big jump. It turned out to be McGuinness International, the Atlanta-based firm that had established itself as a leader in nuclear technology and experimental aviation. McGuinness started a branch company, Skycorp, which would be dedicated exclusively to space development. The parent company immediately sank over $50 billion into the company, building state-of-the-art facilities in Huntsville and combing the aerospace industry to hire the best management, scientists, and workers in the field.

Early on, Skycorp announced that its first major goal would be establishing permanent quarters in high orbit to house over a hundred space workers and construction facilities in both space and at the site of the tiny U.S. lunar base. In the industry—behind closed boardroom doors, on the golf links, in the pages of *Aviation Week* and *Space Business News*—it was rumored that Skycorp's second major goal was to build a network of solar power-plants in space, to operate themselves and sell the electricity to American utility companies. In New York, Chicago, and London, some boasted that Skycorp's upper management would soon be taking swan dives off the Cape Canaveral launch towers, while other quietly instructed their brokers to buy Skycorp stock and get ready to sell it at once if things got too weird.

So far, Skycorp's stockholders had remained happy with their decisions and no one had gone high-diving on Merritt Island.

The Skycorp compound on Saturn Boulevard in Huntsville consisted of the main administration building—an enormous, eight-story A-frame made of white granite and stainless steel—surrounded by dome-shaped laboratory and test buildings and small, squat hangars. The complex included a private airstrip and its own telemetry field, a grove of dish antennae that maintained the communications links with Skycorp's offworld holdings. The complex was located prestigiously close to Marshall Center, close enough that the tops of the Atlas and Saturn boosters on display at the Alabama Space Museum could be seen over the treetops from the administration building windows.

A bronze plaque set in a marble slab by the entrance drive bore the corporate logo, a sphere traversed by a stylized spaceship flying past on a cometlike path. Golden letters below the logo read "SKYCORP A Division of McGuinness International."

Two basement sublevels beneath the administration building was the company's own Orbital Operations Center, which closely resembled the spacecraft-tracking centers at NASA's Houston facility and the Air Force's CSOC facility in Colorado Springs. In some ways, Skycorp's SpaceOps was superior to the Government's centers. The computers represented the latest, fastest advances in artificial intelligence. The work station displays, through satellite relays, gave OOC techs the same information available to Olympus and Vulcan commands. The electronics had EMP protection and the center itself could be sealed off and maintained independently in the case of nuclear war, a major consideration when the center had been built, although that was no longer quite as important.

The center was designed for comfort as well as efficiency. The chairs in front of the tiered consoles were leather upholstered, the temperature in the room maintained at a comfortable 72 degrees. The lighting was dim enough to allow the red and blue light from the computer and TV monitors to stand out, yet not so dim as to make one squint in order to read a printout. On busy days there were polite young men and women working as gofers, gathering hard-copy from the line printers and fetching coffee and sandwiches from the commissary.

It had been one of those days. The blowout of the Vulcan hotdogs had electrified the thirty men and women manning SpaceOps that afternoon. In the hours that followed those critical few minutes of the emergency they had been trying to figure out the exact circumstances of the accident: running simulations through the computers, gathering what scant data could be gained from Olympus and Vulcan, communicating with eyewitnesses in orbit.

The team had, after four hours of feverish work, come up with little more than they had initially learned. No one knew exactly what had caused construction pod Alpha Romeo's fuel cell to explode, and it would not be until Hotdog One was dismantled and shipped back to Earth that a lab team could analyze the wreckage to determine exactly how a piece of shrapnel managed to cause the explosive decompression that had killed the two crew members. Now, as the long twilight of a summer evening settled in, most of the team had gone home for the day, leaving a skeleton crew of five technicians to monitor the boards and a few tired gofers to clean up the mess of coffee cups, crumpled sandwich wrappers, and ashtrays overflowing with cigarette butts.

Kenneth Crespin found Clayton Dobbs in the operations supervisor's glass-walled cubicle at the rear of the operations center, staring at a long sheaf of printout which trailed from his hands into a pile on the floor next to his desk. Crespin stood in the doorway for a moment, looking at Dobbs and wondering how long it would take the young man to notice his presence. Probably never, or at least until Dobbs decided it was time to get up and go home, which from the reports that had filtered to Crespin's attention would be sometime in the wee hours. Like many geniuses, Dobbs apparently had an infinite concentration span, and like many ambitious young men of his caliber, he slept only when it was absolutely necessary.

After a moment Crespin cleared his throat; ten seconds later,

Dobbs noticed, his angular head jerking up from the printout. "Oh," he said. "Hello, Kenneth."

Crespin smiled and took a couple of steps into the cubicle. "I'm surprised you're still here, Clay. I understand your team has figured out everything which led up to it. Are you still trying to find something else?"

Dobbs said nothing for a moment, then dropped the printout on his desktop—the surface of which was invisible, buried completely by paper—and leaned back in his armchair, knitting his fingers together over his negligible stomach. "So how did the press conference go?" he asked mildly.

Crespin shrugged. His eyes wandered to framed pictures on Dobbs' walls, of shuttles lifting off from the Cape, and Olympus Station being built in high orbit. "Well enough, I suppose, considering. I didn't participate, but I spoke with our reps afterwards and was told that it was rough, but at least not quite as rough as when we had that worker killed on Olympus two years ago. The press has come to expect that people can and do get killed in space just as they can and do on Earth. They came away satisfied."

"They came away satisfied." Dobbs blew out his cheeks in a great sigh. "I'm sure those guys' families have also come away satisfied. For Christ's sake . . ."

"Clay . . ."

"You know what I'm looking at here?" Dobbs continued, tapping a finger on the computer printout he had been studying. "These are the results of a computer projection my guys ran on the blowout, taking what we found out about the event and letting the machine run a simulation." He nodded his head toward the terminal beside his desk. "I've compared it with a similar profile I did before we had decided to attach hotdogs to Vulcan, and the numbers match almost exactly. I remember a couple of years ago waving the earlier projection in front of the Board and telling you guys that inflatable crew modules, especially in a construction zone, wouldn't cut it."

"Clay . . ."

"Don't 'Clay' me, Kenneth. We both know the score here. The board pooh-poohed my objections. That horse's ass Roland said that the risk was well within the limits of acceptability, that making temporary crew habitations on the shack was more economic than shipping up a couple of additional hard modules."

Dobbs stood up and shook his head. "I'm sure you didn't do it, but if there was any justice in the world you would have had Roland make the phone calls to those families to tell them that their husbands or sons were dead."

"What do you want me to say, Clayton? That you were right all along? That we should have listened to you, and that we're sorry that this happened, and that next time we'll take the bluster of our resident boy-genius seriously?"

Dobbs grinned wryly and ran his hands through his uncombed mop of curly black hair. "Yes, that would be nice. You could also add, 'And, Clayton, we'll make sure that it never happens again.' "

"Your ego is amazing."

"You know what I think is amazing?" Dobbs turned his head to gaze with wide, angry eyes at Skycorp's vice-president. "That you hired me to be your resident boy-genius with one attitude and are now treating me with this attitude. I remember you telling me that you wanted a trouble-shooter, how space was still a big unknown environment and what Skycorp needed was someone who knew the problems intimately and wouldn't be afraid to buck the system when it was going wrong. 'Don't be afraid to raise hell, Clayton.' You said that. Well, that's what I did, and everyone told me to shut up, and now two men are dead and you're carrying on like this is business as usual. Boy, that sucks."

Crespin closed his eyes and leaned against a wall. Lord help him, he was beginning to regret hiring Clayton Dobbs. The kid—Dobbs was only twenty-seven—had made a name for himself at MIT as one of the foremost experts in the nitty-gritty details of space engineering. Crespin had first met him when Dobbs joined NASA's civilian Space Advisory Board: an unkempt young man wearing jeans, an unironed shirt, and a clip-on tie, who slouched in a chair in the back of the room and systematically pounced on and deflated the wild-eyed extrapolations made by NASA's section chiefs. Dobbs was a hardheaded pragmatist in a field often dominated by hazy-minded dreamers. It was an indication of Dobbs' attitude toward space that he claimed to loathe science fiction, an oddity when one considered that the average Skycorp employee had at least one novel by Clarke or Niven or Brin on his or her bookshelf.

Crespin had recruited Dobbs, offering him salary and responsibilities far and above anything he could have earned in academia. Unlike many child prodigies (and, indeed, Clayton Dobbs had displayed his genius at an early age, first entering MIT as an honors freshman at the age of fourteen), the young man was not shy of the world outside the ivory tower. Dobbs had taken the job because, he claimed, he wanted to make his ideas work, and he dreaded having to teach classes to underclassmen.

But it was at times like these that Crespin felt as if he should have left the rebellious young engineer in Massachusetts, where he belonged.

"Okay, Clayton, okay. *Mea maxima culpa.* We should have listened to you, we shouldn't have sent up untested equipment, we should have heeded your warnings. I can't say that it won't happen again, though, especially concerning men getting killed up there. Three guys have died now on this project, and you know damned well that three more, or three hundred more, may die before those powersats are completed. But what the hell else do you want me to do?"

Dobbs stared down at his desktop, then looked out over the floor of SpaceOps. "Shit, I dunno. I dunno what any of us can do. I just dread having to lie to the union boards and the NASA inquiry boards over the next couple of days."

"You mean you won't tell them what you know about this?"

"No, I mean I won't blow the whistle on Skycorp. I guess I've become too much of a company man to let something stand in the way of the powersats getting completed." He shot a glance at the older man. "Relieved?"

"Yes, though I didn't think you'd blow the whistle, anyway."

"Think of it as a testimony to my own cynicism and character corruption. So what did you want to talk to me about, Kenneth?"

He's sharp, Crespin thought. He knows I don't make social calls at times like this. "Big Ear," he replied.

"What? Oh, that." Dobbs settled back down in his chair and propped his feet up on the desk. "What about it?"

"Have you been keeping up with it?"

Dobbs shrugged. "They had another test today. The NSA boys on Olympus managed to track down and identify a couple of phone calls which contained key phrases. The Fort Meade computers were able to trace the calls to their correct locations. So far, it seems like the system works, which should please the Senate Select Intelligence Committee no end."

"How do you feel about it?"

"Well, besides thinking that they should rename it the J. Edgar Hoover Memorial Spy Satellite Network, I have the typical soulless scientist's reaction of 'okey-doke with me.' "

"Funny to hear that from one of the men who designed the system, to compare it to J. Edgar Hoover. Why, I think it was even you who dubbed the thing Big Ear."

"What can I say? The idea of total social breakdown in this country scares me. Global terrorism scares me even more. I think it's time we started trying to take preventive measures, and if it means compromising the First and Fifth Amendments, hey, Tom Jefferson and James Madison didn't live in a time when Presidents got shot by rifles with laser sights and high school kids were able to build nuclear devices in their basements."

Crespin folded his arms over his chest and gazed thoughtfully at Dobbs. "You have an interesting set of morals, young man."

"Fuck morality," he replied, staring up at the ceiling, "I want to survive in this century."

*Fuck morality,* he said, Crespin thought. *Is this the result of our new age, of our enlightened approach to high technology? Would Dobbs say something like that if he wasn't a pampered, loudmouthed intellectual, or is my son the jock going to come home from Texas A&M next weekend saying the same things?* "Sometimes I think you say things simply for shock value," he said aloud.

Dobbs laughed. "Yeah, okay, maybe so. So what's the point? Why are you asking me these things?"

"Well, you know of course that they're completing the Ear's command and control module." Dobbs nodded. "It will probably be launched within schedule, sometime before the end of the summer. Because of this accident, though, we can probably expect closer scrutiny by the press, as well as the labor unions, over what Skycorp's doing, including what we're sending up at the Cape."

"So you're now reluctant to launch this thing from Cape Canaveral," Dobbs finished. "So what? Ship it over to Vandenberg and launch it there."

Crespin shook his head. "We've already checked with the Pentagon. The manifests for their shuttle launches are full until early next year, and there's too many military cargos for remanifesting. The solution we've arrived at, tentatively, is to subcontract Arianespace and have the thing sent up on one of their boosters from South America."

"Ah, so. And since I've done some work for the ESA in French Guiana, you'd like for me to go down to Kourou to oversee things." Dobbs shrugged offhandedly. "Sure. No problem there."

"Well, there's more. Some of the Board also thinks that the resident boy-genius who helped design the system should follow the module up, and participate in the shakedown on Freedom. That is, in outer space."

Dobbs stared at him, unblinking, for a full minute before he answered. "The Board of Directors is out of its fucking mind," he said at last.

Crespin stared back at the brat for as long as it took him to make up his mind whether to kick over his chair. Too much of a waste, he decided; Dobbs would probably just tell the story around the lunchroom for kicks, and Crespin would only get embarrassment for his trouble. Dobbs knows you're trying to work your way onto the Board, he reminded himself. Don't give the ungrateful little bastard anything to screw you with. "What makes you say that?" he asked stiffly, never taking his eyes off Clayton's.

To his surprise, it was Dobbs' turn to look uncomfortable. He looked away with a growing pout on his face, his shoulders slumping forward. A characteristic Dobbs pose; Crespin had once overheard someone ask aloud if that was how their *enfant terrible* looked while sitting on the throne. Clayton wiped the smirk off his face when Dobbs looked back at him.

"I know it's my design and my baby and I've got some responsibility for it," Dobbs began slowly, "but—and this is going to surprise you—I have no desire at all to go up there."

"I know that," Crespin said, allowing himself a small smile. "We went over that a year ago, with the construction shack."

"I guess I didn't make myself clear then," Dobbs said, keeping his cool, but just so much. "Lemme make myself clear: Going up for myself scares the hell out of me."

"There's little to support a reason why," the Vice-President of Operations said, running his finger idly along the edge of an aluminum paperweight on Dobbs' desktop—a refined sample from the Moon, if he recognized the granular feel of its surface. "You fly just about everywhere you go, and Nicki books you on everything from commuter crop-dusters to Concordes. You've even done a trip on the Vomit Comet, and no one I've talked to told me you disgraced yourself. . . ."

"Hey, where did you . . . who said you could check my medical record?"

It was Crespin's turn for condescension. "Clay," he said solemnly, "I'm a vice-president here. I can look at whoever's record I want. Remember that. I can talk to whomever I want about you. Remember that. Clay . . ."

Oh, cut the crap with him. "Clay, your job here is mine. I can get you dusted off so quick"—he snapped his fingers and put his fist down hard on Dobbs' desk, a foot away from the engineer's foot—"you'd be back to playing with model rockets with your MIT frat brothers."

"That was the International Space . . ."

"Forget it. The point is, Dobbs, without my help you don't get research support from the Board. You know that, but you don't remember it. When I'm not around to pull strings with the Board, whom you yourself charge with insanity, you become another talented and efficient wheel-bearing here. You earn your keep as an assistant operations manager, but you got your reputation in R & D. Yet you take so long, Clay, and sometimes people run out of faith. . . ."

"Okay, can the shit, will you Kenny?" Dobbs' cool was gone, and Crespin could see the fury in his face. "You can cut the bullshit now. You know it's true and I know it's true, so you can quit gloating already." He paused and shook his head, scowling at Crespin. "I don't know why you're doing this, though. After all, you hired me."

"I hired a smart young man," Crespin replied. "It's the spoiled little kid that I enjoy torturing."

"Okay, okay, I can accept that!" Dobbs shouted, throwing his arms up and staring at Crespin with wild eyes. "What I can't figure is why you want to scare the hell out of me? Jesus Christ, haven't I made this *clear* yet? I'm a space engineer! I'm fascinated with designing ships and suits and tools and better latrines, but it's just an abstract with me, a particularly intriguing set of unique variables! *I'm not a goddamn spaceman!* The thought of taking off in a shuttle of any kind—*myself taking off*—shit, Kenneth, it scares me out of my wits. And experiencing microgravity makes me even more ill!"

"You know there's stuff for that—scopolamine, biofeedback, the rest. That's if you get spacesick, and there's no statistical promise that you'll get that. If I were you I'd worry about it as little as I could," Crespin said smoothly.

"You bastard. You're really enjoying this, aren't you?"

"I'd be lying if I said it wasn't funny. Yeah, I'm enjoying this."

"Shit." Dobbs looked out over the operations center. The first of the night shift was beginning to arrive, taking over their stations in the tiers. "Well, it gets me out of here, I guess."

"Do you mind that?"

"I won't miss it. Massachusetts I miss," he said thoughtfully, "but not this Disneyworld. I'm gonna get you for this, Kenneth."

"You're the best man for the job, Dobbs. That's why they want you up there."

Dobbs turned his chair around, swinging his feet off his desk, and faced his terminal again, deliberately turning his back on Crespin. "Get lost. Go away. I gotta work."

"Happy trip," Crespin said. Dobbs didn't reply, but only reopened another file on his system, and Crespin eventually turned and walked silently out of his office.

# PART TWO
## *Welcome to the Club*

Do you remember that rhetorical question you used to ask yourself, or your friends, in those rare philosophical moments when you were a kid: If given a choice, would you rather die by heat or by cold? Would you rather freeze or fry? At this point, the end of my life, I'm faced with that question again, and in spades, because it's become a matter of practicality.

See, according to the heads-up display in my helmet, the life-support batteries are beginning to wear out. I guess they'll probably go before my oxygen supply, although as I've explained before it's really a three-way drag race between air, power, and the duration of this tape. If I want to keep talking—which, frankly, seems the only way to keep myself sane right now—I should try to accommodate power failure. There's both light and shadow in this crevasse, and the difference is within a couple of hundred degrees Fahrenheit. Continuing to sit in the shadowside might save my batteries longer, but my toes are beginning to get cold. However, if I get up and walk to the other side and sit in the sunlight, I'll soon suffocate and roast when the batteries burn out while trying to keep the suit cool. An added consideration is the lifetime of this tape; the recorder has its own battery, I think, but I'm afraid of the tape melting.

I think I'll stay in the shade. I'm made in the shade. Memo to the Almighty: You should include a note with the writers you make in the future, reading: "Batteries Not Included."

Ha, ha, ha.

I think I'm losing my mind.

Where was I? Boredom, right. It didn't get any better after the July accident at Vulcan. Maybe it gave us all something to talk about for a while, and everyone on Skycan had their own views of how it happened, but unfortunately the upshot of the accident was that talking was all it gave us to do. Skycorp got a roasting from the press on the matter of the hazardous equipment the company was using in space, but that was nothing in comparison to what happened when NASA, the unions, and the House Subcommittee on Space Science and Technology got into the act. Between Congressional oversight hearings, NASA regulatory reviews, and the general pissing and moaning by the Aerospace Workers union, Skycorp took a lot of shit for the deaths of those two men. I heard through the grapevine that Skycorp had only barely managed to stop a *New York Times* report from taking a shuttle up to investigate first-hand the safety conditions on Vulcan and Skycan; they did it by claiming that the OTV's had a full passenger manifest for the next three months, which was baloney. It was just as well, I suppose. If the *Times* reporter had not found any more life-threatening design flaws—and actually, there really weren't any; it was boring up there, but it was still reasonably safe—he probably could have discovered enough juicy stuff from talking to the beamjacks to write one hell of an exposé, and no telling what he would have made of a conversation with H.G. Wallace, our allegedly sound-of-mind project supervisor. We didn't need any more bad publicity, thank you.

The problem we encountered was that, as soon as the shit hit the fan downstairs, Skycorp's brass in Huntsville made what they saw as a prudent decision. They ordered a temporary work shutdown on the powersat project. No one except vital supervisory personnel was to be allowed on Vulcan Station, and absolutely no one was to be allowed in the hotdogs until they were deflated and replaced with Olympus-type hard modules, which were being hastily thrown together in Alabama. They called it a paid vacation for the construction crew. We called it two weeks in hell.

*There was nothing to do!* Actually, I didn't mind it so much, because my work in the data processing center went on, and in the extra free time I used the chance to work on my science fiction novel, *Ragnarok Night,* but for the majority of space grunts living on Skycan it was the worst thing Skycorp could have done to them short of ordering Cap'n Wallace to depressurize all the living compartments. As I pointed out before, most of the beamjacks were your basic, Joe Lunchpail construction types, not intellectuals. Some of them had probably never picked up a book since they had cheated their way through high school exams on *Silas Marner* and *The Old Man and the Sea.* Fewer still knew anything about meditation or any of those other mind games one can play to zip away unwanted hours.

Fortunately for a few, there was one guy—I can't recall his name, except that he was a Jewish guy from Long Island who was a first-class Dungeons and Dragons Dungeonmaster. Someone had told me that he was a world-class player until something had happened which made him ship out to work in space. He had gathered a few converts to the game while on Skycan, and during the shutdown they took the opportunity to launch an extensive, wild campaign this Dungeonmaster had been spending months dreaming up. They took over bunkhouse Module 14 and chased everyone else out, and played like fanatics for several days straight until the DM either knocked off the players with his tomato-pulper deathtraps or raised the survivors so many levels that they became near-deities. They had fun.

But for the vast majority, life during those two weeks was the epitome of dullness. Their lives had become built around an eight-hour shift of putting together that huge, spaceborne Erector Set, and without it they were lost. They hung around in the rec rooms watching either baseball games or soap operas beamed up from Earth, or fooled around with the six half-grown offspring of ZeeGee, or played blackjack or poker or solitaire, with Mr. Big checking in to make sure they weren't disobeying Wallace's edict against gambling. They chased after the few female crew members, and getting nowhere they closed themselves off in their bunks and masturbated. They tried to throw Frisbees on the catwalk, which was both absurd and boring. They went low-gravity jumping in the spokes until one guy sprained his ankle badly and Doc Felapolous outlawed the sport. If they had possessed knives they probably would have played mumbletypeg. They wrote long, dull letters to their families and friends, many of which were probably never sent. Sometimes you found them just sitting in chairs or lying on their bunks, staring at nothing, thinking about something they didn't want to talk about. Popeye Hooker was that way a lot, but no one ever knew what it was about except that it vaguely involved his ex-wife.

Maybe the Skycorp executives thought they were saving lives with their shutdown, but they didn't save anyone's nerves.

Only one eventful thing came out of the godawful period, and that was the arrival of Jack Hamilton on Skycan. No one knew it at the time, but the new hydroponics engineer was destined to change life for the beamjacks, and also make history.

# 12

# Milk Run

Lisa Barnhart's alarm clock went off with a sustained whine at three o'clock in the morning just as she felt she was falling asleep. As usual for her on Thursday nights she had gone to bed at seven o'clock, just after dinner, in order to be up and refreshed before dawn on Friday. Annie, however, had decided that it was not yet time for her mother to go to bed. The baby had begun wailing about an hour after Lisa had gone to bed, and nothing Carl could do had been able to soothe her, so it had been Mommy who had to get up and walk her child around their apartment, rocking and singing to Annie all the lullabies she could remember until, an eternity later, the baby had fallen back to sleep.

So Lisa was still fatigued, even after her shower. Talking to someone usually helped wake her up, but Carl was dead asleep on his side of the bed, and she knew better than to even contemplate waking him up. He would either be a complete grouch, or would make an attempt at having sex with her, neither of which would wear well with her for the rest of the long day ahead. And there was even less sense in waking up Annie, she thought as she poured the first of several cups of coffee she would consume that morning. One-year-olds were notorious for not keeping up their end of the conversation.

Lisa pushed open the glass door leading to the balcony and walked outside. Even in the early morning hours it was still hot outside, a reminder of yesterday's broiling heat and a harbinger of today's broiling heat. The balcony overlooked the beach, and as she sipped her coffee she listened to the constant crash of the surf. Far out at sea she could see the lights of freighters prowling the Atlantic coast; or perhaps they were the spy trawlers which the Soviets, to this day, continued to dispatch to the Cape whenever a launch was scheduled.

She turned to her left and gazed up the coast toward the old Eastern Test Range and the Kennedy Space Center. Brilliant blue-white searchlight beams lanced up into the night sky, converging a couple of thousand feet above the launch pads. She clutched her coffee cup and stared at the beams with wide eyes, feeling her pulse quicken. The beams were focused on Pad 39-A; in their center, transfixed in a chrysalis of light, was the *Willy Ley.*

Lisa drank her coffee, reminding herself to hurry. I wonder if I'm treating Carl and Annie right, she thought. Annie needs a mother and Carl needs a wife, and when they need me I'm either off training pilots or in preflight sessions or taking off for another milk run. Carl says Annie cries every Friday morning, when she wakes up and finds out that Mommy's not around to change her or feed her. How do you explain to a baby girl that Mommy's 300 miles up in space?

She put her coffee cup down on the railing and gave herself another moment to stare at the lights on Merritt Island. She could take that extra moment; the techs at Launch Control knew what they were doing, and so did the pad rats and her copilot and everyone else. All she had to do was fly the thing. Shit, she thought, I used to enjoy this job. I had wanted it since I was five years old and Sally Ride and Judy Resnick and Rhea Seddon and old John Young himself were my heroes. Now I've arrived, I'm an astronaut, and all I want to do is be a full-time mother. She smiled grimly and pushed away a tear with her forefinger. Oh, baby, what do you do when the thrill is gone?

Half an hour later she pulled up to the security gate off Route 3 and held up her ID card. The elderly guard shined his flashlight through the windshield and peered in, closely inspecting both her pass and her face. The old guy did it the same way every Friday morning; one would have thought the senile old coot would have remembered her face by now. Finally he stepped back and waved her on. Dingbat, she thought. I wish he would at least get his eyes checked. As she drove past, the armed MP on the other side of the road swept up her arm in a customary salute, which Lisa returned with an absent nod.

Driving down the Kennedy Parkway, she passed the darkened marshes of the wildlife sanctuary surrounding the launch facilities and the industrial area, which had blossomed over the past twenty years to become a small city of its own. She looked out for critters which might appear on the road—two months ago she had been forced to swerve for an alligator which had decided to cross the road just then—although she was sure most of the early morning traffic had already scared the critters away from the road. One day, she mused, she was going to be piloting *Willy Ley* for a touchdown on the shuttle landing strip and there was going to be one of those big lizards sunning itself on the concrete.

The Vehicle Assembly Building was directly ahead, a mammoth white block standing out in stark relief under the spotlights, the American flag and Bicentennial star glowing against the huge alabaster walls. She parked in the lot beside it and walked to the Crew Prep building next to the KSC cafeteria building. Years ago, astronauts had prepared for launches at the training facility in the industrial area near the NASA headquarters building, but once the number of flight-worthy shuttles topped a dozen and the launches became scheduled on a weekly basis, the new building had been constructed. No longer were the crews given steak and egg breakfasts, paraded through the walk out past a battery of journalists waiting in the corridor, and driven to the pad in the company of the launch director, with an escort of security cruisers and helicopters flying overhead. I would have liked to have had that treatment just once, Lisa thought as she pushed through the glass and waved her ID at the security guard standing inside. It might have been nice to have been thought of as a VIP. . . .

Taking an elevator down to the basement, she went into the locker room and changed out of her civvies into her regulation blue jumpsuit with a Skycorp patch over her left breast and "L. Barnhart" on her right. After lacing up her high-topped sneakers and tucking pens, headset, flashlight, and calculator into her pockets, she pulled on her own, nonregulation addition to her uniform: a St. Louis Cardinals baseball cap, a reminder of her girlhood home.

Leaving the locker room, she strolled down the hallway to the Green Room, where the crews waited until the technicians made the finishing touches on the birds.

"Morning, Lisa."

"Morning, George." She stopped at the bulletin board and pulled her clipboard off its hook. "Got my breakfast ready?"

"In the skillet, waiting just for you, beautiful." The old cook hobbled around the kitchenette counter to his stove, displaying the limp he had picked up many years before as a chopper pilot in Vietnam. "I'm through with that newspaper if you want it. Coffee and O.J.?"

"Yeah, thanks." She threw a glance at the Cocoa *Today* lying on the table, but decided not to pick it up; if she started getting engrossed in the Sports and Op-Ed pages, she'd never get to looking over the flight reports and her checklist. She sat down at the table and began thumbing through the sheaf of papers on the clipboard.

The room was nearly empty, except for one other person in a jumpsuit sitting at the far end, a tall guy whom she barely noticed.

George reappeared with her plate: scrambled eggs, toasted bagel, and a slice of Canadian bacon. How the cook managed to keep track of what every shuttle crewman ate before launch was anyone's wild guess; he never had to ask twice. "So what do you think is going to happen with the Cards-Reds game tonight?"

"Are you kidding me? Cincinnati's going to blow it. National League East is having a crummy season and the Reds are at the bottom of their division."

"Chicago's doing okay," he observed, settling down in the chair opposite her and picking up the newspaper. "They stomped the Pirates last night."

"Uh-huh. I watched some of the game. Eight-oh shutout." She shrugged and forked some eggs onto a bagel. "I guess it's about time they had a decent season." She glanced back at the clipboard, at the manifest she had just turned to. "Have you seen the Launch Director this morning?"

"Yeah, Paul stopped by a little while ago to update the board. Why?"

"I seem to have only one passenger going up in the OTV." She looked again at the manifest. Sure enough, besides the usual food and medical supplies and the mailbag, plus a box of personal request items, there was only one name penciled in on the list. "I thought they tried to save on payload expense by sending up the reliefs all at once. Hell, they could just bottle this guy into the nose of a Delta and shoot him up that way, if they're just going to send up one person."

"Beats hell out of me. That's him sitting over there. Why don't you ask him yourself?"

Lisa looked across the Green Room at the man in the jumpsuit sitting at a table alone, picking at his breakfast. She glanced down at her manifest again, then called out, "Hey, is your name Hamilton?"

The passenger's head bobbed up at the sound of his name. "Uh, yeah?"

Just like all the new cannon fodder: lost, hopeless, and with the look of the damned. "Don't have to be a stranger," she said. "Come on over and have some coffee with me."

The passenger got up and walked over to her table, carrying along a nylon shoulder bag. He appeared to be in his late twenties, with longish blond hair and a thin, rather scraggly beard on his chin. He had startlingly blue, clear eyes, and when he got closer he gave her a smile. Not bad-looking, Lisa caught herself thinking. Better watch yourself, dear, or you can end up as one of the other tawdry soap opera cases at the Cape.

"Thanks," he said as he sat down. His eyes went to her breast, and Lisa blushed before she realized that he was reading her patch. "L. Barnhart," he said. "The *L* stands for Linda, and you're the commander."

"Wrong and right," she replied. "The letter stands for Lisa, and yes, I'm the commander." Without having to be cued, George got up to go fetch the coffeepot. "I understand you're the only passenger I'm taking up today."

"I guess that's right. I hope I'm not wasting your time." He stuck out his hand. "My name's Jack Hamilton. I'm the new hydroponics engineer at Olympus. At least you're only taking me halfway, since I'll be in the, uh . . ."

"OTV," she said, shaking his hand. "Orbital transfer vehicle. You're not wasting my time, either. There's supplies which have to go up also. I'm just surprised that they're not sending you up with the two new beamjacks they're sending to replace the guys who got killed last week."

"Holdup in their training," George said, returning with the coffee. "It's getting harder to train those guys in the KC-135's. All they want to do is toss their cookies, eh?"

Lisa saw Hamilton's face blanch as George spoke. "Go read your newspaper, George," she said, giving him a swift, hard look. George shrugged and lurched back toward the kitchen. She looked at Hamilton. "Didn't do so hot on the Vomit Comet, didya, Jack?"

He smiled ruefully. "It wasn't bad after the first time . . . but I don't want to repeat that experience again. Be honest with me. How bad is the liftoff?"

She lifted an eyebrow as she took a sip from her coffee. "It's not bad. Lot of noise and g-force at first, but not even as bad as, say, a takeoff in a small single-engine plane in a crosswind. It's reaching orbit that sometimes gets people, more than the launch. Did you eat a big breakfast?"

"No."

"Good. Smart move." She leaned closer. "George's a malicious bastard sometimes. He gets new people like you and tempts 'em into having a big meal. Last good food on Earth, all that stuff. He tries to fill 'em up with Spanish omelets, smoked sausage, home fries, all that stuff, so they'll get spacesick once we . . ."

"I do not!" George yelled from across the counter. "I heard that, Barnhart, and I don't try to . . ."

"Shut up, George," she threw over her shoulder. "Seriously, though, it's hard to tell. The KC-135 trips are a poor substitute for the real thing. People who were doing somersaults in the cabin on that flight lose it sometimes as soon as they turn their heads or look out a window. They don't even feel sick; one look out the window, and there they go. Sometimes they were borderline cases in the Comet, and when they get up there they're fine, or at least no worse than taking a plane trip during bad weather. How did you do on the training flights?"

"Borderline," Hamilton admitted, fluttering his hand up and down.

Lisa smiled. On impulse, she reached across the table and gripped his wrist. "You'll do fine," she said. "No one as handsome as you could lose it up there."

"Thanks," Hamilton said. Unexpectedly, he took her hand and gave it a squeeze in return.

"Watch it, pal," George yelled. "She's married!"

"Shut *up*, George!" Lisa snarled. She felt her face grow hot. Christ, she was feeling like a teenager sneaking feelies in the lunchroom. She glanced up in time to see Jack Hamilton's face turning red as well. He released her hand.

"Sorry," he muttered, and cleared his throat. "How do you like . . . I mean, how does your husband . . . ah, dammit . . ."

"I like it," she said. "Carl, well . . . I guess he's getting over it, or has gotten over it by now. He teaches gym at Titusville High, and the way teachers are paid these days, what he makes manages to buy the groceries and not much else."

"Any kids?"

"Yes," she said. "A daughter. Annie. Only a year old last month." She smiled, wistfully, and stared off at a wall for a moment. "Like I was saying, spacesickness isn't that big of a worry, as long as you didn't . . ."

"I bet she's proud of her mother."

She stared down at the tabletop. No, c'mon, Lisa. Don't break down crying in front of this guy. "I think she is," she managed to say. "It's hard to tell with babies, y'know . . ."

They were both silent for a little while, and George even managed to keep his mouth shut. After a few moments Hamilton cleared his throat again, a nervous gesture. "I, uh, heard through the rumor mill that the guy I'm replacing had some problems of his own," he said.

He stopped, and quickly added, "Not to say that you have any problems, I mean . . ."

"That's okay," she said. She snuffled back a tear and patted his hand. "We've all got problems, Jack." Lisa sat up a little straighter and picked at her plate of now-lukewarm food. "I don't know much either, but what I heard was that he . . . well, he got unglued, to make it simple. Nothing very serious, not like trying to shoot himself through an airlock or anything, but someone who was shuttling back from Skycan . . ."

"Skycan?"

She grinned in spite of herself. "Skycan. Don't ask. You'll find out why soon enough. Anyway, he started talking to walls or something, and the doctor there, Ed Felapolous, decided that it would be better if he was transferred back to Earth. Don't worry about it. That's rare up on Skycan. I hear it's a little dull, but I've never taken anyone back in a straitjacket."

"Oh," he said, "that's nice to know."

Lisa looked up at him. "Oh, God, listen to me," she said with a sigh. "I'm being honest with you, Jack. There's nothing really to worry about, either with the launch or living up there. It'll be rough, don't let yourself think otherwise, but it's no worse than any place else people have gone. The launch won't be serious. You only . . ."

The intercom near the ceiling announced: *John Hamilton, John Hamilton, please report to Room A-12. John Hamilton, to the bus at Room A-12.*

"Up the elevator, turn right, and straight down the hall to the end," George said in a matter-of-fact tone without looking up from his newspaper. "Can't miss it."

"I suppose that's my cue." Hamilton got up reluctantly, shouldering his bag strap. "I guess I'll probably see you at the pad, huh?"

"No. Actually, you won't," she said. Lisa looked up and smiled at him. "You're going into the cargo deck down below, down the ladder into the OVT. I'll be up on the command deck. I'll arrive after you're stowed away with the rest of the baggage, and the flight's so short you'll be on your way out only fifteen minutes after we've left the ground."

"Oh. That's too bad. I was beginning to enjoy this."

So was I, she thought. As he turned to leave, she said, "Listen, Jack, when they put you into the OTV, get one of the rats to lend you a headset. Um, there's a woman named Crissie who'll be working on the tower. Tell her I said it was okay, because regulations say they're not supposed to do it."

"Do what?"

"Give you a headset," she repeated. "So you can talk to me and I can talk to you. The OTV's under automatic pilot, and supposedly it distracts the pilot to be talking to passengers, but I've done this so many times I won't be bothered. The jack fits into a socket under the armrest, just like on an airliner. I'll give you a ring once we're underway, okay?"

"All right." Hamilton grinned. "I'd like that."

"No problem. Hey, and one more thing. Some of the guys going up think they're supposed to be Iron Man or something. Don't be a jerk. Take the Dramamine tabs they'll offer you, okay?"

"Okay." He turned around and headed for the door. "Thanks a lot, Lisa."

"Have a good flight," she said, and on impulse added, "handsome."

When he had disappeared through the door, Lisa finished her breakfast. She swigged down the rest of her coffee, then picked up her clipboard and walked toward the door. "Have a good flight, handsome," George mimicked as she headed out.

"Gag on it, pegleg," she replied, and let the door slam behind her. Lisa could hear him laughing as she strode down the hall.

She paused on the concrete apron at the bottom of the gantry tower before getting on the elevator, and watched dawn break over the Cape. As a pale yellow glow spread from the east over the Atlantic, she could hear sounds of stirring life in the surrounding wildlife sanctuary: bird songs, the sullen *garrumph* of bullfrogs, the quiet chitter of crickets, even the echoing *gawwmp* of an alligator yawning or whatever it was that gators did when they made that sound, mixed in with the sound of machinery at work and the occasional beeping of a horn from the tower.

This was Lisa's favorite part of Friday morning, the early dawn hours just before a launch. Three miles away, she could see the mellow sunlight shining on the walls of the VAB. Hawks were circling their nests on top of the huge rectangular building. The spotlights were being turned off now; the dawn's light gave everything a crystal-clear clarity, reflecting off the windshields of the tourists' cars and campers parked by the old KSC press mound near the VAB, on the other side of the barge-turning basin. Shuttle launches from the Cape had long since become so routine that the press had given up its once jealously guarded front-row seats to the tourists, who still flocked in from Cocoa Beach and Titusville and Orlando. Lisa smiled. Maybe she wasn't greeted by reporters when she made her walk out to the pad, but it was still nice to have an audience. One day she would have to get Carl to bring Annie out to the old press mound to watch her mommy take off. . . .

She shut off the thought deliberately, and turned to walk toward the elevator. A pad rat, wearing a NASA cap and a headphone dangling around his neck, wordlessly took her up as she studied the white skin of the *Willy Ley* passing by them. The Mark II shuttle was still looking good for an old bird with several thousand flight-hours behind her, but it was only a matter of time now before she would be retired for one of the Mark III's which were beginning to come off the Rockwell assembly lines. Eventually they would get the bugs worked out of the prototype hydrogen ramjet, and an economical HTOL would make these old, history-reeking launch pads obsolescent. By then I'll be too old to retrain to launch off a runway, Lisa thought. Just as well. Maybe I'll take up teaching or something.

A technician, dressed in a white jumpsuit with the Skycorp logo stenciled on the back, escorted her down the catwalk to the white-room at the end of the umbilical arm connected to *Willy Ley*'s main hatch. She made small talk with a couple of more pad rats who helped her into her escape harness, and let them guide her through the circular hatch onto the flight deck, but she insisted on putting on her own helmet and strapping herself into the couch—for no particular reason except that she had always felt annoyed at being treated like baggage.

S. Francis Coffey, her copilot, was already strapped into his own couch behind the wraparound console and going through the preflight checklist. He peered at her through his bifocals, looking as usual like an aging, grandfatherly walrus. "Getting later all the time, sweetheart," he grumbled.

"We're on schedule, aren't we?" she said, plugging in her headset and turning over a page on the notebook strapped to the console between them. Already the spacecraft was shuddering and grumbling, as if it were angry at the long checkout delay and ready to depart at once.

"On seven-thirty, right on the money," he replied. "Sleep well?"

"Is it that evident?" she asked.

*Willy Ley, this is Launch Control,* the voice of CapCom said over the radio. *Radio check, over.*

Lisa touched a switch on the console to her left. "Roger, out," she responded. "Annie was being a bitch last night and kept me up."

"Don't worry, it doesn't show. You look just beautiful."

*What's that, Willy Ley? We don't copy.*

"Never mind, Launch Control," Coffey replied easily, and snapped off his comlink. "For cryin' out loud, Lisa . . ." he began, before they both broke up laughing.

For the next hour and fifteen minutes they went through the systems check, running down the list with Launch Control while the ground crew finished loading the rest of the liquid fuel into the booster and SME's. She wondered briefly during the activity how Jack Hamilton was feeling, sitting alone in the tiny spacecraft in the shuttle's cargo bay and listening to the exchange of jargon over the comlink. She was nervous about launches even after having done them on a weekly basis for almost three years, and the ritual of the checklist was all that kept her from going bananas during these last few minutes until liftoff. No telling how he felt, waiting out his first launch, sitting by himself in the OTV with nothing to do except listen and wait. I'll give him a call after booster separation, she promised herself.

There was an obligatory ten-minute hold before launch; although neither she nor Coffey needed the time to catch up on their checklist, Launch Control used the period to go through its own final check. Lying on their backs, gazing through the windows at the clear blue sky above and the edge of the launch tower overhead, she and her copilot had their usual prelaunch disagreement.

"I want country music," S. Francis Coffey said sternly.

"No. I've gotten tired of listening to Willie Nelson doing 'Whisky River' everytime we launch. I—"

"We've only listened to that two times now."

"The last two times as I recall. I'm really tired of that song, Steve, so—"

"No Willie this time." He grinned and held up a cassette he had pulled from his breast pocket. "Something you've never heard before, darling. A classic Jimmy Buffett recording. *A1A*. Got a beauty song on it, 'A Pirate Looks At Forty.' "

"What's it like?"

"Kind of slow, mellow . . ."

"I'm not in the mood for slow and mellow," she insisted. She unzipped a hip pocket and produced a cassette of her own. "Look, I'm trying to go halfway with you . . ."

"No, no, no," he said, shaking his head and holding his hand up. "Not Paul Winter Consort again. I don't care if they use a fiddle, I'm not going to listen to 'Icarus' one more time when we lift off."

"Philistine. This is Aaron Copland, the 'Hoedown' suite from *Rodeo.* You'll love it."

"Is it country?"

"No, it's last-century American classical, but . . ."

"Forget it," he said sternly, holding his hand in front of the cassette player they had jury-rigged to the console between them months ago, when they had started piloting together and had learned that they both liked to have background music during launches. Strictly speaking, it was against Skycorp regulations, but almost everyone in both Skycorp and NASA looked the other way. It didn't affect their flying performance as long as they kept it at a low volume, and astronauts had been carrying cassette music into space since the Project Apollo days. "I don't want any of that violin and trumpet shit."

"Cut it out, Coffey, you know better than that." Lisa knocked his hand out of the way and slid the tape into the slot. "Besides, you told me that the next time we flew I would get the pick because you simply had to listen to Willie Nelson again when we took off." She reached over and adjusted the digital timer so that the tape would start just after rollover, seven seconds after launch. "Think of it as some culture coming into your miserable, backwoods Kentucky-bred existence."

*Willy Ley, this is Launch Control, we are coming out of hold, over.*

Lisa pushed a switch on the console between them, reopening the radio link to CapCom. "Control, this is *Willy Ley.* Event timer started, over."

*Roger, Willy Ley. We have T-minus-nine minutes and counting.*

Out at the press mound, three miles from Pad 39-A, a hundred and seventy people were waiting in the viewing stands and on the lawn behind the barge-turning basin. Waiting in the area where the national and international press had once gathered for the first flights to the Moon and the initial few dozen shuttle launches before their interest faded—although the public's interest had maintained, one of the first indications by the end of the twentieth century of how the press's influence on public opinion had waned—they watched the distant yet clearly visible launch pad and the shuttle poised on it. The giant digital chronometer on the lawn read seven minutes and counting; over the loudspeakers, the Voice of Mission Control kept up a play-by-play commentary for the benefit of the viewers.

When the press had started forsaking the weekly shuttle launches, NASA had learned that it could keep up public interest and help pay for its operations by selling tickets to the press mound at the Visitors Center. At forty bucks a shot (ten bucks for youngsters and senior citizens and half-price for card-carrying members of the National Space Society), not only could the public see the launches from the edge of the safety perimeter instead of seven miles away on the Bennett Causeway to Merritt Island, but NASA also benefited by circumventing a cynical press's snubbing of the space program.

A middle-aged tourist from Delaware watched through his binoculars as the crew-access arm of the gantry tower was retracted from the spacecraft. He lowered the glasses for a moment, letting his eyes relax. He had been a space fan since he had been a freshman in college and had watched the first launch of the shuttle *Columbia* on the TV in his dorm; now, after all these years, he was getting to see a launch in real life. He smiled and started to raise his binoculars again when a hand tapped him on his shoulder.

"Hey, mister. Wanna buy a souvenir?"

He looked around, slightly startled, to see an old man standing next to him. He had long, iron-gray hair tied back in a braided ponytail and a grizzled beard, and wore cut-off denim shorts, a Hawaiian shirt, and sandals. On his head was a well-worn blue cap with scrambled-eggs braiding on the bill; embroidered on the front were the words "Hornet Plus Three."

The tourist from Delaware had spotted the old guy working the crowd at the press site earlier, carrying a box full of tie clasps, bumper stickers, patches, postcards, and various other knickknacks. The tourist had promised himself that he would pick up a few items for his nephews back home, but he couldn't see himself giving the old geezer any of his business. The bum would probably just waste the money on a bottle of cheap wine, or something worse. "Um, sorry, no thanks," he murmured.

The old man wore a huge grin. "Hey, I got a lot of good stuff here. Cheapest prices on the Cape, too. Authentic NASA souvenirs."

"No thanks." The tourist raised the binoculars again, hoping the gesture would ward off the old coot.

"Really something, ain't she?" the old guy said, making no move to leave.

"Huh?"

The old man nodded toward the distant launch pad. "The *Willy Ley.* One of the first of the second-generations. Let me give you a tip, sir. Don't watch it go up through those glasses, you'll just miss everything. It'll just seem like watching it on the tube, that's all. Lots of people make that mistake, and it's funny how unimpressive it is when you're using binoculars or a telescope. Also, when this is over, go over to the landing strip and watch when the flyback booster comes in. Just glides right in, smooth as silk, just like a big jet. Not at all like the days when they used to drop in the ocean, no sir. A lot different from the old space capsules."

"Um." The tourist barely remembered when space capsules used to make splashdowns in the ocean. That had been when he was just a kid in elementary school. He checked the big digital countdown clock several feet away. Four and a half minutes to go . . .

"Y'know," the old guy said, "I once walked on the Moon."

"Yeah, I'm sure you have, old-timer. Plenty of times."

The old man's eyes narrowed and he stepped back, affronted. "Hey! You think I'm some kinda crazy old geek, but I'm not foolin' ya! I walked on the Moon, back when you were just a little kid!"

"Sure . . . go on, get lost, willya?"

"Hey, look here!" He pointed a gnarled forefinger at his cap. "See that? You read what it says? Now what do you think the *Hornet* was, huh?" He pointed at a patch sewn to the sleeve of his garish shirt. "See that patch? See that eagle landing on the Moon? You read what it says?"

A NASA security guard had suddenly materialized behind them both. Laying a hand on the old man's shoulder, he said to the tourist, "Sir, is this man bothering you?" Without waiting for an answer, the guard gently took hold of the old man's forearm and started to lead him away.

"Enjoy the launch, sir," the old man said with a grin. "Have a nice day."

On *Willy Ley*'s flight deck, Lisa Barnhart's hands moved smoothly across the consoles around her, making final adjustments. The digital timer in front of her read two minutes until launch. Now her reflexes had taken over, sharpened from previous flights and hundreds of hours in the simulator. Both she and Coffey worked without conscious decision, by preprogrammed function like the redundant computer systems in the spacecraft itself. It was as if she was merely functioning in a dream-world, and if she thought about the complexity of her actions, she would be intimidated. But she didn't have time to think much about it, so she wasn't frightened.

Somewhere in the back of her mind, though, she was seventeen years old again, and making her first solo flight in a Cessna 132 from Columbia Regional Airport in Missouri: taxiing toward the runway, alone in the cockpit without her instructor, the thrill and the terror combining to shoot cold electricity up her spine. Whether it was a single-engine airplane or a space shuttle, it was always the same, the first time or the fiftieth time: getting off the ground is always the hardest part.

"Control, this is *Willy Ley,*" Coffey said into his headset mike. "APU to inhibit, over."

*Roger, we copy, Willy Ley,* CapCom responded. After a pause: *Willy Ley, this is Launch Control. H-two tank pressurization okay. You are go for launch, over.*

"Roger, go for launch, out," Lisa replied. Glancing across the console, she saw that the registers on the liquid oxygen tank pressure meter had built to maximum limits. The orbiter had already switched to internal power; her main engines swiveled into launch position. Her eyes went swiftly across the board, a built-in reflex from the old days of flying Cessnas. All systems were green and ready for launch. You're cleared for takeoff, the voice of the control tower in Missouri intoned in her mind.

*Willy Ley, this is Launch Control. APU start is go. You are on your onboard computer, over.*

"Roger, out," she said. Now the control of the launch had shifted from Launch Control to *Willy Ley* itself. *It's all in your hands now. Don't embarrass me,* Lisa's old flight instructor said to her again. She checked the timer. T-minus twenty seconds and counting.

The lights on the console blinked as the computers started the booster's main engine. She heard the sudden roar as the engines ignited, felt the tremor of an earthquake roll through the vessel, the shuttle trembling like a great animal straining at its leash.

*We have main engine start,* CapCom intoned. *Two . . .*

The wheels lifted off the runway . . .

*One . . .*

Oh, dear God, this is great . . .

*Zero . . . FRB ignition . . .*

Green lights flashed across the engine status board.

*Lift off . . . we have lift off . . .*

Now she was firmly pressed back into her couch as the spacecraft trembled and shook and began to rise, and through the windows she saw the launch tower disappear and the deep blue sky moved closer, and the thunder began a steady roar as *Willy Ley* headed for the abyss of space.

Strangely, there was no sound at first as the shuttle rose from the launch pad. It was like a silent movie; flame, a blossom of dark reddish smoke, a bright light which made the tourists squint and involuntarily step back a pace, the shuttle rising from the pad and clearing the tower, but no noise.

It had cleared the tower and was several hundred feet in the air when the sound arrived from three miles away, a bristling crackle like the world's biggest blowtorch being ignited, thundering across the marshes, causing wood ducks and hawks and geese and white egrets and sparrows to take wing from the pines and palmettos. The people standing on the edge of the basin stared up at the spaceship as it streaked toward the sky, as the booster's eight engines sent back a descending pillar of rich, dense smoke which obscured the launch towers and the crackle boomed across the watery plains. A cheer rose from the crowd, all but drowned out by the spaceship's roar.

At the very edge of the basin's steep bank, the old huckster jumped high in the air, thin arms thrust over his head, trinkets of paper stuff showering from the box as it dropped from his arms. *"Go, baby!* he yelled with his hoarse voice. *"Go, baybee, go! We have liftoff, Apollo!"*

Seven seconds after launch and arcing out over the ocean, *Willy Ley* made a 120-degree turn to the right, which put the shuttle with its back down toward Earth. The spaceship hit Mach One a few moments later, with a boom which was heard all the way to the Cape, where watchers were still transfixed on the spear of exhaust still rising into space.

In the OTV tucked in the cargo bay, the noise was incredible. Jack Hamilton grimaced and was thankful for the helmet the whiteroom technician had given him to wear. His body felt flattened into the acceleration couch; three g's on his chest would have made it very difficult for him to move, even if he had wanted to move.

He didn't. Hamilton gripped the armrests, squeezed his eyes shut, and tried hard to concentrate on remembering the comparative oxygen-carbon dioxide ratios for tubers in hydroponic conditions. It was stupid; it was a lecture he remembered Dr. Vishnu Suni of the Gaia Institute giving once at the University of Massachusetts, and in his initial moment of panic upon liftoff his mind somehow flipped to and fastened on that particular event.

"That's great," he whispered through clenched teeth as the shuttle completed its gut-lurching roll, which kept him lying on his back on the ceiling, staring down. Even giving voice to his outrage was too much effort. His thoughts tumbled about wildly: The ship's gonna blow up or crash, I'm getting sick to my stomach, I'm helplessly

strapped into an overgrown beer can, and I'm thinking about goddamn potatoes.

*Completing roll maneuver,* he heard Lisa Barnhart say over the
headset.

*Roger, Willy Ley, you're looking good,* CapCom replied. Oh, go to
hell, Hamilton thought.

*Launch control, this is Willy Ley. Main engines at sixty-five per
cent. Two minutes, forty-five seconds to FRB separation, over.*

*Roger, Willy Ley, we copy.*

Acceleration and flip-flopping; the whole ship shaking; a roar
which worked through his helmet's padding. Hamilton shut his eyes
tight and concentrated on thinking about dumb, safe, pastoral Idaho
russet potatoes. As long as they didn't turn to french fries, it beat
thinking about his roiling stomach.

Sixty seconds after launch, *Willy Ley* had reached an altitude of
four and a half miles and was traveling faster than the speed of
sound. Cape Canaveral had vanished behind the spaceship, and the
sky had changed from blue to dark purple as it raced into the upper
fringes of the atmosphere. The shuttle was now throttled back to 65
per cent of its engine power, and the crew prepared to disengage its
flyback booster.

Lisa and Steve worked with quiet efficiency as Copland's "Hoedown" heralded their arrival on the fringes of space. As Coffey throttled the engines back up to 100 per cent, Lisa consulted the flight
trajectory on the CRT screen of the shuttle's navigational computer,
preparing herself for the separation. A glance at the gauges in front
of her confirmed the computer's signal that the orbiter's tanks were
fully pressurized.

"Launch Control, this is *Willy Ley,*" she said. "We have FRB
burnout. Ready for FRB separation, over."

*Roger, Willy Ley, out.*

Lisa worked the digital control board beside her, bringing the
spacecraft into a shallow, long drive in preparation for casting away
the booster. The change in course was so slight that it was barely
perceptible even within the cabin; on the ground, an observer with a
telescope would detect no change at all relative to the ground. But
they were now traveling four and a half times the speed of sound,
and as the spacecraft began the dive eighty miles above the ground,
she felt the force of three g's push her back again into her couch.

The MECO light flashed on her console, signifying main engine cutoff. "Control, this is *Willy Ley,*" she said. "Main engine cutoff on schedule."

*We copy, Willy Ley. Go for FRB separation in twenty seconds.*

Now the roaring had ceased entirely, leaving only the sound of the Copland ballet reaching its crescendo and the hiss of the cabin's air regulators. Lisa rested her fingers on two buttons on the console beside her and watched the CRT screen as the flight computer counted back; when the countdown reached zero, she pushed both buttons at once.

There was a bright flash of light through the portholes and a *thump,* unheard but felt, as explosive bolts triggered on the underside of the *Willy Ley* and the streamlined booster separated from the orbiter. In her mind's eye Lisa could see the narrow rocket with the stubby little wings angling into a somersault for its reentry into the atmosphere and remote controlled landing on Kennedy Space Center's shuttle landing strip. "Control, this is *Willy Ley,*" she said. "We have FRB separation."

*Roger, Willy Ley, we copy. You are go for OMS-one burn, over.*

"Roger, OMS-one burn, out." Steve's fingers were already gliding over the digital autopilot panel, punching in the instructions to the ship's computers which would start the orbiter's main engines and send *Willy Ley* farther into space.

The first OMS fire occurred less than two minutes later and it brought the shuttle out of the shallow dive. There was no vibration on the flight deck when it happened, no sound, only the instruments showing that the engines, with a combined thrust of 12,000 pounds, were firing to place the shuttle in a low elliptical orbit 300 miles above the planet.

"Control, this is *Willy Ley,*" Lisa said. "We have OMS cutoff, FRB umbilical doors closed."

*Roger, out.*

"Okay," Lisa said, "let's take 'em the groceries."

"Spoken like a true housewife," Coffey murmured, taking off his helmet and stowing it under his seat.

"Yeah," she laughed. "Real housewife." She stowed her own helmet, then checked the notebook held open in the holder in front of her, to confirm that the second OMS burn would occur in half an hour. This one would put them on course for the *Freedom* space station. She shut down the auxiliary power unit while Coffey changed the computer program, resetting for the roll maneuver which would align *Willy Ley* for the deployment of the OTV she carried in her cargo bay.

Oh hell, she thought as she watched Steve punch in the coordinates. I forgot all about Jack Hamilton. She punched the intercom button and said into her throat-mike, "OTV-Four Navajo, this is *Willy Ley.* The button's next to your right armrest, Jack, talk to me."

There was a pause, then she heard Jack Hamilton's voice in the intercom. He sounded weak. *Hi. Lisa.*

"Hi, yourself. How are we doing down there?"

*I don't know how we're doing,* the hydroponics engineer replied, sounding a little surly. *Personally speaking, I'm sick as a dog.*

"Oh, dear," she said. She heard Coffey guffaw and cast him a dirty look. "I'm sorry, Jack. Didn't you take your pills?"

*Yeah. Didn't help once you started doing loops, though. I found the bag, though, so at least I didn't make that bad of a mess. Nice of Skycorp to take that into consideration.*

"Sorry I can't come back there and help you," she said, "but you're sealed off from me."

*That's okay. You wouldn't want to see me now, anyway.* He paused. *They don't have a TV screen or anything back here. What's it look like out there?*

She gazed through the windows at the planet slowly turning above her; the sight of the world upside down would have been enough to upset her own stomach if she wasn't already so used to it, and she was careful not to mention the angle to Hamilton. "Well, we're going over Australia now," she said. "Clear skies in kangaroo land. There's the Coral Sea and the leading edge of the Bismarck Archipelago. . . ."

*New Guinea?* he asked.

"Yeah, I can just see New Guinea," she said. "There's the Great Barrier Reef, and I swear I can see a school of blue marlin . . . no, no, I think that's just waves, maybe a current or something."

*That's great. We've gone halfway around the world already. Bet you love this every time.*

"Ah, I dunno. I get used to it."

*No. You're only fooling yourself. When she gets old enough, you should bring Annie up with you. Let her travel around the world in eighty minutes.*

Inexplicably, she felt her eyes getting moist. She tried to dab at them with her fingertip, but only succeeded in jostling little round droplets, which floated in midair. She snuffled and glanced toward Coffey, who seemed to be pointedly gazing out the portholes on his side of the cabin. Or perhaps he was just as transfixed by the southwestern Pacific.

*You okay?* she heard Hamilton say.

"I'm okay," Lisa said, rubbing at her eyes. "It's just . . . a little post-orbital nasal drip, y'know?" She laughed.

*You're a good woman, Lisa,* Hamilton said. *Damn it that you're married. I could fall in love with you.*

"Yeah," she said. "Happily married."

*Sorry. I didn't mean anything, y'know.*

"I know. I realize that." She paused. "Listen, Jack, I like you. If you ever need anything . . . like, if you ever get sick of the view and want to stow away on a homeward shuttle or something . . . you can call me on the phone. My number's in the directory."

*Call you? On the phone?*

"Sure. It's just like making a long-distance phone call. Same com-sats, only a little more expensive from where you are. Gimme a call if you need anything smuggled up or something, y'know."

*Thanks. I don't know what to say.*

"No, thank *you,*" she said. "I think you've helped me remember something I forgot."

"Payload deployment in sixty seconds, Commander," Coffey said stiffly, signaling her that it was time to knock off the mushy stuff and get back to business.

"Right," she said. "Gotta go, Hamilton. Take care of yourself in that tin can, okay?"

*Got it,* he said. *Thanks for the lift up, sweetheart.*

"Any time, big boy."

# 13

# Hooker Remembers
# (Where Did She Go?)

Three of his bunkmates were sitting on the metal floor, absorbed in a game of Monopoly. The last time he had checked, all the property—including the utilities and railroads—had been taken by one of the three, and most of the houses had been replaced by little red hotels. But it didn't look like any of the three were ready to lose; they were simply trading stacks of hundreds and fifties, each hoping that he would be the one who would land next on the Free Parking square and thus grab the rising mound of play money in the center of the board. A couple of other beamjacks were seated on the edge of a nearby bunk, watching the three-way standoff; one had ZeeGee the cat in his lap and was stroking her fur. He could almost hear ZeeGee's contented purr as well as the sound of the men's voices through his bunk's curtain.

The plastic clatter of dice rolling across the board. "Seven, lucky seven . . . one, two, three, four, five, six . . . shit."

"Ha! Boardwalk! With three houses, that's . . . nine hundred dollars! Pay up, sucker."

A rustle of play money being counted. "That's all the money you got from him the last time he ran through your railroads."

Laughter. "You broke yet?"

"Forget it, pal. I still got a grand or more here, and you've got to make it around my corner here. I'll frisk your ass and send you to the poorhouse."

"Bullshit. You'll land in jail like you always do and won't be able to collect!"

"Hey, I got this Get-Out-of-Jail card. Remember, last time I landed on Chance? Here's your money, now shaddup and roll 'em."

The clatter of dice on the board. "Six."

"That's not a six, that's a five."

"Oh. Sorry. One, two, three, four . . . ah, damn!"

"Property tax!"

It was driving Hooker bananas. Once before, a couple of days ago, he had tried to get them to tone down the noise. No, more than that; he had rammed open the plastic curtain with his hands and had yelled at them to shut up. The crewmen, who had turned to marathon Monopoly out of the boredom which had haunted the construction crew during the long days of the work shutdown, had simply stared back at him in bewildered anger. Phillips had asked him if anything was wrong, with the tone of an adult addressing a mentally disturbed child, and that had made him further blow his cool. He had jerked the curtain shut again, and had heard them snickering a few minutes later. *Popeye's going over the edge. Losing his grip. Better make sure he doesn't get his hands on any sharp objects, man.*

So he didn't bother to object anymore. After all, it was his problem that he was slowly going insane, wasn't it?

Hooker lay on the foam sleeping pad inside his bunk and stared at the narrow walls of what was laughingly referred to in Skycorp's official jargon as his private crew accommodations. Right. Very private. He picked up the dogeared paperback copy of *Moby Dick* he had been trying to force himself to read, opened it, stared at the pages, closed it and plopped it back down beside himself again. Absently, he picked up the phone receiver from the hook inset in the wall, realized there was nowhere or no one on Skycan he particularly wanted to call, and put the receiver back on the hook. He stared at the toes of his regulation sneakers and wondered where he had gotten all those scuff marks, but even that thought was too boring to stay in his mind for longer than a second.

There was a snapshot of Laura taped on the wall near his head. He studiously avoided looking at it.

Impulsively he pulled his terminal keyboard out of its slot in the wall, propped it in his lap and punched in control-S, the code for station general status report. The LCD screen just beyond his feet, at the far end of his bunk, beeped. Words formed on its dark green surface. Hooker read it quickly: With the shutdown in effect, no work crews were going in or going out; it was 1504 hours stationtime, 0804 Eastern Standard Time, 0704 Central Standard Time, so it was therefore morning in most of America and, unlike the crew of Skycan, most of the country was getting ready to go to work, big deal; all life-support systems were working nominally; an OTV was due for docking with Olympus at 1600 hours station-time.

Hooker stared at the last entry. Scuttlebutt had it that the new crew member, the new hydroponics engineer, was arriving this morning, but that wasn't what he was thinking about. The last OTV had carried away the bodies of the beamjacks who had been killed in the accident. Hooker had found himself in the Docks when David Chang and Doc Felapolous had loaded the body-bags into the tiny spacecraft for the long trip back to Earth. He remembered what he had thought then: *only two ways to leave this place—serve out your contract, or get killed.*

It wasn't entirely true, of course—if you read the fine print on the Skycorp contract—but close enough. Hooker closed his eyes. He wanted to go home desperately, but for some reason he had voluntarily extended his contract; he could be thinking about going back to Earth in a few months, but now he was stuck on Skycan for almost another two years. Why?

Involuntarily, his eyes wandered to the snapshot of Laura which was taped to his bunkspace's wall. Because he didn't want to go back.

*A flash of gold disappearing.*

He squeezed his eyes shut, so hard that his head throbbed.

*Her laughter.*

His head sank back against the wall.

"Free Parking!" someone outside his bunk yelled. "Gimme that money!"

Oh, God, I don't want to remember, I don't want to remember, I don't want to think about it, I don't want to remember. . . .

As if he had any choice.

Hooker had not been surprised to find Laura gone when he awoke the next morning. Even when they had been married, it was usual for one of them to wake up and find the other side of the bed vacant—usually Hooker himself, since his fishing generally kept him out until the early hours of the morning, and Laura's teaching job had her in the classroom before nine. Even on the weekends she was up and around long before his eyes opened. She was simply more of a morning person.

Even though he had begun getting up early after their divorce, she had left his place out by Hog Island before he was out of bed at eight o'clock. Wandering naked through the cabin, scratching his groin in time with the throbbing in his skull, he stopped to stare blearily through the front window at the sandy driveway outside. Her battered little Toyota, which had followed his Camaro back from town last night, was gone from the driveway.

Well, what did he expect? Typical of Laura, the sexual pirate. Wham bam thank-you-ma'am, I think. She got what she came for, he thought. Why stay around for the uneasy morning after, especially when it's with your former hubby?

Hooker leaned against the windowsill and stared at the sunlight filtering down into the front yard through the pine and cypress woods surrounding his place. The night before had been great. Spectacular, in fact. Four stars. They had writhed together in bed with a fervor which had left them gasping for breath between rounds. Between bouts they had polished off a bottle of white wine he had found in the refrigerator, and they had told each other funny stories and giggled as they each tickled the other's old, familiar sensitive places, until they finally pounced on each other again and the giggles became soft moans and whispers in the darkness. Good loving indeed.

And she had split before he had awakened, like a pirate who had pulled off another successful raid. One woman on a dead man's chest, yo-ho-ho and a bottle of Gallo.

"Damn, Laura," he mumbled, feeling alone and tossed aside. "You could have at least left a note." And what would she have written on it, stupid? *Claude: last night was great! Let's get married again!* Uh-huh. Fat chance.

He shuffled back to the bedroom and pulled on a pair of ragged cutoffs and tennis shoes, then went out through the back door and crossed around the side of the cabin to the driveway. The morning air was cool and fresh, and he sucked in the smell of pine needles and salt as he walked down the driveway to fetch the morning paper and mail from the mailbox. By the time he got back to the cabin his head felt clear, his hangover less crippling.

The kitchen was still a mess, as was the rest of the house. Hooker promised himself that he would clean up the place before he went into town. If it had been Jeanine he had brought home last night—he wasn't surprised to find that he couldn't recall her last name—he would have been embarrassed. He put the newspaper and mail down on the kitchen table, glanced once through the back window at the edge of the salt marsh which lay in his back yard, and saw the tip of Hog Island a quarter of a mile out on the edge of the Gulf. Once that little chunk of land had been dotted by the summer homes of the rich. Most of the homes were gone now, the fortunes which had built them swept away by the Second Depression. The houses which were left were shells populated mainly by poor Cuban and Haitian immigrants who had found their way to Cedar Key and who commuted back and forth in leaky rowboats and inflatable dinghies. Sometimes at night he could see their bonfires and wondered what they were burning. Maybe a rich man's library and paintings.

Hooker switched on the portable TV set on the counter and listened to *Good Morning America* as he fried a couple of eggs and link sausage and made a pot of coffee. The news was still the same, as most people preferred these days, following the tumultuous end of the twentieth century. California was still trying to raise money to clean up after the El Diablo meltdown of '98. NATO and Warsaw Pact troops continued to eyeball each other across the East German border while Washington and Moscow tried to negotiate the final details of SALT IV and the Space Weapons Treaty in Geneva, but it would still be a while before either country completely forgave the other for the mistakes made during the Polish Uprising. Libyan diplomats were in Israel again, as the two shattered countries tried to recover from their bloody little war. The Presbyterian Church of America had joined the more fundamental denominations in decrying the findings of the Princeton biomedical team which had determined that there was indeed an afterlife and that it lasted for about forty-five minutes. The northeastern United States and parts of Canada were still digging themselves out of a blizzard which had dumped fourteen inches of snow on Boston. A child prodigy in Great Falls was reciting *King Lear* after having read it only once, and Hooker went to the john during a quick report on how Johnny Cash's 3-D simulacrum was packing the house at the New Grand Ol' Opry in Nashville.

When he got back to the kitchen, the pretty anchorwoman, Linda Francis, was introducing her next guest for the morning. Hooker scraped the eggs and sausage onto a chipped plate and poured a mug of black coffee as he watched the set from the corner of his eye.

"Olympus Station has been in orbit over Earth for a year as of this week and is now mostly complete, and Project Franklin, America's attempt to build three solar-power satellites in geosynchronous orbit, is in its first stages," she said into the camera. In the background behind her appeared a file tape showing a cylindrical spacecraft coasting into orbit near the slowly turning space station. "Yet despite claims by the space industry and the White House that the project will be the beginning of the final solution to America's energy needs, skepticism still abounds."

The film clip disappeared from the background and the studio set reappeared. The camera moved in for a close-up of a lean, blond-haired man sitting in an armchair next to Francis. "With us today is

Olympus Station's new project supervisor, Henry G. Wallace, formerly of the NASA astronaut corps and the leader of the first expeditionary mission to the Moon, now working for Skycorp and McGuinness International, the prime builders of Project Franklin. He will be sent up to Olympus later this month to take over as head of operations on the space station. Good morning, Mr. Wallace."

"Good morning, Ms. Francis," Wallace said. He appeared to be in his late thirties; solidly built, hair thinning on the top of his scalp, wearing a dark blue sports jacket with a recognizable Skycorp logo pin on his lapel. He grinned when his name was mentioned, displaying perfect teeth.

Hooker—unshaven, unwashed, hungover—disliked his boyish grin and perfect good looks at once. Oh boy, he thought, look at the space hero. He made a farting sound with his lips and murmured, "Good morning, jerk."

Linda Francis, as rosy and smiling as Wallace, opened her questioning. "Mr. Wallace, there's been some question lately as to the claims Skycorp has made concerning Project Franklin's effectiveness. Do you believe the powersats can completely solve the energy problems of the new century?"

Hooker winced. It was the year 2014, and the twenty-first century didn't look or feel a hell of a lot different from the twentieth (except that it seemed a hell of a lot less deadly), yet the mass media was running the phrase "the new century" into the ground. Fifteen years old and still being thought of as a baby, Hooker thought, as if some wondrous event were taking place. He drank his coffee. Christ. The only wonder is that we didn't exterminate ourselves.

Wallace's perfect smile didn't falter. "Well, Linda, it would not take too much homework to poke holes in some of the more, ah, enthusiastic predictions about the SPS program. That's a tendency even experts have when they're discussing the potentials of space. Right now the power consumption annually of the United States is somewhere around 900,000 megawatts, and that's even with the loss of some utility companies in the last fifteen or twenty years. Since each of the powersats planned, when completed in five years, will only produce 5,000 megawatts, they'll only account for a little less than six per cent of the nation's total power demand."

The anchorwoman's eyebrows rose slightly. "Six per cent? Nuclear power plants accounted for eight per cent in the last century. . . ."

"Yes, but there are not as many of them with us anymore, are there? Remember, the utilities, that went under . . ."

"Went under because the debt burden for paying for the plants became too high," Francis finished. "Project Franklin isn't going to be cheap, either. How can we justify building something this big, when its output is only going to account for six per cent of the national energy requirement each year?"

"Two reasons." Wallace raised a finger. "One, it's an infinitely renewable resource. The sun is going to be with us always, or at least for another few hundred million years. It's an energy resource that's available as long as we have the capability to move beyond the atmosphere's filtering effect and tap into it. Certainly it's expensive. Even with the last few decades of breakthroughs in space technology, it's going to be a while before getting a cargo into high orbit will be cheap. But . . . and here's the second reason . . ."

As he spoke, the studio-set background changed to show a starscape several hundred miles above Earth. Three-dimensional videotape clips showed the big HLV's arriving in orbit near a half-complete Olympus station; spaceworkers unloading the cylindrical crew modules from the cargo bays; a long shot of the station being built; the arrival of the beam-builders at the Vulcan construction station.

"Now that the commitment has been made," Wallace was saying, "the investments from Skycorp and the U.S. Government made which have established Olympus and Vulcan in geosynch orbit and got Descartes Base built on the Moon, most of the work has been done, really. We only have the major components of the scheme online and operating, but once we really get started on this thing, ah, space construction, we'll gain experience and the costs will begin to go down. Actually, Linda, there's no reason why we should stop the project when we've built the three powersats being planned."

"You mean there are plans to build more?" she asked.

"No, not at this time at least. But the capability will be there. In fact, it gets better as we put more time and energy into the project. The cost of each satellite will decrease as the technology is perfected and the raw materials become more available, and so mass production will eventually become feasible. The first powersat will account for only two per cent of the annual U.S. energy requirement, but that will increase exponentially once more powersats are built. The main thing will be making the raw materials more available."

"You're referring, of course, to Descartes Base." As she said that, the film clip in the background changed to show the mountainous Descartes region of the Moon's southern hemisphere: lunar freighters making soft touchdowns on the gray plains, bulldozers shoving lunar soil over the habitation modules, a man in a spacesuit standing near the bottom half of the old Apollo 16 LEM left there since 1972.

"That's right," Wallace replied. "In the lunar highlands. That area, as everyone now knows, is rich in oxidized aluminum and silicon, the main materials required for building powersats. In fact, we discovered that during the Apollo missions thirty years ago. Once the base is expanded, and once the mass-driver is perfected and built, we won't have to use freighters any more, but will be able to shoot the building materials up, making the cost for the girders and the solar cells that much cheaper."

"Uh-huh." Linda Francis held a finger to her slightly parted lips. Hooker's gaze was fixed on her. God, he thought, why haven't I met any beautiful women like that in my life? Was the rumor true that she was married to a dwarf? "Of course, once these satellites are operational, Skycorp and McGuinness will make a fortune selling utilities cheap electrical power."

Wallace's smile thinned a little. "That's a rather loaded statement, isn't it?" She laughed. "For one thing," he continued, "there will be enormous initial costs to be covered—to the subcontractors, to NASA, and so forth—that will have to be settled before McGuinness or Skycorp will be able to make any fortunes. Those will begin being paid when SPS-1 goes operational, but even then, it'll be a while before . . ."

"But if Skycorp builds more powersats . . ."

"That's right. Mass production will cover its own costs. For another thing, what's wrong with the companies involved making that profit? They're taking the risks, their stockholders are taking risks, so why shouldn't they benefit from the end results? Besides, part of the rebuilding of the economy after the last depression means restoring American industry. The Europeans and the Japanese have full-fledged space capability of their own now, but they're not doing anything on this scale. The Russians are on Mars and it looks like they're gearing up for a Titan expedition, so there's a matter of national presence in space to be dealt with. No other country, though, it taking this step, even though people like Peter Glaser and Gerard O'Neill were postulating it many years ago. It's about time we got down to doing it, that's all."

The anchorwoman consulted her notebook, and Hooker poured another cup of coffee. "Tell me a little about the job you're taking," she said. "You're going to be in charge of the whole project. Are you . . . ?"

"Actually, I'll only be in charge of the high part." The smile again.

Hooker winced. What a bloody Boy Scout. "The decisions will really be made in Huntsville, at Skycorp's company headquarters. I'll only be supervising the work and support crews on the project. Lester Riddell—who, you might remember, was my co-commander on the lunar expedition years ago—is to be in charge of operations at Descartes Base. We're basically foremen, making sure that everything stays on schedule. They're putting a pair of old space cadets up there, you might say." The smile again.

"So you'll be up there for two years. What will you do in your free time, when you're not working?"

Henry G. Wallace chuckled. "Oh, I don't know. I haven't had much time to think about that. If I do have any free time . . . well, I'll probably just look at the stars."

Francis put on a plastic smile. "Thank you for being with us this morning, Mr. Wallace." She turned to the camera. "When we return, George Bingham will be giving us today's weather, and Angela Hoffer will be talking with a man who practices ESP with dogs. On 'Good Morning.' "

Hooked grunted and reached for the morning mail as a commercial with Jane Fonda speaking for Geritol appeared. When he was a kid, outer space had fascinated him. That was in the days when the first shuttles were going up and space was big news. He remembered waking up early to catch the TV broadcasts of those launches, and the pictures of the *Columbia* and the *Discovery* and the *Atlantis* he had tacked to his bedroom walls in his family's old house in southern Georgia. He smiled wistfully. There was a time when he had idolized astronaut Pinky Nelson, and wanted nothing more than to fly a space shuttle into orbit just like him.

The good old days, long ago and far away. Hooker shook his head and leafed through the junk mail and bills. *This is the crap that makes us grow old,* he thought. *If only we could forget about the high cost of living, advertisers trying to sell us stuff we don't need, and ex-wives who pull disappearing acts. If only we could jump on a space shuttle for a trip away from Earth.* Occasionally, he did make a rendezvous with his old obsession, at those times when he would find himself on the state's Atlantic side. He would tell himself that Port Canaveral was a good place to make landfall for supplies for the return trip down the intracoastal waterway, but the fact was that the rockets on Merritt Island would call to him as he sailed by. Once, he had anchored off the Cape and had watched an HLV lift off. He had sat in the aft deck, drinking beer as he watched the giant cargo ship thunder into the sky, and had imagined himself as a kid again, his dreams riding on that spaceship. . . .

Hooker frowned at his telephone bill. Damn it, had the rates gone up again while he wasn't looking? He hardly used his phone at home, rarely making long-distance calls. How could the long-distance service charge be so high? Then he remembered the cellular phone he had installed on the *Jumbo Shrimp II*. He had put the billing on his home phone, so that would account for the charge.

He shrugged. It was something he could take care of on the way to the dock, at the phone company's branch office in Cedar Key. While he thought about it, Hooker got up and went into the bedroom, to his desk where he kept his cash box. He had a character flaw—a phenomenal capacity for bouncing checks, so whenever possible he kept much of his expense money in cash, to avoid embarrassments with his major creditors. He had cashed a check for two hundred dollars just the other day, and though it was pegged as grocery money, he had better get it to the phone company before . . .

He opened the gunmetal gray box and stared into it. Empty. Not a green piece of paper in sight.

Hooker shut the box slowly and stared at the top of it. He clearly remembered putting the money inside, and he hadn't touched the stash since then, of that he was certain. The house was always locked when he was gone, and if someone had broken in, a lot of other valuable things would have been missing. No one had visited him, no one except . . .

Laura, who had left the house before he had awakened.

Hooker gritted his teeth, swore silently, and pounded the top of the metal box with his fist. Laura.

Dammit to hell. This was one of the reasons why he had divorced the bitch.

*Attention, all crew members.* Joni Lowenstein's silky voice practically floated over the loudspeaker system, interrupting the continuous melodic mumble of the Muzak. *OVT from Canaveral arriving at the Docks. Docking personnel on standby.*

Popeye Hooker blinked and glanced at the terminal's screen. It was 1600 hours now. Where had that last hour gone? And what did he care?

I'm getting stale in here, he thought. I've got to get out and do something. He eased aside his bunk's curtain and swung his feet out. The Monopoly players barely noticed him, but ZeeGee the cat, startled by his sudden appearance, jerked her head up, stared at him, then bolted out of one guy's lap and bounded up the ladder's rungs to the catwalk outside—a feline feat made possible by the one-third gravity. Hooker followed the cat up the ladder, stepping around the game players as he exited the bunkhouse. Cat's got the right idea, he thought. When in doubt, run it out. Hell with it. I'm going to the meteorology deck and bug 'em into letting me use the telescope again. I want to look at the ocean.

# 14

# Welcome to the Club

Virgin Bruce and Mike Webb were sitting in the rec room in Sky-can's western hemisphere when the intercom announced the arrival of the weekly OTV flight from the Cape. "Ah, now there's a voice that can make a man's groin throb," Virgin Bruce said, and then he belched hugely from the near-beer he had been drinking, startling a couple of video-game players sitting next to them. The beer was nonalcoholic, and to Bruce's palate it tasted like chilled dog whizz, but it was the nearest one could get to decent brew on the station and at least one could get a meaningful, satisfactory belch from the stuff.

Webb looked up at one of the overhead displays and watched the little spacecraft making its final approach maneuver on the docks. "Hey, let's go meet the new man, Brucie," he said. "I'm bored."

Virgin Bruce drained the beer with one gulp, aimed at a nearby trash chute, and lobbed the can toward it. As to be expected, even with a straight-on shot from fifteen feet away, the Coriolis effect from the station rim's spin caused the can to bounce off the bulkhead wall a couple of feet to the left of the target.

The can landed at the feet of Mr. Big, who was standing in the miniature gym at one end of the compartment, with a pair of hundred-pound weights hefted above his head on his pillarlike arms. The big Navajo looked down at the can, then glared up at Virgin Bruce. "Pick it up and put it in the chute, Neiman," the Navajo security chief growled, keeping the huge weights stationary over his head, with no visible strain.

Virgin Bruce turned his head around and stared sulkily at Phil Bigthorn for a moment, then lazily heaved himself out of his chair, sauntered across the compartment, picked up the can and marched it over to the waste bin. With exaggerated fastidiousness he dropped it into the chute, cast a foul look at Bigthorn—who responded in kind —then sauntered back to the table where Webb waited, watching the brief encounter. "Yeah, let's get the fuck out of here," he said, then added, in a louder voice, "the atmosphere's getting a little *strong* in here, y'know."

When they had climbed up the ladder out of the compartment and were walking down the catwalk to the west spoke, Webb said, "You better watch how you're pushing it with Mr. Big, man. He could be bad news if he wanted to jump you."

"Hell with him," Virgin Bruce said, stepping aside to let a beamjack walking in the other direction pass by. "He and I've tangled before. He isn't that tough. Let him try it again, man, I'll send him back to the fuckin' reservation in a bag. Who's the new guy they're sending up, y'know?"

"I dunno what his name is," Webb replied. "All I know is that he's the new hydroponics engineer, the one who's taking over for McHenry."

"Hydroponics engineer, right." Virgin Bruce shook his head. "Either another Air Force type or a college boy. Chances are that once Wallace meets him and talks to the poor sonuvabitch, he'll turn into another dedicated, regulation space hero. Shit."

"Hey, they don't always turn out to be Major Matt Mason," Webb said. Major Matt Mason was a toy spaceman dating back from the 1960's; the term was reserved, in derision, for crewmen who followed in Wallace's approved path, the would-be stellar conquerors. "I mean, look at Sloane. He's college-educated, into the whole space thing, y'know. But I've never heard him talking about this high frontier stuff."

"Yeah, okay, Sloane's a good shit. But for once I'd like to sit down with one of these new arrivals and let 'em know right off the bat what this job is all about. Give 'em the facts of life before Wallace makes his speech and takes him on his inspiring little tour. I think . . ."

Suddenly, Virgin Bruce grinned and slapped Webb on the shoulder. "Hey, what the fuck! Why not?"

"Why not what?"

"We're on the way up there now, aren't we? Well, let's take our little chickadee under our wing and show him the ropes ourselves." Bruce stopped and turned to face Webb. "It's always a few minutes after the new guys get off the ship before Wallace sees them, right? That Harris slug usually tells them to beat it to Command so that Wallace can play his head games first, but H.G. himself never shows up right away. So why don't we head him off, give him the nickel tour of this joint before Wallace can sink his claws into him."

"I dunno," Webb said. "Wallace is going to want to speak to him eventually. What if he finds out that we've already met the guy and . . . ?"

"So what?" Bruce threw up his arms. "What's he gonna do about it? Kick us off the fuckin' station? Hell, he's the one who's always harping about sticking together, making sure the new people get adjusted and all that." He continued walking down the catwalk. "Besides, this could be fun. We could pull a headgame on the poor bastard."

"Like what?" Webb asked, running to catch up with Bruce.

"Hell, I dunno. Lemme think about it."

They reached the end of the west hemisphere catwalk and descended a short flight of steps through a hatch into Module 29, the terminus module where the west spoke connected with the rim. Bruce turned to the ladder and put a hand and a foot on the rungs, then quickly stepped back from the ladder, making room for the long pair of legs coming down the shaft. "Hello, Joni," he said. "Love your voice."

Joni Lowenstein descended the ladder and stepped off, not looking at Bruce. "Thanks," she said curtly. Bruce didn't step aside, but with only a moment's hesitation she shouldered him aside. "You're in my way, Bruce," she added coolly.

"I'm sorry. Let me make it up to you. Dinner tonight?"

She laughed softly. "At the same place all of us eat, anyway? Thanks but no thanks." She walked toward the steps leading to the east hemisphere catwalk. "I get enough grease in my food, anyway."

Webb and Virgin Bruce watched her as she walked up the steps and disappeared from sight. "Ooooh," murmured Webb. "Touchy, touchy."

"I'm in love," Bruce said. He grinned at Webb and slipped a hand under his shirt, pumping his hand up and down against the inside of the fabric. "Women with guts! I love 'em, Mike, I tell you I love 'em!"

"Anderson tells me that she's got it for Wallace."

"Anderson beats off with *Playboy*. He doesn't know what he's talking about."

Bruce glanced up the spoke, made sure no one else was on the way down the ladder, then grabbed a rung and began to climb; Webb waited until he had disappeared through the terminus module's ceiling, then grabbed the same ladder and followed. The slapping of their palms and the soles of their high-topped sneakers on the rungs reverberated in the tube as they climbed, all but drowning out "Don't Worry, Be Happy" as it echoed from the loudspeakers.

Neiman paused next to a recessed wall speaker and glared at it for a moment. He glanced up, then looked down at Webb. "Is anyone coming?" he asked.

Webb checked and looked up at Virgin Bruce, shaking his head. The beamjack reached down to his hip, lifted a Velcro flap on his trousers and pulled out a pair of wire cutters and a Phillips head. Hooking his arms around the ladder, he quickly unscrewed the panel holding the speaker into the bulkhead wall, reached into it with the wire cutters and snipped its wires. The Muzak instantly ceased. Virgin Bruce, grinning like a cat, hastily replaced the panel and resumed his climb, all without saying a word to Webb.

When they had arrived at the hub, the decrease in the gravity gradient had left them in microgravitational conditions; not absolutely weightless, but close enough in effect to zero g to be termed as much. They propelled themselves down the station's core, past the hatches leading to the command decks, to the prep room and the Docks. Bob Harris was on duty, floating near the main control console, watching the TV screen overhead as the OTV inched its way toward a docking collar.

"Hey, San Francisco!" Virgin Bruce yelled, clapping his hand on Harris' shoulder with a force which nearly sent the kid reeling into the console. "What's shaking, man?"

Harris grinned weakly, his chin trembling, as he braced himself against the panel and looked over his shoulder at Virgin Bruce. "Oh, uh—hi, Bruce. We're just, ah, getting the OTV in and, ah, getting ready to bring the new guy in, and, um, send Mr. Honeyman back home."

Both Virgin Bruce and Webb turned around and noticed, for the first time, the two other men in the compartment. Doc Felapolous was escorting Honeyman, the rookie space worker who had been in the whiteroom on Vulcan Station when the hotdog had blown out. Honeyman's eyes were soporific and his limbs hung loosely in mid-air; he was obviously under sedation.

Mike Webb took hold of a handrail and pulled himself closer to the drugged beamjack. "Hey, screamer," he murmured. "So they're sending you for a nice, long vacation on Fantasy Island, huh?"

Honeyman's glassy eyes slowly rose to meet Webb's angry gaze. His mouth worked for a moment before the words came. "F-fuck you," he said numbly.

"Yeah, and fuck you, too. What were you doing when I was trying

to save our hides, huh? How long did you stay hysterical, you goddamn . . ."

Felapolous reached around Honeyman and savagely shoved his
hand against Webb's chest. "Leave him alone," he snarled as Webb
automatically thrust out his hands and rebounded off the opposite
wall of the small compartment. "He's had enough already, Webb."

Virgin Bruce grabbed Webb's arm roughly, holding him back from
both bouncing toward the other side of the compartment and launching himself at the man who had nearly perished with him during the
accident. There was a thick moment of tension and silence, interrupted suddenly by the soft jar of the spacecraft docking and the
simultaneous *ping* of an annunciator on Harris' console. Virgin
Bruce glanced over his shoulder at Harris, who continued to stare at
both Webb and Honeyman. "Ship's in, Bobby," he said calmly.
"Want to do something about it?"

Harris blinked, then checked a couple of displays on his console
and pressed the intercom switch. "OTV docked and secure," he murmured. "Pressurizing airlock." He hit the switches that sent air into
the airlock compartment beyond the connecting hatch.

"You're meeting the new hydroponics man, aren't you?" Virgin
Bruce asked Harris.

"Ah, yeah," Harris replied, visibly relieved by the small talk.
"Wallace wants to see him right away, so I . . ."

"So you've been sent to escort him down?" Harris nodded. "The
red carpet treatment, huh? What's his name?"

Harris glanced at the checklist strapped to his right forearm. "Uh,
Hamilton. Jack Hamilton. I . . ."

"Right. Cap'n Wallace wants to meet him." Virgin Bruce rubbed
his jaw contemplatively. "Listen, Frisco," he said quietly, "Mike and
I really wanted to meet this new guy. Give him the guided tour, so to
speak. Now, it looks to me that your buddy Chang's not on duty, so
that leaves only one person up here, right? It also looks like Doc's
going to need a hand getting Honeyman on his way back home. So
why don't we both cut each other a favor. You stay here and assist
the doctor, and Mike and I will take this guy down, show him the
place and everything, and take him to meet the old captain. How
about that?"

Harris looked uncertainly at Doc Felapolous. The physician
shrugged. "Go ahead, I guess," he said noncommittally. "I need to
have you here to help me with Honeyman. Besides, it'll get these two
out of my sight." He cast a glare at both Webb and Virgin Bruce.

"Sure, Bruce," Harris agreed. "Whatever you say." He glanced at a small sheet of printout he had magnetized to his console. "He's been assigned to Bunkhouse 38. Do you want me to call the command deck and tell them you're going to . . . ?"

Virgin Bruce shook his head. "Naw, don't bother. Henry Wallace won't mind if he's just a few minutes overdue." Felapolous rolled his eyes.

A green light flashed on a display over the hatch, signaling that the airlock was pressurized. Harris pushed himself over to the hatch, undogged it, and pushed it open, then lightly propelled himself into the cool compartment. Felapolous started to ease the drugged Honeyman through the hatch, maneuvering the beamjack in microgravity as if he were an invalid, when Mike Webb abruptly glided over toward them. Felapolous looked up at his approach. "Hey, I told you once," the doctor warned. "Back off."

"Easy, Doc." Webb's demeanor was gentler now. He put a hand on Honeyman's arm, then leaned forward and whispered something in his ear. No one else in the prep room could hear what was said, but they saw Honeyman's eyes close and his lips tighten.

Webb backed away, gently patting Honeyman on the back. "Take it easy, pal," he said softly. "Go home and get well."

"Th-thanks," Honeyman mumbled.

"It's nothing. It shouldn't have happened, and I'm sorry for what I or anyone else said. Get well, y'hear?"

Doc Felapolous gently pushed Honeyman through the hatch, and before he went through himself he caught Webb's eye and gave him a small, approving nod of his head. "That was good of you, man," Virgin Bruce said.

"Yeah, well." Webb shrugged as he grabbed an overhead rail and watched the two men float the rest of the way into the airlock, Felapolous holding onto the back of Honeyman's shirt. "He's been through a lot, y'know. Couldn't let him go back feeling completely bad. He just wasn't cut out for this job, that's all."

Inside the airlock, Bob Harris found himself relaxing as he pulled the protective cover away from the OTV's bow hatch and twisted the locking lever to the left. He couldn't help it; Virgin Bruce made him nervous, even when the guy was in a jolly mood. Virgin Bruce in a good mood was like being in a small room with a cheerful maniac carrying a loaded gun; you never knew when he thought it would be funny as hell if you did a little dance for him. I'll just get Hamilton out of there, he thought, and send him over to the prep room, where Virgin Bruce can have him. Poor guy. He doesn't know what's waiting for him out there.

He pulled open the hatch and peered in. "Okay, Mr. Hamilton, you can come out now," he said pleasantly. "Watch your head and take your time. Just be careful to . . . *aggh!*"

A small, green plastic envelope, with the NASA logo stamped on it, sealed at one end, had floated out of the spacecraft's interior, apparently propelled by the OTV's passenger so that the bag drifted into Harris' face. The kid backed off, horror registering on his face as he recognized the object for what it was. This was not the first time this sort of thing had happened to him.

"Oh, God," he grumbled. "Why do they always send out the sick bags first?"

"Sorry. I was trying to hold onto it, but when we docked, uh, the jar just knocked it out of my hands and it just floated that way before . . ."

"That's okay. No sweat." The kid was wearing baggy trousers, a T-shirt with the San Francisco Forty-Niners logo printed on the front, and a long-billed cap with the name HARRIS on the front. He reached out and plucked the filled vomit bag out of midair, taking it gingerly between his thumb and forefinger, wincing as he did so. "Happens to half the guys who arrive here. What got you, launch or orbit?"

"Both." Jack Hamilton floated with his back on the ceiling of the spacecraft's compartment, waiting for Harris to get out of his way. "I'm okay, as long as I don't move quickly."

"Won't matter even if you move slowly. You'll have it for the next couple of days." He looked over his shoulder as he pushed himself away from the hatch. "Hey, Doc! Another case of Star Whoops for you!"

"Know how to make a guy feel better, don't you, Harris?" Hamilton murmured to himself. He unlatched a locker over his seat and gently pulled out his flight bag, then trailing it behind him he *very* carefully pulled himself along by handholds until he reached the hatch. Making sure he didn't bash his head into anything, he wiggled through the hatch, kicking his legs and flailing with his hands, feeling like an enormous fish. He heard people laughing as he exited the OTV, but didn't look up. I'll maintain my dignity if it's the last thing I do, he thought.

Harris came back and took the flight bag's strap off his shoulder, now that he had disposed of the bag. "Come this way," he said to Hamilton. "Easy. Just push yourself a little at a time, and coast when you don't need to change direction." He reached above his head—

which was to say, in the direction Hamilton's feet were pointing—and grasped one of several rails running the length of the compartment. "Use these to pull yourself along. They're in all the zero g sections."

"How do you stop?" Hamilton asked.

"You don't, son, you just bounce." The speaker was an elderly, heavyset gentleman with a handlebar mustache, wearing an absurdly garish Hawaiian shirt. Surfers riding breakers and volcanoes heaving fire and smoke. He was holding onto a thin young man who, when Hamilton looked at him closely, seemed stoned to mindlessness. "And if you break anything," the heavyset man continued, "just come see me. Modules 19 and 20, east side."

"That's Doc Felapolous," Harris said, heading for the airlock's hatch and dragging Hamilton's bag behind him like a toy balloon. "He's the chief physician."

Nice shirt, Hamilton thought. Maybe he can lend me two next time I want to throw up. "If that's one of your patients, I'll . . . Oh, never mind."

Felapolous' wide smile remained, but his gaze simmered. "My boy, if you get ill, don't bother with me," he said with an edge to his voice. "Just come up here and have Bob give you the old heave-ho."

"Sorry. Didn't mean to insult you."

Felapolous sighed. "No more than anyone else here does," he muttered, shaking his head.

Harris was waiting for him by the hatch. "Ah, there's a couple of the guys up here to meet you and help you get settled in," he said. His voice was mysteriously low. "Let me tell you about one of them. His name's Virgin Bruce, and . . ."

"Oh, swell."

"Oh, no," Harris said quickly, reading the expression on Hamilton's face, "he's not like *that,* but . . ."

A long and thin yet muscular arm reached through the hatch, grabbed Harris' belt, and yanked the crewman through the opening before Harris could do more than squawk. Someone else, wearing an unbuttoned uniform shirt with the name WEBB embroidered over the right pocket, pocked his shoulders through the hatch, grinning at Hamilton. "You must be Jack Hamilton!" he exclaimed heartily. "Come on down! Welcome to the club!"

Then probably the most singularly evil face Hamilton had ever seen looked through the hatch with an expression which the hydroponicist imagined the devils in Dante's *Inferno* must have worn. "This is Virgin Bruce," Webb explained.

"Ah-*henh!*" Virgin Bruce snorted, giving Hamilton the once-over with his eyes. "He's *young!* And he's pretty! *I want him, Mike! I want him NOW!*"

"Don't worry," Webb said to Hamilton with a conspiratorial smile. "He's like this with all the new guys."

Virgin Bruce chuckled. "Ni-i-i-ice," he said slowly. His hands were not in sight, but Hamilton could hear what sounded like Harris trying to shout something through a hand clamped over his mouth. "What I mean is . . ." Webb continued.

Hamilton looked over his shoulder. Doc Felapolous was loading the drugged man into the OTV from which the hydroponicist had just disembarked. "Is that thing going back?" he asked. "Keep that hatch open, I want to . . ."

Then more hands reached through the airlock hatch and fastened on his wrists and forearms. Hamilton screamed in spite of himself, and flashed to a scene from *The Night of the Living Dead* when George Romero's zombies were breaking through the farmhouse door and attacking one of their victims. *"Mine!"* Virgin Bruce was howling. *"He's all MINE!"* Then Hamilton was pulled bodily through the hatch, and this was how he came aboard Olympus Station.

# 15

# Profiles in Weirdness

*Mr. Anderson, has the OTV undocked yet?*

Anderson checked his console. "Yes, sir, one minute ago. Main engine has fired and it's going home."

*Its passenger, the new hydroponics chief engineer. He did arrive, didn't he?*

"According to the manifest, he should have been aboard."

*Yes. You did leave word with the personnel at the Docks that he was to report to me upon arrival, didn't you?*

"Oh, yes sir!"

*Then where is he?*

Anderson looked around the Command deck and didn't see any new faces. "I don't know sir."

*Well.* The voice in his earphones paused. Anderson glanced over his shoulder and saw H.G. Wallace's back was turned to him; as usual, the project supervisor was at his station, monitoring the construction work on SPS-1. *He must be lost,* Wallace said firmly. *The new men usually are when they arrive. If he isn't here in a few minutes, let me know. We'll have him paged.*

"Yes, sir."

"Nice to know you weren't serious," Jack Hamilton said as he leaned against the door of a locker in the west terminus module. He said that just to make Bruce and Mike think that he wasn't a complete wimp, while he was taking a few deep gasps of air.

"Hey, if we had been serious, you'd be in a lot worse shape than you're in now," Virgin Bruce replied. "Are you okay there? We can get you to sickbay if you're really hung up."

"I'm fine. I'll be fine. Just let me—*urrruph!*" He dry-heaved spasmodically, and was glad that he had nothing left in his guts to vomit.

He gasped and waved off his welcome wagon. "Just let me pull my shit together."

That, he realized, was going to take more of an effort than keeping some of his nerve, and humor, intact during and after Bruce's mock rape. After it was all done, he had realized that Virgin Bruce's weird greeting had been an impromptu gag, a kind of initiation, to see how much he could take. A little sophomoric, but not unsurvivable; a good-old-boy gag he could live with.

What had been truly terrifying was the trip down the spoke to the station's rim. He had barely recovered from his bout of Star Whoops —cute name, he thought, very cute—before being subjected to a torture worse than the imagined horror of being molested by a sex-crazed astronaut: the gravity gradient in the spoke. His fragile sense of equilibrium had been turned inside out while climbing down the long ladder. One moment he had perceived himself as horizontal, crawling backwards in microgravity along a tunnel. In the next moment, he felt the slight but unmistakable pull of gravity, and realized he was no longer in a horizontal tunnel but in a vertical shaft. The sudden flip-flop of reality had nearly blown his guts out again, and Hamilton had only barely managed to climb the rest of the distance down the spoke shaft to the terminus module.

He managed to catch his breath. Bruce and Mike were now eyeing him speculatively; they were trying to make up their minds whether the new guy was going to cut the mustard. Well, if I can't, we're all screwed, Hamilton thought. He stood up straight, willed his stomach to be still, and said, "Okay. Lead on."

They grinned and led him up the steps into the west catwalk, beginning a two-sided travelogue, which was both dour and enthusiastic at the same time: old boys showing the street to the new kid on the block.

It was the details that they insisted on showing him, leaving him with many questions about operational procedures and the overall layout of the station, but giving him an idea of what the long-timers considered to be priority matters. A dappled gray cat came bounding out of an open hatch to stare at them with wide blue eyes before fleeing in the opposite direction: "That's Asimov. They're all named after sci-fi writers. Asimov, Heinlein, Clarke, Niven, Anderson, Bear . . ." The notes tacked magnetically on the walls concerning everything from the deadlines for filing income tax forms to this week's movie in the rec room: "Hey, you shoulda met the guy you're replacing. One day he started pointing at these signs, screaming, 'The writing is on the wall! The writing is on the wall!' Damifino what he was talking about, do you, Bruce?" The rec room: "This is where you spend your time off. You can lift weights or ride a bicycle. And there's a tri-vee. We get great reception. You a baseball fan? And here's the video game table, and here's a bunch of books. There's lots to do here. And, um, we've got video cassettes, lots of tapes. Hey, we've got the whole run of *Star Trek* and *Twilight Zone* and *Battlestar Galactica* and . . ."

They had taken him down into Module 38, a compartment roughly the size and shape of a soda can, about a quarter of the way around the circumference of the station, and were showing him everything he needed to know about his bunk, when the Muzak which unceasingly floated over the speakers was interrupted by a woman's voice: *John Hamilton, will you please report to the command center,* the tender voice cooed in a pillow-talk tone. *John Hamilton, please report to the project supervisor at the command center.* Then the canned string-section version of "Like A Virgin" resumed, and Hamilton looked up to see both Bruce and Mike staring at him.

The expressions on their faces were so odd that Hamilton's first impulse was to laugh out loud before he checked it. He had just arrived here, so why did they look as if he were going away? No, it wasn't quite like that; it was as if a door had suddenly slammed shut between them. They both mumbled things about seeing if there was a ball game going on the tri-vee in the rec room, and Mike Webb forgot about showing him how his locker opened and shut, and Virgin Bruce told him how to get to the command center, which was essentially going back the way they had just come. Then they both babbled things about seeing him around and practically shuffled their way up the ladder out of the compartment. Hamilton dropped his bag in his locker, closed it, and leaned against the door for a moment, alone for the first time since he had arrived on Olympus Station. He didn't know where or how to put his finger on it, but he had the feeling that his imminent meeting with H.G. Wallace was going to further alter his conceptions of what life for him aboard the station would be like in the future.

Mike Webb had been right. Hamilton's trip up a shaft ladder to the hub wasn't so bad the second time . . . but it was, after all, the second time in a day he had gone from a gravity field to a state of weightlessness, or near-weightlessness, so his stomach did lurch around some. But he didn't get sick. That was a small blessing.

But if a return to microgravitational conditions wasn't enough to bugger his senses, then the command center was. After Jack Hamilton slid open the hatch and entered, he snatched a handhold and paused just inside the center, trying to give himself a moment to orient himself, for the deck was unlike anything he had so far seen on Olympus.

It was by far the largest compartment in the space station, about twenty-five feet wide and thirty feet high, arranged in a circular fashion around the access shaft at the center of the modified Shuttle Mark I external tank from which the hub had been built. The deck was divided into half-levels, like tiered balconies built onto the bulkhead walls opposite each other. Vertical poles—vertical, that is, in that they ran in the direction of the station's polar axis; they could just as easily be horizontal, depending on one's perspective in zero g —ran through the length of the compartment near each tier, and Hamilton noticed rungs welded onto the poles, indicating that they functioned as "fireman's poles" allowing one to easily climb from one level to another. The floors of each level were open metal grids. Looking up, he could see through the floor above him two crewmen seated in front of a console. Fortunately the chairs were all bolted in the tiers in the same direction—there had to be some consistency here, he supposed, even within these strange gravitational conditions —but he was still a little disturbed to see a woman making her way, hand over hand on the rungs, headfirst down one of the poles, and another crewman floating calmly in a horizontal position next to a seated colleague. All in all, Command looked as if it had been designed by the late M.C. Escher.

After a moment, though, he realized how logically the command deck had been designed. If there's little or no gravity to deal with, why bother with old-fashioned notions like floors and ceilings? Each tier was apparently a work station with its own separate function. The center was dimly lighted by red fluorescent bulbs, with the bluish glow from CRT's at the work stations giving the faces of the men and women sitting in front of them a ghostly look. At least a dozen people were working at various stations on the tiers, but the noise level was surprisingly low. Each wore a headset mike, so they could speak to others at different stations on different tiers without having to shout across the compartment. There was a weird, efficient, and somewhat sterile beauty to the place that entranced Hamilton. This was what he had imagined the inside of a space station to be like.

And, realizing that, he almost instantly took a dislike to it. A place of computers and men welded together in a fusion that took away humanity. Here there were no pegged-up notices for used cars on sale in Des Moines, no shelves of dogeared paperback books. This was a place of cool efficiency, of fingers urgently tap-tapping on keyboards, eyes straining to read quickly moving figures on glowing blue screens, everyone doing their best to make all the little systems go so that the big systems could go. Some people thrived in it, and some, like Hamilton, who disdained using electronic equipment in the growing of plants when his green thumbs and intuition could do it just as well, hated it.

He was still gazing around at the command center when a young guy dressed—as everyone in here was—in a powder blue jumpsuit with Skycorp patches on his chest and shoulders floated up to him from a level above. "Are you the new hydroponics chief?" he asked. Hamilton nodded, somewhat distractedly. "Mr. Wallace is down here," he said, motioning upwards with his thumb. "He's waiting to see you now."

Hamilton nodded, and carefully followed the crewman as they pulled themselves up—or down, according to one's own personal perspective—a pole's rungs to a tier that was two half-levels up and a third of the way across the deck. Hamilton found himself at the largest tier, fifteen feet long, with a long console wrapped concave inside a bulkhead wall. There were three chairs fixed to the floor in front of the console, facing a set of computer and television screens, and in the middle one was seated Henry George Wallace, the project supervisor for Olympus Station and the Franklin Project.

Hamilton nearly did not recognize him.

When he had applied to Skycorp for work and when he had been in training—not to mention when the lunar expedition had happened and when Olympus was being established—Hamilton had gotten used to seeing pictures of Henry G. Wallace. TV interviews, magazine and newspaper photos—all had shown a handsome, smiling man in his mid-thirties, with thinning, stylishly cut blond hair and an athletic build—so good-looking and square-cut, he was almost a throwback to the NASA astronauts of the 1960's, a modern space hero.

This was not the same person. H.G. Wallace had physically changed: His eyes, under which there were now heavy bags due to body-fluid shift in weightlessness, seemed more intense, staring bleakly ahead; he had gained more weight than could be accounted for by fluid shift, and had a pot belly; his hair had been cut back until it was a thinning crew cut. Wallace crouched forward in his chair, his neck tucked down almost parallel with his shoulders. The smile was gone as if it had never existed, leaving only a gaunt, dissatisfied pout.

Wallace looked over his shoulder and saw Hamilton hovering behind him, but instead of saying anything, the project supervisor simply turned his attention back to the station in front of him. A couple of TV screens showed pictures of the SPS-1 powersat from angles Hamilton guessed were shot from the construction shack. An LCD between the screens showed a computer-generated animation of the powersat's gridlike structure, a simulation that periodically changed at the touch of a nearby crewman's fingers on a keyboard. Wallace leaned forward in his chair, his eyes fixed on the TV display, his right hand absently stroking his headset mike, ignoring Hamilton.

Suddenly he snapped, "Hold it!" The crewman seated at the keyboard tapped a command and the animation of the powersat stopped its procession across the screen. "Zoom in on the bottom half of the truss section in the center," Wallace said. "That one there." The crewman glanced at Wallace's pointing finger and at the screen, then quietly tapped out a new command. The animation expanded and rotated until the truss was magnified several times.

"Gimme the specs," Wallace said in a rasping voice, and a cluster of numbers appeared on the left margin of the screen. Wallace peered closely at the figures, then said, "Hank, that truss is off, dammit. Who was doing that section?"

A voice came from an audio speaker above the console. *It's off, Henry, but not by much. Our instruments say it's only .057 centimeters. That's within the acceptable limits of . . .*

"Bullshit!" Wallace snapped with an anger that made Hamilton step back a little. "That's not goddamn acceptable, Luton! Why do you think we've got lasers to make measurements if it isn't going to be *perfect!*"

Wallace calmed down. He rubbed his hand across his forehead in exhaustion. "That section was done on the twentieth?" he asked, addressing no one in particular. He reached to his own keyboard and tapped in a complex command, and a screen to his far right lit with a list of names and numbers. The project supervisor studied it for a moment. "It was either Harwell or Hooker," he muttered. "Figures. Harwell was probably carrying on about baseball and Hooker was probably daydreaming again. Hank, warn both of those dummies that if they don't get it together, we'll start deducting the time wasted in fixing their mistakes from their paychecks."

*I'm telling you, there's no mistakes on that section . . .*

"And I'm telling you that there is and that when we get off of this shutdown it had better get fixed."

*Roger, Command,* the voice said after a barely perceptible pause.

As if he had suddenly remembered Hamilton's presence, Wallace

turned halfway around in his seat to gaze silently at the hydroponicist. He didn't say anything, only stared at Hamilton with an expression which seemed to mix hostility, curiosity, and fear. It was unsettling, and Hamilton knew of nothing else to do but to lock eyes with
Wallace and try not to display any emotion.

There was something singularly disturbing about Wallace's eyes.
They reminded Hamilton of the eyes of a drug addict who had been
driven insane by junk; of a lion he had seen in a zoo, which had
restlessly prowled its cage, looking straight ahead, driven crazy by
the loneliness and the austerity of his existence; of old, nineteenth-
century English engravings of the caperings of the inhabitants of
Bedlam.

In a word: madness. Wallace had crazy eyes. C'mon, now, don't
jump to conclusions, Hamilton thought as a chill crept down his
back. He's overworked, under pressure. Stress. He has a lot of responsibility. He looks that way because it's been a hard day of chew-
ing out people for making fraction of a centimeter mistakes. He *can't*
be crazy, because Skycorp wouldn't *let* a crazy man run this operation.

Suddenly, H.G. Wallace unbuckled the straps holding him into his
chair and gently rose, floating upward only a few inches. His mouth
suddenly arced into a smile, although his eyes remained wary. "So
you're Mr. Hamilton, our new hydroponics chief," he said, ex-
tending his hand. "I was wondering when you would arrive. Welcome to Olympus Station, son!"

Son? Hamilton tried to not smile as he clasped Wallace's hand. At
the age of twenty-eight, it had been many years since anyone had
called him "son" unless they were in their sixties or older, and Wallace was no more than forty. "I was a little held up at the, ah,
docking area," he explained, deciding not to tell Wallace about his
welcome at the Docks by Webb and Virgin Bruce. "I was just shown
to my bunk by a couple of your crewmen and dropped off my . . ."

"Who met you?" Wallace asked, in a less than demanding tone.

"I believe their names were Webb and . . . ah, Virgin Bruce?"

Wallace's face clouded at the mention of their names. For a moment he simply stared at Hamilton, and this time Hamilton turned
his eyes away; that lunatic gaze was a bit much to take at close
range. Lord, what was going through this man's mind?

Abruptly, Wallace gave him a slap on the arm and laughed out
loud. Hamilton was forced to fumble blindly above his head for a
handhold, but he had already sailed five feet away from the project
supervisor before he managed to stop himself, colliding backwards

with a passing crewman as he did. The scientist mumbled an apology and caught a dirty look from the crewman. "Well!" exclaimed Wallace, as if he hadn't noticed the accident. "I suppose they didn't give you a proper orientation to your new home, did they? Come on then, Mr. Hamilton, let me show you Olympus Station!"

Without waiting for a reply, he did a neat somersault, grasped the rungs of a pole and started descending headfirst toward the lower levels of the compartment, leaving Hamilton to clumsily follow feet first. *Son of a bitch,* the hydroponicist thought as he tried to catch up with Wallace, who gave no sign of slowing down for him. *He meant to slap me across the compartment. He might have even hoped that I would run into that guy. There's no way he could not have known what he was doing, if he's that seasoned to zero g.* Hamilton realized that, in his own way, H.G. Wallace had just given him some kind of rebuff, and a warning. But for what?

Once out in the hub's passageway, Wallace began to reel off a lecture about the station as he led the way toward the spoke shafts. Some of it Hamilton had heard before, from the two who had met him at the Docks. It seemed to him that Wallace was deliberately ignoring the fact that he *must* have already learned some of this, since Hamilton had told him that he had been to the rim already. For instance, Wallace seemed compelled to tell him just how he should descend the east spoke ladder and how to cope with the gravity gradient.

It seemed to Hamilton that Wallace was determined to be the first person to show the new man around the space station, even if simple logic dictated otherwise. It was enlightening to hear Wallace's description of things: the Muzak coming from the speakers ("Rather pleasant, don't you think? It's a little unorthodox, but it's soothing and improves efficiency . . . and the men just *love* it."); the food ("Skycorp has a contract with one of the companies which supplies in-flight meals to the major airlines. They're balanced meals, very tasty, and can be sent up with maximum efficiency. The men *love* it!"); and the shortage of water for hygienic purposes ("Most of the time, of course, we have to settle for sponge baths with cold water, but we do try to allow everyone a hot shower at least once or twice a week. The men don't mind.") None of this matched what Bruce and Mike had expressed about annoying music, tasteless food, or the fact that most of the crew stank from having washed infrequently.

They were halfway around the station's rim when they came upon a crewman who was coming the opposite way. Hamilton took one look at him, and realized that he was the saddest example of the crew's morale he had seen so far. Blond hair growing long and unkempt, circles under his eyes, hollow-chested, shoulders bent. When he looked up and saw them coming, the crewman's eyes darted to the floor, but instead of walking past, Wallace abruptly descended on him.

"Hello, Popeye!" Wallace exclaimed grandly. He wrapped an arm in a buddy-buddy way around the crewman's shoulders and turned him around to meet Hamilton. "Mr. Hamilton, allow me to introduce you to one of the best construction specialists we have aboard: Claude Hooker." He looked condescendingly at Hooker. "Claude used to be a shrimp fisherman before he came to work for us, so that's why we call him Popeye!"

The poor wretch winced as Wallace said that. Hamilton looked at him and realized that it had been a while since he had seen a more unhappy-looking person. Not noticing—or, perhaps, choosing not to notice—Hooker's discomforture, Wallace went on. "Popeye is one of our old-timers here on Olympus," he said. "Not only has he been here for one two-year shift already and just signed up for another tour of duty, but he's even turned down the one-week vacation the company offered him when he agreed to sign on again. He's a real professional, hardworking spaceman, aren't you, Popeye?"

"Yeah," said Popeye Hooker, staring emptily at a space somewhere around Hamilton's knees. Hamilton recalled seeing Wallace on the command deck inspecting recent work on SPS-1 and wondered if this man was the same Hooker that Wallace had accused of wasting time and daydreaming.

"This is John Hamilton, Popeye," Wallace explained. "Why don't you tell him a little about life here on Olympus."

For a moment it was as if the crewman had not heard Wallace, and Hamilton thought he was going to mumble off something meaningless. Then, as if a notion had passed into Hooker's mind, he raised his haunted eyes and looked straight at Hamilton.

"It sucks," he said in a hollow voice, without any emphasis or inflection. "It's a fucking purgatory. If I had anything to go back home for, any reason to go back to Earth, I would go, but I don't and that's why I'm here. We're all bored out of our minds, and this guy here is a goddamn maniac, and a couple of weeks ago I had a couple of friends killed out in space, so don't listen to anything this fucker has to say about how swell our lives are up here. It's shit, and the only reason why I'm still here is because I'm just a little crazier than he is, and if I were you, I'd get on the next OTV out and go home before . . ."

Wallace took the arm he had wrapped around Hooker's shoulders and used it to hurl the crewman against the far wall of the corridor. The one-third gravity lessened the violence of the shove, but Hooker still hit the hard plastic wall with enough force to make him crumple to the floor.

Hamilton immediately started toward him, and Wallace roared, *"Let him alone! Let that coward alone!"*

Hamilton stopped and stared, first at Hooker, then at Wallace. Hooker, holding his neck and chest painfully, got up off the metal grid floor slowly. He glanced first in Wallace's direction, then looked at Hamilton and gave a weak grin, which seemed to make him a little stronger than he had been when Hamilton had first laid eyes on him. He didn't say anything else; he simply turned and hobbled his way down the upward-sloping corridor.

Wallace had been staring at Hooker with inflamed eyes. He shut his eyes now and slumped against the catwalk wall. He raised his right hand to cover his face and his chest rose and fell as if he were sobbing silently to himself. Hooker was gone by the time he exposed his face again.

Hamilton saw that the project supervisor had composed himself again. More than that; it was as if Wallace had blocked the incident from his mind. The hydroponicist thought he heard footsteps coming from the direction in which they had been walking, but when he looked he didn't see anyone there. Someone had witnessed this savage episode, and, probably wisely, had decided that discretion was the better part of valor.

"Well," Wallace said. He straightened his shoulders and smiled brightly at Hamilton. "I suppose you want to see where you're going to be working, eh?"

*Oh, don't mind me,* Hamilton thought as he forced himself to nod his head. *I only get like that sometimes.* Wallace said nothing more but simply turned and started striding down the catwalk. Back straight, eyes ahead. As if nothing had just happened.

He stopped after a moment and looked inquisitively over his shoulder at Hamilton. "Coming?" he asked.

*Right,* Hamilton replied silently. He started following the project supervisor—and deliberately kept a few paces behind.

"Of course, you realize that this *is* a difficult environment. We're isolated from everything we've grown up with, in a place where danger lurks at every step, with the crew working eight-hour shifts each day. No one ever said that this was a safe environment, but then, when you think about it, when has there ever been a safe environment for man?"

They had been in the five-module Hydroponics section for the past fifteen minutes, and Hamilton had still not seen much more of his workplace than when they had first come down the ladder. He was anxious to give the section a thorough inspection, particularly the rows of tanks which held the station's vegetable crops, but Wallace was apparently deaf to all the subtle hints he had dropped. This was Wallace's chance, it seemed, to twist his new senior crewman's ear and lecture him interminably about the promise and perils of life in space.

"As you've noticed, Skycorp doesn't have a uniform, although I've *requested* that the men aboard this space station maintain a decent wardrobe. But the thought remains the same. There must be discipline, or everything goes to hell, excuse my language. Otherwise things become lax, and it leads to carelessness, and carelessness kills, Mr. Hamilton, *carelessness* is the murderer in space."

"Right," Hamilton said, for the fifth or sixth time during H.G. Wallace's monologue, hoping again that making sounds of agreement during Wallace's spiel would ease him out of the compartment.

"Absolutely!" Wallace said, smiling broadly with the knowledge that Hamilton agreed. "It was *carelessness* that killed those two unfortunate men a couple of weeks ago. Someone on Earth was careless in making the fuel pod for the ITWS that was near Vulcan Station at the time of the accident, so it exploded. But more importantly those two men were killed because of their own *carelessness,* because they shouldn't have been there . . . I mean, they shouldn't have been . . . they shouldn't have put themselves into that position in the first place, do you know what I mean?"

*No, not at all,* Hamilton mutely responded. "I see what you mean, sir," he said aloud.

"Right!" Wallace exclaimed. He slapped the rung of the ladder with his palm. "Yes! Right! It's a question of discipline! If we're ever going to conquer the final frontier, we're going to need to maintain discipline. We're building a bridge between the heavens and the earth, between America and the stars. We're on the edge of the greatest adventure that man has ever known, and the adventure is only beginning, Hamilton! This requires perfection, it requires discipline, oh, and yes, it requires *carelessness!*"

Wallace stopped. His face turned red. "I mean . . ." he began.

At that moment two things happened at once. First, the overhead hatch leading up to the catwalk opened and a pair of feet in sneakers

stepped onto the ladder leading down into Module 42. "Hello!" a
voice called. "Anyone down there?"

Then another hatch in the right wall of the compartment opened
and a thin man with a mustache stepped through. He stopped and
looked first at Wallace, then at Hamilton. "Hi," he said. "You must
be the new hydroponics man."

"Yeah, I do believe that's who he is." Doc Felapolous climbed
down the ladder and walked over toward Wallace and Hamilton.
"Pardon me for interrupting your conversation," he said amiably to
H.G. Wallace, "but I encountered this gentleman while he was being
piped aboard at the Docks, and I didn't really have a chance to
introduce myself." He held out his hand to Hamilton. "Edwin Felapolous, son. Chief physician. I hope you're over your bout with
spacesickness by now."

Hamilton took Felapolous' hand, but before he could say anything, Wallace butted in. "I'm sure he's over it by now, Edwin," he
said somewhat stiffly. "I was just giving him his orientation tour of
the station. . . ."

The thin man who had come in from the next compartment
walked forward, also holding out his hand. "My name's Sam
Sloane," he said. "I'm chief programmer at the data processing center next door. I heard you come in, and I just wanted to . . ."

"I'm certain you'll have ample time in which to introduce yourself, Mr. Sloane," Wallace said quickly. "As I said, I was giving Mr.
Hamilton his orientation tour of the station, and I . . ."

"Oh, now, Henry, I'm sure Mr. Hamilton knows his way around
here." Felapolous waved his hand expansively toward the tanks of
algae arranged in rows down the length of the module, with feeder
lines dangling from nutrient tanks suspended from the ceiling, and
bright growth lights shining on them from overhead tracks. "After
all, as I understand his record, Jack . . . may I call you Jack? . . .
holds a Ph.D. from Yale in space bioengineering and is a former
fellow in hydroponics with the Gaia Institute at Cape Hattaras." He
turned and patted Hamilton's shoulder. "One of Vishnu Suni's former students, are you not? I seem to recall a paper you had published
in the *Journal* late last year . . ."

"Well, yes, I, ah . . ."

"Oh, you were once with *the* Gaia Institute?" Sam Sloane interjected. "I've read much about that place. They were the innovators
of the Ocean Ark." He pumped Hamilton's hand enthusiastically.
"You're simply going to have to tell me everything about that place.

I once heard a lecture by Suni and I was very impressed by the things he said about . . ."

*"Gentlemen,"* Wallace said, a glowering expression growing on his face, "I was *speaking* to Mr. Hamilton about this space station and its mission."

Felapolous turned his head to look at Wallace. "Oh, Henry, I'm terribly sorry," he said, wide-eyed and apologetic. "I almost forgot the second reason I tracked you down. You're needed up on the command deck at once. Huntsville needs to communicate with you about the timetable for coming off the work shutdown. I believe it's urgent."

Wallace's eyes widened. His eyes darted back and forth between the three men. Then his back straightened and his gaze became self-involved. "Thank you, Doctor," he said formally. "Gentlemen, if you'll excuse me . . ."

He turned, walked across the compartment, and quickly scaled the ladder up and out of the module. Sloane watched him until he had disappeared from sight, then he looked at Doc Felapolous with a raised eyebrow. "Nice improvisation," he said softly. "I'm surprised that he didn't ask why he wasn't summoned over the intercom, though."

"He might in a few minutes," Felapolous replied, resting his hands behind him against the edge of a tank. "But I'm sure he'll think of a reason why he wasn't." He looked at Hamilton with an amused expression. "How are you doing, Jack?"

"Fine, just fine," Hamilton replied. He felt bewildered by the sudden flurry of conversation. His eyes glanced from the two newcomers to the overhead hatch and back to the two men again. "Would someone mind explaining to me what just happened here?"

Sloane and Felapolous looked at each other and smiled. "It looks like we both came to the same conclusion at once," Sloane replied. "That, ah, you might want a little relief from your talk with our project supervisor."

"Well . . ." Hamilton paused. "He is . . . a little intense, isn't he?" he said guardedly.

"A little intense." Sloane grinned, clapped his hands and rubbed them together. "Well!" he said to Felapolous. "That's as diplomatic a way to describe a full-blown maniac as you're going to find, right, Doc?"

# 16

# Seeds of Dissent

Is it too much to say that I anticipated that things would be different from the first moment I laid eyes on Jack Hamilton? I guess so. That type of foreshadowing occurs only as the cheapest of coincidences in pulp fiction, usually written in mauve sentences: *Sam looked at the handsome young stranger who stood before him in the space station and thought, "Yes! He's the one! He'll be the one who shall redeem us!"* I'll admit, I embarrassed myself by sending short stories with shit like that to editors at *Analog* and *Amazing,* but any yo-yo—well, nearly any yo-yo—knows that revelations like that just don't occur in real life. Even Saint Peter doubted who Jesus was until He did his little stroll across the waters. . . .

But I will go so far as to say that Jack Hamilton made an impression on me the moment I walked into the hydroponics section, if only because he was putting up with Cap'n Wallace's rambling ravings while keeping a straight face. A perfectly deadpan look; nary an upturned eyebrow, a rolling eyeball, or a wry or a condescending or a humoring smile. But I also sensed at once that not only was he not buying anything that Wallace said, but he had come to the same conclusion that ninety-five per cent of Skycan's crew had long since reached: that our head honcho, chief, and project supervisor was a certifiable Daffy Duck. A Daffy Duck trying to sound like William Shatner.

I *was* impressed. Not many men can look such flat-out weirdness in the eye and not blow their cool. So forgive me if I can't foreshadow things by saying that I knew at once that our new chief hydroponics engineer would be the man who would soon take the whole apple cart and kick it down Dead Man's Hill.

Doc Felapolous gave me an angry glance. "Sam, don't you think you're stretching things a little by calling your boss a full-blown maniac?" he said in a tone of voice that meant, *You better watch*

*where you're speaking your mind, son. I'm Wallace's friend—if you
don't remember.*

I didn't care. "Doc, I thought the man was only eccentric, until I
saw the way he treated Popeye Hooker a few minutes ago," I said.
"You spent time with Hooker after the accident, so you tell me if he
deserved to be shoved and called a coward."

Felapolous cleared his throat and looked down at the floor. Hamilton looked from him to me. "I thought I heard someone else in the
corridor," he said. "That was you?"

"Entirely by accident," I replied. "Yeah, I saw what happened.
Then I came back here and called Doc on the intercom, told him to
get over to Hydroponics as soon as he could manage. Not a bad fib
you concocted, Doc."

"Only a subterfuge to get Henry back to Command so we could
explain things to our new arrival." Doc stared at the floor for another moment before looking back up at Hamilton. "It's a little difficult to explain, Jack . . . may I call you Jack?"

"Call me anything you want except late to supper." That old saw
seemed to appeal to Doc's country-boy persona, and he grinned.
"Tell you what," Hamilton added, "why don't we talk while I check
out my new workplace? I haven't really had a chance to inspect the
place while, ah . . ."

We both nodded in understanding. Wallace had cornered him
down here, so Jack Hamilton had not really been given the chance to
see the hydroponics section. As Felapolous talked, he began to
wander around the compartment, inspecting the tanks, looking at
the consoles, checking readings and so forth.

"I won't pretend that there isn't something wrong with Henry
Wallace," Felapolous began, "but I'll ask you to bear in mind that his
malady isn't an unusual one for spaceflight. I'll also ask you to remember that I'm a medical doctor and not a psychologist, or at least
not much more than an armchair psychologist with a better than
average knowledge of space medicine. First, you have to keep in
mind the unusual physical environment in which we're living. In
effect, this is a closed universe. There are no windows or portholes
because, in a spinning environment, the sense of momentum can
induce vertigo."

"I can understand that," Hamilton said, dipping a finger into a
tank to check the water level. "I got sick on the way up when the
shuttle did its rollover during launch."

"Happens to a lot of people," Felapolous said. "We call it the Star
Whoops." I started to nose-hum the old John Williams movie theme,

but Felapolous shushed me. "Some people get used to it, and some people never do, so the station was designed as a closed environment, without that distraction. It's cut down on cases of spacesickness, which is good because the crewmen spend less work time in the infirmary losing their lunches.

"Unfortunately . . ." Felapolous paused to collect his thoughts. "Well, there's a side effect, and as I said, it's not terribly unusual for spaceflight. Psychologists call it the solipsism syndrome, and so far no one has come up with a cute name for it.

"It's not unique to spaceflight. It's occurred with submarine crews and with other people who stay for long periods of time in a cooped-up environment. Essentially, it means that a person loses touch with the outside, and begins to believe that the world begins and ends within the confines of his environment, that it is the entirety of his universe."

Hamilton looked up from a tray of carrots he had been examining. "Hey! Sort of like the crew of that starship in that old Robert Heinlein story *Orphans of the Sky,* right?"

"You've read that!" I exclaimed. I warmed to Hamilton even more. Damn if it isn't nice to find a person who's familiar with the classics!

"I don't know the work," Felapolous said, "but I'll take your word for it that you're aware of a literary paradigm. In the case of the syndrome, it poses a paradox for the victim, because it's difficult for someone else to prove he's wrong. In an acute case, moreover, the victim will not only come to believe that his environment is the length and breadth of the universe, but he will eventually come to believe that *he* is the *center* of the universe."

Hamilton grunted and led the way into the next of the five hydroponics modules. This one was mainly filled with growing vegetables: lettuce, onions, bell peppers, peas, more carrots. I got hungry just looking at it all. Considering that our entrees came freeze-dried from Earth, Skycan's home-grown veggies were one of the few luxuries we had aboard. I deliberated over swiping a pepper or a carrot when the other two turned their backs. "But I saw Wallace watching TV monitors while I was on the command deck," Hamilton said, "so it can't be that he's entirely out of touch with the real world."

"Well, no," Felapolous agreed. "Wallace's case isn't quite according to the textbook. Although he knows that there's still space and Earth and so forth, he seems to think that he's the center of it all, that he's the only factor which matters."

"I don't quite follow."

"He seems to believe, from my conversations with him, that his particular vision is the only one which matters. You have to realize what kind of person he is. He's not only spit-and-polish military material, he's also the product of lifetime fantasies of becoming a . . . well, a space hero. Coupled with his record as a famous astronaut, of blazing some frontiers in space, it has reinforced his ego, which has in turn reinforced the solipsism syndrome, to the point where no one can disagree with what he thinks, unless they manage to make him believe that *their* ideas are really *his* ideas. Then he'll listen. Anyone who doesn't agree, exists outside his universe, and therefore becomes an enemy."

"Well, that's paranoia, not this syndrome."

"Yes, well, partly that, too," Felapolous admitted. "You would have had to have been here for a while to understand where it all springs from. From the beginning of his tour of duty aboard this station, Henry didn't fit in with the majority of the crew. While he's had these visions of conquering the high frontier, exploring the farthest reaches of space, et cetera, most of the crew are here mainly to make a living. . . ."

"To make a buck," I threw in, breaking my silence. To hell with shoplifting carrots; this was getting interesting. "These guys are mainly blue-collar, salt of the earth, hard-hat types, with a wild-ass streak that would make them want to take on this particular job. They don't want to hear discourses about manifest destiny among the stars, they want to make a bundle at a high-risk profession and get home alive. When Wallace tried to lecture these guys, they shut him off, alienated him. He came on too intense. Hell, I myself gave him a chance. I tried to eat dinner with him once on the mess deck, and frankly he was boring as hell. Space, space space—that was all he wanted to talk about."

Felapolous nodded. "Sam puts it bluntly, but that's essentially the way that it was. It's now come to the point where Henry spends most of his time either on the command deck or in his private cabin and is rarely seen by the crew. He has his meals brought to him there and discourages anyone meeting him, unless it's a new crewman such as yourself, whom he'll try to convert—without success. I've continued to have informal therapy sessions with him—I'm one of the few persons aboard he trusts. . . ."

"You're Dr. McCoy to his Captain Kirk," I threw in.

"Well, I prefer to think of myself as a confessor. . . . Did I tell you, Jack, that I'm also a Jesuit priest? . . . but, um, yes, you could phrase it that way. As far as Henry now believes, he's still the intrepid and daring commander, backed by a hundred and thirty loyal crewmen, among whom he admits there are a few bad apples whom he is willing to tolerate. Besides his mental health, my concern is also with his physical health, since he spends most of his time in the weightless condition of the command deck, as demonstrated by the facial, skeletal, and body-mass ratio changes he has gone through due to spending so much time floating, and the shift in his internal liquids and metabolism that go with it."

"I noticed that he looks different," Hamilton said.

"Said much more succinctly than Doc could ever put it," I said, giving Felapolous a wink. "But it's not just zero g, it's his mental condition. I mean, his eyes, the way he looks at you . . ."

Hamilton shuddered a little. "Right. I noticed that too. I guess he isn't the only case aboard, either. Like the guy he shoved around back there. Popeye, he called him. And the guy who showed me around earlier, Virgin Bruce . . ."

Felapolous stared at him. "Good Lord," he said seriously, "you've *met* Virgin Bruce? Poor devil."

I broke up. "No, no," I insisted after I got hold of myself, "you've got it wrong with Brucie. He's not crazy . . . or at least not in the usual sense of the word. I mean, he's *crazy,* but he's a sane kind of crazy. Relatively harmless, if you can expect that from an ex-biker. He intimidates everyone at first, but don't worry, he's a good person once you get used to him."

"On the other hand, Popeye Hooker is a different matter." Doc Felapolous shook his head and shoved his hands into the pockets of his shorts. "I haven't been able to figure him out," he said, more to himself than to either of us. "At first I thought he was simply homesick, just as we have several people aboard who are counting the hours till their contracts run out and they can ship back to Earth, but then just a couple of months ago he signed on with Skycorp for another two years. I discussed it with him, tried to talk him out of it, but he was adamant, and since he was then basically healthy in mind and body, I signed the form." Felapolous sighed. "I regret to say I made a mistake. His mental health is deteriorating. He's in a state of depression, and as far as I can tell, it stems from guilt, or feeling guilty, about something he left behind. But he won't say a thing about it, and until he shows some overt sign of mental illness, I can't recommend that he be sent back."

"Like the guy I saw you putting on the OTV earlier, when I arrived," Hamilton said. Felapolous nodded. "And Virgin Bruce . . . Christ, what a name . . . Virgin Bruce mentioned something about the last hydroponics engineer you had aboard, named Mc-Henry."

"McHenry, right," I said. "He went right over the top. One day he started shouting at people in the rec room that the writing was on the wall. Pointing at the wall, screaming, 'It's there, can't you read it!' Doc had to come up and sedate him."

"Shipped him back two days later," Felapolous said. "I had therapy with him up until then, and he still wouldn't tell me what he saw written up there."

"Okay, okay," Hamilton said, leaning up against a wall and folding his arms across his chest. "So here's the million dollar question. You have guys sometimes go crazy up here from the confinement or whatever, you send 'em back. Henry Wallace, the top dog here, is crazy. You've diagnosed that with some certainty. So why haven't you sent *him* back."

I looked at Doc, who was silent for a moment. Our senior physician had painted himself into a corner by explaining all this so openly to Hamilton. Now he had to answer the obvious question. I stood back and waited; Doc and I were friends, but he still hadn't explained that to me, either.

"First off," Doc said quietly at last, "you have to both promise me that this doesn't get beyond this compartment." We nodded, and Felapolous glanced up at the overhead hatch leading to the catwalk, making sure it was closed. "I *have* explained to Skycorp Command about Henry's condition, and I *have* recommended to them that he be replaced."

"So they know Wallace has gone bonkers," I said. "Why hasn't he been replaced?"

"I discussed this with one of their senior planning officials, a young Turk named Clayton Dobbs," Felapolous said. "He argued economics in return. Remember, this whole thing—the station, all the people on it, all the billions of dollars which have been invested—are geared toward one immediate goal, the construction of the Project Franklin powersats. The potential for construction holdups and cost overruns is staggering. There have been both of those, so far, but except for the recent incident of the Vulcan blowout, most of the problems have been ground-based. As far as Olympus, Vulcan, Descartes, and the other space-based operations are concerned, everything has been kept on schedule and reasonably within budget. We're still on the production possibilities curve, as Dobbs phrased it. The economics equilibrium between costs and long-term benefits has not yet been upset. As usual with the corporate system, they have put the credit on the front-line man."

"Oh, shit," I murmured, "I can see it coming."

Felapolous nodded. "Right you are, Sam, and in a sense, so are they. Henry's the man in charge. He keeps everyone on line, keeps operations going smoothly, keeps the project alive. The investors would bail out otherwise, and that would sink the whole ship. Yes, McGuinness and Skycorp are aware that our project supervisor is unhinged, even though they keep it to themselves as a corporate top-secret. But the inarguable fact of the matter is that *he gets the job done.* As long as he does that, they don't give a damn if he wears a pink bunny suit and runs around the station declaring himself the prom queen."

Hamilton let out a breath. "Good economic sense," he said. "If it takes a crazy man to do the job, let the crazy man do it."

"You can't argue with success," I added. Felapolous nodded, and I knew he was right. It was scary, but it was logical.

We were quiet for a moment, each of us immersed in his own thoughts. After a minute Felapolous straightened himself, clapping his hands together. "Well!" he said. "I'm sure you've been given quite an earful, Jack, and I'll trust that you'll keep it all to yourself. If you gentlemen will excuse me, I'll go attend to one of my principal duties aboard the station."

"What's that?" Hamilton asked.

"Feeding the cats." Felapolous turned and walked to a ladder. "Sam here named them all after science fiction writers," he said as he began to climb. "He'll explain it to you. See you later." Doc opened the hatch, climbed out onto the catwalk, and dropped the hatch shut behind him.

"See, it's like this," I started to explain. "I'm a science fiction writer myself, and . . ."

But Hamilton just waved his hand. "Never mind. Virgin Bruce explained it to me already. Nice guy, that Felapolous, isn't he?"

"One of the better people we have aboard," I agreed. "He keeps us sane."

Hamilton crossed his arms and peered closely at me for a moment, as if sizing me up. "Y'know, I don't think neurosis is the biggest problem here," he said. "No one has come straight out and said it to me, but I think your problem—everyone's aboard the station, not you personally—is that you're bored."

I let my eyes roll up. "Oh, gee, what a surprise," I replied sarcastically. "I've been here for almost a year now, working in this can day after day, but I didn't notice that until a new guy came aboard and pointed that out to me on his first day in orbit. Thank you, Jack, for that astute observation."

Well, it *was* astute for someone to pick up on that upon arrival, and perhaps I should have given Hamilton credit for that quick bit of observation. But it was a little like telling the man who's dying of leukemia that he's looking a little anemic. Jack continued to gaze at me, and I shrugged. "I dunno, man. I manage to keep myself busy and entertained, but the guys who have to really face it are the beamjacks. From what I hear, their life isn't all that great. Eight hours a day they take a lot of risks, and then they get to come back here, eat freeze-dried plastic crap, watch TV, and try to get some sleep before doing it all over again. This place reinforces boredom, y'know, and anything that's really fun to do is either discouraged or outright forbidden. Yeah, they're bored. *We're* bored. What can you do, though, right?" I shrugged.

Hamilton returned the shrug. "There's lots of ways you can beat boredom, Sam," he said blandly, "if you're willing to take a few risks."

He had a wry smile on his face and a gleam in his eye as he said that. He was getting at something. "How so?" I asked casually. "You have an idea?"

"Well, what I mean is doing something you've maybe not considered doing before," he said. "Cutting up a bit. Getting a little crazy. Taking a little risk. Know what I mean?"

"No, I don't know what you mean," I challenged. "Tell me about it." He was baiting me, and it was working.

He hesitated. "Depends how much I can trust you," he said. "Do I have your word that you won't let the cat out of the bag?"

"Cat's already out of the bag. Has been ever since Lou Maynard brought Spoker and ZeeGee aboard. No, no, never mind. Stupid joke. I promise, mums the word. What's your idea?"

Jack studied me for a moment longer, then kneeled down and unfastened a pocket on the left leg of his coveralls. Without standing up, he handed me a plastic bag rolled up and secured with a rubber band.

I pulled off the band and unrolled the bag. Inside were a couple of hundred tiny, nut-brown seeds. "Okay. Seeds. So what?"

He looked up at me with a raised eyebrow—a characteristic expression I was soon to become familiar with—but said nothing as he shifted to his left knee and unsealed the pocket on his left calf. He pulled out and handed me another bag, this one bulkier than the first, also secured with a rubber band.

I unrolled that bag and stared at the contents. For a moment I didn't recognize what was inside, but when I did, I almost dropped the bag. I glanced at the bag of seeds, then just to make sure my eyes weren't deceiving me, I opened the second bag, stuck my nose into the opening, and took a big sniff.

What I smelled brought me instantly back to old college days, of sitting around in the dorm after classes and late at night; of cigarette papers and funky-looking plastic pipes with huge briar-and-aluminum bowls caked with dark brown resin which had never known the taint of tobacco; of a funny tingling at the top of my scalp and a loosening of my bowels in a way which made going to the john an unspeakably delightful experience; of finding rare humor in late-night news shows, and revelations on the nature of the universe in the way that the New England rain drizzled down my window pane; of wearing, as John Prine had once aptly phrased it, an illegal smile.

One bag was full of marijuana; good stuff, if my nose told me true. The second bag was full of marijuana seeds. My mind at once made the obvious connections. "My God," I whispered, "you can't be serious."

"I'm serious," Jack whispered in reply. "That's just a sample. It won't last long, but by that time the crop will have grown and we'll have much more like it."

"In *here?*" My eyes wandered over the hydroponics tanks.

He nodded. "In here. In this section. The sample you're holding was raised in a greenhouse, in a hydroponics tank almost identical to these. The conditions were virtually the same, except of course for the higher gravity." He smiled. "The crop I cultivated there grew to maturity in half the usual time, and I'm curious to see what growth rate will occur in reduced gravity."

I took a deep breath and handed the bags back to Hamilton who neatly rerolled them and put them back into the pockets from which they had come. "You know what could happen if Wallace or Felapolous or Phil Bigthorn stumbled across this? You've got to be careful, Jack."

"I'll be very careful. I've already figured the whole thing out. If you'll trust me, and keep your lips tight about it, I'll show you how to beat boredom." He smiled again. "I could tell by the look on your face you've smoked the stuff before. Are you in with me?"

A little bag of marijuana and a little bag of marijuana seeds. Recollections of summer afternoons and irresponsible years, dis-

carded along the road to responsible adulthood. Tantalizing crimi-
nality of the past. I recalled that moist, thick, musky scent I had
whiffed from the bag. How could I, in my approaching middle years,
with the first streaks of gray already appearing in my hair, possibly
consider getting into this type of thing again, here on a space station
thousands of miles above Earth?

"Do you seriously believe you're going to get away with this?" I
asked.

"Yes," he said.

"How are we going to smoke it without anyone catching on?"

"Come back here at 1800 hours tomorrow and I'll show you," he
said.

"Okay. I'm in."

"That's great," he said. "Don't worry. You'll love it."

That was the beginning. I believed everything he said.

# PART THREE

*High Up There*

No rescue yet.

I'm not surprised. Like I said before, it will take the guys back at Descartes Base a while to miss me, longer to get worried, and much longer than that to think about sending out a search party. Virgin Bruce would have fit right in with that crowd; a huge tapestry picture of Jerry Garcia on the wall of the rec room, and hours of loafing around telling themselves what indispensable jobs they were doing and complaining about the overtime hours. I would have liked to seen the look on Henry Wallace's face had he seen Lester Riddell, the Skycorp project supervisor on the Moon and Wallace's co-commander during their lunar expedition back in '01. As opposed to clean-shaven, squeaky-clean, honor- and duty-first Wallace, I remember Lester: long hair, unshaven, lying on the floor of the wardroom, wearing a pair of Bose headphones plugged into a tape deck blasting oldies by Black Flag into his cheesecloth brain. I'm supposed to depend on guys like *that* to save me?

Actually, I suspect, upon examining my feelings closely, that I would actually be disappointed if someone showed up now to get me out of this crevasse. It's not like I welcome death, but . . . well, I'm not scared. I'm rather resigned to the fact that my air will go out in a little while and that I'll perish here. I don't welcome death, but what comes around goes around. We all buy Boot Hill sooner or later, and frankly there's worse ways to go. Besides, I'm down here alone with the Greatest Discovery Ever Made, capitalized, and let me tell you, the view is wonderful.

My only wish is that Doc Felapolous was here with me. No, I don't mean stuck in this fatal situation. I have no reason to wish that on Edwin. He was always good for conversation, for letting you get things off your chest, and the fact that he was a priest would have made things easier concerning my eventual funeral.

Oh, hell. Thinking about that aspect of my demise has made me morbid again. I'll tell you what else I could use now: a joint of Jack Hamilton's weed. Mighty good smoke, that Skycan Brown. The choice of spacemen across the galaxy. Two hits and you achieve free fall even in a gravity area. Three, and you unhook your tether. Smoke it in a water pipe or bake it in brownies, makes no difference; Skycan Brown's damn good weed.

Jack got that stuff going the same week the construction crew came off the company's work shutdown. The Senate Subcommittee on Space Science and Technology and the NASA review boards admonished Skycorp for utilizing flimsy engineering practices on the Vulcan station, but at the same time agreed that it was a freak accident that killed those men. They gave Skycorp three months in which to replace the hotdogs with hard modules, and let the company off with a warning not to let such a tragedy happen again. The political maneuvering that occurred behind the scenes can be left to the imagination. Wallace got word that the shutdown was officially over, and he sent the beamjacks back to work on SPS-1 with an enthusiastic address over the intercom system which barely made the guys lay down their cards or look away from the National League game on the tri-vee set. They all knew it would end sooner or later, and they were a little disgruntled; they had become used to loafing around on company time.

Meanwhile, Jack Hamilton was secretly germinating his little pile of marijuana seeds in an incubator, while taking measures to assure that his privacy in the hydroponics section would not be disturbed. Asserting that a constant temperature had to be maintained in his five modules, he ordered the access hatches to the catwalk sealed at all times. He installed disinfectant mats at the bottom of the ladders to make a hassle for those who did come down, forcing them to rub their feet in the mats for a minute before trodding on his decks. He planted corn in the tanks in Module 2, to grow high and act as shields for the eventual pot stalks, and had the lateral hatch leading from the rec room in Module 39 to Hydroponics Module 40 sealed by Phil Bigthorn, again to maintain the hydroponics section's temperature and humidity on the beam. In this way, Hamilton managed to secure a small spot for a pot crop in a place with closer confines than a men's room john, yet safer than a mountainside in east Tennessee. The boy had genius.

I knew Jack was going to upset things. I knew that the pot crop was the beginning of something big. I just didn't foresee how far things would go, and I know Jack didn't, either. So much for the myth of science fiction writers being able to foretell the future.

Shit, it's getting cold down here.

# 17

# Space

He felt himself slipping, so he grabbed tight to his tether line with his right hand and with his left hand grasped the thin edge of the girder he had been welding, letting the laser torch dangle free, drifting away from his body by its power line. He had already shut his eyes when the first sensation of vertigo hit him. With his eyes tightly closed, the darkness was interspaced only by the faint, retina-remembered red and blue glow of the telltale lights on the inside of his helmet, ghost lights which still danced softly in his field of vision.

There was darkness, but there was also sound. He kept the com-link open for safety's sake; if he started to pass out, he could always shout something and he would be rescued. The selector continued to scan across the channels.

*Freighter on approach, X-ray forty-five, Yankee minus two, Zulu minus ten, over Vulcan Command.*

*We copy, Goddard, you're cleared for final approach, over.*

The channel switched to static, then: *Lemme see if I can reach that, Mick, just lemme get a little more . . . hell, this is a bitch, why don't you . . . ?*

*Hold it, hold it, hold it—! Nyaagh, got it! This sucker won't slip! Here, gimme the torch and hold it and kinda push it . . . yeah, that's right, right like that . . .*

*Team Two-ten, you're not on the beam and we're not reading a joint lock. Bring it down a couple of inches and try it again.*

*For Christ's sake, Vulcan, I'm looking at the thing and it's in the right . . . oops, yeah, let me swing it back this way, how're you, I mean we, set now?*

*Looking better, two-ten. Move it another ten feet and you're there almost.*

Static; the channel changed: *I mean, could you believe that inning? Vincenti was on the fucking base, the cameras caught it from three*

*angles, man, and the ump still called him out. I mean, did you hear
those Jap fans cheer?*

*A-right. Give 'em a smaller field and they think they invented the
game. Wanna hand me my wrench? Oops, thanks. I know. Mets blew
it on this one after that, 'cause Moto got on third and that broke it, but
they're still a long way from the play-offs and they got the Cards to
handle next.*

*Yeah. Hey, you know anybody who has tickets to the play-offs? I'm
going home around then.*

*If it's going to be in St. Louie, ask Bruce. He's from there.*

Popeye wasn't spinning so badly by then. The unexpected torque
from the clockwise spin he'd accidentally gone into when he had hit
the MMU's control handles incorrectly had stopped when he
grabbed the tether and the girder. But he still kept his eyes shut, took
deep breaths, and forced himself to concentrate on the cacophony of
voices coming through his headphones. There was a burst of static
and the pitch of the voices subtly shifted again.

*Truss E as in Edward twenty-two-five finished, we're holding Vul-
can, waiting for the load, over.*

*We copy, boys, hold on for another load by Zulu Tango. Pod Zulu
Tango, do you copy, over.*

Switch, then: weird, something in the background, which made
him listen hard—music that seemed to be coming from a pocket
radio turned down low several yards behind his head. A gentle, lilting rhythm, with a breath of electronic pedal steel guitar blowing in
like a summer breeze off the Gulf.

*Zulu Tango, we're getting interference, over.*

He opened his eyes for an instant, saw the absolute blackness of
cislunar space, the starlight blotted out by the shining hemisphere of
Earth swinging into view from the right. The last time he had looked
at Earth, it had been to his left and below him. Feeling his senses
lurch, he quickly shut his eyes again.

Static. A voice called to him. *Station one-Betty, you copy, over?*

*Zulu Tango, acknowledge, over.*

Static, channel change: *Zulu Tango here, we're in visual range of
Eddie twenty-two-five, this is nice, boys, listen.*

Then suddenly the music rose, and it overcame the static and
flowed into his mind with a backbeat, and a gentle, nasal voice sang
to him words whose meaning became apparent at once:

> "The Wheel is turning and you can't slow down,
> "You can't let go and you can't hold on,

*"You can't go back and you can't stand still,*
*"If the thunder don't get you then the lightning will."*

His eyes opened, and there was space, stretching out to eternity, a vast carpet of fathomless darkness, starless and black as sleep, nothingness that was at once impenetrable and transparent for light-years. Part of him instantly recoiled, and part of him stared at the wonder, saying softly, look, look, this is the true reality, nothing else matters, this is everything, this is God, don't blink or you'll miss the show. . . .

*"Won't you try just a little bit harder,*
*"Couldn't you try just a little bit more . . . ?"*

Static. Then a loud, overpowering voice: *"Neiman! Can it!"*

Snap! There went the music, gone like that. Popeye blinked a few times, relaxed his vision. He looked at his hands, and was surprised to see that he wasn't holding anything. The tether line was floating several inches away from his right hand, and the edge of the girder was many feet from his left hand. He had let go of the powersat, and was held to it only by the tether, and he hadn't noticed that he had let go.

Glancing upward, he saw the powersat stretching away above his head as a silvery grid several miles long pointed almost directly at the three-quarters-full Earth. Not far away to his left, a pair of beamjacks hovered underneath a truss section; he could see the brilliant white flash of a hand-held laser torch spitting against a joint as one of the pair welded in a section held in place by the other worker. Much farther away, another beamjack gently guided himself toward a long stay which was being maneuvered into place by a work pod. Through the grid's square openings, he could see another pod coasting above him and the powersat, carrying long aluminum sections from Vulcan's stores out to another point of assembly on the gargantuan structure.

*Neiman, I'm not telling you this again. You got permission to play your damn tapes in your pod, but you're not going to broadcast them over any of the comlink channels. It screws up communications. Do you copy?*

*Yeah, right, I copy, Hank. Don't get upset.* The music abruptly ceased.

*Station One-Betty, this is Vulcan Command. You copy there, Popeye?*

Oh, hell, Hooker thought, they must have missed me. "Vulcan, this is One-Betty, we read you."

*What's going on, Hooker? I called for you a minute ago.*

"I'm okay, Sammy. I just had a slight case of vertigo, so I shut my eyes till it went away."

He heard laughter over the channels. *Hey, Popeye, don't let that pure oxygen go to your head now, eh?*

*Hey! Popeye! I gotta can a spinach if you need it!*

*Hooker, are you okay?* That was Hank Luton, the construction supervisor. *How're you doing there?*

"I said I'm okay," he insisted. He grabbed his tether and started pulling it hand over hand, reeling himself in toward the beam he had been welding. "I just got the spins for a minute there. Let me get this done, and I'll go work with Hernandez and Webb at their section."

*Nix on that, Popeye. You know the rules. Finish that weld, then I want you back on Vulcan and cycled through into the whiteroom. I don't want anyone dozing off on the job.*

Oh, that's just great, Hooker thought as he grabbed the powersat again. That means he'll put me on medical report to Doc, and Doc'll put me on the couch again. "No, seriously, Hank, I'm okay," he said, trying to keep the pleading tone out of his voice. "I just misfired my MMU a bit and that put me in a spin and I just got a little dizzy. I'm telling you, I'm fine."

*Don't gimme that crap, Popeye. Untether now and head back. Al, go over there and finish what Hooker was working on. Hooker, back to the station, pronto, you copy?*

"Goddammit," Hooker said under his breath. He unsnapped his tether and hit the button on his chest box, which reeled the line back into the metal can on his hip. Then he pushed off from the girder with his leg, did a half-flip backwards and jostled the hand controls on his backpack's arms. The MMU stopped the momentum from his backflip, and a correction on the vernier jets sent him gliding toward the telephone shape of Vulcan, hovering underneath the powersat three-quarters of a mile away, joining the continuous flying circus of men and vehicles arrayed around the shack's open loading bays. Not only was he going to have to take a break now, Popeye thought, but he had little doubt that he was going to have to listen to Hank as well.

"I don't know what to do about you, Popeye, I honestly don't know." Hank Luton paused to suck on the straw leading into his coffee bulb. "I mean, you and I both know you got problems, but I can't do a thing for you if you don't tell me about 'em, right?"

Hooker floated nearby, holding a bulb in his own hand. He had his suit on still, but with the backpack off, his helmet undogged and his gloves shed. He gazed moodily at a display screen; for some reason, he couldn't bring himself to look at Hank. He didn't say anything.

Luton waited for him to answer. Getting no reply, he went on. "C'mon, Claude. You've been on this operation almost longer than anyone else. At least as long as the rest of the work crew. I've appreciated your hard work so far. You're a good man. I like you. If you have something on your mind, tell me about it. It won't go any farther than this room."

"I don't have anything to talk about."

"Oh, *Jesus,* Popeye, get off it!" Luton snapped. "You don't think anyone notices? You hardly say anything to anyone anymore. You're never in the rec room, you eat alone on the mess deck, you don't show any desire to be with other people. You work, you eat, you take a sponge bath, you sleep for a few hours and you go back to work again. A man just can't live like that, Hooker!"

Hooker shrugged. "Doesn't seem to be hurting me so far." He sucked down a little coffee and didn't look at the construction supervisor.

"Aw, bullshit, man. You spaced out back there. If you hadn't had your tether secured, someone would now be retrieving you from your own little orbit." Luton crushed the bulb in his black fist and shoved it down a disposal chute. "To tell you the truth, I don't care if people daydream on the job sometimes, as long as they don't let it interfere with what they're doing. But up here, when you start to space out, that's the beginning of a fatal mistake."

"I wasn't daydreaming, Hank," Popeye said.

"C'mon . . ."

"*No!*" Suddenly, he felt something snap inside of him. He flung the coffee bulb he had been holding across the compartment, where it bounced off an oxygen tank and ricocheted into a Mylar wall. "I had a little bit of vertigo, that was all, I just got a little dizzy and I shut my eyes to get my shit together!" he shouted. At the same time, he had the impression that he was outside his own body, watching himself yelling at Hank Luton, passively examining himself as he lost control. "And I don't want to talk about my problems because I don't have any, so I don't have anything I don't want to tell you about, so just let me do my fucking job. I just got dizzy, that's all! I just got the spins and that's why I didn't answer Sammy, and there's nothing I want to talk to you about, so thank you very much and get outta my life you goddamn *nigger!*"

Hank Luton's right fist wound back for a punch so fast that the momentum sent him toppling backwards and he had to grab for a handhold to keep himself in place. The fist hung parallel to his shoulder for a moment, trembling as if it contained a fury of its own, and Hooker shrank back, waiting for the blow which would probably take his head clean off his neck. Luton's dark eyes bored into his own for a long second; then, remarkably, he lowered his hand, his fingers uncoiling from the bricklike fist he had made.

Luton let out a breath. "Popeye," he said slowly and softly, "I haven't let a white guy live after calling me a nigger since I was a little kid. I know you're not the type who usually says things like that, though, so I'm going to let that one slide by."

"I'm sorry, Hank," Hooker said. "You're right. I didn't mean that."

The construction supervisor nodded his head and looked away. "If you really were a bigot you wouldn't have saved Julian's life when that hotdog blew out," he murmured. "I'm just glad he's not on this shift so he didn't have to hear you say that. I know you're sorry, Popeye. You don't have to say anything else."

Hooker no longer felt detached from himself. He only felt ashamed. It was like what had happened a few weeks earlier, when he had blown up at H.G. Wallace. Something deep inside himself had snapped its reins and had roared loose, but unlike the episode with Cap'n Wallace, this time it had been ugly and obscene and he wanted to crawl away someplace to die because of it. He remembered . . .

*Rocky, fat Rocky, two hundred-plus pounds of manipulative shit, bent over a small mound of soft white powder balanced in the cup of gold-plated balance-beam scales which reflected in the Florida sun like a promise disappearing into the blue; gone, forever gone. "Money's money, man," Rocky murmured as he carefully balanced the scales, "but I hope your lady likes the present you're giving her."*

"I'm sorry," Popeye said. "I guess it just came out."

Luton nodded. "Hooker, you're through for this shift," he said. "I think there's something wrong that you don't want to talk about with me, so I'm going to take you off this shift and let you catch a ferry back to Skycan. I know I can't make you do it, but I want you to go talk to Doc Felapolous and get whatever it is off your chest."

Hooker nodded, knowing that he wasn't going to visit Felapolous. Luton turned toward the hatch leading back toward Vulcan's command compartment. "Just one warning," he tossed over his shoulder. "If you space out again, I'm going to recommend to Doc and Cap'n Wallace that you be sent back to Earth on a psychiatric release. I can't put my finger on it, but I get the feeling that's the last thing you want to happen. You're homesick, Popeye, but you never want to go home."

He sat in the whiteroom for a while after Luton left, gazing at the crumpled coffee container he had thrown across the compartment, which drifted like a tiny rogue asteroid. Luton had been right. *I want to go home,* Hooker thought, *but I can't, and getting shipped back would be the worst thing to ever happen to me.*

Almost the worst thing.

# 18

# Virgin Bruce's Tale

If it had not been for the St. Louis Cardinals throwing away their chance to go to the Series to the Chicago Cubs—a major development in the season, which eventually led to the historic games between the Cubs and the Tokyo Giants—we probably would never have learned how Virgin Bruce came to be on Olympus Station. It took a disastrous defensive play by the Cards in the seventh inning for Bruce to get upset enough to spill the beans about his past.

Of course, no one had ever asked him to tell about himself before, at least not in any detail. That was tradition among the Skycan crew, a tacit agreement by which it was generally understood that a beamjack or any other crewman wasn't obligated to relate his autobiography to anyone.

There were a couple of reasons for this. One, it was rumored, and correctly so, that a few guys had past affairs which were nobody's business but their own. Bad marriages and divorces which had them running from alimony payments, or possible criminal charges concerning God knew what real or trumped-up offenses (remember Tennessee's "Tipper" law against live rock music performances?), or shattered reputations and ruined businesses in wherever one called home—these were the most recurrent stories, when one heard them. Remember, we were all living in close confines on the station, so there wasn't much privacy. A yarn told to a few friends in the bunkhouse could spread throughout Skycan, until someone sat down next to you in the mess deck and calmly asked you if that seventeen-year-old in New York had been any good. The other reason was that some of the guys had psychological scars which were simply too vulnerable to expose in public. Popeye Hooker was one of those people. He had something in his background he didn't want to discuss, and no one really pressed him about it, except maybe Hank Luton or Doc Felapolous.

It was not as if everyone on Skycan were in the position of expatriated Americans living in banana republics under false identities. Many times during the long, dull hours spent in the rec rooms or in the bunkhouses between work shifts some guys would open up, telling their life stories to whoever was nearby. That was another reason for the tradition of voluntary silence: Most of those stories were either tedious drivel or pure bullshit. But while there were many people who spouted dull anecdotes or tall tales, there were also a few who didn't have much to say about what they did before they came to work for Skycorp. Virgin Bruce was among the members of the latter group.

At least before that Sunday afternoon in the west rec room, that is. The baseball fans aboard had been long looking forward to that game. The Cubs and the Cards were rivals way back when dinosaurs roamed the Earth, and in the season of 2016 they were running almost neck and neck for the numero uno standing in the National League, especially after they both kicked the shit out of last season's Series champs, the San Diego Padres, and summarily whomped American League stalwarts like the Royals (whom the Cards had never forgiven since the I-70 Series of '85), the Yankees, and the revived and highly touted Washington Senators. After all these years, it looked like the Cubs were again going to make it at least to the play-offs, and there were enough Midwesterners among the crew to make that particular game of interest even to those of us who really didn't give a damn about baseball, only because we wanted to see if there was going to be a bloody brawl between Cards and Cubs fans by the time it was done.

So a lot of shift-swapping had occurred the week before, which had placed a couple of dozen diehards around the tri-vee table by 1400 hours Sunday, with more swarming in after the fourth inning, when the second shift got off duty. I was never much of a baseball fan—college basketball was my sport, besides boxing—but I ducked out of work at Data Processing and strolled over to the west rec room, where one of the two circuses on Skycan was in progress. With two rec rooms on Skycan, it worked out that most of the Cards fans were in the west hemisphere and most of the Cubs fans were in the east, which probably reduced the bloodshed in the aftermath.

I remember that the compartment was jammed almost to capacity. Most people were standing in a dense circle three layers deep around the table; the lucky few who had staked out seats had been there two hours before the game, and weren't moving for love or money. I recall one surprise: Joni Lowenstein, the beautiful woman who usu-

ally worked Olympus' communications station during the second
shift on weekdays, she who had resisted the advances of every guy on
Skycan, who hardly spoke to any beamjack anymore except as
"Skycorp Command" over the comlink. She turned out to be a true
blue-eyed Cards fan and managed to spirit herself into one of the few
tableside seats to yell for her team throughout the game. The men
present were too astonished to even think about making a pass at
her.

I suspect Joni was there mainly to watch Shelly Smith play. That
sours the memory a little, because Shelly's blowing it at the bottom
of the seventh was what lost the game for the Cards. It was a bad
moment for the first female player on a major league baseball team,
and I was surprised that Joni watched the game through to the bitter
end.

The tri-vee tables were two of the few luxuries Skycorp had sent
up to us. There was one in each rec room and they were blessings,
nice Mitsubishi systems with stereo sound and overhead TV screens
for the close-up shots. A holographic image projected on the tabletop
showed the diamond and the outfields as a three-dimensional di-
orama painted in ghostly translucent light, the players as three-inch
images running across the table. With a little imagination, one could
imagine himself or herself up in the nosebleed section of Busch Stadium squinting down at the field. We had to keep the cats off the
table, because it was so convincing to them that they would bat with
their paws at the players on first and third base or go snatching after
an outfielder running to intercept a pop fly.

It was a good game, which ended in tragic defeat for the Cardinals. The St. Louis team had started off strong with Cox and Bingham taking home in the first two innings and Caruso stealing home
during a stumble by the Cubs' Kelso, but by the end of the fifth the
old Cards curse of early burnout set in when a rookie dropped a base
hit, which the Cards screwed up in catching and thus let two Cubbies
run home. Things got better for the Cubs and worse for the Cards
after that, especially when the Cards coach sent in Ron Lucey as the
relief pitcher. Lucey had been a promising rookie once, but his
megabuck salary had sapped away his drive, and through the rest of
the game he sent erratic pitches to the Cubs batters, who either
ignored them or sent them slamming into the stadium's outfield
walls. The Cards fans in the west rec room became surly around that
time; if there were any Cubs fans in the room, they either kept mum
or had the wisdom to go over to the east rec room, where they were
having a good time.

The killing blow in the seventh happened when one of Lucey's weird pitches was clobbered by a Cub heavyweight named DiPaula, straight into right field. Shelly Smith ran to intercept it, stumbled at the last minute, let it drop, recovered, grabbed the ball and flung it at second base . . . too much too late, because by then DiPaula was rounding second and a schmuck named Lomax, who had made it to third base on luck alone, was prancing across home plate like a sixteen-year-old who had copped a feel on his first date. The error was compounded by the Cards' second baseman missing Smith's throw, which allowed DiPaula to run home a moment later. Shelly Smith crumpled to her knees and the Cubs took the lead, and the screams in the west rec room could be heard throughout the station.

Virgin Bruce, who had been sitting quietly in a chair behind first base throughout the last two innings, crumpled a near-beer can in his fist and chucked it across the table. It fell like an aluminum meteor on a Cubs player, passed through his ghostly miniature body, and bounced off the table. "Sonuvagoddamnbitch," he snarled, getting up from his chair. "I can't stand to watch anymore." He pushed through the crowd and headed for the refrigerator. A few guys eyed his empty chair covetously, but no one made a move to claim it. You don't tempt fate that way.

It was just as well that Bruce stayed away for the next two innings. Smith's bad play was the end of the game for the Cards; the Cubs managed to repulse them from bringing any more men home for the rest of the game, and the final score was 4–3 in favor of Chicago. We let Asimov the cat onto the table to maul the 3-D image of Fred Bird as he pranced around the pitcher's mound, and most of the crowd climbed up the ladder out of the rec room, probably bound for the east rec room to take their frustrations out on the Cubs fans there.

That left a few people sitting around the now empty tri-vee table: Joni, Dave Chang, Mike Webb, Claude Hooker, and myself. I had pulled out my Tandy PC and unfolded the screen, preparing to finish the chapter of *Ragnarok Night* I had been suffering over for the past week, but somehow a bull session got started and I didn't get more than a line written. A few minutes later Virgin Bruce, who was getting over his apoplexy from watching his team lose, came back to the table and sat down in a vacant chair.

Somehow—and don't ask me how; you know the way bull sessions tend to go—the subject drifted to home towns. I remember Mike Webb telling a long story about his juvenile delinquency down South, and Chang telling some anecdotal tale about a Chinese restaurant in Boston's Chinatown which used to serve up cat as an entree, which didn't amuse Joni, who was stroking Asimov in her lap. Everyone seemed to take turns in relating their favorite tall tales except for Popeye, who as usual was reticent about his past. We didn't push him on it; there was something dark and ugly in Hooker's past, and the beamjack was within his rights to be secretive about it. The unwritten rule and all that.

However, that didn't stop Joni from turning to Virgin Bruce, who was seated to her right, and saying, "Bruce, you grew up in St. Louis, didn't you?"

I could see Bruce shift uncomfortably in his seat. He was being put on the spot. Any guy who would have tried to pry something out of Neiman about his past probably would have been told to go to hell. However, Joni was the best-looking of the few women aboard Skycan, and Bruce had been pursuing her since anyone could remember. Lowenstein had always been cold to our resident ex-biker, calling him a greaseball and a motorhead and so forth, but now here was a rare circumstance—probably arising from the fact that they appeared to have at least one thing in common, both being Cards fans —in which she was actually addressing him in a civil tone. The only problem was that she was subtly asking him to talk about the one thing Bruce *never* talked about: what he had done before becoming a beamjack. She was breaking the rules, but how could Bruce cry foul, when it was his first, and perhaps only, chance to win some points with the object of his desire?

Virgin Bruce looked down at his hands and cleared his throat. "Yeah, I used to be from there," he said. "Outside of it, actually. Little town called Wentzville, right outside the county line."

"You were with a bike gang there, weren't you?" Joni prodded.

"Uh-huh," he replied slowly, and paused. "Satan's Exiles. I used to ride with Satan's Exiles."

Joni nodded. "I heard of them," she said. "I went to college at Washington University." She pointed at the tattoo on his left bicep, the dagger stuck through a heart, with the words "Virgin Bruce" written underneath. "Is that where you got the tattoo?"

"Uh-huh," he said without looking at her.

Joni leaned forward in her chair towards Bruce. "How did you get the name?" she asked teasingly. "Are you a virgin?"

Oh, my God, I thought. I glanced around the table and saw that everyone's eyes were as wide as mine. If there was ever a question which was guaranteed a punch in the mouth from Bruce, it was that one, as a few unsuspecting green crew members had learned in the past. "Lowenstein, you like to live dangerously, don't you?" I murmured. Someone had to warn the poor girl, after all.

To my surprise, Virgin Bruce shot me a dirty look. "Clam it, Sloane," he said in that calm but ever-so-deadly voice he used to intimidate people aboard Skycan. Then he smiled and looked back at Joni. "You want to find out for yourself, babe?" he replied in a soft, challenging tone.

Now I thought it was Joni who was going to punch *him* in the mouth. She turned beet red for a moment. But then she apparently decided to up the ante in this psychological poker game. She shook back her blond hair, leaned back in her chair, and lifted her long legs to place them across each other *in his lap.*

"Tell me about it, Brucie," she said. "Tell me your life story, and we'll see about that."

For a moment the beamjack and the communications officer stared at each other, while the rest of us tried to make up our minds whether to move our chairs closer or duck for cover under the table. To this day I still haven't decided if Joni Lowenstein really knew what she was doing, playing with fire like that. Maybe she was just bored like the rest of us and was looking for amusement. Or maybe she secretly had the hots for Bruce after all—as Tom Rush once said in a song, ladies love outlaws—and wanted Virgin Bruce to do something to prove himself to her.

Whatever her motivation was, it worked. Bruce clasped his hands together and rested them on Joni's ankles—she didn't move her legs —and began to talk about himself.

It wasn't his whole life story, of course; he skipped the Charles Dickens routine of starting with his childhood, and picked up the story with him being a helicopter pilot in Nicaragua, mainly flying as an ambulance pilot supporting the 514th Medical Company. He left the service with a Purple Heart and a couple of citations for bravery under fire, and went back to his home state of Missouri, no longer the green, innocent eighteen-year-old kid who had been drafted shortly after leaving high school.

He didn't say how he fell in with the Satan's Exiles except that he had been riding motorcycles all his life. "A lot of the guys in the outfit were vets also," he said, "and after getting back from Central America I wasn't ready to put on a suit and tie, go work for an insurance company, y'know, act like nothing had happened. I used to wake up nights, still flying in with rockets zinging all around the cockpit. I needed something more real than a desk and a home in the suburbs and ten kids, if you know what I mean."

By his account, the Exiles were relatively tame for a bike club. Although they had all the regalia and attitudes of a "one-percenter" group—their colors on the back of leather vests, the customized Harley Davidsons, the crazy women who hung around with them, and the disdain for helmet laws—they weren't in the hard-core class of the Outlaws or the Hell's Angels. "I mean, we weren't pseudo-bikers either, like the weekend bikers who had straight jobs Monday through Friday and wore Nazi helmets Saturday and Sunday," he said with a sneer, "but we weren't into the badass stuff that the big groups did."

Joni had to prod him some more before he finally told how he got his handle of Virgin Bruce. He seemed reluctant to let that loose. "It was during the initiation," he said at last. "One of the things we had to do was go out to this whorehouse which operated in Callaway County off I-70. There were lots of nice chicks there, y'know, and some of the boys who weren't hitched seriously to their old ladies would hit the place frequently. But there was this one fat old lady, the one who ran the place. Her name was Cecilia, and man, she had a face that could stop a clock. Never bathed either. She was bad news, man . . ."

"Let me guess," Popeye said. "You had to lay her, right?"

"Uh-huh. But with all the gang watching." Everyone laughed, and Bruce shook his head. "Oh, man, it was *bad,*" he said ruefully. "The boys would get you drunk and stoned downstairs first, with all these good-looking women with hardly any clothes on walking around acting like they were waiting for you, y'know, and the boys would be promising that all you had to do was satisfy this *one* woman, right? And then, when you were about ready to pass out, they'd march you upstairs to this little bedroom and open the door, and there *she* was, lying on a bed which looked like it was ready to break under her. 'There she is, Bruce!' they yelled. 'Go for it! She's all yours!' "

I laughed, and so did the rest of the guys sitting around the table, but I glanced over at Joni and noticed that she wasn't smiling. She gazed at Virgin Bruce with an expression that suggested she was not at all amused. However, she didn't remove her feet from his lap, and she didn't say what was on her mind at that moment. As if I couldn't guess. No one else seemed to notice, however. Least of all Bruce, who kept on with his story.

"So the whole gang, y'know, is standing around watching and drinking beer, and what can you do, man? I got nekkid and climbed on top and started to do my best, right? And I got to admit, she was pretty good, as long as I kept my eyes shut. . . ." That brought on more laughter, except from Joni, who at least smiled. "And there she was, stroking my ass and breathin' in my face, and I could tell what she had eaten for dinner that night. . . ." Laughter. "And then she . . . she . . ."

He stopped and took a deep breath. *"What?"* Chang howled. "Tell me, you sonuvabitch, or I'll break this goddamn chair over your head!"

Virgin Bruce looked down at the tabletop for a moment. "She said, 'Oh, Bruce!' " He turned his voice into a feminine, breathy snarl. " 'Ohhh, Bruce! You make me feel . . . like . . . like a *virgin* again!' "

It was then that we saw Popeye Hooker do something we had never seen before. We watched him crack up and lose it. Or at least I did; the rest of the guys, and Joni as well, were busy losing their own cools. Popeye split his so badly that he fell over backwards, keeled over in his chair, hitting the deck so hard that the wind got knocked out of him. "Virgin . . . virgin . . . virgin . . ." he gasped.

It took a few minutes for any of us to recover ourselves. "So, ah, the name stuck," Dave Chang said at last, wiping the tears from his eyes.

"Yeah, it did," Virgin Bruce said, red-faced. "That became my handle. The next day they took me to a tattoo parlor in St. Louis and had it put on my arm." He lifted his left bicep to show us. "And that's how I got in the gang."

"So how did you end up here?" Joni asked, once we had all quieted down again. "I mean, it sounds as if you were doing all right with the Satan's Exiles. What put you up here?"

Bruce gazed at the tabletop for a few silent moments, a frown on his face. We all realized that the funny stuff was over and if we wanted to hear any more, we had better stop laughing. We stifled our lingering giggles and sat quietly, waiting to see if Virgin Bruce would tell us the rest of the story. I figured out at once that if there was anything that he didn't care to expose, it wasn't a tall tale about a whore in the backwoods of Missouri, but something much deeper and not as amusing.

"This doesn't get beyond this room, okay?" he said at last, staring at each of us in turn. We nodded, and he let out a sigh and continued:

"I didn't get along so well with everyone in the gang. When I was initiated into the Exiles, the Treasurer was a guy everyone called the Fish, and don't ask me why, except that he sorta looked like one. The Fish and I didn't like each other from the word go—no real reason, I guess, just that we rubbed each other the wrong way—and he was the only one who voted against letting me in, but the majority ruled and I was let in. He still didn't like it, but he stayed outta my way and I stayed outta his.

"The Exiles weren't entirely clean. We all paid monthly dues, but most of the money we used for booze and gas and pot came from a kitty the Fish was responsible for, as Treasurer. He managed to keep it full by selling dope, dealing all sorts of shit to wholesale dealers in St. Louis. He'd skim off a percentage for himself, of course, and we all knew that and let it go, because it kept us in the money and the guys in the gang who did drugs had a constant, reliable source." He paused, and added, "Not me, though. I smoked a little weed, but I didn't have any use for coke or crank or any of the other heavy shit.

"About two months after I was initiated and started running with the Exiles, the Prez, whose name was Rodney and who everyone called Big Wad 'cause of—ah, never mind—got killed. He was coming back from a bar on the Landing in St. Louis one night on Route 40, probably drunk, and the semi he got in front of too fast wiped him off the road. Anyway, an emergency election was called under the club's constitution, and guess who got elected?"

"The Fish," I guessed.

Bruce gave me a shooting motion with his right hand. "Bingo. He had seniority, and he had lots of blow, which made the snowheads in the group happy, and so he got elected. And guess who was the only guy who voted against him? No, don't even bother to guess.

"I was surprised, though. I thought the first thing President Fish would do would be to kick me out of the gang. As the Prez, he had the autonomous privilege to do that, no vote necessary. But he didn't. In fact, he even started to chum up to me a little. I was edgy about his sudden friendliness, 'specially since I was the sole dissenting voice in his election, but after a few weeks I thought, well, what the fuck, maybe giving him some power has mellowed him out. So I stopped looking over my shoulder, y'know?"

Virgin Bruce stopped for a minute. He got up and walked to the refrigerator to get another can of fake brew, saying nothing until he had popped the lid and settled back in his chair. I could tell he was thinking over his words, and wondered again why he was telling us this story. Perhaps everyone has to lay down his or her particular burden sooner or later, because I had the sense he wasn't telling us this solely to impress Joni.

"Then, a few weeks after he got elected, Fish came up to me during a party at his place, with a couple of his closest cronies at his side," Bruce continued. "He comes up to me real casual and says,

Bruce, there's a job I need you to do. Yeah? I says, and he says, there's a shipment which is coming in for me from down South, which arrived yesterday in Illinois. It's a bunch of coke which is worth a few grand, and I need someone I can trust to go get it for me. I asked him why he couldn't go make the connection himself, and he told me that his bike was in the shop and that was why someone else had to make the run. So I said I would do it."

"You didn't question him?" Mike asked. "You just said, 'sure, I'll do it'? To someone you didn't like?"

Bruce glanced over at Webb with a condescending expression. "In this club, pal, if the Prez gave an order, there was no question about it. You did it. That was why he had his friends with him, to back him up and to act as witnesses in case I disobeyed an order from the Prez. Besides, like I said, I had stopped worrying about him. I really didn't think he was going to screw me.

"So the next day I got on my bike and headed for a little town just across the Mississippi called O'Fallon, about twenty-five miles from St. Louis. Out in the farmland sort of near Scott Air Force Base. I followed Fish's directions to a little broken-down place just off the I-64 ramp, where this skinny guy whose name I don't remember was waiting for me with the stuff." I wondered if Bruce really didn't recall the name of his connection, or if he was simply covering up that point. "He was nervous, but so was I, so I didn't think much of it. I handed him the roll of bills Fish had given me, and he gave me the stuff—two big plastic bags of white mindfuck, which I squeezed into a pair of saddlebags I had lashed over my rear wheel's mudguard. Fish had told me that he would take care of the testing when I got back but that this guy was usually dependable, so not to sweat it. He and I had a quick beer together, then I hopped on my bike and away I went, back down a short stretch of highway to the interstate."

Virgin Bruce rapped his knuckles on the table. "That, my friends, was when the shit hit the fan. I had barely hit the westbound lane of 64, doing the speed limit, when I looked in my mirror and saw an Illinois state trooper coming up behind me, coming off the exit I had just left. I barely had time to check my speed and start to sweat, when his lights came on and he started to speed up."

"A trap," I said.

Virgin Bruce nodded slowly. "A trap. The dealer in Illinois was being watched and I guess Fish knew it, and that was why he sent me. If I made it through, fine, he'd get his coke—and if anyone got popped, it would be me, not him. All that went through my brain as

I gunned the throttle and took off down the highway with that trooper right on me.

"I knew I was in big trouble. Doubtless the trooper would be radioing ahead for reinforcements, and if there weren't cops waiting on the Poplar Street Bridge into St. Louis, then there would be someone on the Illinois side, like in Centreville or East St. Louis. I thought, maybe if I can make it to East St. Louis, I'll be okay, because the area around the interstate and the river was a combat zone and even the cops didn't like to go in there because some nut might blow their car away with an Army surplus grenade launcher. If I can make it to East St. Louis, I figured, I'll be fine, they'll lose me in that ghetto."

He shook his head. "Then they started firing on me. I heard the shots, and looked in my mirror to see that they had opened the sun window and one of the cops was braced in it and trying to line me up in his gun sight. I started to zigzag but there wasn't any traffic to duck behind. It was in the middle of the afternoon and no one else was on the road.

"So I said to myself, Bruce, you're in trouble. You're holding enough dope to send you to jail for life, the exits ahead are probably blocked, and the cop on your tail has opened fire on your ass, so you'd better take radical measures *real quick.* I don't really recall how I made up my mind, y'know. I guess it was just reflex.

"I twisted the bar to the left, gunned the gas, and went *right across the median!* Right across the left side of the road, in front of a truck, getting on the far shoulder. An overpass came up and I saw, in a second, what I *knew* I was looking for, a break in the wire fence along the road, near the top of the overpass. I *gunned* that mother and went off the road, *into* the weeds, *up* the embankment, and hit the hole in the fence doing maybe thirty-five.

"I hit the fence hard, man, scraped the side of it with my bike, and my Harley laid down on the road on top of the overpass. Scraped the shit out of my leg, but I got up, got on the bike and tore the hell out of there. Didn't even look back to see what the cop was doing, just got the fuck out of there. I saw a little dirt road come up and I took off down it, kept right on going till I stopped about fifteen miles away and looked to see if anyone was still behind me."

Virgin Bruce took a deep breath. "Well, I'd lost the cops, but that wasn't the only thing I had lost. The saddlebags. I'd lost them too. They had torn loose when I laid the bike down, I guess. They were gone, with the coke in them, but I wasn't about to go back and look for them because I knew the area would be crawling with cops by now. I'd gotten out of there with my skin, but a couple thousand dollars in cocaine was the price I'd paid for my escape."

"I guess the gang wasn't happy about that," Joni said.

"Yeah, but how could they blame you?" Chang threw in. "You were only trying to get away from the cops, so . . ."

Virgin Bruce shook his head. "They did blame me, thanks to the Fish. I can't prove it, but I think I know what happened. The Fish set me up for the bust. If I got busted, he knew that I wouldn't rat on the rest of the gang."

"But it wasn't *your* coke!" Joni said. "You just said you didn't even use the stuff! Why wouldn't you have . . . ?"

Then she stopped. Like the rest of us, she knew how seriously Virgin Bruce took being loyal to his "gang," whether they were bikers or beamjacks. We had all seen how he had risked his own life, not to mention the ire of Cap'n Wallace and Hank Luton, to attempt to rescue Webb and Honeyman when the hotdog on Vulcan had blown out. Fish had picked his mule well. If Virgin Bruce had been busted by the Illinois state troopers, bamboo shoots under his fingernails or the rubber hose treatment wouldn't have forced him into betraying his friends. Some might call it criminal. I called it being damned brave.

"I had on a wristphone so I called the clubhouse," Virgin Bruce continued. "As my luck would have it, Fish picked up the phone. There must have been others in the room, because even as I told him what had happened, he began to threaten me, saying that he knew I had stolen the junk and that if I didn't get it back to him in five hours, the gang would kill me. I have no doubt that he told the others that I had split with the coke. I didn't even bother to argue. I just clicked off. That was the last I ever heard from them.

"I had gotten a job as a welder at the Big Mac plant in St. Louis by then—that's McDonnell Douglas, the big aerospace contractor— and I headed there because I had some clothes and a few extra bucks stashed in my locker at the plant. My first intention was to grab the stuff and get out of town, not even return to my apartment 'cause the boys might be waiting for me there. While I was getting my junk, I spotted a poster on the bulletin board. Said 'Career Opportunities On The High Frontier,' showed a picture of Olympus. Skycorp was hiring out of Big Mac then.

"As luck would have it, one of the supervisors in the Space Division at the plant and I were on pretty good terms since I had fixed his bike the week before. I immediately went to him and told him that I wanted a job in space *now,* that I was sick of Missouri and the sooner I could go to work for Skycorp, the better. He made a call to Alabama while I was in his office and found that they were just about to interview and start training another bunch of beamjacks for work on the station, and that they'd be glad to take on a Big Mac employee at the last minute provided that he had the right recommendations. Chuck put in a good word for me on the phone right there, and twenty minutes later I was hauling ass out of the parking lot, heading to Huntsville. I had the clothes on my back, a couple of hundred dollars in my pocket, my bike, and nothing else but a gut full of fear."

We were all quiet for a moment. "Why here, man?" Webb asked at last. "What made you decide on Skycan? I mean, there's other places you could have hid out, so why did you . . . ?"

"Why did I pick this place?" Virgin Bruce crumpled his empty beer can in his fist. "Mike, I have this nightmare, pal. I'm in a cheesy little hotel room somewhere—doesn't matter where, in Mexico or Canada, someplace you've never heard of—and I hear a knock on the door. I get up to answer it, and when I open the door, the Exiles are standing there, with Fish in front of them. They all smile and say hello . . . and then they come in and kill me. That vision came to me when I last talked to Fish. I knew at that moment there was no place on Earth that was safe for me. So when I saw that poster in the locker room, I knew the only way out was to get off the planet."

There wasn't much any of us could say after that. Bruce looked at the cat, who was still playing on the table, and the rest of us looked at Bruce. It had taken a lot for him to break the traditional silence, but I suppose the time comes when even a marked man has to unload his guilt. I noticed that Joni had a little Mona Lisa-like smile on her face when she looked at him. That was maybe the first indication anyone had that our space station's resident ice-goddess was falling for a scruffy, crude greaseball like Virgin Bruce. Opposites attract, so they say.

I was so fascinated with watching Joni's eyes on Virgin Bruce that I didn't notice someone climbing down the ladder from the catwalk, so I jumped a little when Jack Hamilton put his hand on my shoulder and said, "Hi, Sam, what's going on?"

Everyone laughed a little at my reaction. I ignored them and looked up at the hydroponicist. Hamilton had been on the station for several weeks by then, and as with everyone living in reduced or zero g he had gone through some of the usual changes: his face widening a little, gaining a couple of inches in height as reduced gravity caused his spine to stretch. Like a lot of crewmen, he had cut the sleeves off his uniform shirt and begun wearing shorts. He now wore a baseball cap on his head, stenciled with the words "Fat Boy's." There was only one place where you could find a cap like that: Fat Boy's Barbecue on Route A1A in Cocoa Beach, Florida, a favorite sandwich-and-suds joint for astronauts since the days of Shepard, Glenn, and Grissom. There had been a rumor circulating that Hamilton had some kind of thing going with a female shuttle pilot who made regular runs to Freedom Station, so that might have been how Hamilton got the cap. I hadn't seen him wearing it in the station up until that point. Maybe she had sent it to him.

Hamilton said, "Hey, you wanna come over to Forty-Two with me? I want you to take a look at something." Then he casually brushed his right index finger against his nose. It was a move that he had copped from that old Newman-Redford movie, *The Sting,* when the good-guy crooks would signal to each other that the game was afoot. Hamilton had adapted it for his own purposes. When he did that, he meant: *hey, you wanna go smoke some pot?*

By this time, I had come to enjoy a smoking session in the Hydroponics bay two or three times a week. I kept from smiling, and raised my hand to casually brush my nose with my fingertip, when I saw that Hamilton wasn't looking in my direction. I glanced that way, toward the other crewmen sitting around the table.

Mike, Joni, Chang, and Virgin Bruce . . . all had their index fingers raised and each was halfway through the motion of casually brushing off the tip of his or her nose. They all stopped and stared at each other in bewilderment, then each in turn stared back at Jack Hamilton, everyone having the same thought as I had initially held: *Hey, I thought this was between you and me only, Jack.* Hamilton himself was having a wonderful time, watching the silly looks on our faces as comprehension dawned on us. He had corrupted all of us. Virgin Bruce wasn't the only outlaw in the room.

In the midst of that timeless moment, Popeye Hooker quietly rose from his seat and walked toward the ladder. Nobody seemed to notice that he was leaving, except for Jack and me. As the others broke up laughing—at themselves, not at Popeye—Jack and I traded a look. We both knew we had done something wrong. Of all the people on Skycan, Popeye was the last one who needed to be alienated from the bunch. He had recognized that an in-joke was being passed, and he wasn't in on it, so that brief instance in which he had forgotten his own past and enjoyed a few minutes of friendship, of sitting around a table trading tall tales, had been ruined. Virgin Bruce could talk about his sins, but Popeye had something under his skin that prevented him from discussing his own sorrows. We had to face it: We had just kicked a cripple's crutch out from under him.

Jack watched Hooker climb up the ladder out of the rec room, and I could tell that he wasn't about to let his mistake slide. Jack was going to pull Popeye into the gang. Hamilton was that kind of a guy.

# 19

# Hearing Aid

If anything, it was even hotter in French Guiana than it was in Huntsville, which did nothing to improve Clayton Dobbs' disposition. The space engineer had to admit to himself that he was bred for cool, air-conditioned environments. If he had sweltered in the Alabama summer heat, then the tropical climate of this godforsaken South American country made him feel like he was standing in a blast furnace.

Once more, Dobbs wiped a sheen of sweat off his forehead as he again glanced over his shoulder at the Guiana Space Centre's launch preparation and control center three miles away. From that distance he could only clearly make out the Vehicle Assembly Building, the new structure which had recently replaced Arianespace's original VAB built in the 1980's. Not only had the Europeans lifted the design of the building from NASA's identical structure on Merritt Island, but they had also blithely swiped the name. At one time that had bothered Dobbs, even though he harbored no great love for NASA. Now it didn't matter; their VAB marked the location of the launch control center, the nearest accessible place that was air-conditioned. Jesus Christ, it was *hot!*

"Kenneth," he said, still looking at the VAB through shimmering waves of heat rising from the long pavement leading from there to the launch pad. Not hearing a reply, he turned back around and said, more loudly, *"Kenneth!"*

Kenneth Crespin was still talking to the German launch technician, both of them carrying on a casual conversation in the technician's mother tongue. Crespin irritably waved off Dobbs; the German glanced over his shoulder at him. "Clayton," he said, "you know the rules concerning the launch pad personnel. Please, put on again your helmet."

Dobbs looked down at the white plastic hard-hat dangling by its adjustment strap from his hand. He had taken it off because it was too warm. He glowered at the German, whom he had privately nicknamed Von Schmuck, and clapped the hat back on his head. Crespin was still staring at him. "And it would appear a little more couth if you would tuck in your shirttails and adjust your tie," the vice-president added sourly.

"Damn it, who cares," Dobbs muttered under his breath. He turned around and angrily shoved the bottom of his Brooks Brothers shirt into the front of his trousers, but ignored his tie. It was too hot for closing one's collar. Turning around again, he found some pleasure in noticing the spreading sweat stains under Crespin's arms and on his back. You're not cool either, are you, Kenny?

Dobbs checked his watch. Less than an hour to launch, thank God, so at least they would soon be returning to the launch center. Once again, he studied the giant Ariane 5 HLV poised beside its umbilical mast. Cold steam rolled off the flanks of its cryogenic liquid booster, streaming down past the two strap-on boosters on its sides. The catwalk leading to the Hermes spaceplane was still in place; inside the whiteroom fitted over the trim little spacecraft, technicians were doubtlessly still getting the two-man flight crew ready for launch. The servicing tower had been moved back on its tracks five hours earlier, and only a skeleton crew of workmen still roamed around the mobile launch platform and the mast. Like the Americans and the Russians, the Europeans had long ago conquered the necessity of multiple holds and some of the old uncertainties of whether or not the birds would get off the ground, but he had to hand it to Arianespace: The efficiency of their launch operations made Skycorp look sloppy.

Dobbs found himself looking at the servicing tower. Several hours earlier, in the dark hours before sunrise, he had been in that tower, crouched on a platform pressed against the Hermes' open cargo bay as he went through the last-minute inspection of the spaceplane's cargo. Only a couple of technicians had been with him then; one from Skycorp, the other from the European Space Agency, both with security clearances of the highest order. With the necessary exception of the French flight crew, only a handful involved with this routine launch from Kourou knew exactly what was being ferried to orbit in the Hermes. Just before the cargo bay hatches had been closed and sealed, Dobbs had reached out with his plastic-gloved right hand and had gently stroked the module's side, bidding it goodbye.

Or rather, he reminded himself savagely, *hasta luego* rather than *adios.* In only a matter of weeks he would be reunited with his creation, on the Freedom space station out in space. Absently he kicked at the cinders under his feet, a cold clutch of fear in his gut temporarily—but not completely—offsetting the heat. Out in space. Shit, he thought. I'm an engineer. I live in front of a CAD/CAM terminal. What the hell am I doing going up into outer space?

A whistle sounded over the loudspeakers surrounding the launch site and a voice said a few words in French, which Dobbs didn't understand, but he noted a subtle increase in activity around the tower. It was time to vacate the pad. Crespin and the German began striding toward the van parked nearby, where several workmen were already gathered. One of them had produced a bottle of Dom Perignon from the cooler Dobbs had glimpsed in the van's rearmost seat earlier and was untwisting the wire cage which held down the cork; the others were waiting around expectantly with paper cups in hand.

"Oh, for God's sake, now the launch crew is going to get pickled," Dobbs murmured in Crespin's ear.

"No, they're going to drink a toast," Crespin replied, giving Dobbs an annoyed glance. "It's a long-standing tradition. If it gets their rockets launched on time to celebrate each launch as a victory, then who are we to complain?"

"Oh, no, we can't complain at all!" Dobbs said aloud. Several of the technicians looked up as the bottle was passed around. "It's only that it's our five billion-dollar module that's riding on this!"

One of the technicians stepped back from the bunch, sloshing a little champagne from his Dixie cup. "If you don't like it," he said with a smile, in thickly accented English, "get a horse!"

"Clay," Crespin said, no longer dropping his voice, "please remember who taught NASA a few things about getting rockets off the ground. If you've never seen anything like this at the Cape, just stop and ask yourself why."

The technicians all stepped back from each other, raised their cups of champagne—first to each other, then to the Ariane 5—and said, *"Santé."* Dobbs watched them, then after casting a baleful glance at Crespin, marched over to the technicians. He took the bottle from their hands and raised it toward the spacecraft, which smoked and wheezed on its railed launch platform. *"Santé,"* he said, then added, *"Vaya con Dios."* When the French and Germans looked at him in confusion, he solemnly affixed, "Rise, you bastard." The technicians laughed, Dobbs and Crespin traded mutually hostile looks, and they drank. Dobbs felt less overheated after that.

*"Neuf . . . huit . . . sept . . . six . . . cinq . . ."*

Dark black smoke tinted with the colors of the rising South American sun billowed from the base of the rocket; the image was transmitted onto the massive screen, with the colorful, digitally reproduced surreality of a high-tech dream. Dobbs never got used to the sight; he felt a lump in his throat.

*"Quatre . . . trois . . . deux . . . un . . ."*

The four main engines and the two strap-on boosters fired at once, creating an orchestrated blast of light and thunder which caused him to wince and—imagined or real, he couldn't tell—the floor beneath his feet to tremble. *"Lancez,"* the Launch Control Supervisor intoned, almost unnecessarily, as the Ariane 5 broke loose from its launch platform and sprinted toward the deep blue sky.

The roar of the liftoff was carried into the launch center over the PA system, although dampened by the hand of a mindful technician who made sure it didn't drown out the overlapping conversations in the room. On the giant TV screen overhead, the camera was tilted back to scan the rocket as it beelined toward space; already it was becoming not much more than a hexagonal dot surrounded by a white-hot corona at the head of a billowing contrail. In the observation booth, Dobbs could see the launch technicians as they huddled over their control stations, peering carefully at the readouts on dials and computer screens. By any standard, it was a good launch. European efficiency, he thought. Good old German rocketry know-how. Oberth and Von Braun and the rest of the original Peenemunde scientists began the tradition years ago, and their descendants—in spirit, if not by bloodline—carry it on today. He found himself grinning. By Volkswagen to the stars, he thought.

A hand clapped his shoulder suddenly. "Well, Clay," Kenneth Crespin said. "It looks like your 'J. Edgar Hoover' satellite is on its way at last, eh?"

Dobbs at once soured. Jerk. "Spare me," he replied. "I'm only enjoying the launch."

Crespin shrugged. "I would think that after having watched a couple of hundred launches you'd be bored with one more."

Dobbs looked over his shoulder at Crespin. "Ken, only an idiot takes these things for granted. Ever since the *Challenger* accident, no one in the space business can afford to take a successful launch with men aboard as something which just comes naturally."

Crespin snorted. "Son, you were born two years after that happened. I think you're a little too young to have any lasting memories of that, don't you think?"

"Didn't Santayana say something about ignoring the lessons of history?" Dobbs replied.

"*Touché.* I hope this doesn't mean you're going to back out of your own trip up in a few weeks."

Dobbs said nothing, but stood up and stretched. Glancing at the imaging screen on the wall overhead, he saw that the Ariane had jettisoned its strap-on boosters and had gone transsonic over the Atlantic just above the equator. The digital countdown clock was counting down the seconds to first-stage separation. "I'd love to," he said. "Would you mind writing them a note and telling them that I'm too sick to come out and play?"

"Yes."

"I kind of thought so. See if I'll do anything nice for you again."

"You know the reasons. We need to have the best person available up there to give this thing its final systems check and bring it on line. Obviously, the principal designer is that person, when he's available." Crespin shook his head as he stood up and put his hands on the back of his chair, leaning on them. "I don't see what you're so frightened about," he said. "Space travel was relatively safe even before the *Challenger*. It's become radically safer since then. There's hundreds of people living in space today because of the advances made in space engineering. Hell, it's *your* profession, *you* of all people should know that."

Dobbs didn't reply. The first stage had separated, and the countdown clock was recycling for the second-stage burnout and jettison. Judging from the calm on the launch-center floor, all was going just as planned. "It's not a matter of fear," he said firmly.

"Then what is it?"

"I just don't want to be the one who turns the key and starts this thing up. Perhaps you find that paradoxical coming from the person who designed Big Ear, but I'd just as soon let someone else do the dirty work." He managed a quick smile. "I'd rather be at my workbench, figuring out an electronic countermeasure to the Ear. I'm sure that once the system's existence becomes public, some bright person will design . . ." He stopped, and laughed. "An Ear plug," he added.

Dobbs looked at Crespin and noticed the frown on the older man's face. "Don't worry, Ken. I'm not about to call the *Times* or the *Washington Post* to leak the story. If there's going to be a security risk anywhere, it won't be me. I'm not going to risk a prison term only for the sake of soothing a guilty conscience."

"I should certainly hope not," Crespin said stiffly.

"Not that it will matter who does it." Dobbs started to walk away slowly. "I'm just in it for the love of building the thing. It'll work fine, and when it does, when the day comes that someone *does* call a reporter to tell him what the government and Skycorp have done to civil rights in the name of peace, you'll be able to know just who it was and where they called from."

He paused just before he left the room. "Who knows? Maybe it'll be your phone number the NSA will catch." He gave Crespin a wink and walked out.

# 20

# Popeye Goes to Heaven

*He had recognized the fat man as soon as he had walked into the filthy apartment in which he lived: Rocky, who wrestled with nurse sharks to impress tourists. But Rocky didn't look like the type of guy who would make a fool out of himself dancing on top of the bar at Mikey's Place. Sitting on the couch in the room, with Venetian blinds pulled down against the early afternoon sun, his hands resting not too far away from the place on the polished coffee table where a Smith & Wesson .45 automatic lay, he smiled in a way which probably signaled genuine amusement for himself, but which probably would have made Hooker afraid—if Hooker had not been too pissed off to feel fear in anything but an abstract, unrealized way.*

*"That's an unexpected question," Rocky said. "I thought you had come here to do business with me, not to ask me about a chick I may or may not have ever met. I thought you had something else on your mind when I let you into the house."*

*"Maybe I do," Hooker replied evenly. "But I want you to answer my question first. Has she been here?"*

Popeye absently tapped the edge of the mattress with his fingertips. His bunk was dark, the curtain closed, the only light coming from the little computer screen near his feet and the green-tinted readouts which constantly flashed and changed on it.

*Rocky stared at him silently for a moment, then leaned forward on the couch, fixing him with his dark, menacing eyes. "I want you to listen to me," he said in a low voice. "It doesn't matter whether your ex has been here to see me or not. What I do here, who I see, and with whom I do business . . . whatever that business may be . . . is none of your concern. Their right to privacy is mine, too, so I don't appreciate your questions. I don't care who told you about me, but if you don't want to do business on my terms, then get the hell out of here right now and don't let me see you again."*

*Hooker knew that the tall, thin kid who had answered the door and let him in was standing directly behind him. He knew that it would only take a word from Rocky—maybe not even that, just a flutter of his languid eyelids—for the kid to pounce on him, to dislocate his shoulder or slug him unconscious, or maybe even use the folding knife he carried on a strap on his belt. The kid was skinny, but there was something in the way he carried himself that made Hooker realize that he was a born, efficient, remorseless killer.*

*"Then I'll do business your way," he said, "and then we'll do it mine."*

*Rocky blinked. "How's that?"*

*"I'll buy what you have to sell," he said. To show he meant it, he pulled his wallet out of his back pocket and showed the fat man the money stuffed inside. "Then you tell me what you know."*

Suddenly the bunk's curtain was yanked aside. He had just enough time to squint and blink at the glare of the overhead lights and raise his hands halfway to his face, when a bunch of people he could only barely make out shouted, *"Happy Birthday!"* and a dark blue blanket from another bunk was thrown over his head and shoulders.

Popeye instinctively grabbed at the blanket and tried to throw it off, but strong hands thrust into his bunk to hold down the blanket, pinning his arms to his side. He kicked his legs as the hands pulled him out of his bunk. He fell to the floor of the bunkhouse in a heap, and for a moment he had a chance at freedom as the hands disengaged from his arms. But as he tried to struggle out of the blanket, several people swiftly pulled his arms back to his sides and kept the blanket yanked taut over his head.

Someone knelt on his chest, pinning him to the floor. The voices around him were raucous; everyone was laughing, and a disjointed chorus of "Happy Birthday" began to swell. "Son of a bitch, get this thing off me!" Popeye yelled, and more people began to laugh.

"Hold him down, hold him down!" he heard a voice—Virgin Bruce's—shout. Apparently it was Bruce who was kneeling on his chest. "Gimme the rope!" Popeye panicked, began to fight, flailing his arms and legs, but there were too many of them. He felt a length of nylon rope pass around his ankles and tighten as unseen hands bound his ankles. The hands holding his arms strengthened their grip as the rope was passed around and under him, binding his arms and holding the blanket over the upper part of his body. "Hogtie the bastard!" someone yelled. "Throw him out of the goddamn airlock!"

The only light he could see was through the fabric of the blanket; vague, shadowed forms passed between him and the overhead lights on the module's ceiling. Now he couldn't move at all; his arms were lashed to his sides, his ankles were bound together, and Virgin Bruce was sitting on his chest. "Airlock! Airlock!" a voice he recognized as Mike Webb's began to chant. Others in the compartment—he estimated at least half a dozen—picked it up: *"Airlock! Airlock! Airlock! Airlock!"*

The hands which had grabbed him from his bunk hoisted him off the deck and began to carry him. As they began to carefully push him up the ladder, he said, "You get this thing off me, damn it." He knew it wasn't worth the effort to raise his voice, and everyone laughed anyway and did nothing, so he didn't bother even to struggle anymore. Someone grabbed him underneath his armpits and raised him the rest of the way out of the well, laying him on the cool metal surface of the catwalk floor. Several pairs of feet in sneakers padded up the ladder behind him, and a moment later he was hoisted again and was carried down the length of the catwalk, two men carrying his torso, one carrying his legs.

"Shhh!" someone whispered through the blanket near his face. "Don't make a sound, or we'll make it worse!"

"Wouldn't dream of it," Popeye murmured, and heard a few of them laugh. They're going to throw me out the airlock, Popeye thought. How the hell can you make it worse than that? He knew that they weren't serious.

The gang who had kidnapped him—Virgin Bruce, Webb, and a couple of others whose voices he recognized—had obviously thought their scheme through well. It was between work-shift changes, so the catwalk and the access shafts to the station's hub were abandoned. A pulley had been jury-rigged in the access shaft so that his bound body could be raised with relative ease. Once they got him to the central shaft at Skycan's core, of course, they didn't need to carry him, only push him along the way. However, by the time they got Popeye to that point and began to propel him through zero g toward the Docks, the beamjack began to seriously suspect that his abductors might actually be intending to throw him out the airlock.

He shouted, *"Help!"* and a hand was jammed over his mouth, through the blanket. "Shut up, for Christ's sake!" he heard Virgin Bruce hiss angrily. "You want someone to hear you?"

"If you're going to throw me out the airlock, hell yeah!"

He didn't hear anything for a moment. "Look, Popeye," Virgin Bruce said. "It's . . . we're not going to throw you out the airlock. You're going out all right, but we're not throwing you out. Today's your birthday, okay? So we're giving you a birthday present. It's nothing worse than that."

"Then get this blanket off my head," Popeye said.

"But then you wouldn't get the surprise," Webb said.

"I don't want a surprise," Popeye snapped. "I don't . . . I don't want something for my birthday. I didn't want this. I just want to be left alone in my bunk, for chrissakes, so . . ."

"Popeye, man," Bruce said softly, "we leave you alone in your bunk all the time. We give you all the time you want to sit by yourself and mope. We like you, man. It's your birthday, okay? Let us get you out of your bunk for once, do something different for you. If you don't want that . . . well, then the hell with you, go back to your goddamn bunk."

Popeye thought about it for a moment. No, he really didn't even think about it; he only weighed the choice, between lying alone in his bunk again, confronting his memories again, or . . .

"What's the surprise?" he asked.

Virgin Bruce and Webb chuckled, and recommenced pushing him toward the Docks.

He heard the hatch open and David Chang say, "Hey, it's the birthday boy! Number four, gentlemen, she's all yours. He's here."

"Is everything set?" Webb asked. Popeye felt his feet bump against the side of the hatch as he was pushed through the prep compartment, and heard the sigh of the airtight hatch into the Docks easing open.

"You're all set. Signed out and cleared. And remember our deal," Chang added, as Popeye was eased into the chill environment of the airlock compartment, "if any shit comes down, you forged my name on that form. *Comprende?*"

"We copy," Bruce replied. "Where's Bobby?"

"I told him he was sick and told him to go lie down for a while." Laughter. "He said he was feeling fine, but I told him he was looking pale and that he shouldn't worry, he should just take a couple of aspirin and rest and he would feel better. I wonder sometimes what that boy uses for brains, man."

"Damn if I know. Good deal. Close the hatch behind me, willya?"

"Okay. Have a good trip."

Popeye heard the hatch slam shut behind them and lock shut, then Bruce turned his body around so that his feet were leading first. A moment later he felt the soles of his feet bump against an open airlock hatch, and realized that he was being pushed into a spacecraft. He also realized that he didn't hear Mike Webb anymore.

Someone in the spacecraft reached forward and grabbed his ankles, pulling him inside. He felt Virgin Bruce climbing in after him and heard him shutting the hatch. Whatever kind of craft he had just boarded, it was small; he could feel three bodies, his included, jammed closely together.

Hands began to untie the ropes, and suddenly the blanket was pulled off. It was dimly lit, so his eyes didn't have to adjust. Jack Hamilton was bending over him, a wide grin spread across his face. "Welcome aboard, matey," he said. "Arf, arf, arf!"

He realized then that he was inside the construction pod which was kept at Olympus for use on inspection and repair missions for the station. Virgin Bruce was buckling himself into the pilot's seat, lashing the carry-strap of Doc Felapolous' cassette deck to a hand rung. Through the canopy, Popeye could see space. "Find some place to scrunch into behind me," Bruce said as he adjusted his headset. "We'll be taking off once I get clearance."

Hamilton and Hooker eased themselves into crouching positions behind Bruce; they were so close together that their shoulders were squashed against each other's and their knees were jammed against the back of Bruce's seat. Virgin Bruce flipped a few switches, and lights went up on the control boards surrounding him as the spacecraft powered up, giving the inside of the craft a warm, Christmas-like feeling. Bruce unsnapped a small clipboard from below the canopy windows and began running down the preflight checklist, pressing buttons every few minutes. "I've never carried passengers before," he murmured to them, "so you'll have to be careful where you move your arms and legs, okay?"

"What are we doing?" Popeye asked.

"Going for a little ride," Hamilton said breezily. "It's Sunday. Didn't you ever go for a ride in the park on Sunday? We're going for a little Sunday drive."

"Why?"

"Because it's also your birthday. We wanted to do something a little special for you."

Hooker shrugged as best as he could. "I go on EVA almost every day of the week. What's so special about this?"

"This is different. You'll see."

"Why is it different?"

"You'll see." Hamilton gave him a smile. "Trust me. You'll love it to death."

"Okay, you guys, pipe down," Virgin Bruce said. "I've got to call in." He adjusted the headset mike in front of his face and touched a

switch. "Olympus Traffic, this is Pod Beta House Olympus, request-
ing permission to undock and to proceed to coordinates X-ray incon-
stant, Yankee three, Zulu three, do you copy over?"

There was a pause. "I'm on a maintenance check, Traffic Control,
cleared by Chang. Please check your log." He snapped off the radio
for a moment and looked over his shoulder at them. "Anderson is
such a shithead," he sneered, before snapping the radio on again.
After a second he said, with sarcastic politeness, *"Thank* you, Traffic
Control. Beta House Olympus out."

He flipped off the radio, muttering, "Only good for taking up
space on the food chain. Okay, hang on." He grasped the control
stick and throttle and pulled them both back a little, and there was
the tactile *thump* of the pod uncoupling from the station. Through
the canopy Popeye saw the stars move slightly; it was the only indication that the pod was moving away from the space station. Bruce
worked the controls, and the pod tilted as the RCR's fired. Suddenly,
they were looking at Olympus Station from a north polar perspective, a giant wheel from which they were gradually backing away.
Over Virgin Bruce's shoulder, Popeye could see a nearly identical
graphic display of the station on the blue LCD screen.

"Oh, hell," Hamilton murmured. Popeye glanced at him and saw
that the hydroponics engineer had his eyes tightly closed.

"You okay, Jack?" Bruce murmured, not taking his eyes from the
controls. "I've got a bag in here if you want it. I think."

"I'm fine. Just have to get myself reoriented. Don't do anything
too radical, that's all." Hamilton slowly opened his eyes, blinked a
few times, and took a deep breath. "I'm okay. Going from sideways
to vertical just throws me, that's all."

He grinned and unsealed a hip pocket on the shorts he was wearing. He pulled out a plastic bag filled with brown squares: brownies.
He opened the bag and pulled out a brownie, then from another
pocket he produced a single pink wax candle. He stuck the candle
into the brownie's frosting and handed it to Popeye. "Sorry we can't
light it," he said, "but Bruce says that even if we didn't have an
oxygen atmosphere in here, it would be too dangerous to have flame
and smoke inside something this small."

"Fuckin' A, buddy," Virgin Bruce agreed. He had eased the controls into a neutral position, and was tapping instructions on the
navaids computer's keypad. Glancing through the canopy, Popeye
could see that they were now off-center from Olympus Station's axis,
moving slowly toward the rim, although keeping the same distance.
Bruce glanced over his shoulder at Popeye. "Just put her on auto-

matic, man," he explained. "Polar orbit. We're just going to glide along here and have us a little birthday party. Yo, Jackie! Gimme one of those *fine* brownies. And let's hear some music."

He reached up and punched the playback button on the tape recorder. The Grateful Dead's lilting rock poured out, and Jerry Garcia's voice sang:

> "A lotta poor man make a five-dollar bill,
> "Keep him happy all the time.
> "Some other fellow's making nothing at all,
> "And you can hear him cryin' . . .
> "Can I go, buddy, can I go down,
> "Take your shift at the mine?"

Virgin Bruce's hands gently slapped his thighs in time with the music. "They don't make music like that no more." He accepted a brownie that Hamilton handed to him, and hoisted it toward Popeye in a salute. "Happy birthday, Popeye the Sailor Man."

Without realizing it, Popeye found himself smiling. He waved his brownie at Bruce, then gently pulled the candle off and let it drift in the air in front of him while he bit into the soft square. A few crumbs broke off and danced in front of his face, and his mouth was filled with the taste of chocolate. He let his eyes close in satisfaction. Real chocolate; not like the watered-down, antiseptic chocolate pudding that was served on the mess deck, but the real McCoy. However, there was an odd crunchy texture to this brownie, and a funny, aromatic taste to it. He ignored it. It was hard to find a good brownie in outer space.

Hamilton was munching on a brownie of his own, a small nebula of brown crumbs dancing in front of his face. "Got one of the cooks on the mess deck to whip these up," he said, and added, "Secret family recipe." He winked at Virgin Bruce, and Bruce winked back. Popeye decided to ignore that, too.

"How did you guys know it was my birthday?" he asked.

"Oh, I just happened to ask Doc Felapolous if anyone's birthday was coming up soon," Hamilton replied. "He looked up his records and, lo and behold, it was yours which was coming up. The guys decided that, y'know, you're a nice guy and you're quiet all the time, so it was high time someone did something nice for you. So here we are."

"So here we are." Popeye shrugged and polished off his brownie. "I appreciate it. Thanks." Without his asking, Hamilton pulled another brownie out of the bag and put it in his hands. "Good brownies," Popeye said, and took a bite out of it. "Been a while since I've had anything this good."

"Glad you like 'em," Hamilton said. "Hey, can I ask you a personal question?"

Hooker hesitated. "Yeah. Sure. What's your question, Jack?" he said through a mouthful of crunchy, weird-tasting chocolate.

"Maybe it's none of my business, but why are you so quiet? I mean, what is it that you have on your mind?"

*"I'm not sure if I should be telling you this, Hook," Whitey said, hunched over a beer at the table in Mikey's. "I got a family, right? I try to keep my nose clean, but you hear things, y'know? But I try to stay away from that stuff. You understand."*

*"No, I don't understand," Hooker said angrily. "Laura took off this morning with a couple of hundred bucks that belonged to me. Okay, so you tell me that you know where she might be and what she's doing with it, but you also say you don't want to tell me about it because you want to keep your nose clean. I mean, why the hell haven't you told me anything before?"*

*Whitey clasped his fists together on the tabletop. "C'mon, Hooker," he mumbled, "don't put that shit on me. I didn't know she'd use your money." He looked over his shoulder. The bar was almost vacant; only Kurt the bartender was in there, reloading the cooler with a case of beer. Late morning sunlight streamed through the windows. "Remember that guy who was dancing on the bar last night? The guy from Louisiana, the shark-fishing guide? Rocky, Fat Rocky?"*

*"Yeah, I remember the feep. What about him?"*

*"He doesn't just guide. I hear he's a drug dealer." Whitey lowered his voice. "He sells the stuff from a place out near the beach. Someone told me that Laura's one of his regular customers. You know what I mean?"*

*"I know what you mean. You're a real asshole for not telling me. Don't say anything," he added coldly. "Just tell me where he lives."*

"I don't have anything on my mind. I just like to be by myself. What's wrong with that?"

"Not a thing. Unless it starts to get to you." Hamilton gobbled down the rest of his brownie. "It's like cabin fever. I once heard a story about a trapper who lived alone in a cabin up in Alaska. As the story goes, the guy would only come down out of the cabin once or twice a year, to this little town to buy a truckful of groceries and supplies, then head back to his cabin. He had a radio, but rarely did anyone ever hear from him. Nobody even seemed to know his name.

Well, a winter passed and no one saw this guy, so a state trooper or a friend or somebody went up into the mountains to try to find him. He found the cabin, and . . ."

"He found the guy hanging from a rope from the rafters," interjected Virgin Bruce. "Yeah, yeah, yeah."

*A flash of gold disappearing . . . gone . . . gone, forever gone . . .*

Hamilton looked at Virgin Bruce balefully. "No. The trooper, or whoever he was, found the guy in his cabin. He stopped outside the door and listened to him talking to himself. He was telling a joke, and at first it sounded like he was telling it to someone, except that the trooper knew that the guy was alone. The guy told this long, complicated joke, and when he got to the punch line, he cracked up. He broke up laughing, but he didn't finish the joke . . . and then he started to tell it all over again."

"Weird," Virgin Bruce said flatly. "Gimme another brownie and promise you won't tell us any more bullshit stories."

"I promise I won't tell any more bullshit stories," Hamilton said, reaching into the bag for another brownie. "But do you see what I'm getting at, Popeye? You're setting yourself up to be like that trapper. All you're doing is telling yourself the same thing over and over, whatever that thing is. But you're not in a cabin in some godforsaken part of Alaska, man, you've got a hundred people here with you. There's no reason for you to hide. Tell us what's bugging you, Popeye."

Popeye didn't say anything. He put his back against the bulkhead behind him and gazed through the canopy. Olympus' rim was coming into view, a ring of cylinders reflecting the sunlight off their sides. When he looked closely, he could see the ring moving. In the background he could see the Moon coming into view from the far right, one-quarter in shadow. He felt lightheaded, and wondered dully if something was wrong with the oxygen-nitrogen mix in the pod's atmosphere, but almost as quickly as the thought occurred to him, it went away. He was beginning to feel good, whatever the reason.

"I don't like my nickname," he mumbled.

Virgin Bruce whooped. *"You* don't like *your* nickname! Jesus H. Christ! You think I like *mine?"* His head went back and he howled with laughter. "Do you know what it's like to be called a virgin all the time, when you probably qualify for a gold medal in the Sex Olympics?"

Hooker saw what Bruce did, even though Bruce himself didn't realize what he was doing; he saw Virgin Bruce's finger punch the activation button on the communications board. He howled into his headset mike: "Sex! I want sex *now!*"

A second later his eyes went wide and he settled back into his seat. "Ah, negatory on that, Olympus Control," he intoned. "I think we have a communications dysfunction, ah, malfuck, um, malfunction here. No, we're . . . I mean, I'm in good shape, Beta House over."

He punched out of the comlink, closed his eyes, and let out a sigh. "For the love of Mike," he murmured, rubbing his eyes while the others laughed, "we must be getting stoned on that stuff."

Hooker laughed for a few more seconds until what Virgin Bruce had just said sank in. "Getting stoned on what stuff?" he asked.

"Don't change the subject," Hamilton said. "C'mon, Popeye. It's just between the three of us. Virgin Bruce told everyone in the rec room last week about his sordid past. Now it's your turn. You used to be a shrimp trawler, right?"

"I was never a boat," Popeye said, laughing. Remarkably, he *was* feeling good. For the first time in weeks, maybe months, he felt relaxed. It was an easiness he used to feel when he looked through the telescope in Meteorology, until he gave that up, following the blowout of the hotdog. As the pod rounded the rim of the space station, Earth swam into view, half in shadow, half in light. Automatically, his eyes sought the Gulf of Mexico.

"C'mon," Hamilton prodded. "Tell us about it and I'll let you in on the secret ingredients for that brownie you just ate."

"My wife," Popeye said. "My ex-wife, actually, though I kept on sleeping with her after our divorce." Somehow, he felt detached from himself, as if he were standing outside his own body, looking in, listening to himself speak. "I loved her a lot, even after I found out she was stealing money and using it to buy cocaine."

*He was sure the fat man had cheated him on the deal, though he couldn't be sure. He had never bought coke before; it was one thing he had always tried to stay away from. But it didn't matter, even if you could prove the little cellophane wrapper in his hand contained less than the two grams Rocky had promised or if it was considerably less pure than claimed. It didn't matter.*

*"To be honest with you, I'm surprised that you're buying from me," Rocky said as he counted the tens and twenties Hooker had just handed him, "but if you're interested in trying it, I assure you that you'll like its quality and tell you that it's always available from me. However, if you're just trying to set me up for a bust, I'll also be candid and let you know that's a foolish thing to do. The cops have been bought and paid for, and if you go to them with an accusation,*

*my friend behind you will gladly visit you at home and break your
arms."*

"That's bad news," Virgin Bruce said sympathetically. "It's that
shit which got me in trouble, too. So what'd you do?"

*Hooker flipped the packet around a couple of times between his
fingertips, then slipped it into the breast pocket of his denim jacket. "I
don't plan to do either. It's for her."*

*"Ah." Rocky smiled at him. "It's a present for her. I can dig it. I'll
give you a little bonus, then, since you're a new customer. She hasn't
been here yet. If you want to give her your present, I'll let you wait
here." He smiled his treacherous, hungry smile, which had probably
made little girls smile and made their mothers wonder if he should be
reported to the police for suspected child molestation. "I have everything you need right here," he added.*

"Did you bake pot into those brownies?" Popeye asked. From the
smiles he got from Hamilton and Virgin Bruce, he knew he had
pegged the funny consistency and taste of the confections correctly.
"Thought so. They're not bad." He sighed and settled his back
against the rear bulkhead again. "Man, I used to enjoy smoking pot.
Got into the stuff some nights when I'd be out on the ocean alone.
Midnight on the Gulf, letting the nets drag with the *Jumbo Shrimp*
at one-quarter throttle, drinking beer and smoking reefer, listening to
jazz on the radio. Watching the Coast Guard boats' lights going back
and forth along the eight-mile mark, looking for smugglers or immigrants. That was a lot of fun."

"How long were you a fisherman?" Hamilton asked.

"Most of my life, I guess. Parents died when I was young, in a jet
crash at Miami International. I barely remember them, I was so
little. Spent a few years in the orphanage before being adopted by a
shrimp fisher who lived on St. Simon's Island in Georgia. When he
died, I took over his boat, the *Jumbo Shrimp*. Second biggest boat in
the state, next to the old *Georgia Bulldog*. A couple of years later I
sold it and used the money to buy a smaller boat I could handle by
myself without having to hire a crew. Named it the *Jumbo Shrimp II*
and moved to Cedar Key, Florida." He smiled at the fond memory.
"Those were good days. My wife was a bitch, that was the only
problem, but I enjoyed myself."

"So why did you give it up?" Hamilton asked.

*He sat on the gunnel on the aft deck, drinking beer and watching
the other sailors getting ready to head out for the evening. At four
o'clock the sun was still high in the summer sky. She'd be there soon.*

*Unless she still wanted to blow his money away on Rocky's trash. It was hot, so he unbuttoned his shirt.*

"I just got sick of it," he lied.

Now the station's south pole was coming up. Looking at it, he could make out the telescope fastened to the hemispherical bulge of the Meteorology section, the rectangular casing pointed toward Earth. "Wonder what those CIA guys are looking at today," Virgin Bruce said, as if reading his thoughts.

"Submarines off Cuba. Troop movements near the Canal. A spaceport being built in Haiti." Popeye shrugged. "Go in there sometime and look over their shoulders at the reports they're filing back home. You'll wonder about this Century of Peace everyone's proclaiming." He raised his knees an inch or so up the back of the pilot's seat, trying to relieve the growing cramps in his legs. "So where did this pot come from, Jack?" he asked. "Did you smuggle some up or what?"

"Well, yeah, I did, but I smoked that stuff up a little while ago. Ah, you promise not to tell anyone else?"

"I promise."

"Well, I also brought up a little stash of seeds and I planted them in the hydroponics bay. What you're smoking now . . . I mean, eating . . . is from the first crop. How do you like it?"

"Pretty good." Actually, it had been so long since he had last smoked marijuana that even lousy pot could have made him high, but this stuff *was* good. He found himself staring at the Earth again. Down there is the Gulf of Mexico, and on it is a boat, he thought. And on that boat is a woman. She's lying on her back under the sun, and there's a little bead of sweat running down her left breast, down under the cup of her bra where the sun hasn't turned her skin brown, and the warm sun feels like a lover's hand so she arches her back slightly, her flat stomach rising up and her round buttocks pushing flat against the wooden deck. Her lips part slightly and her eyes open, and she sees me walking toward her; she smiles, so I push my thumbs underneath the waistband of my trunks and push them down, and she sits up and reaches for . . .

"Hey! Popeye!" Hamilton snapped. "Come back here!" Instantly he was back in the spacecraft. Hamilton was grinning at him and offering another brownie. Hooker stared at it for a moment, then shook his head. "I just asked you a question," the hydroponicist said, putting the brownie back into the plastic bag.

"I asked you when was the last time you saw your ex-wife."

*Gold disappearing . . .*

"I haven't seen her in a while," he said shortly. He thought for a moment, then quickly added, "I don't know where she is." Another lie.

"You mean she hasn't written to you or called or nothing?" Virgin Bruce asked.

*"No, I don't want to stick around," he told Rocky. "Just tell her that I've been here and I've got something for her, and if she wants it, she can come down to my boat. I'll meet her there."*

"No, I haven't heard anything from her since I've been here," Popeye replied.

Virgin Bruce snorted. "Ain't that like women? I swear, sometimes I think they were put here just to drive men crazy, you know what I mean?"

"Yeah," Popeye agreed most sincerely, "I know what you mean."

Just then, Virgin Bruce sat forward intently and cupped his hand over his headset's earpiece, waving his other hand urgently for silence as he listened to the comlink. "Keep it down," he half-whispered, then jabbed the transmission button on the communications board. "Ah, yeah, we copy, Olympus Traffic. I'm winding up my first orbit now. Everything looks good. Do you want me to continue? Olympus Beta House over."

He listened for another second, then his lips pulled back into a grimace. He looked over his shoulder at Hooker and Hamilton and shook his head, then said, "We copy there, Olympus Traffic. Beta House proceeding for docking at Olympus a-sap. Beta House over and out."

He punched off, then sighed. "Son of a bitch. They want us to come back in. One of the hub antennae has gone out of alignment and they need this pod to send a guy to go fix it. Fortunately I don't have the right equipment and they know it; otherwise I'd have to come up with a reason quick to stop them from sending me."

Popeye nodded. There would have been no possibility of Virgin Bruce doing the errand; to fix the antenna on the south pole of Skycan's hub, he would have necessarily had to have gone EVA, which meant that he would have had to depressurize the pod. There was only one suit in the pod, though. Not that Bruce could have pulled off such a delicate mission, in his present state of mind . . .

"Bruce," he asked, "are you sure you can dock this thing?"

" 'Are you sure you can . . .' " Bruce repeated, then stopped and glared back at Popeye. "Popeye, son, do you know who you're speaking to? I'm the best pod pilot in the whole company! You're talking to the hotdog man, brother! The ace of aces himself! I can dock a pod with my eyes closed! What the hell do you mean, 'Bruce, are you sure you can dock this thing?' "

He turned back around, snapped off the autopilot and switched to manual, then hit a couple of switches and pushed the throttle arm forward. The pod eased forward, falling out of its orbit, but instead of going straight, it began to roll toward the left, taking a spiraling course toward the station's hub. Red lights began to flash on the LCD simulation. Virgin Bruce muttered something unintelligible and hastily corrected his course, firing RCR's to stop the rolling. "Nothing serious," he said aloud.

"Bruce," Hamilton said in a calm voice, although Popeye noticed that the hydroponics engineer had his eyes tightly closed, "I think I should rephrase Popeye's question. The question isn't whether you can dock this thing. It should be, can you dock this thing *stoned?*"

"Hey. Hey." Virgin Bruce's voice took a defensive edge. "This is no more difficult than riding my bike, and I used to do that all the time after smoking reefer. Man, they were good days. Driving down 40 on a summer day, high on good Jamaican weed, doing seventy through rush-hour traffic. No helmet, no nothing, just you and the road, man." He giggled. "Man, I used to have fun with those big trucks. . . ."

# 21

# Strange Tales of Space

Virgin Bruce's near-crash landing at the Docks wasn't the first indication that things were getting a little loose on Skycan, but it was the most obvious. He ended up slam-docking his pod so hard that later a repair crew had to be dispatched to the airlock compartment to patch the small leaks in the seams which he had inadvertently sprung. Bruce himself got chewed out by both Chang and Anderson . . . especially by Chang, who was the only one who knew that more than one person had been in the pod, or what the three of them had been doing.

It's worth noting that H.G. Wallace didn't hear about the incident for a couple of hours, because the project supervisor wasn't in the command center when Neiman, Hooker, and Hamilton took their joy ride. Lately, Wallace had not been his usual omnipresent self. He had, over the past few weeks, become a hermit, sequestering himself in his private quarters in Module 24, delegating most of the authority to Hank Luton and Doc Felapolous. Despite what Felapolous had said about Cap'n Wallace being the force which kept the SPS construction project on time and within budget, Wallace's presence was not really missed. Work continued on the giant satellite without missing a beat; in fact, the beamjacks seemed to be enjoying themselves, now that they didn't have to worry about Wallace constantly haranguing them over the comlink. It was possible that Wallace was still monitoring them from his cabin, but if he was, the only evidence he gave was a once-a-day whirlwind tour of the command center, during which he would harass everyone on duty about the sloppy jobs they were doing, before disappearing back to the isolation of his cabin.

Perhaps it was because Wallace was becoming invisible that things were getting looser on Skycan, but I think that there were some other factors. For one thing, there was Hamilton's pot crop. I don't want to give the impression that the crew of Olympus overnight became a gang of stoned-out twenty-first century hippies, but just having that stuff aboard had an effect on the crew. Hamilton tried to keep Skycan Brown—as he dubbed the particular, fast-growing strain he had developed in Hydroponics—a secret within a close circle of friends, but for how long could anyone keep anything a secret within the station? Not very damn long. He soon found himself in the position any well-known supplier of contraband materials on Earth has had to face: Crewmen started approaching him at all hours, looking for a joint or two, referred to him by "friend of a friend of a friend" connections.

Somehow, he got lucky in that word of his crop didn't leak to the wrong people, like Phil Bigthorn or Wallace. But before things got completely out of control he harvested the last of his crop, cured the marijuana and hid it away, and didn't grow any more. In fact, the day after he did that, he had an unexpected visit from Doc Felapolous, who said he was just "wandering by and decided to drop in for a little socializing." After Doctor Feelgood managed to mosey through each of the five Hydroponics modules and peer closely at everything, he left Jack in a cold sweat—especially after Felapolous mumbled something about there being "a lot of careless little accidents lately." At that point, Hamilton decided to go out of business. Like every smart dope dealer, he decided that it wasn't worth the risk, let alone the paranoia.

There had been a lot of little accidents, and some of them had been caused by a lot of the beamjacks smoking pot. Things like that inside Olympus could be controlled. Stoned crewmen loosing their balance and falling down, and various other little incidents that happened when two or three guys were jammed together in a curtained bunk with a smokeless pipe, exhaling into a towel that had been liberally sprayed with deodorant—those things didn't matter much. It was even funny when you would see somebody in the mess deck giggling uncontrollably at the food on his plate (or, better, someone who had always complained about the food, wolfing down his meal and mumbling with a mouthful about how great the slop seemed to taste), or a bunch of guys in the rec deck transfixed by a *Star Trek* or *Twilight Zone* rerun which they must have already seen a dozen times.

But it was a sign that the situation was getting out of hand when accidents started occurring during the work shifts out on SPS-1. Just before going on a shift a couple of guys would hole up in a john with one of the little water pipes Hamilton had at first obligingly whipped up from the chemistry apparatus in his lab. Then they would ride the ferry out to Vulcan. Julian Price would have his hands full in the whiteroom, catching the careless mistakes these jokers would make while suiting up—the disconnected hoses or partially pressurized tanks or the unsealed suit seams. We were lucky we didn't lose any guys that way. We were doubly lucky that no fatalities resulted from numerous other pot-induced errors: Beamjacks firing their MMU's in the wrong direction and colliding with the satellite or each other, tethers improperly fastened. Once, a laser torch was fired in the wrong direction and damn near put a hole through the faceplate of the beamjack's helmet. Oh, man, we were just *lucky* no one got killed!

If there was anything that Jack Hamilton's experiment with cultivating marijuana in space proved, it was that dope doesn't belong in space. Hamilton knew it, so he stopped passing out loose pot and his homemade brownies to the beamjacks. He told them that he had run out—a lie which no one could prove, since he carefully hid his remaining pound of cured pot somewhere in the hydroponics bay—and that he wasn't going to grow any more, which was the truth after Doc's visit. Fortunately, Doc didn't get suspicious enough to start making spot checks of the crew's blood and urine. He chalked up the rumors of drug use to the number of painkillers he had formerly handed out, figuring that some of the crew had been hoarding the pills, and started prescribing aspirin instead. After a little while, the accidents began to ease off in frequency and crewmen stopped laughing at their food.

But the long-term effect, far more benign, was that the morale of the people aboard Skycan had improved. It was a synthesis of pot use by the minority, the contact-high which the nonsmoking majority had gotten from them, and the absence of Cap'n Wallace's brooding presence that raised spirits a little on the station. Since Hamilton had accumulated a small hunk of money from his short career as a reluctant dealer, he used that cash to have a few luxury items shipped up to Skycan, things that had been officially forbidden by Wallace until he had become a modern version of Captain Ahab. Through his friendship with Lisa Barnhart, one of the shuttle pilots who made runs to LEO from the Cape, Hamilton got us a few cassette decks, tapes, video cassettes that weren't G-rated, Frisbees—little stuff that was taken for granted down on Earth but had been made unwelcome on Skycan by Wallace's vision of a perfect space crew. They went a long way toward making people feel better. You could walk down the catwalk and see off-duty crewmen tossing the friz to each other, hear the Byrds coming from this bunkhouse, the Talking Heads from the next, Miles Davis or Stanley Clarke coming from the next. People stopped being uptight about sex as well. A few of Virgin Bruce's bunkhouse mates were surprised when Joni Lowenstein started crawling in and out of Bruce's bunk, but Command didn't raise any objections. Wallace would have been upset to see all this going on, but Wallace seldom emerged from Module 24 anymore; he was completely self-immersed in his own private world which no one except Doc Felapolous was allowed to enter, and Doc wasn't telling anyone what was going on inside Cap'n Wallace's head.

No one cared. SPS-1 was still being built on schedule; the crew was happy, Skycorp was happy, the stockholders were reasonably satisfied. Things were good there, for a while.

And Jack still had a secret cache of marijuana to which he once in a while treated himself and a half-dozen carefully chosen friends. In the long run, it was fortunate he had not obeyed his first instinct, which was to chuck the rest of that stuff out an airlock after Doc Felapolous' surprise visit. We would not have been able to learn about the Big Ear if there had not been pot available aboard Olympus.

But then again, maybe he should have heaved that junk when he had the opportunity, for it was partially responsible for ending the good times for us all, just as it had been partially responsible for starting those good times.

# 22

# *Ear Ache*

*The Ugarian star-destroyer came out of warspace in a dazzling explosion of color. It was followed closely by a handful of smaller explosions, signaling the arrival of its sister attack ships. For an instant they
shimmered in space with the aftereffects of their pangalactic jump,
then resolved into hard, menacing reality.*

*On the decks of the warships, Ugarian warriors in exoskeleton armor raced to their battle stations. On the bridge, final computations
commenced for the sneak attack on the human-colonized planet before them. Within a dome on the highest point of the star-destroyer,
T'Hhark in his black armor raised his arms as if to embrace the blue-
green world which swam before him.*

*"Let the assault begin," he whispered, his voice carrying to all levels
of each ship. "Take no prisoners."*

Sam Sloane heard a knock on the hatch behind him and hissed
under his breath before he realized who it was that could be knocking. "Yeah, come in," he called irritably, and typed a command on
his keyboard, which saved Chapter 15 of *Ragnarok Night.* Not until
he had swiveled around in his chair and seen the connecting hatch to
Module 5 swinging open, did he realize that this was an interruption
of the welcome variety. Jack Hamilton didn't drop by very often,
although his Hydroponics modules were adjacent to the Data Processing bay; when he did, it was usually an amiable visit.

Hamilton stepped through the hatch and carefully closed it behind
him. Walking into the compartment, he stopped and quickly looked
around. "Are you alone?" he asked in a soft voice, looking over
Sam's shoulder at the open hatch leading into Module 7, the other
half of the computer deck.

Sloane nodded. Hamilton quickly stepped over to the ladder and
peered up at the overhead hatch leading to the catwalk. As usual,
that hatch was closed. Like Hydroponics, the computer bay's

hatches were usually kept sealed due to necessary environmental considerations. Just as Hamilton's plants had to be kept under hot-house conditions, the mainframes of Skycan's computer systems had to be kept in a lower-than-normal temperature. In fact, Sloane's working section was one of the few compartments on the space station in which privacy could be assured. The overhead hatches could be locked, and could be unlocked only with a coded key-card. Data Processing was the nerve center of Olympus, and Skycorp had not taken any chances with possible sabotage when it had worked out the fine details of Skycan's design.

Still, Hamilton climbed halfway up the ladder to reach up and yank the locking handle, making sure the hatch was secure. Sloane watched him with surprised amusement. "Worried about air guns, Holmes?" he asked casually.

"Huh?" Hamilton hopped off of the ladder, which was an unfortunate move. The Coriolis effect, combined with one-third normal gravity, caught him off-balance when he landed, and he staggered slightly. Sloane snickered behind his hand. Even after a couple of months, Jack Hamilton had not managed to coordinate himself to space. On Earth he was undoubtedly athletic and even catlike, but up here his clodlike blundering was a standing joke among the crew. Even the station's resident cats were better adapted than the Chief Hydroponics Engineer.

Hamilton grinned sheepishly. "What was that about air guns?" he asked.

Sloane waved it off. "Literary reference," he said. "Never mind." Then he frowned. "Look, um, if you want to smoke something, why don't we do it over in Hydroponics? Smoke doesn't agree with the equipment here."

Hamilton shook his head, and walked to the chair next to Sam's. "Not here to smoke," he said, his face lapsing back into the serious expression he was wearing when he had entered the compartment. "Am I bothering you?" he asked quickly.

Sloane shrugged. "Not really. Can't get my shit together behind my novel anyway, so the only thing you're interrupting is a badly written scene." He stared thoughtfully at the blinking cursor above the main menu displayed on the terminal's screen. "Goddamn," he murmured thoughtfully, "no matter how hard I try, these friggin' aliens end up sounding like every bad-guy alien invented since the Boskone, and their captain just sounds like Darth Vader with . . ."

He stopped when he noticed how Hamilton had practically fallen into his chair. If the chair had not been fixed to the deck, he would have toppled over backwards. As it was, the hydroponicist slumped into the padded metal seat like a dead weight. When he looked up at Sloane with a dazed expression, the computer chief noticed that his eyes were mildly bloodshot.

"Jack," he said, "you're stoned."

"Clever deduction, Watson," Hamilton replied. Then he chuckled. *"The Final Problem.* Moriarity's air guns. I remember now. Very clever, very clever." He waggled a finger at Sloane, grinning foxily.

Sam sighed. "Jesus, you're fried." He glanced at his watch. "Look, you've got about an hour before dinner. I suggest you go back to your section and straighten up if you want to eat. You'd better not show up on the mess deck in the shape you're in."

*"No!"* Once more Hamilton turned serious. He waved his hands in front of his face and shook his head. "No, I don't need to straighten up . . . no, yeah, I admit, I'm stoned, but you've got to listen to this, it's important!"

"Sure it is." Sloane stood up and gently took Jack's arm. "Tell me about it while I get you . . ."

"No, dammit!" Hamilton exclaimed. He shook off Sloane's hands. "Sit down, Sam! I'm stoned, but this is important. This is real, and it's important, and I'm not becoming paranoid and you need to listen to me. It's *because* I'm stoned that this is important. I mean, if I wasn't high, then this . . ." He took a long, deep breath. "Now just sit down and hear me out, okay?"

"Okay." Sloane sat down again. "But if I heard what you just said correctly, pal, what you're about to tell me wouldn't be important unless I was as high as you are. Since I'm not high, and you are, what's there to make me think this isn't bullshit?"

Hamilton let out his breath and put his head in his hands for a second. After a moment he lifted his face and looked Sloane square in the eyes. "Look, Sam," he said slowly, "forget my present condition. Forget all that. Just listen to my story, okay?"

Sloane started to tap a command into his terminal. "Why don't you let me read you some of my novel instead?" he asked. "I guarantee that it'll be . . ."

"Dammit, Sam!"

"Okay, okay!" Sam lifted his hands away from the keyboard. "Tell me your story, for crying out loud!"

Hamilton let out his breath and settled back in his chair, looking up at the ceiling to collect his thoughts. "It happened about a couple of hours ago," he said, "while I was working next door in my lab. Someone called me on the intercom and asked if he could come down to Hydroponics to see me. I didn't recognize his voice and he wouldn't be specific about why he wanted to see me, but I've been less finicky about letting people come down since I got rid of the pot crop, so I said, sure, c'mon down.

"When the guy finally showed up and climbed down into the bay, I recognized who it was. It was Dave."

"Dave?" Sam shook his head. "Which Dave? There's at least a dozen Daves on Skycan, Jack."

"Yeah, there are, but which of those Daves do you know the least about? I mean, which Dave do you even know his last name?" Impatient with the confused look on Sloane's face, Hamilton hurried on. "Dave the phony meteorologist, dummy. Dave of Dave, Bob, and John, the spook trio."

This perked Sloane's attention. "Dave, the NSA agent, came down to see you? C'mon, those guys don't talk to anyone except themselves."

Hamilton nodded, smiling. "Right. They don't even share the same commode with anyone for fear of risking national security. That's why I was so surprised to see this guy coming down here.

"He was really antsy about it, too. He secured the hatch behind him on the way down the ladder, and once he was there, he was nervous. Had his hands in his pockets, kept looking around to see if anyone else was in the bay, all the while keeping up this chitchat. Y'know, like 'We've never met, decided to drop by—So this is Hydroponics, huh?—I certainly like the veggies you grow here. Are those beanstalks?' and bullshit like that. I sat down in a chair and said yes and no and asked him how things were in Meteorology, all the while wondering what was going on.

"It took him a few minutes to get down to brass tacks, and when he finally did, I was kinda surprised to hear him ask the same thing I've heard a couple of dozen of the beamjacks ask me over the past couple of months. He said, almost in a whisper"—Hamilton's own voice dropped to a whisper—" 'Hey, I've heard that you've got some *marijuana.*' "

"Oh, no," Sloane said softly, feeling the blood drain from his face. "How did this guy . . . ?"

"I asked him that. I said, 'Now what makes you think that? Who told you something like that?' He wouldn't tell me any names, but said that he had just heard it through the grapevine that Jack Hamilton down in Hydroponics had some pot. Then he says . . . I couldn't believe this . . . Dave says, 'I want to smoke some.' "

*"What?"* Sam nearly shouted. "He wanted to—!"

"Shh! Dammit, Sam, keep your voice down." Both men momentarily forgot that the modules were soundproof with the hatches shut. "Right. Oh, of course I was suspicious as hell as well as being surprised. After picking my jaw off the floor I decided to be straightforward with him. I said, 'Well, assuming that I do have something like that, why should I tell you? I mean, let's lay down our cards here, man. You're no meteorologist any more than I'm George Washington. Everyone knows you're with the National Security Agency. *If* I did happen to have some marijuana, how am I supposed to know that you're not trying to set me up for a fall?' "

"Good question," said Sloane, "though I'm surprised that you didn't just turn him down flat. I mean, you've been telling nearly everyone you've learned to trust that you've run out."

Hamilton looked down at the floor and shrugged. "I don't know. I guess I was intrigued with the whole thing. Low-life tokers, like you and I, are a nickel a gross, but you always hear these stories about Secret Service agents and sons of Presidents and Senators who smoke dope. I was wondering if this was one of these cases."

Sloane grinned. "Okay, sure, I can understand that. So go on."

"Well," Hamilton continued, "Dave says real slowly, 'I suppose there's no way I can really make you trust me, no way I can prove to you that I'm not here to bust you except to say that pot isn't one of those things which the NSA enforces. We're an intelligence-gathering agency, not the FBI.' Hell, Sam, he practically started to plead to me! 'C'mon, if you've got some, I want to smoke it with you. No one else is gong to know, I promise.' "

Hamilton put up his hands. "So what could I say? It was like walking on broken glass, but I decided to go ahead and take the risk."

Sloane closed his eyes and shook his head in disbelief. "I can't believe you did that," he murmured. "For all you knew, he could have been working with Mr. Big to get the goods on you."

"The thought did cross my mind," Hamilton admitted, "but somehow my sixth sense, if you want to call it that, told me that this guy was on the level. Anyway, I escorted him over to Module 42—y'know, that part of the bay where I had blocked some of the vents off—and pulled out a bit of my stash and the little water pipe I'd made, and we hunched down behind one of the racks and lit up.

"Okay, for one thing, this guy had unusually low tolerance to the stuff. Maybe it was because the Brown is a potent hybrid, or because like most other people I've smoked with on Skycan, he hadn't smoked pot in a long time, or maybe it was because of my pet theory that the one-third environment gets you high more quickly because of the overall physiological impact. But in any case, Dave got ripped in a hurry. He was talking a mile a minute by his third hit. I mean, I thought it was a miracle that he had admitted to me that he was with the NSA when he had first come in, but we had hardly finished one bowlful of the stuff before he was telling me not to call him Dave and that because we were friends I could call him Jack." Hamilton grinned. "Jack Jarrett, that's his real name. He got a kick out of the fact that we both have the same first name. Also, his home state is New Hampshire and I used to live in Massachusetts, so he figured that we have a lot in common. Weekends at Hampton Beach, going to restaurants and nightclubs in Boston, swimming on Cape Cod, trips to the Berkshires and the Whites for the fall foliage season. We started to talk about a lot of that stuff."

"Uh-huh. Homecoming day for you two," Sam said blandly. "So you smoked dope with a guy from the NSA. Boy, I haven't heard of such daring since I sneaked a joint under the bleachers in high school. Is that the important stuff you wanted to tell me, Jack?" He glanced at his watch. "Almost time for dinner."

"No, no, no!" Hamilton waved his hands frantically. "You haven't heard the rest of it, Sam! Just let me get to the end of the story!"

"Do tell," Sloane said. Novelty or not, stories about people getting stoned on Skycan were beginning to wear on Sam after a couple of months. The peculiar conditions and the precautions that had to be taken notwithstanding, the tales had long since begun to sound alike.

"So as I said before," Hamilton went on, "the pot hit Dave, or whatshisname, pretty hard. I like to think it was because of Skycan Brown's unusual potency thanks to my horticultural talents, but . . ."

"But he got solidly stoned," Sloane said impatiently.

"Right. And then he started to *talk.*" Hamilton drew the last word out meaningfully. "He started to talk about how crummy his job was, how he was becoming disillusioned with the whole role that the NSA was playing in spying on the rest of the world, how he really felt that a lasting world peace could really be accomplished if we only learned to trust each other the way he and I had learned to." Hamilton noticed the pained look on the computer chief's face. "Yakety-yack like that," he said shortly. Then he leaned forward in his chair. "Then he said, 'And it's such a bitch, that the government can't even trust its own citizens anymore, that it's starting to spy on the people themselves.' And I said, 'What do you mean, Jack?' And he said, 'Hey, you wouldn't believe what they've got cooked up with this Big Ear project.' "

"Big Ear," Sloane said. "What did he mean, Big Ear?"

"C'mon, Sam," Hamilton chided, "you know what that is. It's the comsat system that's being set up. The ring of communications sats that are being established in geosynchronous orbit, interconnecting with each other. A telephone in every tribal village, bringing about the Global Village, all that stuff? C'mon, it's been in the news for at least the last couple of years."

"Oh, right, the Big Ear project the multinationals were bringing off." Sam shook his head, wondering at his own forgetfulness. DBS technology had been old hat in the United States since the 1990's, when coaxial cables had been rendered obsolete by dishes and when wristphones had been first made available to the general public. Once that had occurred in the U.S., Great Britain, and Japan, the Third Wave countries had largely forgotten about the impact such advances could have upon the Third World countries. Until, eventually as it must, the multinational corporations saw the benefits of expanding DBS technology worldwide, realizing the longstanding dream which Arthur C. Clarke, R. Buckminster Fuller, and other visionaries had of uniting humanity through satellite-based communications.

"Right. The Big Ear. But from the way he talked about it, there's something going on with that thing which the NSA is involved with. Something that he and those two other guys have been testing."

"Something?" Sloane asked, his interest was aroused again. "You mean he wouldn't say, or what?"

Hamilton shook his head. "I don't know. You have to remember, he was very stoned. I don't even think he was talking to me. He mumbled something about a test they had done on the day of the Vulcan blowout, which allowed them to tap into phone calls in California and Tennessee. Then he said something like, 'Once the Ear is brought on-line, there isn't going to be any privacy left in the world and we can flush the Bill of Rights down the toilet.' I asked him what he meant, and he just looked at me and shut up completely. In fact, in a few minutes after that, he put down the pipe, thanked me for getting him high, and left." Jack snickered. "Poor sap was so rocked out of his skull he banged his head on the hatch while climbing up the ladder. I think he went to his bunk to sleep the rest of it off."

Sloane rubbed his jaw. "Well, if he's that stoned, you might try finding him and asking some more questions."

Hamilton shook his head. "I sincerely doubt it. He told me that stuff while he wasn't aware of what he was saying to whom. If anything, he's probably worried sick that I might have made sense out of it." Hamilton paused. "I dunno, Sam. Stuff about using the Ear to tap into telephone calls. Ending the Bill of Rights. Am I just high, or is there something here to worry about?"

Sam Sloane sat back in his chair and propped his feet up on the arm of Hamilton's chair. "It's hard to say," he said thoughtfully, pulling on one end of his mustache with his fingertips. "We've had spy satellites capable of monitoring phone conversations on the ground since the '80's, but that's always been something that's been part of the NSA's mission. Why would anyone want to listen in on phone calls in the United States? Maybe they were just making a test run on California and Tennessee lines."

"Yeah, maybe that's it, but why that line about there not being any privacy left and flushing the Bill of Rights?" Hamilton cupped his face in his hands and shook his head. "Oh, man, this is bizarre."

Sloane pondered the problem for a moment. Then, on impulse, he pulled his legs off the armrest, swiveled his chair to face his terminal, and typed in a command that exited him from his own program. "What are you doing?" Hamilton asked.

"I'm not the computer chief on Skycan for nothing," Sam muttered. "I've never tried this before, so I hope . . ." His voice trailed off as he typed: CD/NSA.

INVALID COMMAND, the computer replied.

CD/METEOROLOGY, he tried.

INVALID COMMAND, the computer responded again.

"Trying to get into their files?" Hamilton asked, peering over Sam's shoulder.

"Yeah. So much for the obvious logons." Sloane pulled on his mustache some more. "Okay, it has to be something easy to remember that they've entered." CD/BIGEAR, he typed.

INVALID PROTOCOL, the computer responded.

"Okay, we're getting somewhere," Sloane said. He thought for a moment, then typed, CD/STORMKING.

STORMKING LOGON, the computer printed out. ENTER PASS PHRASE NOW.

"Hot damn," Hamilton said. "How did you guess . . ."

"Old brand name for a cigarette lighter," Sloane snapped. "Hush! It sounds like I've got only a few seconds to come up with the pass phrase, or we're screwed."

"How about 'Zippo'?" Hamilton inquired.

"Damn it, Jack, don't bug me!" Sloane pounded his clenched fists against the side of his own head. "I've been lucky so far, but this thing probably won't take a wrong answer at this point . . ." He stopped, then snapped, "What did you say that guy's name was?"

"Ah . . . uh, um . . . Jack Jarrett. Hey, what the hell."

"Worth a shot. Can't think of anything else logical." Sloane quickly typed in JARRETT.

PASS OK, the computer replied. ENTER FILE NAME.

"Hallelujah!" Hamilton yelled as Sloane sagged back in his chair, suddenly exhausted. "I can't believe you just did that!"

"A computer whiz's skill and a writer's sense of the obvious," Sam said with a weak grin. "Okay, let's see what this bugger has to tell us."

He typed in, BIGEAR, and suddenly the screen filled with print. Both men leaned forward and began to study the screen.

They missed dinner, and it didn't matter to them. The file was short and it took them only a couple of minutes to read it through the first time, but they found themselves studying its scrolling copy on the screen, again and again. Finally, Sloane made a hard copy on the printer, closed the file, and exited the program, being careful not to log himself as the last user.

"Well," Hamilton said simply.

"Well," Sam said in a near-whisper. Rubbing his eyes, he stood up from his chair and arched his aching back, stretching. "We've just stumbled onto a secret, and a big one at that. Question is, what are we going to do about it?"

Hamilton stared at the blank screen. No longer stoned, he now had a throbbing headache and his own eyes felt sore from staring at the screen so long and so intently. "Jesus, I don't know," he replied. After a moment he added reflectively, "When I started growing pot up here, I did it strictly for recreation. I stopped dispensing it when I realized people were beginning to get hurt. Now it turns out that getting one guy high has opened up this whole mess. I don't know if I should regret smoking with him, or being glad Jarrett happens to be as bored as everyone else and wanted to have some kicks of his own."

"I don't think the pot had anything to do with it," Sloane said. He leaned against a hardware rack on which he had magnetically tacked a print of an old Frank Kelly Freas painting. "Sounds to me like our friend Jarrett has a guilty conscience about what he's aiding and abetting. He might have told anyone, anyway. It just so happened that your dope helped him say what was on his mind at this time and place." He thought for a second, then added, "Though if I were you, I'd dump the rest of that stuff out the airlock the first chance you get."

"Yeah. You might be right. If someone finds out that we've discovered what they're up to . . ."

"Exactly," Sam agreed, "but we can't let ourselves linger on that now. If the timetable on that file is correct"—he pointed a finger at the terminal—"then the command module for the Ear has already been joined with the Freedom space station and there's only a matter of days before the system as a whole goes on-line."

If their mood wasn't already somber, that thought definitely sobered them. They looked at each other for a few seconds before Hamilton cleared his throat. "Well," he said, "what are we going to do about it?"

Sloane shrugged, knowing already what had to be done. "Someone has to take responsibility, I guess. I mean . . . somebody's got to put a stop to it."

Hamilton nodded. "Yeah." He hesitated. "So who's it going to be?"

Sam closed his eyes. "I don't think we have much choice."

"Right," said Hamilton. "We've got to think of something."

Sam kept his eyes closed. He felt one hell of a headache coming on. Shit, he thought. All I wanted to do is write a science fiction novel.

# PART FOUR
## 300-Mile Fade-away

I really have no idea how much time I have left. It looks as if my suit batteries are going to outlast my air supply, but that's because I've switched off all the nonessential stuff, except for this recorder, and turned down the thermostat to about 60 degrees Fahrenheit. It's a little cold, but what the hell. I'll be dead before I get frostbite.

As far as my air supply goes, I haven't the foggiest how much I have left. One of the nonessentials which got switched off were all the gauges. Since they all worked off the same switch on my chest pack, that means the heads-up displays inside my helmet are dark, including the one which would normally warn me when I'm breathing my reserves. The oxygen pressure needle on the chest pack is lying flat, but since I'm still breathing, there's obviously still some air left. The only thing I haven't been able to switch off is the digital chronometer, because it runs off its own battery, but it's set into the cuff of my suit's right sleeve, so I don't have to look at it. And I won't.

Two reasons why I've switched off everything. One, I don't want to know. When I die, I don't want to have an amber warning lamp blinking on and off in my face while watching the pressure indicator's needle making a slow plunge toward the zero mark. I can spare myself the possibility of living those last few minutes in blind, helpless panic. Give me a little dignity, please. Second, I'm trying to preserve the batteries to power the recorder, in the slim hope that I can finish this chronicle before I croak. It's my last testament, after all. Certainly more worth the reader's time than *Ragnarok Night*, which—I have to admit, in my dying hour—was unmitigated dogshit.

Hey, if anyone does decide to transcribe and publish this thing, at least I won't have to live with a lot of things writers have to cope with. Editorial demands to rewrite. Publicity tours. Agents. Royalties. Fame. Awards. The groupies the pros attract at SF conventions.

Notice that I'm not laughing any more. God damn it. I think I'm actually becoming scared of dying.

Let's get back on the track here. Take a deep breath. What the hell, let's splurge. . . .

Y'know, the thing which always got me about the exploration of space was how naively the human race—but Americans particularly —has approached the whole thing. I mean, because we'd proven to ourselves that it was possible to send men and machines into orbit, we always assumed that everything would always work *right,* that people would always do the *right* thing out there, that just being in space would make everything so *right.* Jesus, you would have thought that after 1986, after the *Challenger* blew up and killed seven people because some people at NASA disregarded good advice not to launch that day, that after SDI was proven to be a monstrous sham which knowledgeable people who knew that it couldn't work as advertised tried to foist upon the world anyway, after the L-5 colony bullshit which even more so-called reliable sources tried to present as being economically feasible and practical . . .

Whoa. Gotta watch it on those long-winded speeches. Let's not splurge too much, Sam. You've got to finish the story.

But there is an underlying point that has to be made, if only to clarify the reasons for what we did. Mainly, we did what we did because we were the only ones who could—the only ones who *would* —do anything about it. The Big Ear should have been the instrument which destroyed the global status quo, not the bludgeon which reinforced it. It should have acted as a global switchboard, a ring of satellites that united every city, town, village, and hamlet, making it possible for anyone to trade information with anyone else. National borders rendered obsolete, political ideologies of secondary consideration, even differences in language of a lesser priority. Do-it-yourself world government, established not through a League of Nations, but through the everyday act of picking up the telephone, and dialing New York, Thailand, Japan, the U.S.S.R., Botswana, Brazil, the Aleutian Islands, wherever . . .

But instead, those who didn't want to have the power of information access spread decided to use the Big Ear to consolidate their own power. They did it, unfortunately, with the blind endorsement of the system's original supporters, just as the architects of the Strategic Defense Initiative managed to shanghai the grass-roots supporters of space development into advocating the "Star Wars" plan. The democracy of one Big Ear plan became the technocracy of another plan by the same name.

Except that we managed to stumble upon it. We: a small group of pot-smoking, fornicating, seditious working-class Joes. It fell to us, the responsibility of making certain that a dream didn't become corrupted, as so many others in the past had, into yet another Cold War weapon, with the only difference being that the Cold War was being waged this time against ourselves.

In a way, it was not right that it should have been us. It should have been someone else who had to wage the good fight. Maybe an earlier generation should have recognized the threat, and done something about it before the eleventh hour. But they didn't, and we did; we got stuck with the dirty end of the stick.

Someone had to do it, and that's why we did it. Looking back, I would have done it just the same way again, if I had been given the chance. But with one difference: I would have found some way to prevent Popeye Hooker from getting killed.

# 23

# The Weirdo Summit

Later on, when he got a chance to think about it more, Popeye decided that it was unfair that the first good day he had been given in a long time—how long, he couldn't remember—should be kicked out from under him.

It wasn't fair, that was all there was to it. For once, he had gone through a day without thinking about Laura. For once, he had actually gone on shift without having his mind elsewhere. For once, he had been able to look at Earth without having feelings of remorse. For once, damn it, for *once,* he had gotten through the day without wondering if he was losing his mind.

More than that, he had actually enjoyed his work, and that had never happened before. He got away from the edginess he had always felt while on EVA out on the powersat; he had jetted from section to section, stopping to weld beams here and there on direction from Vulcan Command, feeling like an agile kid playing on the biggest monkey bar in all the universe. He caught himself humming at one point, and at another time he actually had to restrain himself from untethering and doing somersaults with his MMU just for the hell of it. Popeye had no explanation for how he felt that day, except that perhaps he had gone for so long feeling miserable that his mind had finally overloaded and given him—yes, *given* was the operative word —a day to feel good about himself and things in general.

Popeye supposed it was Hamilton's advice, to yank himself by his bootstraps out of his self-perpetuating misery, which had finally sunk in and had made sense. Or maybe it was just a set of cerebral circuit breakers snapping in, saying, *Okay, time out! Enough self-searching pity, Hooker, it's time to party!* Whatever it was, he didn't try to analyze it too closely, for fear that the good feeling of feeling good would vanish as mysteriously as it had appeared.

But if it had been Hamilton's advice, freely given on that day when he and Virgin Bruce had gone for a joy ride in the pod, which had helped turn things around for Popeye's disposition, then it was ironically unfair that it should be Hamilton who should appear to ruin it.

The hydroponics engineer caught up with Hooker as he was coming off the second shift, in the west terminus module while Popeye was depositing his work gear in his locker. The rest of the second-shift beamjacks were banging their lockers shut and talking about the upcoming Series playoffs, when Jack Hamilton slid up beside Hooker and murmured, "Hey, Popeye, do you got a few minutes?"

"Sure," Popeye replied. "Why not? What's up?"

"There's a few people getting together in the hydroponics bay, Module One." Hamilton's voice was very low, almost a whisper. "It's very important, and I think I'd like to have you there."

Popeye grinned. "Sure. I could use a little R and R right now." He gave Jack a wink.

But Jack didn't return the smile or the wink. His solemn demeanor was Popeye's first indication that things were going to get sour again. "I'm afraid it's not like that," Hamilton said softly. "Sorry to disappoint you, but it's kind of important. Um, I hope this won't mean that you're not going to be there, 'cause it's something we can only trust a few people with and we really need your help in particular."

Popeye blinked. It was completely unexpected, and he was already beginning to have misgivings . . . but Jack did trust him, and Popeye realized that a key part of getting over his misery was to stop alienating himself from his crewmates. "Sure. Sure. When are we going to meet?"

"We're doing it right now. Module One. You'll be there?" Hooker nodded, and Jack gave him a slap on the shoulder. "See you there. . . . Hey, and don't let anyone know you're coming," he added.

Popeye watched Hamilton as he walked up the gangway leading to the catwalk, heading toward Module One. He noticed Jack pausing for an instant to say something to Virgin Bruce, who was also coming off shift. As Hamilton disappeared onto the catwalk, Virgin Bruce looked at Hooker and nodded in a knowing way. Intrigued now, Popeye nodded back, then closed and locked his locker.

Yet his mood was still buoyant as he strode down the catwalk. For the first time in weeks, he found himself noticing things that he must have heard and seen previously but simply ignored while immersed in his personal blue funk. Crewmen passing each other on the catwalk as they either headed for work on the third shift or returned to the bunkhouses before heading for the mess deck, saying things as

they dodged around each other: "Take it easy out there, pal"
"What're they serving down there today, Ike?" "Watch the feed from
the number two Grumman, man, it's putting out some warped sections today" "Hey, Hildebrant! You use up all the hot water again or
what?" From the open hatches leading down into the habitation
modules he could hear music from the tape decks that had suddenly
proliferated through the space station, the twentieth-century rock
music that was suddenly enjoying a revival among the crew: the
Band's "Rag, Mama, Rag" coming from Module 33, "California
Girls" by the Beach Boys from Module 34, the grating thump of the
James Gang's "Funk #49" from Module 35, the tender sigh of the
Youngbloods' "Darkness, Darkness" from Module 36. He saw the
notices taped up on the catwalk's tubular walls: "Wanted: Led Zep
tapes. Buy or trade. Rockin' Joe, Module 12, East" and "Dungeons
and Dragons! James Bond! Traveller! Need fresh blood for new
games! Roll your own characters and put them thru my tomato-
pulpers! DM Dick, Module 31. No wimps!" and "Movie Saturday
night. Two Stallone classics: *First Blood* and *Rambo.* 2000 and 2200,
East Rec." He passed the rec room, hearing the metallic clanging of
the exercise machines being worked out and the buzz of conversation
from below.

Things had changed on the space station in the past months. People were much more relaxed, now that Cap'n Wallace had gone into
hiding. They were beginning to *enjoy* themselves. I wonder why no
one thought of locking away that pompous bastard before, Popeye
thought. Would have saved everyone a lot of grief, especially me. He
smiled at the recollection of his encounter with Wallace on the day
Jack Hamilton had arrived on Skycan. In an odd way, he felt he
could credit himself, at least in part, for Wallace's self-alienation
from the rest of the personnel. It had probably been the first time in
his career that Wallace had ever had anyone tell him off.

He strode past the first three Hydroponics modules with their
brown color-coded signs and stopped above the sealed hatch of Module 1. He kneeled and twisted the locking wheel to lift open the
hatch. Conversation in the module paused as he climbed down the
ladder, shutting the hatch behind him. As Popeye stepped off the
ladder and turned around, he took a quick accounting of the bunch
gathered in the compartment.

Everyone was familiar to him, of course; Joni Lowenstein, the
communications officer, leaning against a rack of seed trays with her
arms resting on the shoulders of her new-found lover, Virgin Bruce,
who was seated in front of her; Dave Chang, the Docks operations

chief, standing next to a bulkhead with his arms crossed over his stomach; next to him, sitting at a lab bench, Sam Sloane, the Data Processing chief; and, of course, Hamilton himself. All of them nodded or murmured greetings to Popeye. Six people in a compartment already filled with plant beds, consoles, benches, and furniture made the module small indeed, so Popeye rested his butt on the bottom rung of the ladder. Looking around, he noticed at once that the lateral hatches connecting to Module 42 and 2 were sealed and locked, adding to the mysterious nature of the meeting.

"Thanks for sealing the hatch, Popeye," Hamilton said. "You're the last one who's been invited, so if you'd do us a favor and climb up and lock it, we'll get started."

Popeye did so as the hydroponicist cleared his throat formally, ending the small talk which had resumed once Popeye had entered the compartment. "As the saying goes, I suppose you're all wondering why I've called you here today," he began.

"To smoke dope and have an orgy," Chang said. As the others laughed, he noticed Joni turning red. "Sorry," he said, genuinely apologetic. "Didn't mean to imply anything about the lady's character."

"Better not, bubba," Virgin Bruce replied, wearing an expression of good-natured menace.

Even Joni laughed at that. However, Popeye noticed that neither Jack nor Sam had laughed. Hamilton shook his head. "Sorry, folks. This isn't going to be a smoking session." He paused. "It hadn't occurred to me that it might occur to you, when I invited each of you here, that this might be the reason. Each of you was picked to be here for a particular reason, and each of you are needed. However . . . well, if smoking pot is all you have on your mind, if that's all you want to do, you might consider going someplace else. That's not what we're here to do."

"What Jack is saying," Sloane added, "is that we've got some important business to discuss, and that there's a reason why all of you—Bruce, Joni, Dave, and you, Popeye—were asked to be here. You're crucial, but . . . well, if smoking pot is all . . ."

"We get what you mean, Sam," Virgin Bruce interrupted. He held up his hands. "Hey, I'm probably the biggest junkie of the bunch, but I know when it's time to get serious. Whatever it is, I'm sticking around."

He looked at the others meaningfully, and they either shrugged or nodded their heads. "But it does have to do with pot, doesn't it?"

Bruce continued. "Let me figure it out. Cap'n Wallace and Mr. Big
have finally wised up, and we're all in deep shit."

"Oh, hell," said Chang. "Does it mean we have to *eat* the rest of
that stuff now?"

That cracked everyone up, even the taciturn Jack and Sam. "No,
no, no," Sloane said. "Pot has something to do with it, but only
peripherally. What it is, is . . ."

He stopped, and looked at Hamilton. "Well, Jack told me about
this yesterday, so it's probably best that he explain things himself.
Jack?"

Hamilton crossed his arms. "All right," he began. "Yesterday at
about 1500 I was down here when I got a call over the intercom . . ."

As Hamilton was wrapping up his story, Hooker was beginning to
feel grim again, despite being intrigued with the disclosure of what
"Dave" the phony meteorologist had leaked to Hamilton, and how
Sloane had managed to crack the rest of the secret through the station computer. He wondered privately how much had been just under his nose during those visits he had made over the months to
Meteorology to peer through the telescope at Earth. Perhaps if he
had only listened harder, knowing—as everyone on Skycan did—
that John, Dave, and Bob were attached to the National Security
Agency. Thinking how much his own obsessive behavior had blinded
him to the truth only served to make him feel worse, if he wasn't
already disturbed by what Hamilton had just said.

"Okay, all right," Virgin Bruce said, bending forward in his chair.
"I've been following along, but I'm a little slow to pick up on all this
spy stuff, so tell me in simple language what this Big Ear thing is all
about."

"Well, better yet, I can show you." Sam Sloane turned about in his
chair to the computer terminal on the lab bench. "I did this up last
night just to show you, Bruce, so I hope you appreciate it." He
tapped in commands, and after reaching a file in his own directory he
punched it up.

A graphic simulation of the Big Ear appeared on the screen. With
Earth as the nucleus, it resembled a model of a heavy-element atom.
A network of circular orbits surrounded the planet, arcing on, above,
and below the equatorial plane, sometimes bisecting one another. As
the earth rotated in the simulation, so did the orbits. "This, of
course, is the Ear," Sloane said. "It's twenty communications satel-

lites established in geostationary orbit in the Clarke Belt, a couple of them not relatively far from Skycan's location."

He typed in another command, and a series of black dots with red lines connecting them appeared in the orbits. "The satellites can cover practically every inch of the globe," Sloane continued. "That is to say, through uplinks and downlinks with Earth stations now based in virtually all corners of the globe, they can send and receive messages to and from every continent. But as well, they can communicate with each other, so that a signal sent from, say, Zaire, can be 'bounced' from comsat to comsat until it reaches its destination in, for example, San Francisco. Each satellite is capable of handling several thousand phone calls, television signals, computer messages, and radio transmissions simultaneously, so there is practically no ceiling on the network's communications capability."

Sloane typed in another command, and another orbit appeared on the screen, this one closer to Earth than the orbits of the Ear satellites. "Now, that much is public information which the Ear's primary builder, Skycorp, has released. The deep, dark secret is that the NSA, through Skycorp's cooperation and that of no telling how many friendly governments, has established a way of tapping into the Ear. You see, the comsats are also capable of transmitting their messages to the Freedom space station in low-Earth orbit. We found out that a new module has just been added to Freedom, which acts as a sort of orbital 'switchboard,' or funnel if you want to call it that, for all those tens of thousands of simultaneous signals being bounced around the Ear."

Sloane turned around in his chair to face the group. "In short, that module is the biggest telephone bug ever conceived, except that it can also tap TV and radio communications and patch into stuff being sent computer-to-computer through modem. Through another series of Earth stations—these ones based worldwide and operated by the NSA—those signals can be relayed to the agency's headquarters in Fort Meade, Virginia. What happens then is interesting. The signals are fed through the agency's computers, which are programmed to translate or decode the messages. The computers are also programmed to pick out certain key words or phrases."

Hamilton jumped in again. "Those key words or phrases, of course, are those which the NSA and its clients consider to be dangerous or unpatriotic or un-American, whatever. If one of those words or phrases pops up during a conversation, the computer does two things. One, it traces the origin and the destination of the signal and identifies it according to the phone number or frequency it has used. So it gets the name of the parties who sent and received the message, whether it be by telephone or radio or computer. At the same time, it logs the call and its identification and alerts someone that a so-called dangerous conversation is taking place."

"All right, I think I understand," Joni interrupted. "Say I was in New York and I called a friend in, oh, England . . ."

"Or it could be across town, or in Akron," Sloane added. "Once more satellites are added to the network, they could probably patch in on telephone calls from one house to the next one on the block."

"Whoa, wait a minute," Chang said. "Local calls aren't relayed by comsats, so how can anyone patch into them?"

Hamilton and Sloane both shrugged. "We're not sure," Sam replied, "but the file we read specifically mentioned the capability to tap into local-to-local communications. Our guess is that the Ear is, or will be, interfaced with SIGINT-type satellites. Those are satellites which are capable of listening in on distant telephone communications. They've been with us since the 1980's, when the superpowers used them as spy satellites."

"This is the likelihood," Hamilton added. "If the NSA is going to scheme something this big and extensive, they're not going to leave local communications untouched."

"Okay, I got that," Joni continued, holding her hands up. "Here's my example: I called a friend in, okay, Akron, and I said something like, 'Let's shoot the President tomorrow,' or 'Let's bomb City Hall. . . .' "

"Or, 'The President is a scum-sucking rat fink,' or 'Do you know where I can buy some pot?' " Sloane shrugged. "You don't even have to be serious. You could wish aloud that the King of England be run over by a garbage truck or that your friend's town be used as a test site for the neutron bomb, and somebody might pay attention."

"Right, so I say something nasty and seditious," Joni continued, nodding her head. "Does that mean the computer will pick up that phrase, trace both me and my friend, and alert someone that possible sedition or criminal conspiracy is taking place?"

"Right," Sloane said. "That's exactly what would take place."

"So what would be considered a dangerous word or phrase?"

"Anything they damn well please," Sloane replied in a low voice.

There were a few moments of silence as everyone considered the implications. "Well, it's not necessarily a bad thing," Virgin Bruce said at last. "I mean, they could cut down on a lot of crime that way, or stop terrorism before it starts, or . . ."

"Ah, *c'mon,* Bruce!" Jack slapped his hands on his knees in anger.

"This way *anything* could be made into a crime! *Anyone* could be cast as a potential criminal or terrorist! Innocent people would be hurt as much as the guilty."

"He's right, Bruce," Popeye said.

Everyone turned to look at Hooker, who had not said a word during the whole meeting. Realizing that he was suddenly the center of attention, and why—he seldom said anything—Popeye felt himself blush, and look down at the deck.

"Go on," Hamilton said, his voice at a normal pitch once again. "What's on your mind, Popeye?"

"Well . . ." Popeye spoke slowly, unaccustomed to speaking his mind before a lot of people and wondering how he had become so shy over the past months. "It would be like in Orwell's *1984*, with the Thought Police monitoring what everyone said, inferring treason from casual conversations. I mean, we've had it happen again and again in history. The Salem witch trials and the McCarthy hearings and the Accuracy in Academia movement. Shit, they arrested a lot of people in America a hundred years ago, during World War I, for violating the Alien and Sedition Acts, just for saying things which seemed to support Germany."

"Goddamn," Virgin Bruce said, visibly impressed. "I didn't know you were so educated, pal."

Popeye shrugged, feeling a bit proud of himself. "When I used to trawl for shrimp, there wasn't much to do sometimes. I took books out on the water and read a lot. Uh, and I did a correspondence course with the University of Florida. But the thing is, despite the First Amendment and the principles of free speech, there has always been a history of the U.S. government listening in on the people and taking the names of those who said things which were politically disagreeable. However . . ." He shook his head in amazement. "This is the worst yet, if it's true. No one will be safe. It'll end freedom of speech."

"Nice speech." Virgin Bruce leaned back in his chair and crossed in his arms in a gesture of nonchalance. "Okay, assuming that everything you've found out is true, why did you tell us about it?"

"Because we've got to put a stop to it," Hamilton replied.

"Ohhh," Virgin Bruce retorted, rolling his eyes, *"we've* got to put a stop to it." He shook his head. "Look, Jack, I agree with you that this is serious stuff, but what the hell do you expect us to do about it? I mean . . . shit, I'm just a grunt spaceman. Do you think I look like the type who gives a shit about the fate of democracy or something?"

"Frankly, yeah, I do," Hamilton said calmly. "A couple of months ago you risked your own butt to save the lives of Webb and Honeyman. You did that because you cared, and you were able to do that because . . . well, I don't mean to offend you . . . but you're a natural-born spaceman."

This broke everyone up, and Hamilton grinned in spite of himself. "Well, admit it," he said, gesturing toward Virgin Bruce. "Look at this clown. Look at yourselves. Fifty years ago it was only test pilots and scientists who went into space. Now it's slobs like us . . ."

"Like *him!*" both Joni and Chang shouted in unison, pointing at Virgin Bruce.

"Okay, like him."

"God'll get you for that, Jack," Bruce murmured, red-faced but grinning.

"If the NSA doesn't first," Hamilton replied. "But now it's people like us who are living up here, doing all the things which were only dreamed about years ago. I mean—and I don't want to ring in those hoary old clichés—but we're the pioneers, folks. We're the ones who are really opening up space for the world, for everybody in the human race."

"God help the human race," Chang said with a snicker.

"If you like, but I'd rather it be us. Look, if we're up here, we're the pioneers. Take a look at history. It's always been the misfits, the losers, the weirdos, the people running from the law or the tax collectors or their wives who've started things. Look at most of the people who colonized America. Look at the people who ended up colonizing Antarctica. The weirdos do it eventually, not the governments or the military, and if they don't like what's going on, they change the rules."

"What Jack's trying to say," Sloane continued, "is that if we don't make the decisions for what goes on in space, who will? The guys on Earth? There's Skycorp, who have this P.R. thing going about how the powersats are going to release the world from the energy crunch, and cooperating with the NSA to bug everyone in the world. The government? They're the ones who started the whole thing."

"So? Let's send a letter to the *New York Times,*" said Bruce. "Tip them off. Get something to CNN or CBS. Fuck, that's what the press are there to do, to expose stuff like this."

Joni frowned pensively and gently thumped her fist on Bruce's shoulder. "I don't think so," she said thoughtfully. "I'm sure a newspaper would be interested, yes, but we'd have to transmit anything we said to them. If this satellite system is what it's rumored to be, then it could intercept our message as soon as we link with the normal communications channels, which we'd have to do eventually. I could figure out how to do it, but I can't see any means of getting a message through to any public channel without being caught."

Hamilton nodded. "Sam and I thought of that when we were talking about this yesterday. Besides, if it got into the papers, how much real good would it do? Let's face it. People down there have become apathetic after all the shit that hit the fan in the crazy years. How many people would pay attention? Hell, come to think of it, how many would even take Bruce's stand and say that this kind of surveillance was a good thing?"

"Hey, I get your point," Bruce said quickly, waving his hands. "I see where this is something really twisted, y'know. But why are we the people who have to stop this?"

"Who else do you have in mind?" Jack replied. "NASA? If they're not in on it, then think about what a bang-up job they've done as a regulatory agency. They rubber-stamped the Vulcan blowout as being an unforseeable accident and dismissed the whole thing. You think they'd do much differently this time, when they're renting launch facilities at the Cape to Skycorp and helping them with R & D?"

"You've got a point," Popeye said.

Hamilton nodded. "Then who've you got left, who can be trusted? Which senators and congressmen who might not potentially be involved? How do you contact them if you think they could be trusted?"

"The Russians," Joni said.

Virgin Bruce blew out his cheeks. "I ain't cooperating with no fucking Commie."

"The Japanese," Chang said.

"Who knows? Maybe this is their revenge for Hiroshima." Sloane shrugged. "I mean, there's a chance that they could be involved, since there's apparently some cooperation involved with other countries. When you think about the Tokyo riots and all the stuff that's gone down over there . . ."

"So what does that leave us?" Hamilton shrugged. "It comes down to us, guys. We've been thinking about it, Sam and I, and we have an idea. It's risky as all hell, but the people in this room . . . which is why we picked just you few . . . could pull it off."

"Everyone here has a certain specialty," Sloane said, leaning closer. "All of us can do something which could help . . ."

"Hey," Virgin Bruce said, pointing a finger at Sam's face. "I'm not asking you, I'm asking him. Stop playing boy sidekick, okay?" He looked at Hamilton. "Let's hear it from you, Jack. How do you think we can do something about this, if we can do anything?"

"There's no reason to be nasty about it," Hamilton said, casting a glance at Sloane. "But if you want it from me, then here's the low-down. Besides the fact that everyone here has demonstrated them-selves able to keep one secret, and therefore able to keep another . . . we hope . . . there's also the fact that each has a certain area of specialization aboard the station. You and Popeye are used to working in space, Joni is a communications officer, Dave's the Docks chief, and Sam's a hacker. All this figures in a scheme Sam and I have figured out, of how we can put the Ear out of commission before it goes on-line."

He stopped and looked around at the others. "This is the point of no return, friends. If you don't want to be in on this, go ahead and leave now. We'll trust you to keep your mouth shut. But if you give a damn about little things like freedom of expression and the right of pioneers to decide what happens on the frontier, then I'd suggest that you stick around. But if you do, I'll let you know now that you're part of the conspiracy. There's no backing out after this."

Jack fell quiet, and it was silent for a few moments in the compart-ment. Hooker stared at the seed racks and at the tomato vines grow-ing at the far end of the module. I can leave now, he thought. This really shouldn't involve me. I've got enough problems of my own. He noticed Dave Chang moving restlessly, as if he, too, were trying to make up his mind. I should go, Hooker thought. I should stay. I should climb up this ladder right now. But if I do, all the stuff I said a minute ago, what does that mean? He closed his eyes. . . .

And he didn't get up to leave.

When he opened his eyes, he noticed that no one else had left and Hamilton was looking directly at him. He nodded his head, and Jack nodded back, smiling. "Okay," the hydroponics engineer said. "I'm glad to hear it. Sam?"

Sloane turned back to his computer terminal and typed in another code. A graphic image of the respective orbits of Skycan and Free-dom Station appeared on the screen. "We know that the Ear's com-mand module, the switchboard, arrived at Freedom a few weeks ago," Jack began, "and that they'll be using it to put the Ear on-line in a few days. . . ."

# 24

# Labor Day

The crew of Olympus got Labor Day off. There were not many similarities between working on Earth and working in space, but one was that a few of the holidays—Memorial Day, the Fourth of July, Thanksgiving, and Christmas—were observed as paid days off by Skycorp. Labor Day was another. Vital functions, such as life-support, command, and communications, were kept going of course, operated by a skeleton crew who were given triple-time holiday pay according to the company's agreement with the union, the International Association of Machinists and Aerospace Workers. However, most of the crew was off, which gave the conspirators time to get organized.

For Popeye, there wasn't much to do. He and Virgin Bruce spent a couple of hours in the Docks with Chang, checking out the spacesuits they planned to pilfer from the prep room's lockers. A freight OTV from Freedom Station had arrived at the Docks at 0800 earlier in the day, and once Chang had told Bob Harris again that he wasn't looking well and that he should go back to his bunk and take care of himself, he and Bruce went to work on the little cargocraft—stripping the hold of everything unnecessary, lashing inside three extra oxygen tanks, and juryrigging a latch handle to the inside of the hatch so that it could be opened from the inside. By this time, though, it had become apparent that Bruce and Chang could manage better on their own; a third man simply got in the way. So Popeye was excused from any more duties in the Docks.

"I'll go see if Sam and Jack need any help," Popeye said on his way out of the airlock.

Virgin Bruce shrugged, holding onto a rail with his right hand and cradling a welding laser under his left armpit. "Unless you really know your stuff with computer programming, I wouldn't bother," he replied. "Why don't you go back to your bunk and get some shut-eye. You'll need it."

Popeye glanced at his watch. It was only 1200; they weren't scheduled for departure until 0300 the next morning. "I'm not that tired," he commented.

"Then go down to west rec and watch the baseball game," Bruce replied, turning upside down as he prepared to enter the OTV's open hatch. "Or go read a book. I dunno." He pushed himself off and glided toward the hatch, while Chang reached up to take the laser from him and pull it down into the vehicle. "Geez, take it easy. That's what I'd do."

But Popeye was too wound up to think about taking it easy. Every nerve felt like a stretched guitar string; he wasn't in the mood to watch a baseball game or read another dog-eared paperback or magazine. As he shut the hatch of the prep room behind him, he realized that the thought of returning to Earth bothered him far more than anyone else in the conspiracy.

He had always thought about that day, whenever it came, when he would go back home. It had been something for which he had longed over the course of the many months he had lived in space, but at the same time it filled him with a secret, half-recognized dread. When he had imagined the event in his mind's eye, it had been that vision of getting off a shuttle at the Cape with a hot salt breeze blowing against his face, of a slow, carefree stroll down the tarmac away from the spacecraft, of someone from Skycorp shouting after him, asking if he wanted his check, and him shouting over his shoulder to fold it and feed it to an alligator. He had never permitted himself to think about what would happen after that, but now he wondered: What would he do once he arrived home in Florida? He didn't have the *Jumbo Shrimp II* anymore. He had sold his house long ago. And, of course, there was the question of Laura. . . .

*Gold, gold, gold . . . little gold ring, twisting and turning, disappearing into the aquamarine, reflecting the setting sun as it disappeared . . . gone, forever gone . . .*

He shut his eyes tightly. Don't think about it, he said to himself. Going home would not be the way he had always imagined.

Hooker opened his eyes and pushed himself down the axis shaft, heading toward the spokes and the access ladders which would take him back to the modules. He looked ahead, and saw at the far end of the shaft the hatch to Meteorology, the pit at the south polar end of the station, where the bogus meteorologists worked. He found himself staring at the hatch as he drifted closer. Even before the meeting in Hydroponics and Hamilton's disclosure of the NSA's involvement with Big Ear, he had not been to Meteorology in many weeks; only a couple of times, in fact, since the day of the hotdog blowout at Vulcan Station. Since then, his desire to look at Earth through the telescope had diminished considerably, but now he felt an impulse to haul himself down there, push the intercom button, and ask if he could come in and spend a few minutes with the telescope.

No, he thought, that would probably not be a good idea. He and the others were too close to the start of the deed which would destroy the Ear. It was conceivable that, in some unforseen way, his trip to the weather station might somehow tip off Bob, John, and Dave that a plot was afoot. He squelched the notion almost as soon as it occurred to him, although, he thought, it would be funny if Dave knew the consequences of his stoned conversation with Jack Hamilton.

It was therefore blind, dumb coincidence that, as soon as Popeye reached the open hatch leading to the west spoke's access shaft, who should push himself through the same shaft with a plastic bag full of sandwiches in his hand but Dave the meteorologist, a.k.a. Jack Jarrett, agent for the National Security Agency.

Dave, or Jarrett—Popeye couldn't think of him by any other name than Dave—nearly bumped into him before he recognized Hooker. Then it was with quiet surprise that he looked around at the beamjack. "Hey, Popeye!" Dave exclaimed. "Long time no see!"

"Hi, Dave. Fetching lunch for the boys?"

"Yeah." Dave held the bag of sandwiches up, regarding it glumly. "Wish some more food would get up here soon. Third day in a row we've been stuck with tuna. Haven't seen you down here lately. What's the matter, become tired of looking through the telescope?"

"Something like that." Hooker felt himself getting a little uneasy in Dave's presence, and he did a slow somersault to ease his feet in the proper direction for entering the access shaft. "I'll come by sometime, if you're not too busy."

"Well . . ." Dave seemed to hesitate. "You're welcome to visit, but not for the next couple of days. We're going to be pretty busy down here."

Yeah, I just bet you will be, Hooker thought, and he suddenly felt a surge of anger rise in him. Son of a bitch has a big mouth when he gets high, blabs everything to someone about the Big Ear, and still he tries to put on a front about being a meteorologist. Unbelievable gall . . .

Impulsively, Popeye said, "Getting your ears checked, huh, Dave?"

The NSA agent's eyes went wide and Popeye was immediately sorry he had said anything. "What do you mean?" Dave said, staring at Hooker. Then, recovering himself, he said, "I don't know what you mean, Popeye."

It was so absurd—Dave's first and second reactions to a simple comment—that Hooker had to laugh contemptuously. "Shouldn't talk so much when you're ripped, *Jack,*" he said, eschewing caution as he enjoyed the dig. "I'm surprised that the Agency hasn't briefed you guys about the dangers of smoking dope while on duty."

Jarrett's face went red and his eyes bored into Hooker's. He started to stammer, then managed to collect himself. "If I were you," he whispered angrily, "I'd keep your goddamn mouth shut, sailor!"

"About what, spook?" Popeye whispered back, enjoying himself. Screw caution. This was too good to miss. "You smoking dope, or the Big Ear?"

"I never said *anything* about the Ear to him!" Jarrett hissed.

Popeye was about to make another sarcastic remark, but looking into the phony weatherman's eyes, he was struck suddenly by a startling, absolutely bewildering revelation: Dave actually looked as if he were telling the truth.

Popeye looked at Dave suspiciously. "Okay, let's be straight with each other. If you can be straight with anyone. You got stoned with Jack Hamilton, didn't you?"

Dave returned the suspicious look. "If I did, why should I tell you?" he said, hesitating.

Popeye nodded his head. "I'm going to take that as a confirmation."

"How would you know?"

"Because word travels fast around Skycan," Popeye replied. "Maybe you and your buddies keep out of arm's reach of everyone here, but if you didn't know by now, there isn't much that's secret in this place. No, don't let it bother you. Only Jack, you, and I know about it."

Dave visibly relaxed. "Okay, so maybe I did." He seemed to be studying Popeye's face. "So what's this about . . . um, what are you talking about with this Big Ear business?"

"You mean you've never heard about the Big Ear?" Popeye asked.

"No," Dave said, "I don't know what you're talking about."

"You said you did, just a moment ago."

Dave's face turned red again. His mouth opened and closed in confusion as he tried to muster an answer. Finally he glared at Popeye. "Listen to me, pal. I don't know where you've heard about the Ear, but if you were smart, you'd keep your mouth shut about it. Understand? If I hear you make another sound about it . . ."

"I heard about it because you told Jack," Popeye interrupted. "I heard about it because you told him . . ."

"I didn't say anything about it to Hamilton," Dave said. "That's the truth. And if you say anything more about it to anyone . . ."

"Back off, Jack!" Popeye snarled, feeling both angry and bewildered. "Who are you trying to threaten? You try anything with me, and word gets back to your bosses in Washington, or wherever, that one of their agents has been blowing joints with civilians!"

Dave's lips pursed in a thin, tight line. He stared at Hooker for a moment longer, then swung his body around so that he faced the Meteorology compartment. "Just keep your mouth shut, asshole, or you're going to be sorry." Then he pushed himself away, carrying his bag of sandwiches.

Popeye watched him go, then propelled himself down the spoke shaft, heading for the rim modules at a pace which was literally breakneck. He would grab the ladder rungs when he needed to stop himself from falling, but right then he needed speed.

Jack Jarrett had not told Hamilton about the Big Ear. That much was practically certain in his mind. If Jarrett was indeed telling the truth, then that made Hamilton a liar.

A liar, at least, about everything except the NSA's interest in the Big Ear. Jarrett had overlooked an important fact in his anger: The existence of the satellite network, in itself, was not a closely kept secret, and the only thing he could possibly be upset about Hooker's knowing was the true purpose of the Big Ear. So that part of the story which Hamilton had told Popeye and the others was apparently true.

What was apparently a lie was how Hamilton had found out about it. Popeye intuitively felt, and had at least circumstantial evidence to prove, that Jarrett had not spilled the beans about the Big Ear to Jack Hamilton.

So how did Hamilton know about the Ear's secret? Hooker intended to find out.

Popeye thought he would find Hamilton and Sloane in the computer bay, where they were supposed to be working on the program, but when he got there, he found the Data Processing bay vacant. It was 1218 by this time, so he took a shot in the dark; he jogged down the catwalk until he reached Modules 25 through 28, the mess deck. As he had figured, they had gone over there to get lunch.

He found them in Module 27, sitting across from each other at one of the long tables near the serving counter. Many other members of the crew were also in the three compartments which made up the dining room; behind the counter, Emil the Slob was placing another tray of chicken-flavored grease out for the guys to dig into. The smell did its usual trick on Popeye, revolting him and making him hungry at the same time, but he ignored it and went to the table where Sam and Jack were hunched over their trays.

The mess deck was one of the few sections of Skycan left where Muzak was still piped through the speakers, since no one had yet dared to cut the wires there as had been done throughout the rest of station. "Promises, Promises" floated through the compartment, ignored by the crewmen who apathetically chewed on their reconstituted repast. As Hooker sat down next to Sloane, Hamilton lifted a forkful of lumpy mashed potatoes and quietly murmured, "There aren't going to be many things about this place I'm going to miss. . . ."

"But you're really going to miss the food, right?" Sloane shook his head. "Jack, if you'd been here as long as I have and seen as many guys come and go from here as I have, you'd know that's hardly an original observation. Hi, Popeye."

Hooker ignored Sloane. He wasn't in the mood for social graces. "You lied to us, Jack," he said in a ragged whisper, a little out of breath from his run halfway around the circumference of the catwalk.

Jack looked blandly at him. "What?" he asked with an innocence that made Hooker want to punch him in the nose. "Pardon me?"

"You *lied* to us, asshole," Hooker said, his voice rising along with his anger. "I just talked to Jarrett and he told me that he didn't say anything to you about the Ear. He got stoned with you, but he didn't say *anything* to you about that shit. . . ."

"Jesus!" Sloane said, dropping his fork. "You talked to Jarrett? You dumb son of a bitch, how could you . . . ?"

Popeye turned and stuck a finger up to Sam's face. "Shut up," he hissed. "Just sit there and eat your crap and don't say anything, or so help me after I get through ripping this bastard's lungs out I'll work on yours next." He turned back to face Hamilton, leaning halfway over the table. "I want the truth this time. What do you know about the Ear, and where did you hear it from?"

"I told you," Hamilton said, his eyes nervously shifting from

Popeye to Sloane and back again, his voice an almost inaudible whisper. "I heard it from Dave when he came down to see me in Hydroponics. He told me then, all . . ."

"Stop lying right now," Hooker muttered, the building fury in him making his hands quake, "or so help me, I'm coming across this table and wrapping that fucking tray around your head. One more chance. Where did you hear about the Ear?"

Hamilton stared back at him, then sighed and looked down at his tray. "I'll tell you, but I won't tell you here," he whispered. "We'll go back to the lab and talk about this. There's too many people who can overhear us now." He glanced significantly toward the others seated around them.

Hooker nodded. "Okay," he said. "We'll take it to your lab."

Nothing more was said on the way from the mess deck to Hydroponics, but as soon as the three men had climbed down the ladder into Module 42 and Hamilton had closed the hatch behind them, Popeye again took the offensive. "Okay, I want it straight now," he snapped. "What's going on with the Big Ear, and how come you lied to everyone about hearing it from Jarrett?"

"Now wait just a minute, Popeye," Sloane said. "How can you expect Dave to do anything but deny that he got high with Jack? And what makes you think that Jack's not telling the truth?"

"Because Jarrett *didn't* deny that he had been smoking pot," Popeye said. "That's one thing. And for another . . ."

"Okay, okay, hold it," Hamilton said calmly, putting up his hands in a placating gesture. He settled himself down in a chair and took a deep breath. "I want to get this all straightened out, Popeye, because this is too important to let any misunderstandings get in the way."

"Yeah, right." Hooker leaned against the compartment wall and folded his arms across his chest. "C'mon, Jack, let's hear the rest of your story."

Hamilton shook his head. "No stories, Popeye. You're right. I did lie to you and the others and it was because I saw no other way of telling you about the Ear."

Sam turned and stared at Hamilton with a look of absolute surprise. "Are you saying that . . . ?"

Jack nodded slowly. "That's right. There's some fiction in what I said to you guys the other day. I didn't think anyone would catch on, but that was because I didn't expect anyone to attempt to confirm the story." He let out his breath and looked down at his hands. "I guess that was a mistake, and I'm sorry I had to deceive you guys, but I had to put some credibility behind the source."

"Then the whole thing about the Ear," Sam said. "Is that a lie, too?"

"No, that part is not a lie. Hell, you saw the file yourself. You should know better than that. No, Popeye's right. Dave smoked pot with me down here, but even though I did try to squeeze some info out of him, I didn't get anywhere. He didn't say a word about it. I got my information from another source." He looked up at Popeye. "Hooker, I'm real sorry. But when I tell you just how I found out about the Ear, maybe you'll understand."

"Go ahead," Hooker said stiffly. "But you'll have to understand me if I say I might not trust you this time, either."

Hamilton stood up from his chair and sauntered over to a vegetable tank, reaching up to absently fondle a plastic feeder tube between his fingers as he spoke. "Have either of you ever heard of the Gaia Institute?" he asked. "No? It's located on Cape Hatteras in North Carolina and it's . . . well, it's somewhere between a school and an independently funded think-tank. It mainly functions as a place for biotech research, which is how it originally got its start back in the 1990's, but since then, it's branched off into several different directions." He paused. "Some of them not very public."

"I don't understand," Hooker said. "What's this got to do with . . . ?"

"GI is where I got my real start in hydroponics," Hamilton continued, ignoring the interruption. "I went there to do a two-year postdoc program and ended up staying for about five years. The reason I stayed for so long is that I got involved in some of the Institute's less well-known projects. One of those is something called Globe Watch."

He pulled a ripe tomato off a vine and juggled it thoughtfully from hand to hand. "Did you ever wonder where all the old radicals who were around in the last part of the twentieth century disappeared to? Yeah, right, some of them became reactionary conservatives or reactionary liberals, and some of them sank from view, and a lot of them have gone out mumbling of discarded values and cursing the generations which succeeded them. But a few of them, whose ideals outlived fashions and trends, have ended up in important positions in government and industry, still dedicated to certain goals, still networked with each other. They make up the core of Globe Watch. They're nerve ends, lying dormant, hearing things, seeing things, and secretly conveying their reports to its nexus, the Gaia Institute, which over the years had recruited them. The objective over the years has been simple: to watch and record the decisions that others make, evaluate their impact on contemporary society and, if necessary, act in secret to either accelerate or forestall the circumstances." "Globe Watch found out about the Big Ear," Sloane supplied.

Hamilton nodded. "We found out about the Ear, first through rumor, then through documents located by a highly placed source at NASA. When we were certain that the project was a reality and not just another paranoid rumor, we turned the information over to a GI think-tank. I was one of the people involved, and we made the decision that the Ear had to be stopped if free society was to be preserved."

"Then why didn't you just come to us?" Popeye asked, his anger diminished but not entirely gone. "We would have believed you."

Jack shook his head. "No. Even if you had believed me—and I'm not entirely certain you believe me now—it's Globe Watch's policy to keep its existence secret. Telling you would have blown my cover. Believe me, we considered that option when we were thinking about how to handle this."

Sam's eyebrows knitted together. "Then there's another reason why you came aboard Skycan to be the chief hydroponics engineer."

Hamilton laughed. "The *only* reason I came up here was to do something about the Ear. We had the whole timetable for the implementation of the project, all the details of how it would operate, everything. The tricky part was getting me up here in time once our contact in NASA helped slide my application through the proper channels at Skycorp. Fortunately the last hydroponicist up here, McHenry, went crazy, so I was able to get up here in enough time to get the ball rolling." He turned around to gaze at the others. "To win your hearts and minds, as it were."

Sam and Popeye gave him blank expressions in return, and Jack snorted. "C'mon," he said. "Did you really think it was a coincidence that the guy who brought marijuana seeds aboard was also the guy who happened to discover the Ear and got a handful of people who just happened to have been smoking pot to agree to a mutiny?"

The blank expressions became those of utter surprise.

"That's right," Hamilton said. "I can't say that I didn't enjoy myself, either, but the whole game was planned from the start. The idea was to cultivate a small cluster of people, lower their guards a little with the pot, select a handful who seemed trustworthy and whose skills fitted in with the general plan of how to plug the Ear, then spring the plot on them. We figured we had about a one-in-ten chance of succeeding." He shook his head. "Up to this point, that is. Having Dave stumble down here looking for a good time was a lucky break which I had hoped to use to my advantage. I guess I screwed up there, because I didn't consider the possibility that someone might actually talk to Dave about it."

"You didn't consider the possibility," Popeye repeated. He looked first at Sloane, then at Hamilton. "Did you hear that?" he asked Sam. "This goddamn son of a bitch has been manipulating us every step of the way. He gets us all into using drugs to soften our minds, he lies to us about a government project and talks us into doing the dirty work for a bunch of crazy old granola freaks, and then he *apologizes* because one of us managed to find out it was all a scam. . . ."

"Now, wait, I wouldn't call this a . . ."

*"That could get us all killed!"* Suddenly Popeye launched himself at Hamilton. He grabbed the hydroponicist's shirt with both hands and rammed his back against a tank. Water sloshed out of the tank and splashed across the metal floor; a tomato fell out and splattered on the floor in a red pulpy stain. *"I should fucking kill you, you know that?"* Popeye howled into Jack's face, shaking him back and forth.

Sloane rushed Popeye and grabbed him in a half nelson, wrenching him off the hydroponicist. "Cut it out, goddammit!" he said hoarsely. He looked over Popeye's shoulder. "Is this true?" he demanded of Hamilton. "Is that what this is all about?"

Hamilton weakly pushed himself off the side of the rack, the back of his shirt damp from where he had half-fallen into the tank. "Yes. No. Somewhere in between." He shook his head and absent-mindedly straightened his shirt. He motioned for Sloane to let Popeye go. "If you think you ought to kill me, Claude, you should go ahead," he said to Hooker. "If I really cheated you like that, I guess you're right to do so. But I swear to you, that wasn't the intent."

Hooker took a few deep breaths, and his shoulders and arms relaxed. Sam released his grip reluctantly, but kept his arms up and ready to grab the beamjack again. "Then what was the idea, Jack?" he demanded. "Was it to brainwash us or what?"

Hamilton shook his head vigorously. "No. No, that wasn't the idea at all. Bringing aboard the pot and growing that stuff down here was an afterthought, as . . . like offering a bribe, that's all. You can't get a stoned person to do something he doesn't want to do, any more than you can talk someone who wants to live into committing suicide. We weren't trying to soften your minds or anything like that."

He looked down remorsefully at the ruined tomato on the floor, then kneeled to pick it up. "Anyone want a tomato?" he said. When neither Sam nor Popeye laughed, he slowly walked to a nearby disposal chute and dropped it in. A push of a button and the quiet *whoosh* of compressed air sent the vegetable on its way to Reclamation. "Ashes to ashes, tomatoes to compost," he mumbled.

"I want to hear your answer too, Jack," Sloane said.

Hamilton continued to stare at the chute. "The pot was only because we knew that the people aboard Skycan were bored," he said. "We thought that if the person from Globe Watch who came up here were to bring something which would distract them from that boredom, perhaps he would win a degree of acceptance they wouldn't otherwise have given him. We would have brought up bottles of whiskey and gin, if the chances of discovery hadn't been so great. As it was, because of my availability as a hydroponicist, marijuana was selected as the . . . well, forgive the pun, but the ideal peace pipe.

"Nor was the intention to deceive anyone, or make someone else do the dirty work," he continued. He turned away from the disposal chute and leaned against the adjacent bulkhead, thrusting his clenched fists into the pockets of his shorts. "But we were afraid that, if the group I chose to approach about the Ear were to know that a secret organization was behind this—a twenty-first century Masons or Hellfire Club, or a bunch of old hippies if you want—then the chances of being rejected would be greater, because people still remember all the trouble that groups like the Heritage Foundation and the LaRouchians got us into years ago. If the Skycan people made up their minds for themselves, the think-tank reasoned, then the chances for succeeding would be increased."

"Wait a second," Sloane said, stepping from behind Popeye's back and pointing a finger at Hamilton. "You talked us into this. *You* were the one who convinced us to go after the Ear."

Hamilton smiled and shook his head again. "I didn't talk you into anything, Sam," he said. "You can't *talk* someone, or a bunch of people, into doing anything if they don't want to do it. That's what we were counting on. We were gambling that, if people aboard Skycan were simply made aware of the situation, and told what the circumstances of that situation were, then they would make up their own minds to do something about it for themselves."

He walked toward them, his hands spread apart, pleading for their understanding. "Don't you see? The people on Skycan, the group who agreed to go along with this thing, *me* for chrissakes . . . we're the frontier, not the companies or NASA or Russia or Europeans! It's the people who are out here who ultimately make the decision which way the chips are going to fall! You knew that in your heart of hearts when we agreed to go through with this. I could have had you guys blowing joints until your eyes were crossed and you wouldn't have agreed, or at least until you had straightened up, to go along with this. You think you're up here just to make some dough and that's all, but the fact of the matter is that you're the ones who decide where we go from here. I think that's the reason why we're doing this."

He paused letting his hands drop to his sides. "If you still want to do it," he finished. "You've got the whole truth now. No more lies. At this point, if you two guys want to bail out, then the whole operation's finished because there's no one else who can do the job. I'm sorry for the things I told you before, I truly am, so . . ." He stopped and swallowed. "Well, anyway, there it is. There's your answers, Popeye, Sam. You're right in that it's dangerous as hell. Sam and I have just about completed writing the program, and Joni has already helped me contact my friend at the Cape. But if you guys decide that you've been brainwashed and that all this is bad craziness, then . . ."

His voice trailed off, and Jack stood there, awaiting their answer.

# 25

# Freedom Rendezvous

By the time the United States built Freedom Station in the late 1990's, it was not the first space station in low-Earth orbit, nor was it to be the last. By then, the Soviet Union's Mir station had been permanently manned for several years and had been expanded with six pressurized modules. As well, Space Industries, Inc. had successfully orbited a two-module industrial space station, and Skycorp was planning Olympus Station to support future industrial activities. Yet Freedom, although it was not unique, did fulfill its main purpose—serving as the major springboard for Western activity in space.

Freedom started operation with three modules; by 2016, its pressurized capacity comprised thirteen modules, spread along the station's twin aluminum-lattice keels and connected to each other by access tunnels. The photovoltaic-cell wings and solar dynamic generator dishes had increased in both size and number to accommodate the energy demands of McDonnell Douglas, Rockwell, Johnson & Johnson, Honda, Lily, BMW, and the other corporations which had bought or leased the modules, and the servicing hangars were connected by access tubes and refitted to permit pressurization in order to handle traffic from OTV's.

What had begun as an underfunded attempt to produce a viable space station had in time become an orbiting industrial park. Although free-flying modules in parking orbits nearby did most of the mass production of chips, pharmaceuticals, alloys, abrasives, and novelty items, the companies who could afford R&D in space had taken advantage of a deregulated NASA space station. Members of Congress and a former President who had opposed the few billion dollars spent on the development of the space station during the 80's and 90's had either switched allegiances or had shut up by the time the year 2004 rolled around, when the *Wall Street Journal* reported that gross profits from space-based enterprises aboard Freedom had begun to rival those of some major companies on Earth, including a couple on the Fortune 500 list.

Eleven years after Freedom Station reached that landmark, the station had come to resemble a small city in space: a long frame of cylinders, girders, solar cell wings, and antennae circling Earth at an altitude of 300 miles, serviced by shuttles from the U.S., France, Great Britain, and Japan, with OTV's being retrieved or dispatched by docking crews. Many prominent persons and groups—from the Prince of Wales to a U.S. Secretary of Commerce to a Japanese trade minister, from the Board Chairman of Honda to a research contingent from Data General to a Pulitzer Prize-winning journalist—had been up to visit the station. Three hundred miles-up was no longer a formidable distance; even the insurance companies, who had shied away from underwriting manned space travel thirty years earlier, were reconsidering the tourist trade.

Although Olympus Station had in recent years taken away much of the attention—with its far larger crew capacity, one-third g capability and Project Franklin—Freedom remained as proof that space was a viable habitat for humanity, that the high frontier could be conquered by private industry and the public sector working in concert for the betterment of all people. Especially those who had purchased the right stock at the right time. Who could argue with success?

"Shit," Virgin Bruce said from somewhere in the darkness. "My legs are getting cramped."

"They shouldn't be," Jack Hamilton said over the comlink. "Your muscles shouldn't be tight in zero g. How many times have you been in your pod? That thing's even tighter than this."

"Ah, go throw up," Bruce muttered, "then tell me about zero g."

"Don't even mention that," Popeye Hooker said sharply. "If he gets sick, there's nothing he can do about it." In a softer voice he added, "How're you doing there, Jack?"

"I'm okay. I'm over it now. Jesus."

Popeye checked the chronometer on the heads-up display inside his helmet. "Fifteen, maybe twenty minutes. We should be decelerating any minute now."

"That's right," Virgin Bruce said. "Keep reminding us. God damn, can't we loosen these straps any?"

"No, don't do that," Popeye said. "The shift in inertia might throw the guidance computer off, and I don't want to spend another half an hour in this thing waiting for a recovery crew to retrieve us."

"Yeah," Hamilton said. "I second the motion."

"You mean the lack of it."

The three men laughed. After a moment the laughter died out, and it was quiet over their radio link once again. "Anyone got any more stupid stories to tell?" Jack asked.

"Oh, *fuck!*" Virgin Bruce suddenly snarled.

"What's wrong?" Popeye snapped.

"I just farted," Bruce said in disgust. "Oh, geeze . . ."

"That's what you get for eating," Hamilton said after allowing himself an evil chuckle. "And for wishing Star Whoops on me."

Popeye and Jack laughed again, and then the laughter died out. "You want to recharge your suit air again?" Hamilton asked. "It might help a little."

"Naw. I'm at max pressure already. I'm just going to have to live with it."

More silence in the darkness. Hamilton sighed after a little while. "Once I was on a camping trip in the White Mountains," he began, "and we heard this bear rooting through the brush outside our tent . . ."

"Is this your stupid story?" Virgin Bruce asked.

"This is my stupid story. Anyway . . ."

Suddenly they all felt a slight but discernible *thump.* "There go the RCR's," Popeye said. "Okay, gang, we're going in."

The cargo OTV from Olympus fell a little short of its expected rendezvous point with Freedom's orbit, which meant that the station's tug had to go out a little farther than expected in order to retrieve it and bring it in. Neither the space traffic controller at Freedom nor the docking crew thought much of it; even with no payload to be calculated into the equation, the trajectory of a returning OTV was sometimes off by a couple of degrees in either direction. The shift controller decided not to even bother logging the incident, it was that minor.

Thus, it took a few extra minutes for the pod to tow the OTV to Freedom, where a spacesuited crew member in an MMU latched onto the cylinder with his grappler and gently wrestled the thing down through the open hatch of the Number Three service hangar and onto its cradle. The crew member glided up and over the little spacecraft to its bow and secured its docking adapter to that of the hangar's, making sure the hatches had an airtight fit. Then he jetted out of the hangar and let the command module personnel close the garage doors behind him.

It was another ten minutes after that, at 0710, when another crew member, whose name was Magic Johnson Jones and who was still pissed off that his father, an L.A. Lakers fan, had given him such a silly-ass name when he had been born, undogged a hatch and schlepped his weary ass down the access tunnel to garage Number Three. Jones—who preferred the nickname Joe, and screw what any-one said—expected the chore of checking in the just-arrived OTV to be the last thing he had to do on his shift before he went back to his berth and tucked himself into his sleeping bag for six hours of sleep.

He floated up the tunnel, stopped in front of Number Three and pressed the switch on the wall beside the hatch which would pressur-ize the empty OTV. As he watched the digital indicator which would tell him when the robot spacecraft's cargo bay was fully pressurized, Jones felt the stress of the past week settle over him. Normally his routine as a spacecraft maintenance engineer—NASA's longwinded jargon for what was essentially gofer work—was light, but ever since the new Skycorp module had been attached to the station, he had found himself increasingly involved with putting it on-line. The weirdest part was that he still didn't know exactly what the module's function was, only that it was jammed with electronic equipment. When the team which was to oversee Module 13's operations had arrived by shuttle a couple of days ago, Jones had tried to ask about the module's purpose. He had been rebuffed by the team's leader, a skinny guy named Dobbs, who was not much older than Jones.

"It's an electronics system," Dobbs had said, as if that answered everything. Jones had wanted to say, Hey, you think because I'm Haitian I'm stupid or something? What he said instead was, "Oh, what kind of electronics?" And Dobbs had replied, "Very sophisti-cated electronics. If I explained, I doubt you'd understand," and Jones had wanted to punch the wimp in the teeth.

"So screw it," Jones said to himself as he recalled the incident. Punching out someone important like that would only get him shipped back to Earth. He hadn't struggled down there for years for the chance to go to work in space just to blow it on something stupid like that. No way he was going to return to L.A. now; he was still working on getting transferred to Olympus Station, where the bucks and the action were.

Magic J. Jones saw that the pressurization of the OTV was com-plete, and was about to head back down the tunnel to his quarters in Module 3 when he thought he heard a sound coming from the other side of the hatch, as if something were shifting inside the OTV. He stopped and listened, but heard nothing more. He shrugged and was about to write it off as an auditory illusion brought on by overwork, when he looked down and saw that the locking wheel was turning counterclockwise all by itself.

Now what the hell was *this?* Fascinated, he bent forward and watched the wheel as it slowly turned until there was the loud *click* of the bolts sliding back. It was something he had seen several times when he had been at the service hangars to assist arriving OTV's whose impatient crews had not waited for someone to unlock the hatch for them. But this OTV was an unmanned cargo craft. There was no way to unlock the hatch from the inside unless . . .

The hatch was pushed open by an arm encased in a spacesuit sleeve and gauntlet, and Jones instinctively pulled back. "Hey! Yo!" he shouted, suddenly feeling scared. "What the hell is going on here, man! Who . . . ?"

A helmet was flung straight out of the hatch, hitting Jones in the stomach, even as he reflexively reached up to catch it. He grunted and doubled up over the helmet, his back bouncing off the tunnel wall behind him. Through a wave of pain and surprise he glimpsed a man in a spacesuit, sans helmet, launching himself through the hatch . . . then, in the next instant, the guy's thick, gloved hand grabbed Jones' neck and rammed his head back against the metal wall of the tunnel. The impact made him see tiny pinprick explosions in front of his eyes; he would have gasped, but the hand was tight against his throat.

Through mixed pain, confusion, and outright fear, Jones dimly perceived that others were climbing out of the OTV behind the man who had attacked him. "Works every time," the man holding him by the neck said in a low voice. Jones squinted at him, saw a gaunt face rimmed with a beard, then dark eyes which turned to stare balefully into his own.

"Okay, buddy, one chance," the intruder growled. "Where's the Ear?"

"What?" Jones didn't know what he was talking about. Unfortunately, his attacker didn't buy that excuse. The hand tightened around his throat.

"I said to you, where's the Ear? Where's it located?"

"I don't . . . what are you talking about?" Jones gasped.

He shrank back as the man with the beard pulled a clenched fist back to hammer his head into the curving tunnel wall. Then one of the others behind him—there were two, he now realized—said quickly, "Easy on him, Bruce." This one, who had also removed his helmet, had long blond hair. He said to Jones, "There's a new module here on the station. Came in last week. Where is it?"

Jones' mind was racing. They could be terrorists. PLO, or IRA, or American Christian Army, or one of any number of left- or right-wing extremist groups. But the OTV hadn't come up from Earth; it had come from Olympus, and as far as anyone knew, there weren't any terrorist cells on that place, so how could . . . ? Never mind, never mind. The point was that he now knew what they were searching for, so should he tell them where it was? If he told them, would it later come back to him that he had released that information? Oh, Christ, he didn't want to go back to L.A. . . .

"He knows," the guy with the beard said. "Okay, bub, one more chance. Tell us where it is, or I'm taking you to the nearest airlock and pitching your ass out. One, two, three . . ."

Oh, the hell with all this! "Module 13!" Jones would have yelled, but with the hand around his throat, all he could produce was a weak rasp. "Thirteen! Tunnel One, all the way to the end!" He pointed down the way he had come, where their access tunnel, Number Two, intersected Tunnel One. "That way, that way!" he rasped. Jesus God, he couldn't breathe!

The bearded man, the one the other guy had called Bruce, reached forward, grabbed Jones' left arm and yanked him around. "Duck your head," Bruce commanded, and Jones did so. "A little more," Bruce said. Jones put his chin against his sternum. Bruce let go of his throat, and before Jones could take a good breath, the bearded intruder and another man had grabbed the soles of his deck shoes and shoved.

Jones found himself being pushed into the OTV's cargo compartment. He didn't resist; there wasn't any point in trying. His shoulder banged against something; reaching around, he realized that it was an oxygen tank. But he didn't say anything, even as the hatch shut and he heard the locking wheel turn, sealing him into the cold, dark little chamber. He wasn't a stupid person. His foot rubbed against the hatch, and he felt what had to be an inside unlocking level. Wait a few minutes, he said to himself, then they'll be gone and you can get yourself out of here, and you can go get help. They wanted Module 13, he made himself remember.

Jones smiled. Maybe he wouldn't lose his job after all.

Once the black guy was locked into the OTV and the hatch was closed, Popeye quickly studied the airlock's pressurization controls as he unsnapped the seals on his gauntlets and pulled them off his hands. Then he touched a switch and watched as the digital pressure gauge sank by a fraction, about 1 psi, before he touched the switch again and stopped the depressurization. There. The slight drop in pressure wouldn't matter much to their prisoner—make his ears pop, at worst—but it would prevent the hatch from being opened from the inside, since the airlock's sensors would detect the pressure differential and would keep the hatch bolts from sliding back.

Hooker allowed himself a moment to relax. Okay, the second iffy part of this thing was over. They had managed to successfully rendezvous with Freedom Station, and someone had been on hand to pressurize the OTV from the outside and thus allow them to escape. Two *if's* down. He had lost count of how many more they had to go. . . .

"Okay, now what?" Virgin Bruce said. He was removing his own gauntlets and clipping them to his belt. He glanced over his shoulder, down the access tunnel into which they had emerged, as if expecting another crew member to appear at any moment. "C'mon, Jack, get your shit together. This is your plan, dammit."

"Okay, okay. Just gimmie a minute, will you?" Hamilton was floating in the tunnel, doubled halfway over in a fetal position with his eyes closed. "Just a little disorientation. I had just gotten used to what was up and down in that thing; then I came out and found you and that guy upside down." He opened his eyes slowly and blinked a few times. "Jesus, Bruce, did you have to treat him so rough?"

"We don't have time for this," Virgin Bruce said. He hooked his helmet to his belt, then checked the chronometer on the right sleeve of his suit's overgarment. "It's about 0715. What did she say . . . ?"

"She'll dock at about 0800." Hamilton took a deep breath. "I'm fine. Okay, Module 13, Tunnel One, eh?" He nodded toward his right, where the tunnel they were in ended in a hatch. "The shuttle will be docking down here, which means that where we're going is the opposite direction."

He patted the left thigh-pocket of his suit, making sure that the thick envelope which Sloane had given him was in place. Satisfied that it was—he would have thrown himself out the airlock if it had not been there—he glanced at Popeye and Virgin Bruce. "Let's go."

Virgin Bruce grunted and pushed himself off a wall, guiding himself headfirst, deeper into Freedom Station. Jack was about to follow, but Popeye suddenly reached out with his arm and blocked him. The two men stared into each other's faces for a moment.

"You've gone this far with me," Hamilton whispered. "You're going to have to trust me just a little bit longer."

Popeye nodded slowly. "I know. I just wanted to tell you that if you're yanking us around . . ."

"Well, you're just going to have to take that chance, aren't you?" Hamilton pushed Hooker's arm aside and started after Bruce. Popeye watched him pass, then pushed himself off in their direction, saying nothing in reply.

# 26

# Captain Crunch

I had always wondered how Michael Collins had felt, and now I knew. Michael Collins, the Command Module pilot of the Apollo 11 mission back in 1969, who had sat out the long hours in the spacecraft *Columbia* while Neil Armstrong and Buzz Aldrin made history at Tranquillity Base. For about twenty-five hours Collins was alone in the *Columbia;* once every forty-five minutes, as his ship swung around the far side of the Moon, he had no one to talk to except his tape recorder.

I wasn't that alone, sitting down in the computer bay, but I was just as nervous, waiting for Joni Lowenstein on the command deck to relay to me a signal that Bruce, Popeye, and Jack had managed to make it to the Big Ear logistics module on Freedom Station and that she had managed to patch through a clear comlink for me to send the virus program. We had figured that it would be sometime between 0700 and 0800, if our finely developed timetable worked out, so I really should not have been that anxious. And, after all, I had the easy job: When the comlink was opened, all I had to do was push a few buttons and run the program which was in Skycan's computer system. All things considered, I should have had my feet up, calmly reading a paperback while awaiting Joni's go-code.

I wasn't calm. I paced the floor, I nervously picked my nose, and I constantly checked my watch, because I had the most awful, inescapable premonition that something was going to go wrong. The plan had been worked out carefully. We had taken everything we could imagine into consideration. But I still had serious misgivings about the whole thing. Murphy's Law and all that.

We were relying on the fact that the Ear module was essentially one big, integrated communications switchboard, loaded with enough gear to make any sort of space-based telecommunications possible in Earth orbit. Once the three of them made that module and—by force, most likely—took it over, Hamilton was supposed to transmit a message directly to Skycan. Since Joni had arranged to be on duty at that time as the communications officer, she personally would intercept that message. Without informing anyone, she would then patch me and my computers through. It was Hamilton's responsibility to make sure that he had the radio and the module's computer interfaced as well. To make sure he didn't miss a step, I had carefully written instructions on how to do this, which he was carrying in an envelope in his spacesuit.

Once that was done, I would send a program, which Jack and I had worked out on Skycan's computer, down the comlink. It was a rather sophisticated virus program, which we felt sure would screw up the Ear's program and, by extension, the Ear itself.

We knew the main purpose of the Ear logistics module and its computer: Receive all laser signals sent by the Big Ear communications satellites, remodulate them, and retransmit them to the National Security Agency's headquarters in Fort Meade. My virus program was something which, when locked into that computer's memory, would essentially say to the system: Ignore your primary programming; scramble everything you send to Virginia in a random pattern; erase all records of the origins and destinations of the telecommunications you have intercepted; forget where you heard this order; erase from your memory everything except this program should anyone ask you what you're doing, and have a nice day. This is an oversimplified explanation, of course, but take my word for it: It was a beautiful piece of hacking. I wanted to add a signature, calling myself "Captain Crunch" or something corny like that, but Jack had talked me out of it.

We could have put the whole thing on a diskette and just had Jack boot the little jewel up as soon as he had made it into the computer, but that would have meant leaving it in drive while he, Bruce, and Popeye made good their escape from Freedom. But someone could later access the program and read the sourcecode to figure out how to debug our bug. Thus, it would have only been a temporary nuisance. This way, with the virus program transmitted from a remote location directly into the computer's ROM memory and CPU, it would mean that a computer engineer would have to tear the thing apart to eradicate the program entirely.

On Earth, that wouldn't be much of a problem. In space, it would be nearly impossible, unless Skycorp and the NSA wanted to shuttle up a couple of engineers and a boatload of testing equipment and replacement software and hardware. The cost of that would probably be so prohibitively high that they would likely throw up their hands and have the whole damned thing sent back down to Huntsville to be completely refitted.

The virus was only a short term solution, but it did allow for time to be bought, while Globe Watch made sure that a more permanent solution was developed—such as leaking the news of the Big Ear's covert mission to trustworthy news people and politicians who could blow the whistle on the whole jazz band.

But who was I kidding? It was fun. It was playing space pirates. Maybe we would not have even considered doing this except for the fact that all of us were bored, and you know what Grandma used to say about idle hands. Besides, the guys who were doing the dirty work were getting a free ride home for their trouble, and even if Virgin Bruce and Popeye had their stated and unstated reasons for not wanting to go back to Earth right away, Virgin Bruce had been long since fed up with being a beamjack and Popeye had been wrestling with homesickness for longer than he could remember. I knew that Popeye still had some private demon with which to contend, but . . . well, no one knew, except himself, what was going through his mind.

I knew what was going through mine, though, in that last hour of anxiety. However, I wish we could have known what was tumbling through the twisted cerebrum of Henry George Wallace, the demented project supervisor of Olympus Station.

Edwin Felapolous had been making it a point, for the past couple of months, of making regular house calls on H.G. Wallace. He tried to arrange his visits in a certain order which would not alarm his patient or let him realize that Felapolous was not merely dropping by for social reasons. So Felapolous had learned to stagger the times of his visits; skipping a day here and there, stopping in during the morning on one day, an afternoon the next, waiting a day and then dropping by the following morning.

It was the only time that Felapolous had the opportunity to see Wallace. In fact, it was probably the only regular occasion that anyone on the station had for seeing the project supervisor since Wallace had begun his self-isolation. Hank Luton had moved out of Module 24 weeks ago, preferring the crowded conditions of a bunkhouse module in the east hemisphere to luxury shared with an obvious paranoid, and Phil Bigthorn was now delivering Wallace's meals on a tray from the mess deck.

It was becoming evident that Wallace was going over the deep end.

As Felapolous touched the intercom switch next to the hatch, just above the orange sign which read "Administration," he wondered how much longer it would be before he was obligated to advise Skycorp's management in Huntsville that their veteran space hero was bordering on a complete mental breakdown.

*"Who is it?"* Wallace's voice barked through the intercom.

"Edwin, Henry," Felapolous said, making the effort to keep his voice easy: Shucks, friend, just decided to pop down for a visit. Hiya doing? "Mind if I come down?"

*"Enter!"* There was an audible click as the electronic lock on the hatch was disengaged, and Felapolous kneeled, cranked open the hatch, and climbed down onto the ladder. That in itself took an effort; the compartment was almost totally dark, and he had to be careful that his feet didn't miss the rungs, which he could barely see.

The only lights in the compartment came from a gooseneck high-intensity lamp arched over a desk, the small reading lamp which was switched on in one of the two bunks, and the blue and white glow from a computer screen and a TV monitor at the end of the compartment. Wallace was seated in front of the terminal, his back turned to Felapolous. "Come in, Edwin," he said in a voice which was more relaxed than the one that had come over the intercom, but which still held a ring of self-conscious authority.

Over Wallace's shoulder, Doc Felapolous could see that the TV screen displayed a shot of SPS-1's long grid, stretching out for two miles from a camera angle which was obviously from the side of Vulcan Station. The computer screen held tabulated lists, data relayed from Olympus' command deck. Wallace wore a communications headset, and he was hunched forward, studying the computer and the TV screen. "Make yourself at home," Wallace said. "I'll be with you in a moment, old friend."

Felapolous walked a few feet into the compartment, looking around as he did so. It was doubtful he could make himself at home here. The place was a wreck: food trays containing half-finished meals on the floor and the desk, a long scroll of computer printout lying unfolded across the floor like a tapeworm, clothing scattered here and there on the floor, on the back of a chair, on the unmade bunk. One of the station cats—Clarke, or was it Asimov?—leaped from its perch on the bunk, sprinted between Doc's legs, and bounded up the ladder, raising one of Felapolous' eyebrows, because Henry had always claimed to detest "the inbred little creatures."

Wallace's fingers tapped at the keyboard in his lap. Felapolous noticed a few paperbacks lying on the desk, their covers illuminated under the lamp, and walked over to see what Wallace had been reading. An ancient edition of *The Third Industrial Revolution* by G. Harry Stine; a fairly recent spy-fiction bestseller; *The First Three Minutes* by Steven Weinberg; a science fiction novel. He spotted another book, lying open with its spine broken, on the crumpled pillow underneath the reading light over the bunk. He tiptoed over and raised the cover to peer at the title. *Dianetics* by L. Ron Hubbard. Felapolous grimaced and carefully put the book back in its place.

"There's something rotten in the state of Denmark," Wallace announced.

"What?" Startled, Felapolous jerked up from his bent position over the bunk. Wallace, to his relief, was still facing the computer, his finger pointed at the screen. "What do you mean?" he asked.

"Price's report," Wallace said in a dead voice. "Chang claims in his report that a full second-shift crew was dispatched to Vulcan at 0700 today. But here, Price reported that two men didn't go on EVA at Vulcan. Hooker and Neiman."

He tapped another command into the keyboard and leaned closer to study the screen. "The list of comlink channels being used," he said softly. "The frequencies assigned to Hooker and Neiman for this shift aren't being used." He continued to stare at the screen. Then, suddenly, he barked a laugh. "Ah, so," he said with cynical humor.

He pushed a tab on the right lobe of his headset. "Mr. Bigthorn? I want you to make a quick search of the station. Look for Hooker and Neiman. That's right, Popeye and Virgin Bruce." He rolled the nicknames off his tongue with disgust. "Search all the obvious places, and don't forget the Hydroponics bay. In fact, see if you can find Jack Hamilton also. If they're around, find out why Neiman and Hooker didn't report for their shifts and write it up in a report. If you don't find any of them, let me know at once. Over and out."

Wallace cut out, then picked up the keyboard and put it in its slot on the console. He then turned around in his chair to face Felapolous, and looked straight at the doctor. "So it begins," he said in a hollow, solemn voice. Then he stood up from his chair.

Felapolous couldn't help but notice that Wallace was stark naked. The only thing he wore was his headset. "I'm not sure I understand you," he said, trying not to appear as if he noticed Wallace's uncharacteristic nudity, or the fact that Wallace's physique was shot to hell; where once he had firm muscle, now there was flab and uncontrolled paunch.

Wallace didn't seem to notice. He walked past Felapolous and bent to pick up some trousers left dumped on the floor. Neglecting to put on underwear, he stepped into the legs and pulled up the pants. "Because I've been doing my work, and my studies, down here doesn't mean that I haven't ignored the situation on Olympus, Ed," Wallace said. "In fact, I would have to be pretty stupid if I didn't admit how much the environment has deteriorated over the past few weeks."

He reached for a short-sleeve uniform shirt and slipped it on. "Rock music playing in the crew quarters," he murmured. "Graffiti on the walls. Uninspirational films being shown in the rec room, even pornography. The men smiling. Sex with the female crew members. It's a disgrace." He looked in the direction of the ladder. "It started when we brought those cats aboard. It wasn't entirely your fault, Ed, but I said that there was no room for animals up here, and especially not cats. It was the cats that started this mutiny."

"Pardon me," Felapolous said. "Did you just say that the cats are inciting a mutiny?"

Wallace brayed laughter, which sounded just slightly hysterical. "No, no, no. You misunderstood me, Doctor. The cats were only symptomatic of the problem." He shook his head. "No, the real problem is that these men have become adjusted to living in space. They've come to enjoy themselves, and that's the way to disaster."

Felapolous tried not to return Wallace's stare. Instead, he absently studied his fingernails and said calmly, "Ah, yes. I agree."

Wallace nodded quickly and began to pace. "It wasn't the cats that started this, it was Skycorp, and before them, NASA. It was all the space experts like Clarke and O'Neill, the groups like L-5 and the National Space Society, claiming that outer space was meant to be colonized by the so-called common man." He laughed again. "All the common man is good for is to pave the way for *homo superior,* those who have disciplined themselves—trained their minds, hardened their bodies, become ready to live in this environment. This frontier was never meant for the common man, Ed, it was meant for . . ."

He searched for the right word, waving his right hand in the air. "The master race," Felapolous supplied slowly.

Wallace smiled and jabbed an index finger in his direction as he walked away, his eyes searching the floor of the darkened compartment. "Yes, although not by the classic Hitler definition. I would hate to have my theories compared to his."

"No, of course not," Felapolous murmured.

"But that hasn't been the case, now has it?" Wallace bent suddenly, opened a cabinet door and began rummaging inside, not bothering to switch on the lights. "So now we have a crew of people up here running from taxes or their wives or the law, trying to make a fast buck, playing out simplistic romantic fantasies, without the slightest consideration that what they might be doing could advance the destiny of the human race. I thought Hamilton was different, that he was one of us, but I know now that he was a clever impersonator. Indeed, he's the head of the conspiracy."

"What conspiracy?" Felapolous asked, beginning to feel nervous now. He had to take this step by tentative step, leading Wallace but not putting ideas into his mind. Use objectivity, he reminded himself. He was little more than an armchair psychiatrist, with only the basic med school training in psychology, but he had to have more definite proof that Wallace had flipped before he recommended to Huntsville that the project supervisor be replaced on grounds of mental incompetency.

Wallace looked around at him with an expression of surprise. He studied Felapolous for a moment before turning back to his search of the locker. "No, of course not," he said. "You wouldn't know. But I have put it together. There's a mutiny afoot on this station, with Felapolous . . . I mean, with Neiman and Hamilton and Hooker as the prime conspirators. There may be others, but they are the nucleus of the conspiracy to overthrow this station and take control for themselves."

"What proof do you have of this?" Felapolous asked.

"I'll show you my hard evidence in a moment. But ever since I noticed the degradation aboard Olympus, I put myself in semi-isolation in this compartment, while covertly keeping track of station personnel, both through careful monitoring of roll-call records and reports and through having Security Chief Bigthorn watching and reporting. I've observed that the principals have been absent for long periods of time—once they even went so far as to crowd into a pod together, to avoid prying ears while concocting their plot—and they have attempted to recruit others. I suspect that Communications Officer Lowenstein and . . . um, what's his name, Chang, are also involved."

"Why haven't you said or done anything?"

"Because I've been biding my time," Wallace replied evenly. "I wanted to wait until I had all the evidence, and until I thought the moment was right. With the events of this morning, I know for certain that a mutiny is imminent."

He twisted around on his haunches so quickly that he lost his balance and fell over. As he put out his hands to stop his fall, an object in his right hand fell out onto the floor. Felapolous knelt and picked it up; it was a loosely wrapped plastic bag containing something soft and crumbly.

"Marijuana," Wallace explained tersely as he struggled to his feet. "Hamilton brought it up here, and used it to brainwash the crew. I'm not saying that people like Neiman or Hooker wouldn't have turned to treason sooner or later, but Hamilton's drugs helped accelerate the process. Through him, they became drug zombies."

"Then why didn't you . . . ?"

"Because I was waiting for this moment!" Now Wallace was scurrying around the dark compartment, fitting his feet into sneakers, putting on his cap, and grabbing a vest with a number of Velcro-sealed pockets. The communications headset had slid down around his neck, and Felapolous heard a tinny voice coming through the earpiece. Wallace slapped it to his ear, listened for a moment, then snapped, "Good work, Bigthorn! Continue to search and await my command!"

He ran toward the ladder. "Come, Doctor!" he shouted. "The conspirators are absent and unaccounted for! There's no time to lose!" He started to climb the ladder.

Felapolous stared at the bag of marijuana in his hand, then looked up at Wallace. "Wait a minute!" he yelled. "How can you be sure that this is the cause?" He shook the bag at Wallace.

Wallace paused at the ladder and glanced back at him. "Because I smoked some in a piece of rolled-up printout a few hours ago," he hissed. "It's marijuana, Doctor! And believe me, it *can* bend your mind!" Then he scrambled the rest of the way up the ladder and disappeared, leaving Felapolous staring at the empty ladder, not even noticing that the bag of pot had slipped from his hand and fallen to the floor.

# 27

# Snafu

Clayton Dobbs was bent over the master terminal, punching up another of the long series of test programs he had been performing over the past couple of days, when the module hatch swung open. Assuming that it was Dougherty reporting for this, the day when the Ear was to be put into operation, he didn't look up from his work until he heard McGrath say, "Pardon me, but this area is off limits, you'll have to leave."

Dobbs swung his head around, slowly and carefully. Two previous bouts with spacesickness had already taught him that even simple head motions were enough to bring on instant nausea. Through the open circular hatch he saw two men, both wearing spacesuits with their helmets and gloves off. One had longish blond hair tied back in a ponytail; the other man was dark and unsavory-looking, one of the scruffiest characters Dobbs had ever seen. The ugly one was already halfway through the hatch and was smiling at McGrath in a way which made Dobbs think of snakes.

"Yes, yes," he said, pulling his torso through the hatch, grabbing a rung with his left hand and swinging his legs inside. "Module safety inspection, sir. We're here to check for air leaks, electrical shorts, that sort of thing."

"What the hell is this?" Dobbs complained. Irritated, he slapped a hand against the console and was immediately glad that his feet were slipped into stirrups on the floor; otherwise, that slap might have pushed him against the ceiling of the long, narrow compartment. "You guys were here yesterday looking for leaks and you didn't find anything. Don't you know this is a secure area?"

The swarthy one shrugged and the guy with the ponytail, who was pulling himself through the hatch after him, smiled sheepishly. "Sorry, but that's the regulations. Any module which has been here for less than six months has to be given daily inspections. It'll be just a few . . ."

"Bullshit," Dobbs said. "I don't know who told you that, but I helped write the revised code book for this station, and those inspections are done once a week, not every day. Now get your ass out of here."

"This is a secure area," McGrath repeated, turning completely around to face the men, raising his chin and crossing his arms. Dobbs let his eyes roll up. Self-important little government schmuck, he thought. You can't get away from these pricks any more than you can escape from semi-retarded Joe Sixpack types, even up here. He shook his head and started to turn back to his test—only a dozen more to go—when he did a double take.

"I know, sir, but . . . ah . . ." The swarthy one hesitated for a moment, and looked at his companion. "That's what the checklist said, didn't it? This place was due for inspection?" Dobbs found himself staring at a round patch on the sleeve of the man's spacesuit, which, after a second, he recognized as a mission emblem for Project Franklin. The guy with the ponytail had one also. And both wore square Skycorp patches, which only a few industrial specialists on Freedom wore on their coveralls. No one except shuttle pilots or cargo specialists on secure runs from the Cape should have Skycorp insignia on their spacesuits . . . and there was no reason why anyone on Freedom should be wearing insignia which belonged on Olympus Station.

"Hey, who the hell are you guys?" he demanded. McGrath looked around at him, with an expression which showed the government man's irritation at having his authority superseded by someone else. Dobbs pointed at the ugly guy's shoulder patch. "You guys aren't supposed to even be here," Dobbs snapped. "What are you doing here, huh?"

"What?" the man with the ponytail stammered. He stared at the patch on the ugly man's arm, turned red, then quickly averted his gaze toward an overhead display screen. "The patch. Well, we were short of spacesuits here on Skycan and so we borrowed . . . I mean, on Freedom, so we had to get Skycan, I mean Freedom . . . *Olympus,* I mean . . . to ship a couple . . ."

"Oh, goddammit!" the ugly one snarled. "Just clobber 'em!"

He threw back his legs, touched the soles of his feet against the module bulkhead, and snapped his knees, bringing his straightened arms up in front of him. A human projectile, he shot across the module, hurling himself straight toward a startled and unreacting

McGrath. *Pow!* Ugly's right fist sailed into the government stooge's face even as his momentum slammed them together in a zero g tackle which lifted McGrath's feet out of his stirrups.

Dobbs barely had time to kick out of his own stirrups and dodge aside as the two men flew by him and hit the end of the compartment. Floating free of the foot restraints, he instinctively grabbed for the nearest handhold . . . and was stopped by the impact of the ponytailed guy tackling him in midair. The air left his lungs in a loud *whoof*, and as he doubled over he felt hands grabbing his powerless wrists and forcing them behind his back. As Dobbs attempted to yank his hands free, Ponytail shoved him brutally against a console, hard enough to knock the wind out of him for a moment.

"The tape! The tape!" Ugly yelled from behind them. Dobbs felt a hand release his wrists. Instantly, he attempted to struggle loose, turning himself half-around . . . then a balled fist connected with his chin and he staggered back again, his eyes going out of focus.

A few moments later he felt something cool and sticky being applied to his wrists. He was being bound with something that felt like duct tape. He realized that four hands, not two, were restraining him. Glancing up, he could see that another person besides Ponytail was behind him, a guy with a scraggly mustache, who had apparently been waiting outside the hatch.

The hatch. Dobbs wondered if it was still open. "What do you guys want?" he asked, turning his head around to see if the hatch was open, while hoping to distract his captors with a stupid question.

"Yours is not to ask but only to wonder," Ponytail replied in a near-whisper. The tape made a final revolution around Dobbs' wrists, then he felt a final tug as it was cut from the roll. Someone gave it an experimental yank to make sure that it was tight.

"Good enough," Ponytail said. Dobbs bit the inside of his lip to keep from laughing or even cracking a smile. Good enough, like hell! The tape was not that tight. Given a few seconds, he knew he could work his wrists free. Wait, he told himself. Pull your shit together— stay calm, and just wait a couple of minutes for them to get even more careless.

The one with the ponytail was looking anxiously around the module, apparently searching for some function on the consoles arrayed along its walls. He pushed himself off and drifted to the console where Dobbs had been working. He studied the keyboard for a moment, then pulled a folded sheet of paper out of a thigh pocket of his suit and consulted something written on it. Dobbs watched him as he tentatively pushed a key which cleared the screen, then looked over his shoulder and grinned as he spotted the module's communications board.

"Popeye!" he shouted. "How's it looking?"

A second later the one with the mustache reappeared in the hatchway. "Coast's clear," he said. "And I found the wardroom just down the tube. It's vacant."

Ponytail nodded. "Good." He checked his wrist chronometer. "Okay, let's move it. Popeye, help me out in here. Bruce, take these guys to the module and . . ." He stopped and looked at Dobbs and McGrath. "I dunno, just do something to keep 'em out of the way. Haul ass."

"Okay, just a second." The one called Bruce pulled the roll of duct tape out of a pocket, slid behind McGrath, and sealed his mouth with it in a single, swift movement which caught the little man by surprise. As Bruce stepped toward Dobbs, ripping out another few inches of silver tape, Dobbs turned his head toward Ponytail, the one who seemed to be the leader.

"Just what *is* going on here, anyway?" he asked calmly. What the hell; it couldn't hurt to ask.

"Putting a banana in your Big Ear, my friend," Ponytail replied. Then the tape was spread over Dobbs' mouth, its sticky gluelike taste making him want to gag. That, plus the realization of what these men wanted to do, made him feel sick.

They were after the Ear. But with that revelation came questions. Even though they had somehow managed to get aboard the station undetected and had managed to take him and McGrath by surprise, it seemed to Dobbs that these men were not exactly professional terrorists, even if the swarthy one, Bruce, looked sinister enough to be a *summa cum laude* graduate of a Palestinian terrorist school. Enough of that, he commanded himself. If they're not pros, then you've got an even better chance of getting away.

"Okay, boys, let's go." Bruce pushed them one at a time toward the hatch, where Popeye—not exactly a name for a terrorist, Dobbs noted with brief amusement—grabbed first McGrath, then Dobbs himself, and guided them through the opening. Bound as they were, Dobbs and McGrath were little more than long, cumbersome parcels in the microgravitational environment.

Out in the access tunnel, with his back momentarily turned away from Bruce, Dobbs began to quickly, furtively wiggle his wrists against the duct tape. He'd been right; he could work his wrists free. Good; only Bruce was escorting them, leaving the other two inside the module. His captor was beginning to look genuinely nervous now. Looking quickly back and forth along the access tunnel, he grabbed the back of McGrath's shirt and kicked off the wall with the tip of his boot, heading for an open hatch just twenty-five feet away. Left alone for a few more moments, Dobbs began to wiggle his wrists frantically against the tape. C'mon, c'mon, *c'mon—!*

*Snap!* there went the tape, along with a little bit of his skin. Dobbs was glad that the tape was still on his mouth; it kept him from crying aloud. Bruce's back was turned to him, he was trying to push a futilely struggling McGrath through the hatch. But the way to the command module was that way, past Bruce.

No time to even think about it. Dobbs pushed himself against one wall, doubled his knees, balled his fists and, with a violent kick, lunged straight at Bruce, sailing through the air like a human lance.

He was able to do it only because he took Bruce by surprise, with his back turned and distracted by McGrath. Dobbs fell onto Bruce, depending on his mass and momentum to do what his weightless condition could not. His right fist slammed into the back of Bruce's neck, his left into the side of his ribs. Bruce grunted as his head bounced off the side of the hatch and, for a moment, Dobbs thought he had knocked him senseless.

Then Bruce's right hand grabbed his left ankle and his left fist flew toward Dobbs. Dobbs twisted at the last moment and the fist struck his pelvis instead of his stomach. Damn, the son of a bitch was tough! Already Bruce was recovering, trying to grab him again. . . . Dobbs arched his right knee back, took half a second to aim, then kicked *hard* into Bruce's face.

Bruce's head and torso flew backwards, striking the open hatch, and his hand let go of Dobbs' ankle. Not waiting to see if Bruce was going to recover as swiftly this time, Dobbs propelled himself off the wall and flung himself down the length of the tunnel. He heard a sudden yell from behind, from the Ear module. Damn it! They were onto him! Not only that, but his nearest place of safety, the command module, was at least fifty or seventy feet away!

But just ahead of him was the access tunnel hatch, the emergency hatch which could be manually or automatically shut in case of decompression. That was it. Dobbs grinned in spite of himself, kicked off a tunnel wall again to increase his momentum, and threw himself through the hatch. He flung out his hands and slapped his palms against the walls to stop himself, whirled around and faced the hatch.

Bruce was already pushing himself, clumsily and in obvious pain, toward him, his dark eyes glinting with fury. Dobbs didn't let himself wonder at the man's stamina. He hastily sought out and found the hatch controls on the wall beside the opening, flipped open the cover, and stabbed at the red switch marked "Emergency Override."

The inner emergency hatch began to quickly iris shut, but not before Bruce, only twenty feet away, got in one last howl. *"You goddamn son of a—!"*

*Clang!* The hatch sealed shut, and an instant later Dobbs heard a heavy thud as Bruce's body smacked into it from the other side. Dobbs felt his muscles sag. He felt suddenly nauseous and fought against it—goddamn zero g, goddamn spacesickness—and for the first time heard the brash honking of the warning Klaxon, set off automatically when he had pulled the emergency override switch.

Dobbs reached up and carefully peeled the tape off his mouth, feeling it rip against the skin of his lips. He licked them gingerly with his tongue and murmured, "Your momma."

"Hey! What the heck is going on out here?" Dobbs looked around, saw a station crewman in a blue jumpsuit emerging from an open hatch a short distance away. Dobbs recognized the hatch. It belonged to the station's command module.

Felapolous found the command center in complete chaos. Along its tiered levels—lit in surreal shades of blue from the computer screens and red from the emergency lights—some of the personnel were moving frantically, yelling into their headsets, their hands moving in blurs across their consoles. Others were frozen in disbelieving inactivity, staring at the havoc which had broken loose around them. The doctor closed the hatch behind him, and hung for a few moments to a handhold as he tried to figure out what was going on. He listened:

"Modules 31 through 38, no signs of them, sir . . ."

"All modules report stable pressurization. Repair crews on standby."

"Vulcan reports that construction is on standdown status, awaiting final . . ."

"Bigthorn says that Module 10 is vacant. He's proceeding to Lunar Resources and the astrophysics labs for a check . . ."

"Modules 11 through 18, nothing there, sir, but they're still . . ."

"Meterology reporting, sir. They have something to report on Hooker's recent activity."

"Patch it through to me, on the double!"

Hearing Wallace's voice, Felapolous' eyes whipped around the huge, weirdly lighted compartment, trying to locate the project supervisor. He spotted him near the communications station, hanging upside down to Felapolous' perspective, a headset clamped over his skull. He stared intently over the shoulder of Joni Lowenstein, the shift com officer, as he listened to something being said to him through the headset's earphone. As Felapolous began pulling himself up a "fireman's pole" to Wallace's tier, he saw the corners of his mouth suddenly turn up in a wide, unsettling smile.

"Very good!" the project supervisor shouted. As Felapolous climbed to his level, Wallace turned and winked slyly at him before shifting his gaze again in the direction of Lowenstein's station. "Very, very good! Thank you for communicating that, we'll be in touch. Command out."

Wallace touched a stud on the headset control attached to his belt and turned to face Felapolous, his face red and radiant. "Great news!" he boomed at Felapolous. "The NSA boys . . . that is, the men down in Meteorology . . ." Suddenly self-conscious, he dropped his voice a few decibels before continuing. "They tell me they've been suspicious of Hooker for the past couple of days, and also Hamilton, and that they took it upon themselves to check into their FBI files." Wallace's teeth clenched together within his smiling lips, and his voice dropped further. "Well, Hamilton's been involved in subversive activity groundside, and Hooker was once involved in a criminal investigation in Florida relating to . . ."

"Henry, what's going on here?" Felapolous asked, staring into Wallace's eyes. "Why have these people been put on emergency alert?"

Wallace's eyes grew wide and his mouth dropped open. His lips moved soundlessly for a moment, as if his mind could not react to an absurdity which had been flung in his face. "These . . . this station has been put on alert, Ed," he said slowly, speaking to the doctor as if Felapolous were a backward child. "There's a mutiny happening here. Hooker, Hamilton, that scumball they call Virgin Bruce . . . they're plotting to take over the station, or sabotage it. As the project supervisor, I felt it was my duty and in my power to put Olympus on . . ."

Felapolous quickly shook his head. There was no point in asking for Henry's reasons. "Have you told these people what they're on alert about?"

Wallace's eyes shifted warily toward the communications station. "Didn't you hear what I told you in my quarters?" His whisper was barely audible over the hubbub around them. "Lowenstein is with them. If I tell everyone here what's going on, she might tip off her fellow conspirators and they might . . ." His thoughts seemed to wander. "They might . . ."

"Flee?" Felapolous interjected. He felt himself getting weary of Wallace's paranoid fantasies. He realized that at one time he had been entertained—shamefully, that *was* the right term—by observing Wallace's private universe, but now he knew that the worst-case scenario had abruptly come about, and it was his job to inject some sanity. In that role, Felapolous was quickly becoming frustrated and angry. "Where are the conspirators going to flee, Henry? We're thousands of miles above Earth."

"No! Not flee!" Suddenly Wallace was shouting again, but his eyes pleaded with Felapolous for understanding. "That's why I've had the inspection and repair crews mobilized! They might be planning to stick limpet mines around the station so they can blow it all up, or threaten to hold us hostage while they . . ."

*"Gimme that!"* In a convulsive move born of frustration and disgust, Felapolous found himself reaching out and tearing the headset off Wallace's head. Wallace reached forward with both hands and tried to grab it back from Felapolous, but the doctor angrily shoved him aside. Wallace fell against a couple of crewmen seated nearby, who fumbled to stabilize the station's head officer. Several other command-deck personnel had turned to stare at the sudden violence, including Lowenstein.

*"Hold* him!" Felapolous shouted at the crewmen hanging onto Wallace, as he pushed the headset onto his own head and pushed a button on the headset. Impulsively, he whistled a soft but shrill "C" note into the mike and observed with satisfaction that all the heads in the command center bobbed up at once, a few of the faces wincing in pain.

"Okay, now hear this," he said with forceful calm. "This is Edwin Felapolous speaking. The station is no longer . . . I repeat, no longer on alert status. You're all to revert to previous operating status, and recall all emergency proceedings, and uh . . ." He glanced around the compartment and saw many sets of eyes fastened on him from tiers above and below. ". . . and, uh, go back to normal. Just do your jobs, ladies and gentlemen. I'm afraid that . . ."

He looked around, and saw Wallace's hate boring into him like a laser beam shot from Hell. Felapolous blinked, and said, "I'm afraid the captain isn't feeling too good today."

If he had made a joke, he wasn't aware of it. He was surprised, then, to hear a few unseen people quietly chuckling. Felapolous winced, with embarrassment for both himself and Wallace.

The project supervisor, however, was no longer glowering at him, but was staring intently at something off to his side. Felapolous followed his gaze to the communications station. A red light was flashing on the console, and as Felapolous watched, the printout on its LCD screen suddenly disappeared and a single line of electronic type replaced it: 0169 PRIORITY INTERRUPT—EMERGENCY TRANSMISSION, FREEDOM.

Lowenstein made no apparent move to acknowledge the signal. She stared straight at the screen, her hands resting on the console a couple of inches from her keyboard. She didn't seem to be paying attention to the crisis happening behind her—the only person in the command center who wasn't—but she wasn't making any effort to respond to the message.

"Acknowledge the transmission, Lowenstein," Wallace said, staring at her back. "What's the matter, woman? Don't you see a priority message coming in from Freedom Station?" His voice took on a taunting edge. "Why don't you do your job, Communications Chief?"

"Cut it out, Henry," Felapolous whispered.

"Don't you *see?*" Wallace snapped at the doctor. "She's one of *them.* She's part of this whole . . ." Suddenly, Wallace's face turned pale and his eyes went wide open. "Of course! The *Ear!* They've gone after the Big Ear! They're on Freedom Station, and they're going after the *Big Ear!*"

Felapolous became confused. What the hell was the Big Ear? He swiftly glanced around the command center and saw nothing but bewildered pairs of eyes. Then he looked at Lowenstein again and noticed that she had not yet turned to look at Wallace, even while Wallace was accusing her. She was trying to look calm, but her hands were shaking and she was beginning to sweat. . . . What in the Lord's name *did* she know about . . . ?

Suddenly he heard a loud, pained gasp, and he looked back at Wallace. The crewman who had been holding him was doubled over in pain, holding his solar plexus, where Wallace's elbow had apparently jabbed him. Free now of his restraints, Wallace was straightening up and thrusting his right hand into an inside pocket of the utility vest he had shrugged on when he'd left his quarters.

"Shit!" the doctor snarled as he tore open his belt pouch, fumbling for the syringe gun filled with fast-acting sedative he kept for the rare but recurring freakout situations. As time seemed to slow down, he saw Wallace's hand whip out and point a strange-looking weapon at Lowenstein, who was just beginning to turn around. . . .

Felapolous propelled himself headfirst toward Wallace, the syringe held straight out in front of him. He was a half-second too slow. Wallace squeezed the trigger of his odd-looking gun, there was a high, metallic *twang!*, and something red, blue, and silver shot through the air. As Felapolous collided with Wallace and shot a compressed-air dose of sedative into the other man's neck—no time to cleanse the spot with alcohol, he silently apologized to Wallace— he heard Lowenstein scream.

"Grab him!" he shouted at a crewman, chopping at Wallace's right wrist with the edge of his palm. The gun spun away from Wallace's fingers, and Felapolous immediately grabbed it before it floated away. Two other crewmen were already on Lowenstein, and as Felapolous pushed himself toward her, he saw thick, spherical droplets of blood rising up from the wound just below her left collarbone. He shouldered one of the crewmen aside—Tate, he recalled irrelevantly, the joker who always sprains his ankle while trying to jog on the catwalk—and quickly examined her wound.

A dart, one of those used in the rec room dartboards, was sticking out of Lowenstein's upper chest. She was still conscious, but was pale and in danger of going into shock. "Get her down to sickbay," he snapped at Tate and the other crewman who had jumped to her aid. "Don't remove the dart until Maynard can deal with it. I'll be down there in a minute." The two men nodded and began to carefully carry Lowenstein toward the airlock.

Felapolous turned and looked at Wallace. The project supervisor was out cold, floating limp in midair, with one hand raised halfway to his neck. The other two crewmen on that tier were edging away from him, reflecting the age-old superstition that insanity was somehow contagious.

Felapolous pried open Wallace's hand and examined the weapon with which he had had shot the communications officer. It was an improvised gun, similar to the zip guns that street hoods had been making for years: The handle and trigger belonged to a torqueless screwdriver used by beamjacks while working on EVA, the chamber was a small, unrecognizable cylinder he guessed once belonged to an electronics conduit, the firing mechanism a thick metal spring which could have come from any damn thing. "Jesus Christ," Felapolous whispered with uncharacteristic blasphemy. It was just luck that Wallace, when he had jury-rigged the zip gun at the height of his paranoia, had not had access to a bullet. Felapolous knew that street gang zip guns often blew up in their users' faces. They also had a fifty-fifty chance of killing their intended victims.

"Doc," someone said behind him. He turned and saw that another communications officer, LaFleche, had taken over Lowenstein's station. She had a headset clamped on and was apparently listening to the emergency transmission from Freedom Station. Her face registered shock.

"It's Freedom Command," she said. "They say someone . . . three people . . . from here, from Olympus, are aboard their station. They say they're . . . I don't know, but it sounds like they're trying to sabotage something down there."

Felapolous stared at her, then stared at Wallace. But the project supervisor, drifting unaided in his own private limbo, couldn't help him understand.

It was exactly at 0750 that I realized there *was* a fatal flaw in our plan. But by that time, there was nothing I could do about it.

But that time I knew something had gone wrong. If the plan had worked, by now I should have received a signal from Lowenstein on the command deck, informing me that Jack had managed to take over the Ear module and was transmitting to Olympus, enabling me to downlink the virus program. With only ten minutes left until their deadline, though, I intuitively felt that *something* must have gone wrong.

However—and here was the fatal flaw—there was nothing I could do, because everything depended upon them transmitting to me. *I could not transmit to them,* nor could Joni. Jack had to select a particular frequency from the Ear module, one which he deduced was not presently being monitored. There were hundreds of frequencies from which to choose, but Joni had to get the right one, the only one, before we could coestablish the computer downlink to Freedom. A particular frequency, to be decided upon at the last minute, before . . .

"Hell with it," I murmured to myself, reaching for the intercom phone on my console. My nervousness was such that I was talking out loud. "She's just going to have to scan them all, find the one Jack's using, that's all." I picked up the receiver and began to punch in the three-digit number for Command/Communications. "She's just going to have to take some responsibility, y'know, do a little bit of hard work here. . . ."

Suddenly a hand reached past mine, and an outstretched finger pushed the intercom's disconnect button. I yelped, dropping the receiver in my lap and jerking back in my seat as I looked up and saw who it was that had managed to sneak into the compartment unnoticed.

Phil Bigthorn. The sequoia that walked like a man. The Navajo security chief was wearing his Skycorp Security uniform shirt and had his taser holstered to his turquoise-studded leather belt. That meant bad news; Bigthorn only wore that outfit when he was out on business. He was also smiling, which really meant bad tidings; Mr. Big only smiled when he was preparing to rip your heart out and hand it to you.

"Hi, Phil," I said brightly. I thought I did pretty well to get that out without much stammering. If I was lucky, maybe I could bluff my way through this. "What's the buzz?"

Phil only grunted and stepped back a pace, letting his arms drop to his sides. I noticed that his right hand was close to the handle of his taser. For a few moments he stood there silently, studying me while I felt cold beads of sweat sliding down from my armpits.

"I've been standing behind you for a couple of minutes," he said at last, his voice a perfect monotone. "Sounds like you're having trouble hearing from Jack. I'm looking for Jack, too. Do you know where he is?"

"Jack?" My own voice hit the high end of the scale. "Don't know who you're . . . Oh! Jack! Don't know where he is . . ." I shook my head vigorously, and stared at the blank screen of my computer. I could see Mr. Big's humorless smile reflected in it. "No, no," I said, trying to behave appropriately befuddled, like some simple, absentminded computer programmer who didn't know shit unless it was stored on a diskette. "Why, is there something wrong?"

Bigthorn nodded once, slowly. The smile had disappeared completely from his face, leaving an expression as stolid and unforgiving as the Navajo reservation desert. "Command's received an emergency signal from Freedom Station," he said. "It sounds as if three persons from Skycan got down there somehow and are trying to do something. So you don't know where Jack is? Virgin Bruce, or Popeye?"

I shook my head. He nodded toward the intercom and the receiver lying in my lap. "I saw you punch in the number for Communications," he said in the same droll tone. "Were you calling Joni about something?"

I shrugged. "Maybe I was. Maybe I wanted to ask her for a date? Whose business is it?"

That was probably a mistake. Mr. Big stared at me for a moment longer. Perhaps he had already put all the pieces together even before he had soundlessly crept through the connecting hatch from Module 42 and had listened to me talking to myself. But he just sighed, and without taking his dark, watchful eyes off me he reached with his left hand to his belt and unsnapped his pair of chrome-plated handcuffs. Like the uniform shirt and the taser, the handcuffs only appeared when he was out on business.

"What's the charge?" I snapped.

He just glowered at me and lifted his chin a little to motion me to lift my wrists. Up here, he didn't need to read me the Miranda. I knew it, and he knew it. The jig was up.

Something had *seriously* gone wrong on Freedom Station.

"Gentlemen," Hamilton said, bending over the computer terminal with a headset cupping his right ear, "I do believe we are screwed."

"Yeah, no shit!" Virgin Bruce yelled back. He was still holding the back of his head where it had been kicked into the hatch cover. "Do you know what's happening? The tunnel . . ."

"The tunnel to the docking chamber has been blocked," Hamilton finished, punching into another frequency code. "We can't get to the airlock where the *Willy Ley*'s docking. That, plus we can't raise Skycan. I'm trying all the channels Joni told me she would monitor and I'm getting nothing."

"Oh, for Christ's *sakes!*" Bruce shouted in spite of the throbbing in his head. "You've snafued the whole goddamn thing, you know that? The whole fucking thing is . . ."

*"Will you shut your mouth!"* Jack yelled. Virgin Bruce quailed and Popeye looked up from the console over which he was bending. It was the first time either of them had heard Hamilton raise his voice. Hamilton's head snapped toward Popeye, who was monitoring communications originating from Freedom. "What's going on there?"

Popeye stared back at him for a moment. If he hadn't been so preoccupied and trying to figure a way out of their predicament, he would have been tempted to give Hamilton a chop in the jaw, on general principles if nothing else. "They're talking to Skycan," he said. "It's mostly coded, but it's an emergency message. You can guess what about. I've also picked up some uncoded transmissions to other parts of the station. It sounds like they're trying to stay off the intercom to reduce the chance of us hearing them. They're isolating this part of the station and getting ready to undog that hatch and send men in."

"What about. *Willy Ley?*"

"It's reached orbit and is on course for rendezvous. They've informed the shuttle that there's an emergency aboard station but they're telling your friend to come in." He blinked. "ETA in about nine minutes. I guess by then it won't matter much."

It had been an ingenious plan. Hamilton told himself that to keep from completely losing his mind over how easily it had fallen apart— gone snafu, to paraphrase Virgin Bruce—although Jack still refused to blame himself. Although he hadn't realized it himself at the time, Hamilton had been working on the plan even before he had boarded the *Willy Ley* months ago for his trip up to Skycan. His meeting and resultant friendship with Lisa Barnhart—from the time they had encountered each other at the Cape, through weeks of correspondence and a couple of long-distance phone calls—had resulted in her agreeing, albeit reluctantly, to help in carrying out the scheme. Lisa had deliberately been kept in the dark about some of the details, and she knew little about the exact nature of the Big Ear, but she had been willing to take on three stowaways from Freedom Station when she made her weekly milk run.

Hamilton had blessed her willingness—almost blind willingness, considering that she knew so little and had so much to risk—but he also understood the stipulation she had placed on the agreement. *"I can't get caught,"* she had written in the notes she had stuck in the sweatband of the Fat Boy's Barbecue cap she had shipped him. *"Be there or get left behind—5 minutes! or I cut you off and I cut loose. Sorry."*

He shook his head, stabbed in another code at random—he had already tried that one a dozen times—and listened to another shift in static pitch. Where the hell was Joni? What had happened to Sam? Good old *Willy Ley,* his friend in which he had spent a couple of terrifying hours throwing up. The shuttle would only dock for a short while, so that the station's orbital trajectory could carry the shuttle to a precoordinated point above Earth for its maximum-efficiency re-entry window. If all had worked well, by now they would be receiving Sam's virus program and feeding it into the Ear computer, and be getting ready to head back to their entry point on Freedom to intercept *Willy Ley.* While the station's Canadarm operator would be loading the payload canister into the shuttle's open cargo bay, they would squeeze through the docking tunnel in the bay's forward end and climb into *Ley's* middeck passenger section. That part would take less than five minutes. It had to—because it took only a few minutes more than that before the station would swing into the right orbital bearing for *Ley's* separation. Any delays,

Lisa had explained, would cause someone to ask questions. Freedom traffic control was a tight operation.

"There's no way," he murmured. Even in weightlessness, he felt the weight of everything he had attempted settle across his shoulders. "We can't get there from here. Not before they get us. We're screwed."

"You said that already!" Virgin Bruce yelled. "C'mon! You're the goddamn genius! Get us out of here!"

Hamilton, feeling drained, stood up from the console in his stirrups, gazed at Bruce with weary eyes, and let his hands rise of their own volition. "You know the score," he said quietly. "What's your idea?"

"What's . . . what are you saying, man?"

"I'm out of ideas," Jack said urgently. "This whole scam depended upon a number of variables working out. I fucked up. I guessed wrong. It's going kaput. In a couple of minutes we're screwed. No way to . . ." He shook his head, ending his rambling apology. "If you've got a way out, let's hear it. Or you, Popeye. Otherwise, we're dog food."

"Dog food." Virgin Bruce let the word roll off his tongue and the syllables dropped into a whisper, the voice of someone suddenly made aware of inevitable and impending defeat. "Fuck. You're right. We're dog food." He suddenly smiled, and chuckled dryly. "Gainesburgers," he mumbled.

Hamilton found himself smiling, and as he let out a short, involuntary laugh, he heard that laugh echoed by Popeye Hooker.

The beamjack, grinning, shook his head in obvious disbelief. "This is really too much," he said. "You got us into this situation with the idea that everything would work out exactly as you planned, like some perfect bank robbery, and now that the chips are down you're looking to us to bail you out. I swear, Jack, I'd strangle you if I thought we had the time."

Hamilton shrugged. "We've got the time. We can't get to the airlock to escape, we can't get through to Skycan . . ." He threw up his hands. "We're trapped. Unless you've got some great idea to get us out of this mess, you might as well go ahead and strangle me. I deserve it."

Popeye studied him. "You mean that, don't you?" he said wonderingly. "You got us into this because of your Globe Watch gang's intelligence reports, lied to everyone about your conversation with that guy . . ."

"Whoa! Hold on a minute," Virgin Bruce interrupted. His dark eyes flashed from one man to the next. "What are you talking about, lying to . . . ?"

Popeye shook his head and waved him off. "Never mind, Brucie. It would take too long to explain. Let's just say that everything isn't as it seems." He looked back at Hamilton. "I'll make you a deal, Jack. I know a way to get out of this mess, and I'll let you in on it . . . if you can tell me one thing."

"What do you want to know?"

"Why was all this worth it?" Hooker said. "Why was it worth putting him, me, and all those other poor suckers into this situation? Why is it worth my risking my life to get you out of this jam?"

Hamilton's eyes dropped to the compartment floor. He suddenly felt small and tainted, like a kid caught shoplifting or a married man caught by his spouse in an indiscreet act with another woman. He was nailed; he could tell no more lies.

"I . . ." He stopped.

*"Why?"* Popeye roared, and both men flinched. *"What goddamn good has this done!"*

"We *tried,* goddammit!" Jack howled back. "We *tried* to make a difference! Shit, that might not be good enough, but we made the fucking *effort!"* He ripped his headset off and, in what even he realized in part of his mind was a childish tantrum, flung it at Hooker. "That's why we did this, you son of a bitch!"

"We tried and we blew it!" Hooker yelled back, swatting Hamilton's headset away with the palm of his hand. "You asshole, we were doomed from the *start!* What was the good of making the effort?"

Hamilton's face was hot, and every nerve in his body screamed for him to throw himself at this goddamned redneck shrimp fisher from Florida. "You've got some fuckin' nerve, you geek!" he shouted. "You've been lying around for months in your bunk, bothered about something too dark to tell anyone about! You've been a basket case, pal! You couldn't give a crap about anyone until this happened, and now you've got the . . . *Jesus,* you've got the nerve to ask why we've made the *effort?* You've got to ask that? Holy shit, pal, you've got it wrong! The effort is *everything!"*

Popeye had a sudden sensation. He couldn't have described it if he had been asked, but it was like flipping on a light switch in a dark, familiar room; the light flashes for a millisecond, enough time for the eyes to react, then the filament pops in a silent, microscopic explosion that surges through your nerves as the room plunges into darkness. But this time, there was no . . .

*A gold band, shaped for a lady's finger, splashing into blue crystal water, twisting, falling, going, gone . . .*

This time there was no darkness.

"All right," he said in a calm voice. "Okay." He looked up into Hamilton's hate-filled face—he had never seen Jack like this before —and then at Virgin Bruce, and was doubly surprised to see the beamjack looking frightened. "Okay," he repeated, this time for his own benefit.

He felt himself smiling. It was clear now. He couldn't put his finger on it, but . . . something Jack had said made things seem *clear* now, more sane than he had known in months. There *was* a way out! Not just for Jack and Bruce, but for him as well. . . .

"Popeye." Hamilton's own voice had dropped, from spite to worried concern. "Popeye, are you all right. I'm sorry, I . . ."

"Never say sorry," Hooker said. He let out his breath. "Someone close said that to me once. Never say sorry. Look back all you want, but don't say you're sorry."

He pulled off his own headset and quickly reached for the gloves hanging from his suit utility belt. "Suit up," he said. "Helmets too. You're getting out of here in a couple of minutes."

Compelled by the urgency in his voice, Hamilton and Virgin Bruce reached for their own gloves, unclasping them one at a time and thrusting their curled fists through the wrist rings. Then Jack looked up. "What do you mean, '*You're* getting out of here'?"

Popeye's eyes met Hamilton's, and for a moment Popeye felt like breaking down and telling the hydroponics engineer—the first person he had met in many months whom he felt he could trust, or at least until the day before—everything that he felt and knew. Popeye blinked. No. The truth upon which he had stumbled could not be told to anyone.

"You're going out on the *Willy Ley,*" he said. "Don't worry about me. I'm hitching another ride home."

# 28

# Orbital Decay

"What the hell are you waiting for?" Dobbs demanded. "Rush that compartment and get 'em out of there!"

"Mr. Dobbs, we'll do that," Paul Edgar said calmly, "as soon as we've got the people in place and we know what we're doing. Until then, you're going to sit quietly and not tell my people what to do."

The command module seemed twice as crowded as it actually was, mainly because its narrow interior was filled with Freedom Station personnel trying to keep control of the situation. Men and women were seated in front of the various stations, but most of the action was centered around the communications console, where several different conversations were going on at once: with Olympus Command, with Skycorp headquarters in Alabama, with the NASA military liaison at Cape Canaveral, and—unsuccessfully—with the three intruders who had forced their way into the NSA logistics module. The last was unsuccessful because no contact had been made with the interlopers, despite repeated attempts to reach them on the intercom system.

In fact, the hijacked module had been silent for the last few minutes. The radio signals which had been sent on several different frequencies to Olympus Command from the module had ceased, and no one on Olympus Station seemed to know what was going on any more than Freedom Command. Station Commander Paul Edgar had received a classified, coded message from the National Security Agency shortly after the crisis had begun; he had destroyed the message, printed on a sheet of flimsy, immediately after reading it, and had told his crew that they were to exercise extreme caution in dealing with the three strangers who had taken over the NSA module.

As for Dobbs, who had escaped to give Freedom's command personnel their first warning of the crisis, he found himself in the irritating position of being ignored and shunted aside. Practically pushed into a corner of the command module, he could only watch as Edgar and the others tried to deal with the situation. Edgar had placed several crewmen by the sealed hatch leading to the access tunnel to the NSA module, but he was hesitant to have them unseal the hatch and storm the module.

"There's reason to believe that those men are dangerous," Edgar had explained to Dobbs minutes ago.

"Good God, man, I could have told you that," Dobbs had retorted. "At least one of them is a maniac. We've got to get them out of there!"

Edgar had nodded his head slightly. "We'll get them out of there, sir," he had said in a voice which at once dutifully acknowledged Dobbs' position as an important visitor representing both Skycorp and the U.S. Government, and diplomatically sought to remind Dobbs just who was in charge here. "But I won't have either this station or its crew endangered. I want to first attempt to contact these men and negotiate with them. Get them to come out of there on their own accord. They don't have much choice, so it's in our favor."

It had been a couple of minutes since then, and the officer who had repeatedly tried to make contact with the intruders had still failed to reach them. Dobbs sweated and clung to a handhold, trying to contain his anxiety. The thought of his personal responsibility for the logistics module, with its crucial and costly payload, had never escaped his mind.

"Skipper, I've got Olympus again," the communications officer said. "They say they've had some problems of their own, probably related, and that the security officer aboard has made some arrests. They're also searching for three missing crewmen—John Hamilton, Bruce Neiman, and Claude Hooker."

Edgar glanced at Dobbs, and Dobbs nodded his head quickly. "That's our boys," Edgar replied. "Tell them we've got tentative identification and keep in touch."

"Paul, *Willy Ley* is on final approach for docking," the traffic engineer called over his shoulder. "Should I tell them to hold and make another orbit before they rendezvous?"

The station commander thought for a moment. "No, no, they might need that fuel," he said. "Rendezvous and dock as planned, Charlie, but inform them we've got . . . Oh, hell, just tell 'em we've got an emergency and skip the details. Lisa and Steve will understand. I hope, anyway."

He tapped the man at the intercom station on the shoulder. "What's the scoop, Renaldo?"

"Nothing, Skipper. If they're listening, they won't tell us so."

"Damnation," Edgar muttered, leaning his hands on the back of Renaldo's seat. He glanced once more at Dobbs, then turned back to the communications officer. "Okay, tell Patrick to wait a minute, then open that hatch and wait for my word."

Renaldo punched a button on his console and said into his headset mike, "Code 21, this is Red Rider. Count from sixty and open it, but await go-code, repeat . . ."

Suddenly a loud, harsh buzz sounded from a station behind him and Edgar. As they both looked sharply around, the environmental engineer stared at her board and snapped, "Airlock Three depressurized and opening, sir! We read depressurization in AT-1 registering sudden pressure drop." At that moment a warning Klaxon went off in the compartment.

"Explosive decompression?" Edgar shouted over the alarms.

"Negative!" she shouted back. "The airlock's outer hatch has been opened, and the controls have been set for trickle decompression of the access tunnel." As she shouted, her eyes flicked across the readouts and her hands flew across the panel's switches. "All compartments sealed!" she shouted. "Pressure dropping to 4 psi in AT-1, all other compartments registering minimal drop!"

"What?" Edgar shouted. He then yelled to no one in particular, "Shut the alarms off! How is . . ."

"Skipper, it's Patrick and his men!" Renaldo snapped. "They can't get their hatch open!"

Hamilton wanted to squeeze his eyes tightly shut and at the same time keep them wide open. Earth lay below his feet like a vast, curving plain. Although his mind told him quite reasonably that he couldn't fall those 300 miles to the cloud-flecked West African veldt below, his hands were locked in a death grip on the magnetic plates which held him to the outer surface of the space station.

*Jack.* Virgin Bruce's voice crackled through his helmet's earphones. He was about ten feet ahead of Hamilton, making his own way hand-over-hand across a module, toward the aluminum truss which ran the length of Freedom Station.

"Right behind you, Bruce," Hamilton said, hearing himself gasping hollowly in the confines of his helmet.

*Don't look at the Earth, Jack. Just concentrate on your hands and keep your eyes straight ahead.*

"Right." Hamilton jerked his gaze away from the planet, looked up at his gloved hands and the magnetic grippers clasped in each hand. The grippers had come from a locker Virgin Bruce had found near the airlock through which they had exited; they were normally used by inspection and repair crews who were working EVA and didn't want to fool with either tethers or MMU backpacks. He released the thumb of his right hand from the button on the gripper's handle, moved the gripper forward a few feet, and pushed the button again; the gripper's electromagnetic charge held to the metal skin of the module. Then he released the button on the left-hand gripper, swung it in front of the right hand, and pushed the button again.

*Hurry it up,* Virgin Bruce said. *I can see the shuttle. It's on final approach now. No, don't look for it! Just keep your mind on getting to the truss. We've got to get to that thing before they figure out what we're up to.*

"We're not going to make it," Hamilton said. Their progress with the grippers was slow, only a few feet at a time, and at least a hundred feet separated them from the docking bay where *Willy Ley* would connect with Freedom. In the time limit to which they were confined, there was no way that they could make it.

*We'll get there,* Virgin Bruce replied. *Once we get to the truss we can get rid of these things and the climb will be much quicker. But you've got to . . .*

Suddenly they both felt a small but violent jarring of the station's superstructure, as if something had just smacked into Freedom. At first Hamilton thought it was *Willy Ley* making an exceptionally hard dock. Then he looked down at Earth again.

A long, fat cylinder was moving away from the station, trailing bits of metal and fiberglass debris which glistened with reflected sunlight. It only took him a moment to recognize the cylinder as being one of the space station's modules, and he knew which module it was.

"Adios, Popeye," he said.

The firing of the explosive bolts had been a little more violent than Hooker had anticipated. Seconds after he had thrown the detonating switch and hit the timer, he had grabbed onto handholds with both hands and had silently counted back from ten. The engineers who had designed the modules—which were essentially the same as Olympus modules, although with some important variations—had apparently left nothing to chance when they had added the emergency option for module separation. The explosions kicked the Ear module completely free of Freedom Station, and they also nearly kicked Hooker's teeth out of his head.

At the instant the module sheared away from the station, the lights went out inside the module as the power connection was severed. Hooker had already donned his helmet and gloves and had repressurized his suit. He now flicked on his helmet lamps and went immediately to work on the next, crucial phase of his desperate ploy.

Uncoiling a nylon cord from his utility belt, he quickly looped one end around a ceiling handhold, knotted it, then did the same with the other end through the tether ring on the front of his suit. After testing both knots, he then pushed himself toward the module's sealed hatch. Grabbing the locking arm with both hands, he pushed it down, unlocking the hatch, then did a backward half gainer and kicked the hatch open with both feet.

Instant decompression flung all the loose objects in the module through the hatch. The silent explosion would have thrown Hooker out into space as well had it not been for the rope. His chest hit a console and he grabbed in the darkness for something to hold onto against the torrent. His fingers fell across and instinctively snagged a foot restraint. Hooker held on tight, and turned his head around inside his helmet to watch as a communications headset—probably the one which Hamilton had thrown at him in anger—whipped through the hatch like a mass of ganglia.

Then, as quickly as it had begun, the rush of air ceased. Vacuum had replaced the module's atmosphere. Hooker released the foot restraint and pushed himself toward the open hatch to look outside.

The module was now in a slow tumble, end over end, and he saw Freedom Station swing up and away, far away now, its tiny lights and Erector-set construction making it look like an elaborate kid's toy. Earth then swam into view, much closer than it had been before.

Popeye smiled. So far, so good. The sudden decompression had given the Ear module that extra boost it needed to greatly reduce the likelihood of its being recaptured by a tug from the station. Now it was plummeting down Earth's gravity well, following a course of orbital decay which would bring it to a fiery end in the upper atmosphere. Hooker figured that the trip would take about ten or fifteen minutes.

"And now it's your turn, Sweet Pea," he murmured to himself. Hooker had no intention of escorting the nerve center of Big Ear to its death by friction. Although, he knew, his only alternative for escape was less suicidal only by a matter of degrees.

Turning his back to the hatch and pushing himself further into the module, he searched with his hands and his helmet lamps until he found the candy-striped locker he had spotted before. It was marked with a red arrow reading ESCAPE. He twisted the recessed locking wheel and lowered the compartment's door. Inside was a trunk-sized package wrapped in clear, heavy-duty plastic. Hooker unsnapped the securing belts, unzipped the plastic bag, and reached inside as his mind raced across details he recalled from a technical briefing he had received at Skycorp's training center at Cape Canaveral.

During the formative years of manned space exploration—even before the disasters and near-disasters which had plagued the American and Soviet space programs during the first decades of the push—NASA had been developing ways of rescuing astronauts stranded in space. One was the rescue ball, which became standard equipment aboard American spacecraft in the 80's. Another method was one which was kicked around for decades by designers before finally becoming accepted around the year 2000. It was developed by NASA but considered by them too unsafe to use. Then, private industry further refined it and began putting it aboard manned spacecraft used in LEO operations. At first NASA's regulators hemmed and hawed at the idea, until it was pointed out that for an astronaut, in a life or death situation, a slim chance of survival was better than no chance at all.

The words of the Skycorp instructor who had taught Hooker's class in the use of the rescue device came back to haunt him as he shrugged out of his life-support jacket. "Frankly, fellas, if I had a choice between using this thing and freezing to death or suffocating in my spacesuit, I'd probably opt for the latter," she had said candidly after her demonstration. "Your chances of getting out alive using this thing are about as much as surviving a ride down Niagara Falls in a barrel. Half of the dummies they used in tests either burned up or crash-landed at about 1,000 miles per hour. As far as I know, no one living has ever used it. It scares the hell out of even the Navy test pilots. If you're stranded in LEO, do yourself a favor. Zip yourself into a rescue ball and wait it out. This is probably the dumbest, most dangerous thing built for spaceflight."

Popeye tried not to think about it. He clamped off the air intake/outtake valves, removed the hoses from his suit, and quickly strapped to his stomach the little oxygen cylinder which contained about thirty minutes worth of air. It was more than enough to see him through, regardless of the outcome. When he had clamped on its hoses, he took a deep breath, then reached into the bag and pulled out the miniature rocket engine.

*Rocky had apparently given her the message, because she appeared at the dock shortly before sundown. He was scrubbing the aft deck, down on his hands and knees with a stiff brush and a pail of soapy water, when he felt her presence. He didn't hear her coming, but he knew she was there. Love is like that; you know when your mate is nearby. As he sat back on his haunches and looked up at Laura, who stood on the pier framed against the setting sun, he realized that the same could be said to be true about someone you've come to hate. . . .*

The control mechanism with its built-in gyroscope fitted directly below his helmet, just above the rocket where it mounted on his chest. Working in haste now, he pulled the bag off the rest of the package and cast it aside. In the shimmer of his helmet lantern it floated at the edge of his vision like a formless, translucent ghost. Hefting the bundle, he slid his arms through the shoulder straps and tightened them, then fastened the belt and crotch straps. It fitted to his back like an oversized expedition backpack, with almost the same mass as an MMU.

Hooker looked around once more at the darkened compartment, then focused his mind quickly again on what he had to do: get out of there. Get out because the ship is sinking, the ship is sinking . . .

*"Hi,"* she said. *Her voice would have been bright if it was not somehow numbed, the greeting casual if the tone not guarded. "What's happening, sailor?"*

*She was so beautiful; blue halter top, brown skin, brown hair, faded jeans . . . he could make out all that even with the bright orange sun behind her shining in his eyes, making him squint. She was so beautiful. I love you, he wanted to say, but he couldn't. He was unable to see her face. "Nothing,"* he said. *"C'mon aboard."*

Popeye pushed himself to the hatch and held on to its circular rim with both hands, lowering his back and pushing his shoulders forward, remembering Helen Myricki's instructions from way back when. From here on out, timing had to be right. He waited until the module's pitching motion brought the huge, shining rim of Earth into view. Then he pushed himself out into space.

Earth was much closer now. The module was quickly descending now, its drag increasing as it began contact with the uppermost reaches of the ionosphere. He kicked away from it gently, keeping his back turned against the planet, and watched as the fat cylinder— for the first time, he saw that it was painted with an American flag and U.S. Air Force wings—slowly fell away behind him, seemingly pushed away by his legs, although it was him, not the module, which had been pushed.

His breath was coming hard now, and his hands felt sloppy with sweat inside his gauntlets. He had an urge to pee, but he had disconnected the recirculation tubes to his crotch when he had taken off his life-support pack, so he couldn't whizz into the cup because the urine might bottle up in his suit, potentially causing a short in his auxiliary power unit or, probably worse, seeping up through the neck rung into his helmet. He forgot the urge and stared hard at the register on his control unit, at the glowing digits and the tiny artificial horizon. This was the critical part, the gauging of the reentry path. Then he remembered the pack's firing controls; how could he have missed that? Hooker reached with both hands, down to the back of his hips. His hands found the pack's two arms, and he grasped them and pulled them level with his waist, locking them in place.

His right thumb slid open a tiny compartment on the inside of the left armrest, and he gently pulled a thin cable from the armrest and fitted it into a socket on his chest control. A light on the readout below his face turned yellow. His right hand went to the chest control and flicked a tiny toggle switch. The light switched from yellow to green: the system was armed. Hooker's eyes went back to the artificial horizon, watching as the dark cross's X and Y axes slowly drifted toward a parallel with the Earth's curve. Just a second closer, just a few more fractions of an inch . . .

Impulsively, he glanced back up at the black ceiling of space. His eyes ran back and forth, searching the darkness. He could make out a tiny fusion of bright red and white stars, irregularly spaced, near the edge of his visual horizon, and he guessed it was Freedom. But that wasn't what he was searching for. It was crazy to become nostalgic at this point for a place he had always detested, but in spite of that he searched for a tiny ring of light. Where was Skycan?

With Virgin Bruce leading the way, Hamilton managed to crawl along a structural brace, down along the side of the airlock module to where the *Willy Ley* was docked. They were careful to keep the module between them and the adjacent command module, whose rectangular portholes overlooked the shuttle. The long, jointed Canadarm was gently lowering a payload canister marked with the Johnson & Johnson logo into the shuttle's open cargo bay as Bruce and Jack pushed themselves off the station module and gently glided into the cargo bay.

An astronaut in a spacesuit bearing the Skycorp patch and a black name-patch reading S.F. COFFEY was in the bay, his boots hooked into foot restraints on the deck. He was in the process of attaching the leading end of the station's orbital tether into a bolt inside the bay, and his mirrored faceplate swung around to face the two men as they alighted nearby. After quickly making sure that the tether cable was firmly anchored to the shuttle, he slipped his boots out of the restraints and pushed himself toward Jack, who was holding onto the bay's side.

He touched his helmet to Hamilton's and his voice vibrated through—barely. *"Mmmummarm mummum rarumrum mmma-murum rum!"* was what Hamilton heard.

"What?" Hamilton shouted back.

*"Whomm! Mamarum rum rum whap aharumra!"* the crewman said, and jabbed his finger toward the airlock at the forward end of the cargo bay leading into the *Willy Ley's* crew compartment. "Oh, okay," Hamilton said. "You want to take me to your rum rum."

*"Whaharum."* S.F. Coffey pushed off and drifted toward the airlock, pulling himself along on his tether. Jack and Bruce followed, avoiding the tether, which was suspended in the bay's center like a straight, wrist-thick silver pylon leading up to its enclosed reel on the station. As they moved toward the airlock which Coffey was opening, Hamilton glanced up at the lighted porthole at the end of the command module, about thirty feet above and to the right of the shuttle bay. The crewman in the porthole—positioned at a right angle to the shuttle—seemed to be looking directly at them, although he was probably much more engrossed in maneuvering the Canadarm. No problem there; everyone wearing spacesuits looks alike.

After cycling through the airlock—a tight squeeze for all three of them—they emerged into *Willy Ley's* middeck. S.F. Coffey took off his helmet at once and craned his head around to shout up the egress leading to the flight deck. "Babe! Two for tea!"

"First intelligible thing I've heard you say," Hamilton said as he pulled off his own helmet.

"Sorry," Coffey said with a grin. "It always works in the science fiction novels. I didn't have your frequency."

"Who are they?" Lisa Barnhart called down from the flight deck.

"Hey, Lisa!" he shouted back, overjoyed. "It's your favorite spacesick case!"

"Hi, Jack!" she shouted. "That's Steve. He'll show you up when you're ready."

" 'Hi, Jack,' " Coffey rumbled as he started crawling out of his suit. "I couldn't have phrased it better myself."

"What do you mean?" Hamilton said as he unhooked his suit's waist and began to clumsily work his chest and shoulders out of the suit's top part.

"Meaning . . ." Coffey sighed. "Forget it. If you've got something to do with all the hell that's broken loose here, I don't want to know anything about it."

It took a few minutes for the three of them to climb out of their suits and undergarments, stow them in lockers near the galley, and dress in baggy uniform trousers and polo shirts Coffey produced from another locker. Then Coffey led the way up the shaft in the middeck ceiling onto the flight deck. As he settled into the copilot's seat, Lisa Barnhart looked around from her pilot's station at Hamilton and smiled. "Welcome back," she said.

"God, it's nice to see you," Jack said. He bent forward and kissed her on the forehead, and she gently pushed him back.

"No time for niceties," she said. Lisa looked over at Virgin Bruce. "You're the biker guy," she said. "I can tell just from looking. And I can figure where your third man is."

"What? Where is he!" Jack demanded.

"Well, I'm not sure, but I figure he has to have something to do with the module which just jettisoned itself." She turned back to her flight station. "No time for any of that. Strap yourself into those seats there and keep quiet. We've got to get going without them realizing that you might be aboard. From what I've overheard, they still haven't repressurized that access tunnel, and they figure you might be in the runaway module." She peered over her shoulder at Hamilton. "I figured so, too, when I heard what happened, but I told Steve here to keep an eye peeled for you while he was out there."

"What have you heard about Popeye?" Virgin Bruce demanded as he buckled himself into one of the passenger seats behind Barnhart and Coffey. "What's going on with the Ear module?"

"Hush," she said. "We've got to work quick. I've got to call Freedom Command. Steve . . . ?"

"APU's powered up and systems are go for OT deployment," he murmured, his hands working on his own consoles. "Optimal reentry approach green at sixty-five seconds and counting."

Lisa pressed a button on the console between her and Coffey. "Freedom Traffic, this is *Willy Ley,*" she intoned. "We're go for OT deploy in sixty seconds, mark. Do you copy, over."

She listened for a second. Then she quickly cast a worried look at

Hamilton over her shoulder. "Trouble," she said. "If I give the word, you two get middeck pronto and snuggle into the sleeping berths with the curtains closed."

"Are they asking questions?" Coffey asked, and Lisa nodded her head quickly. "Great," he murmured. He looked over his own shoulder at Hamilton and Virgin Bruce. "This was not my idea," he said shortly. "If I didn't love this woman, I would have left you . . ."

"Clam it, Steve," Lisa said. "Ah, that's a negatory, Traffic. We've got a short countdown . . ." She suddenly reached to the clipboard attached to the console above the yoke and flipped back a page, scanning the cargo manifest. "And we've got perishable pharmaceuticals aboard. I don't see what this has to do with us, anyway. Deploy in forty-five seconds, do you copy?"

Hamilton could see her holding her breath. Then she said, "Roger, Traffic. Thank you. *Willy Ley* undocking on the count. Five, four, three, two, one . . ." She reached above her head and pulled down a red lever. A red light blinked on. "*Willy Ley* is loose. Countdown for tether deploy commencing. Thirty, twenty-nine, twenty-eight . . ."

Jack let out his held breath and looked over at Virgin Bruce. The beamjack—former beamjack now—looked back at him and grinned widely within his spade beard, then held out his left hand. Hamilton reached out his right hand and clumsily shook it. Then he turned his gaze to the line of portholes in front of Lisa and Steve. Through them he could see Freedom's command module. The crewman who had been operating the manipulator arm was now seated before its long window, intent on the controls before him.

Lisa reached the end of her countdown, and Steve tugged another switch, firing the preprogrammed set of RCR's which moved *Willy Ley* away from the space station. Without any perceptible sense of motion, Freedom Station rose up and away from the shuttle's windows; there was no jolt as the shuttle was released from its docking adapter and began to lower itself on the station's tether cable, letting Earth's gravity pull it down the gravity well. At a distance of 40 miles and on a course already established by the shuttle's onboard computers, the cable would release *Willy Ley* in the uppermost part of the atmosphere, there to begin its final reentry maneuvers. Since the computers had plotted it to the last second, the tether cable's release would put the shuttle on an exact reentry and glide approach for the Kennedy Space Center at Cape Canaveral, Florida.

Lisa Barnhart switched off her radio and looked back at Jack and Virgin Bruce. "Boys, you're going home." Her smile faded a little then. "So how did you talk that guy into pulling the crazy stunt he's doing?"

He touched a switch on the unit's control arm and felt a slight bump as dense pressurized foam spewed from its globular container into the pack, inflating the aerobrake/heat shield into its curving, oblate form.

*He found a bottle of Cutty Sark in the wheelhouse and poured her a shot into a cheap plastic cup filled with packing ice which smelled vaguely of shrimp.*

As the pod inflated, he rested his left hand on the chest rocket's firing switch and watched as the artificial horizon slowly settled itself into position, millimeter by millimeter. His breath was rasping in his throat.

*While she drank, sitting on top of a locker on the aft deck, he untied and cast off the ropes, then went into the wheelhouse and started the engines. The* Jumbo Shrimp II *rumbled deep within and her dual inboard diesels plowed a white froth of water from her stern, and she pulled away from the dock as he pointed her blunt bow toward the cool blue Gulf waters beyond the harbor. Laura bitched about the way her drink tasted and asked if he had any coke.*

When the heat shield was fully erected—a huge, stiff umbrella behind his back—he watched his gauges, waiting for the moment to come. Moments later it did, and he pressed the rocket's firing switch.

*He looked at her, and said, "I'm sorry."*

*Laura shook her head. "No," she said, her voice a lazy, stoned drawl. "You should never say sorry. Sorry is how you'll always be if you keep saying you're sorry, so never say you're sorry. Never, never, never." She shook her head vigorously back and forth, her hair flying across her face, shrouding it with fine, moving wisps of brown. Then she gazed at him with smiling lips and hungry eyes and said, "Well, do you have any coke?"*

The miniature rocket engine flared, a nova exploding against his chest, and its sudden thrust kicked him backwards; his eyes squeezed shut, and for a moment he thought that he had mounted it on his suit incorrectly, that the engine would stamp through his body or scorch a part of his suit. Then he opened his eyes and saw that the engine had already died, its white-hot parasol of liquid fuel exhausted. That single thrust was all he needed to escape from orbit. Now he was falling to Earth. He unstrapped the engine and tossed it away with one hand.

*He had intended, first, to throw away the cocaine he had bought*

*from Rocky, and second, to tell her that he had thrown it away. He
had even intended to dump it into the water as she watched, to show
her how easily the precious dope dissolved in common salt water, a
demonstration of how little it was worth compared to the money he
had spent on it. But he did neither. He told her where to look in the
wheelhouse, and she grinned and took it out of its hiding place next to
the fire extinguisher while he watched, cursing his own weakness. As
he steered the* Shrimp *out into open water, he observed Laura out of
the corner of his eye: carefully tapping a tiny white mound out onto the
glass dial of his compass, using a rusty scaling knife to cut the mound
into four uneven white lines, rolling a limp dollar between her fingers
into a tube, all with the practiced ease of someone who knew how to
use this stuff. Meanwhile she kept up her side of a conversation in
which only she participated, a monologue about movies she had seen
and how much she loved old Dustin Hoffman films and how she was
thinking about sending in an application to the University of California at Los Angeles so that she could take graduate level courses in
filmmaking, if only she wasn't so involved with teaching herself, and
God, Claude, this stuff is dynamite, you want some? He shook his
head slightly, no, and couldn't help but notice the avarice in her eyes
as she bent over the two remaining lines on the compass—she had
saved the smaller ones for him—and inhaled them greedily through
the dollar tube: snuuuuf, sigh, snuuuuuuuff! sigh.*

It seemed as if it was only a couple of seconds after he had released
the rocket that he began feeling the first hints of turbulence, the signs
that he was making contact with the upper atmosphere: a jar to the
left, a jar to the right, a sudden dipping sensation which felt as if he
had been suddenly thrown backwards ten feet, then bounced back
out again. His stomach felt cramped and roiling; he willed himself
against nausea, knowing that within minutes it was going to get far
worse. Through either side of his helmet he could see flat planes of
incandescent white; straight ahead, a narrowing cone of starfield. He
gasped, feeling suddenly afraid, and gulped down his panic. Concentrate on something, he told himself. Anything. His mind burped up a
fragment: a line from a song Virgin Bruce used to croon sometimes.
"Goin' home . . . goin' home . . ." he whispered, trying to recall
the tune. "Goin' home . . . goin' home . . . by the water's . . .
by the waterside I will rest my bones . . ."

Then he was pitched into the maelstrom and he screamed.

*They were out on the aft deck . . .*

Oh no, oh God, don't focus on that, don't think about that. He
clutched at the hand controls, useless while he made his journey to

Hell, clenching his teeth until he could feel his molars grinding and his jaw muscles turning to iron, his eyelids fluttering as he fought to keep them open, his guts turning into a stiff, hollow cavity as he shook violently and dropped backwards into a bottomless pit all at once. Was that a warning light going off inside his helmet? He couldn't see it long enough to be sure. Don't think of Laura, don't think about the boat, don't . . .

*She kept on talking as they cruised out toward the setting sun, the boat's prow cutting through the whitecaps, staring through the salt and fly-specked windows of the wheelhouse at the silver-blue sea under the sun, which was now only the width of two fingers from the straight flat horizon: how she liked the kids in her class except for a trio of boys who played terrorist and stole other kids' lunches and wrote things on the bulletin boards, and why the PTA meetings were a hassle, where she and Doug the gym teacher whom she suspected had a little crush on her went for a drink after work—a garbled mishmash of sense and fantasy and bullshit that warbled somewhere on the outermost externality of his consciousness as he refilled her Scotch and water and stared at her tits.*

*Then, in the middle of Doug and kids and movies and "Gee did you know it was Bob Dylan's birthday last week? I always loved listening to that stuff"—in fact, while she was saying that Dylan was the greatest love-song writer of the last century—came the hurriedly murmured, just-barely understated: "You got any more coke?"*

Damn her for laughing, he prayed through the vibration and the roar that he heard in his ears and felt through his backside. Then in horror he realized for what he had been praying. Oh, no . . . oh no, Lord, she's not damned. Give me to Hell, not her. Not her. *(Wham!* he pitched backwards another hundred feet in a fraction of a second.) *Not her!*

"God!" he screamed, in that instant as his one-man heat shield was enveloped in a cushion of white-hot plasma, as four gees piled on his chest and his personal fireball reached a velocity of 600 miles per hour.

*"You think I enjoyed this?" She held up her right hand, displaying the gold wedding band in front of his face. "You think I ever enjoyed it? Don't you accuse me of using you! All you ever did was use me, you bastard!" She yanked the ring off with a sudden, twisting motion, then whirled and threw it overboard. He ran to the side of the boat and leaned over in a vain attempt to save the ring, but saw only a glint of gold disappearing into the blue. Gone, forever gone . . .*

The heat was becoming unbearable; searing, broiling, sweat pouring down his face, stinging his eyes, as the turbulence buffeted his body like pile-drivers impacting against the oblate shield.

*He swung the boathook, and although he closed his eyes at the last moment, he could see in his mind's eye its steel end crash into the back of Laura's skull at the same instant as the dull thunk of metal connecting with soft flesh and bone transmitted itself through the long handle. . . .*

"Oh, dear God, forgive me!" he shouted against the roaring around him, and knew that forgiveness was out of the question. He was a falling angel, a Lucifer in transit from Heaven to Hell. Just as he had attempted to escape his conscience by going into space, now he was confronting ill-buried memories in the last instants of his life, in his long, violent plummet back to Earth.

The night was dark and moonless, the sea was calm, the stars shined with an icy, fragile beauty in a clear sky. He lay in the bottom of the inflatable life raft, exhausted, his feet and arms propped up on the sides of the raft, the plastic paddle lying in his lap. His clothes smelled of gasoline, and he knew that he would have to jump overboard to get the incriminating stench out of his clothes before he reached shore or was picked up.

But then again, maybe not. He looked back over his shoulder again at the small, burning shape on the horizon, like a funeral barge on the Gulf waters. His alibi would be believed; he knew that already. A blocked fuel line. Laura with a lit cigarette, standing too close to the open fuel tank while he was below decks trying to clear the line. An explosion that killed her instantly; he himself with only moments to ditch into the water with the raft, with not even enough time to radio a Mayday while the *Jumbo Shrimp II* was going up in flames.

He wouldn't have to pretend his horror.

Why did she have to laugh? he asked himself again. Why did she have to tell him that their love was, and always had been, a joke, their marriage a convenience? Why had she stolen from him to support her habit? And, oh Jesus, Laura, why did you have to take the last measure of my self-respect, the last ornament of my delusions, and throw it into the sea?

"I didn't need to kill you," he murmured, as his head sank back against the cold wet plastic of the life raft.

Hooker knew that he would reach shore by morning. The tide would carry him in, and he could be an appropriate shipwreck victim, a man who had lost his ex-wife to a tragic mishap on the high seas. The Cedar Key police and the Coast Guard would believe his story. But now there was the future to consider. His life had effectively ended at the same instant as he had ended her with the boathook; he had destroyed his source of livelihood when he had soaked the boat with a can of gasoline and dropped a lit match on the deck near her body. In more ways than one, he was adrift.

Gazing up at the night sky, he made out a tiny ring of light, not much larger than the diameter of his little finger. Fascinated, he stared at it for a minute before he recognized it for what it was. The Olympus space station. He recalled the newscast he had watched only that morning (had it been only such a short time ago?) in his cabin.

He gazed at it, his head resting on the raft's side, fixed upon it with a growing sense of wonder that he had not felt since he was very young, when he had tacked up pictures of space shuttles and floating astronauts on the walls of his bedroom, when his dreams had been alive and he felt his destiny was not as a fisherman but as an astronaut. A pure feeling that seemed to ripple through him again, bringing back an aura of innocence which now seemed well beyond his grasp.

Out of grasp, perhaps, but not beyond reach. Skycorp, the company which had built Olympus Station, was now hiring men to build the world's first space solar power satellite. Hooker had seen the advertisements in the newspapers, knew that the company was not restricting the job search to trained pilots or mission specialists. There was the possibility that even he could qualify. . . .

He continued to stare up at the tiny little ring in the sky. Yes. There was an escape. There was a way to run from himself, from his unforgivable crime. He could leave Earth and the ashes of his past far behind, take up a new life in the cosmos. Claude Hooker: astronaut, pioneer of the high frontier, builder of the future.

He would make a new life for himself in space. He would never look back.

Suddenly, the heat was gone, the violent shocks had diminished in strength to be replaced by a smooth sensation of falling.

Hooker opened his eyes, and saw deep blue sky and a sun which, although bright, was nowhere near as intense as he had come to expect. Through his helmet he could hear a high-pitched keening whistle, as the wind whipped past him.

His eyes went wide, and he didn't have to check his gauges to know where he was. He had survived the initial reentry and was now tens of thousands of feet above the ground, somewhere in the stratosphere.

Hooker pulled a handle on the control arm, and felt the heat shield lift away from him like a carapace being discarded by an insect. As he tumbled forward, he caught a glimpse of its blackened, scarred round shape before the cold winds of the upper atmosphere snapped and folded its fragile structure.

The world stretched out before him, the uppermost cloud layers still miles below him. He had no idea where he was falling, and he didn't care. The parachute was still strapped to his back. Maybe it would work. Maybe it wouldn't. Maybe he wouldn't even bother to find out.

Hooker spread his arms and legs wide, transforming himself into a human kite, and embraced the world below him, feeling the wind drag at his limbs and torso as he made his long, long fall. Nice day for flying, he thought.

There's no such thing as summer out here, you know; not unless you're keeping track of the baseball season. That's how we counted the passage of the hot months. Summer began when the first ball was thrown out in Riverfront Stadium in Cincinnati and ended with the final game of the regular season and the beginning of the play-offs; the cold hand of winter was upon us when the final inning of the World Series was over. So it was near the end of our astronaut's summer when it all came apart.

You know most of the story now, of course. It was impossible for the NSA and Skycorp to cover the existence of the Ear module when its fragments rained down on the Indian Ocean and the Australian outback following its disintegration in the upper atmosphere, nor could they keep Mike Webb, Joni Lowenstein, and Dave Chang from talking to the press once they had been brought back to Earth to await prosecution on charges of conspiring to destroy U.S. Government property. About two weeks after the Ear's command module was destroyed, the Senate Select Intelligence Committee began closed-door hearings on covert space operations by the National Security Agency. It was a reunion on Capitol Hill for a lot of former Skycan personnel: Not only were Dave, Joni, and Mike present, but also subpoenaed down from GEO were the station's resident spooks, "Dave," "Bob," and "John."

Probably the most damaging testimony came from former project supervisor Henry G. Wallace, who was escorted to the hearings by two staff psychiatrists from Walter Reed Hospital in Bethesda, where he had been undergoing treatment since his nervous breakdown on Olympus Station and his attack on Joni Lowenstein. Wallace—now a broken, humbled shadow of his former imperious self—verified that Skycorp had cooperated with the NSA in establishing the Big Ear satellite system as a SIGINT-type global telecommunications monitoring system . . . and then, as unnamed witnesses later told the *Washington Post* and the *New York Times,* launched into a disjointed, rambling screed about humanity's manifest destiny in the stars and the American spiritual mandate to conquer outer space, which wasn't halted until Wallace was quickly, quietly ushered out into the corridor and allegedly sedated in the men's room.

If that wasn't bizarre enough for the solons on the committee— particularly the venerable senator from Vermont who had made a name for himself as chairman of the committee and who was the Democratic front-runner in the coming Presidential election—then there was the flustered testimony of Clayton Dobbs, a principal designer of the Ear, who was aboard Freedom Station at the time of the incident. In response to a question from the Vermont senator, Dobbs defended his role in designing the Ear because "scientists are not responsible to the people, they are responsible to whoever has bankrolled their research." When the senator pressed further, asking if that responsibility still held if the intent of the "bankroller" was basically immoral, Dobbs snapped, "Senator, that's not my department!"

Unfortunately, I wasn't there to witness any of it, though I wished I could have been, if only to hear Wallace's and Dobbs' testimony. But my role in the events of September 2, 2016, ended at the moment when Phil Bigthorn put the cuffs on me in the computer bay on Skycan.

That's a long story in itself, and I'll try to make it short. No one in the media or in Congress ever established my connection with the events, because Skycorp kept me from testifying. I never made it to Washington, D.C. I never made it back to Earth. I was sent to the Moon instead.

It was relatively easy for Skycorp to keep me from testifying. When the shit hit the fan—you know, it's getting so hot in this suit that even talking about fans makes me uncomfortable—some people at the company and at the NSA apparently decided that having three damaging witnesses from former Olympus personnel was enough. All they had to do was not acknowledge my presence, and get me to someplace I wouldn't be found when the General Accounting Office inspectors arrived. Hank Luton had been given temporary (later permanent) command of Skycorp's GEO operations, and when he broke the news to me, it went something like this:

Hank—You want to write some sci-fi stories about living on the Moon, don't you?

Me—No, not the way you're suggesting, Hank.

Hank—Well, we're not asking, anyway, Sam. You're getting your bag packed and ready to board an OTV for Descartes Station at 0100 hours tomorrow. Sorry, Sam.

No kidding, Hank. You always were a sorry bastard.

They didn't get everyone who was involved, of course. The disappearance of Jack Hamilton and Virgin Bruce has continued to be an unsolved aspect of the case. The shuttle *Willy Ley,* which investigators later fingered as their getaway vehicle from Freedom Station, made its landing at the Cape before anyone deduced its role in the events, even while the Ear module was breaking up in the stratosphere above kangaroo-land. Witnesses at the corporate Shuttle Processing Center later told investigators that they had seen two men matching Jack's and Bruce's descriptions, wearing flight jumpsuits, exiting the spacecraft after it had been towed into the hangar. Nobody paid much attention to them, assuming they were flight personnel looking over the *Willy Ley* for its next launch in three days. Steve Coffey, the mission's copilot, later swore that he didn't know what was going on until the flight commander, Lisa Barnhart, revealed her intentions while at dock with Freedom Station.

As for Virgin Bruce and Jack Hamilton . . . no one has seen them since. Like Barnhart and her family, they disappeared within days of the event. No one has seen them again.

As for Popeye . . .

You know what happened to Popeye. No one needed a fried skeleton to determine that the man who uncoupled the Ear module and rode it to reentry in the atmosphere died when it broke apart. There is evidence to suggest that he might have tried to use the unproven escape system that was in the module—a brief trail of smoke in the stratosphere spotted by satellites, the absence of the escape system among the debris that was recovered—but no one was ever really uncertain about his fate, including myself. Popeye was one person who never made it to Washington. And . . .

Hold on, dammit.

Sorry I had to do that.

I just sneaked a peek at my suit's chronometer. I guess I've got a few more minutes left in my air supply. I might just finish the story, even if I do get a little long-winded. No, there haven't been any rescue crews through here lately, and it makes me feel better to go out talking. No, I don't have a rope to use for climbing out, in case you're wondering. Wouldn't know how to use one even if I had it. What do I look like, Doc Savage?

Descartes Station looked like three turtles hunched together in the gray lunar highlands. Each of the humps was two cylindrical modules, much like the ones Skycorp manufactured for Olympus Station, buried under an envelope of aluminum scaffolding, Mylar tenting, and about five feet of soil. It was designed to protect crews from radiation until the day a more permanent mining facility is built, which I guess will be in another ten or twenty years. It's much like the lunar installation built at Tranquillity Base by the Americans, and the polar base used by the Russians, as far as the way it's constructed.

Virgin Bruce would have liked the crew of Descartes Station; they're his kind of degenerates, and they love listening to old Grateful Dead tapes. They spend eight-hour shifts bulldozing the regolith and sending it through the "dirty factory"—the electrostatic separators and microwave processors which separate the oxygen and hydrogen we live on and the aluminum we process into sheet rolls from the soil. Grinding, dirty, hard work—no one on Earth ever truly anticipated how hard it was to work like the Skycorp crew did until the company started that kind of industrial activity.

There are twenty men and five women living at Descartes Station. Twenty-five people living in an environment even more closed and crowded than on Skycan. Unlike the NASA and Soviet bases, the crews are not frequently rotated back to Earth, because of the high cost of sending people there. Morale was bad on Skycan, but it was even worse on the Moon, all but destroyed by the lack of privacy in the base's modules and the bleak, monotonous landscape of the lunar highlands.

Making the situation worse is what the crew here has done to alleviate the boredom. Someone at the Cape has been pipelining drugs to the Moon inside the sealed supply canisters which land every few weeks. Nothing as relatively harmless as Jack Hamilton's marijuana, either, but uppers, downers, bioengineered hallucinogens, and occasionally heroin or cocaine. Lester Riddell, the base commander and Wallace's former copilot on the first lunar expedition, is more than tolerant; he's become a druggie himself, and allows the men to use whatever they want as long as they don't get high while working. Some of them do, anyway; this is the real reason why some of the shipments have been delayed. The living quarters are almost perpetually trashed; routine and vital tasks alike are done on an almost accidental basis. Fortunately, at least the base's power source, the SP-100 nuclear reactor secluded within a crater just outside the base perimeter is designed to function automatically, but I hope I'll never be here when something . . .

Um. Just occurred to me. I won't, will I . . . ?

I was welcome to join in during "party time," the happy hour drug and sex escapades which started in the commons module at about 1500 and continued until everyone was either passed out or the next work shift started. Instead, during the two-week daylight periods, I began my own explorations of the Moon, traveling the lunar highlands on a fat-wheeled rover and rediscovering the strange beauty which the others had long since been conditioned to overlook and forget. My range of sightseeing was the Descartes region; I triangulated my tours around the base and the two life huts, or emergency shelters, which had been established south and west of Descartes Station during the initial months of exploration after the base had been set up, and seldom used since. My favorite place to visit was the Apollo 16 landing site: the bottom half of the LEM still blackened by the exhaust from the upper stage's liftoff forty years ago, the footprints of Charlie Duke and John Young undisturbed in the soil, the sampling and measuring equipment still deployed near the old lunar rover they had used. I would sit on a boulder nearby, never venturing in close to the LEM for fear of disturbing the footprints, and look at Earth rising over the horizon and watch the sun reflect off the artifacts. Then I would go on.

It was during this last safari that I ran into trouble. I was out near South Ray, an impact crater not far from the Apollo 16 site, when I drove into the shadow of a small hill. With no atmosphere to diffuse and bend light rays, the shadows on the Moon are dark and impenetrable, like being outside in the darkest moonless night you've ever seen. Thinking that I only had to skirt fifty yards around the side of the hill, I didn't bother to switch on the headlights. My laziness cost me. The rover found the crevasse hidden in the darkness, and down I went—here.

Radio destroyed, vehicle totaled, no way out . . . and now it's my turn to die. Air's getting thin and stuffy, suit's become a broiler . . . it's only a matter of minutes now.

Wait. Forgot it almost. The Greatest Discovery . . . ha, ha, the Greatest Discovery Ever Made. I mentioned that before, didn't I? Well, maybe I lied. Sorry, folks, but there's no dead alien in a spacesuit, or a robot probe, or spaceship, or black monolith. Maybe one day they'll find the little green men, but not today, José.

Let me tell you what the Greatest Discovery Ever Made was. I'm looking at it now, high above the edge of the crevasse. It's the view of Earthrise, the way Borman, Lovell, and Anders first saw it on Christmas Eve, 1968, as Apollo 8 came around the far side of the Moon. The sublime message of that sight resonates down through the years: No matter how far away we go, no matter what we do out there, we have only one real home, one common heritage.

And now I'm going to die, which is just as well, because I'm getting maudlin as hell.

That rhymes. I'll be goddamned. I could never rhyme before.

Lemme try that again. The air is getting thick . . . thick as a brick, as a brick . . . getting thick as a brick, can't beat it with a stick . . . and the Moon is made of green cheese . . .

What rhymes with cheese . . . ?

The gringo who walked into the roadside Navajo bar in the tiny town of Mexican Hat wasn't dressed for the desert night; that was the first thing that attracted the attention of the regulars. Shorts, blue nylon shirt, and a pair of funny-looking, thick white metal boots so bulky that he could hardly walk normally in them. The Indians elbowed up to the long wooden counter silently eyed him as he stepped over the mongrel dog at the top of the steps and opened the screen door.

Of course, they also immediately noticed that he was white. Mexican Hat was located just across the river from the boundaries of the Arizona Navajo reservation. Since drinking was illegal in Navajoland, and beer wasn't sold at the stores on the reservation, if you wanted a drink you had to go to Flagstaff or Mexican Hat or one of the other towns just outside the reservation. The bar in Mexican Hat had no name; it was an Indian bar, simple as that. The only white people who came by were out-of-state tourists on their way into Navajoland looking for directions, and if they had any sense at all, they didn't stay around for more than one beer.

But this guy simply shuffled in his thick boots to the bar, dug into his pocket, pulled out a crumpled dollar bill, and dropped it on the counter. The men at the bar watched him with the neutral implacability only the red man is capable of maintaining, a silent watchfulness that makes most gringos nervous. A rerun of a popular soap opera nagged from the dusty TV above the bar, and flies settled and buzzed around the spilled beer and potato chip fragments littering the bar top. The bartender opened a Coors longneck and put it down in front of the newcomer, and he lifted it and drank deeply, all while the Navajos silently watched.

He put down the bottle—more than half-emptied by his one swig —and looked at the three Indians wearing cowboy hats, seated on the adjacent stools. He glanced up at the TV, and watched it while a commercial came on, then the call-sign of a Tuscon NBC affiliate. He then looked down at the bar, studied it for a moment, and said to the regulars, "This is a stupid question, but is this Arizona?"

They all nodded their heads. He nodded his own head in acknowl-
edgment, then took another swig of beer. "What's the name of this
town?" he then asked.

"It's called Mexican Hat," the bartender said after a moment.

"Oh," the white guy said. "Mexican Hat."

After another long moment, one of the customers said, "Where're
you from?"

The white guy smiled and traced his finger around the edge of a
small puddle of beer on the bar. "I'm originally from Florida," he
said, in slow, carefully chosen words, "but lately I've lived in outer
space."

"I guess that explains the boots," another man said, *sotto voce.*

"Yeah, it does."

There was another long silence between them before the white guy
said, "Do any of you know Phil Bigthorn?"

They all shook their heads, not taking their eyes off him. "That's
good," the white guy replied. After another moment he asked, "Does
a bus come through here?"

"Where do you want to go?" one of the regulars said.

"Wherever the next bus goes."

The bartender pulled out a Greyhound schedule and told him that
the next bus was due in three hours, destination Flagstaff. He could
catch it at the Texaco station across the street. The gringo nodded
his head, finished his beer, then bought a bottle of cheap red wine
and some freeze-dried beef jerky. As he finished his beer and headed
for the door, one of the customers said offhandedly, "Going back to
space now, man?"

The gringo turned and smiled as he pushed his back against the
screen door, stirring the dozing mutt just outside. "Nope," he replied. "Thanks for the directions home."

As he walked clumsily down the steps, the dog yawned and
stretched and, having nothing better to do that late afternoon, followed him down the stairs and across the sandy parking lot. The
man walked across the cracked highway to the Texaco station and
bought a ticket to Flagstaff from the fat old Navajo woman, who also
tried to sell him some turquoise jewelry. Then he climbed up on a
gravel-and-sand hillock overlooking the highway and sat down, putting his back against a mesquite tree. The dog followed and lay down
nearby, his tongue lolling moistly out of his mouth as he eyed the
strip of jerky in the man's hand.

As the sun began to set, the man opened the bottle of cheap red
wine and stripped off a little bit of jerky to feed to the dog. That

morsel was all he needed to win the dog's loyalty; he crawled closer and lay his head in the man's lap, his dirty tail thumping in the dirt as he gnawed on the tough jerky.

After a little while the sun blazed out in a haze of orange and yellow, and the stars began to appear. The man put the back of his head against the wiry trunk of the tree and stared up into the sky. Once his eyes had become adjusted to the darkness, he could make out a tiny, twinkling constellation, a round sparkle of starlight, like silver appearing against the black. He smiled and raised his bottle to the little constellation in a silent toast, then drank deeply. The dog stirred a little, tail swishing once, twice, in the dirt, and the man petted him as they both contented themselves with the warmth of each other's company. It was a good night to be out in the desert with a friend.